Praise for Jane Sigaloff's
Name & Address Withheld:

"This book is the perfect antidote to Christmas get-togethers. Escape to a comfy chair and enjoy!"
—Company

"Sigaloff's first novel is without doubt an engaging romantic comedy!"
—Booklist

"Witty, juicy and romantic—a clever, controversial comedy about finding love in all the wrong places."
—Bestselling author Sarah Mlynowski

"Moving and cleverly written…
a great present for a girlfriend in need of some love advice (we all have one of these)."
—handbag.com

"4½ stars… Sigaloff has an interesting take on the relationship conundrum."
—funkybitch.com

"Unusually daring in its approach…"
—The Big Issue

Jane Sigaloff

was born in London and, despite brief trips into the countryside, Jane has always been a city girl at heart. After studying history at Oxford University she entered the allegedly glamorous world of television, beginning her career as tea and coffee coordinator for Nickelodeon U.K. After she progressed to researcher and then to assistant producer, her contracts took her to MTV and finally to the BBC where she worked for over three years.

Since 2000, Jane has enjoyed a double life as a part-time P.A., which has given her more time to write and feel guilty about not going to the gym. She lives in London with her laptop and ever-expanding CD collection. Lost & Found is her second novel.

Find out more about Jane at: www.janesigaloff.com

By the same author:

Name & Address Withheld

LOST & FOUND
jane sigaloff

RED
DRESS
INK
™

First North American edition January 2004

LOST & FOUND

A Red Dress Ink novel

ISBN 0-373-25045-2

Visit Red Dress Ink at www.reddressink.com

Printed in U.S.A.

ACKNOWLEDGMENTS

In a concerted attempt to be more concise than last time, immeasurable thanks and much love to my friends and family for their unwavering support, for listening (or at least making encouraging noises while thinking about other things), for their positivity and for ensuring that the life of this writer is by no means a solitary one.

In particular:

Omi—my PR granny extraordinaire. Kate—for always being there for me (and for valiant shelf patrol). Charlotte—for indispensable and immediate fast-talking advice. Louise, Alice, Gemma, Mandy, Fred and all at the Barnes Ladies Writing Circle—it wouldn't be as much fun without you. Marten Foxon, the most flexible boss in London—for employing the only part-time part-time P.A., for being grammatically pedantic and for tales of the city. Melissa, Stuart and Clodagh—for providing insight into life as a lawyer and answering all my questions with due consideration. Peter French and Alex Tscherne at the Carlyle Hotel, New York, for unrivaled hospitality.

As always, thanks to my agent, Carole Blake, to Sam Bell for editorial prowess and keeping me focused, to Claire Sawford for PR duties and to the whole Red Dress Ink team who have worked so hard on my behalf both in the U.K. and North America.

For my parents—
all of them

and

for Paul—
my little big brother and partner in crime
since 1975.

Chapter One

'Something to drink, sir?'

'We'll have champagne…'

Sam hid behind her eyelids. She'd closed them for the steep climb from JFK and must have slipped straight into a power nap. But now she was very much awake. And listening. Taittinger + senior supervising partner (flirting) + altitude of 38,000 feet = certain recipe for disaster.

'Just a still mineral water for me, please.' Opening her eyes, Sam automatically ran a finger along her bottom lashes to remove any smudges of mascara, whilst flexing her calves and curling and uncurling her toes to prevent the onset of DVT. If she focused on her legs she was almost sure she could feel that the blood flow was a little sluggish in the bended knee area. Hypochondria in action. Sometimes knowledge was definitely not a good thing.

'Oh, come on, let's celebrate.' Richard punched her arm playfully. Regrettably, despite the extra room in business class, he was still well within touching distance.

'No, really. I might have some red with supper. You go ahead.' She still couldn't believe he'd flown out for the meetings. As for his behaviour last night—she was generously going to attribute it to the martinis. Yet he was sitting next to her. For the next seven hours. Twenty-first century purgatory.

'Couldn't you squeeze in one glass? We're not billing them for this hour.'

Now he was trying lawyer jokes. 'No, thanks.' Champagne invariably gave her a headache at sea level. 'Just the water.' She exchanged an esoteric smile with the flight attendant as another waft of his Eau de Testosterone threatened to choke them both.

'Great work this week. Very impressive. You know how highly I rate you.'

Typical ambiguity on the personal-professional line. But, while Sam could feel her flesh starting to crawl, her demeanour gave nothing away.

'They were always going to take our recommendations.'

Determined to avoid prolonged eye contact, Sam rummaged in her bag for her lip balm and wished she could be teleported back to London. Business trips were one thing, but a night in New York with Richard Blakely was in a different league altogether. Especially given that the only merger she was working on didn't involve him.

'Maybe, but I'd forgotten how good you are round the table…'

'I enjoy it. Especially when things go our way.'

Wallet, passport, make-up, hairbrush, mobile phone, PalmPilot, perfume, chewing gum, hand cream, dental floss—come on, come on. If her lips were to survive the brutal in-flight air-conditioning she couldn't give up now. She was sure she could actually feel cracks forming.

'…and you've always been a bit of a ball-breaker. I wouldn't trust you with mine…'

Definitely not the impression he'd given her last night.

'Cheers…'

Richard raised his glass and, hang on, was that a wink? Sam

wasn't sure. Watching as he tipped his head back åand took a long sip, she forced herself to think positive. Maybe a stray beam of light had caught the edge of his trophy Rolex as it peeped out from underneath his stiff made-to-measure Jermyn Street cuff. Not a glimmer of embarrassment from him. Nor any sign of a hangover. Amazing.

Picking her bag up from the floor, Sam continued her search in the upright position just in case he thought she'd been aiming for his lap. She'd never so much as given him a modicum of encouragement—unless wearing a just-above-the-knee-length skirt to her final interview at City law firm Lucas, Lex, Lawton six years ago could be cited as foreplay—but her lack of interest didn't seem to bear any relevance to his level of enthusiasm or dedication to her cause. His confidence levels were as unnaturally high as the balance of his current account.

'...we could teach them a thing or two about drinking, though.'

'Mmm.' Sam wasn't listening. She'd heard it all before. But she knew she should be grateful that at least she wasn't expected to provide the in-flight entertainment.

'So, what have you got planned for the weekend?' Richard's tenacity on the conversation front was commendable. 'What does one of London's most eligible women get up to when I let her out of the office?'

'Oh, not much...'

Her choice. Sam refocused on the methodical check of the pockets of her bag, which should have been a dedicated site of special scientific interest. It would appear that they were breeding Biros and tampons.

'I haven't had a clear weekend at home in...' she paused '...well, with the three-ringed circus of hen weekends, weddings and work, we're probably talking months...'

Still sifting through the contents of her shoulder Tardis, Sam squinted at the screen showing their route across the Atlantic. To her dismay the computer-generated plane had barely left the Eastern seaboard, and was creeping north at the sort of pace that had given snails a bad name.

'...and I've got loads to sort out—you know, all that life laundry that always has to take a back seat...'

She was craving a marathon gym session followed by an evening in and a long soak in an aromatherapy bath with the current men in her life: Paul Mitchell, Charles Worthington, John Frieda and, of course, her oldest and most loyal shampooing partner Tim O'Tei. Candles. Chill-out CD. No more having to make polite chit-chat. A bowl of bran flakes. Bliss.

Sam's bathtime bubble burst and her stomach knotted instantly as she realised her bag was emptier than normal. The plight of her lips paled into insignificance as, uninvited, a cold sweat crept up the back of her neck.

A furtive glance to her left. To her relief Richard appeared to have finally taken the hint and was now staring out of the perspex window, apparently mesmerised by the blackness of the night sky. Or perhaps checking his too-perfect teeth in the reflection. Sam peered into the dark folds of her bag before unzipping the myriad compartments one more time, just in case she might have misfiled or overlooked it. Not that she did 'overlook.' Fuck.

'Everything Okay?' Richard sensed a change in the force. A tell-tale furrow had appeared in her brow between her perfectly shaped eyebrows.

'Fine.' Sam forced a smile and, leaning back stiffly in her seat, closed her eyes to create a few seconds of personal space. Maybe it was in her laptop case? A spark of hope followed by a dash of reality. She knew it wasn't. And none of this would be happening if he hadn't interrupted her routinely obsessive check of drawers and cupboards earlier.

She had to move fast. Only right now she was on a plane which, even with a complementary tailwind, was hours from Tarmac and a private telephone opportunity. Forcing herself to take a sip of her water, she reclined her seat, headphones on, volume off, pretending to watch the screen sprouting from the end of her armrest. But while the images flickered enticingly, they failed to penetrate her thoughts. The water felt like a river of neat acid as it burned its path down to her stomach. Internal turbulence. But in nineteen years her diary had never let her down, never told her it was too busy, never not been there for her...until now.

Ben refused to open his eyes. Having tossed and turned for most of the night, typically he'd only finally managed to drift into a proper sleep moments before the alarm had gone off. Yet it appeared, from the generally high activity levels going on around him, that his sister was well and truly up. On a Friday morning. On vacation. He must have been adopted; there was no way they could share genes.

Doing his utmost to pretend he was still asleep, he willed the steady hum of the air-conditioning to lull him back into unconsciousness, and was practically knocking on nirvana's door when a very familiar voice started up right next to his ear. He should have read the small print. This had been sold to him as a free weekend away, not some sort of boot camp. But there was always a catch.

'Ben...jy.' The sing-song pre-school approach to his name was quickly cast aside in favour of an impatient bark. 'Ben... Come on.' If he'd had four legs he'd have known he was in trouble. 'Look, I know you're awake—your breathing's changed. Come on, will you?' No wonder David hadn't minded him taking his place. Ben wondered whether his clients really were in town this weekend.

Ali poked his arm and Ben faked a somnolent shrug and murmur before opening one eye—partially and deliberately obstructed by his arm over his face—giving him a restricted view of his sister, who was squatting down at the edge of the bed. He tried not to smile. Things hadn't changed in twenty-five years. Then on Sunday mornings she'd physically prised his eyelids apart to prove that he was awake before forcing him to play stupid games—usually involving dressing up in clothes their mother had charitably donated to their cause—he suspected now, merely so that she hadn't had to actually throw or give them away.

'Ha! Stop pretending. I just saw you open your eye. Your arm shield needs work.'

Ben stretched indulgently before propping himself up on the pillows. 'Give me a break.'

'I know you.'

'I'd hope so.'

'Better than you know yourself.'

'Hmm, I'm not sure about that.'

'Well, I know that this pretending to be asleep ruse is a) gym avoidance…'

It was fair comment. But the sight of Ali in full Nike regalia before nine on a Friday morning was inducing acute narcolepsy. After hours of sleep deprivation, his eyelids felt incredibly heavy, and a vortex of dizziness was threatening to pin him to the mattress.

'…and b) because you're still worrying about Julia. Come on. You should come for a workout with me.'

'Are you insane?' Ben yawned and stretched before springing back into the foetal position.

'You could do with it.'

Ben clenched his stomach muscles and stabbed at his T-shirt-covered torso to reassure himself that he still had some muscle tone, even if it was currently a few centimetres below the surface.

'Maybe later. I've never been any good at physical exertion first thing. And I've only had about ten minutes' sleep so it might just kill me.'

Ali rolled her eyes.

'Okay, maybe a couple of hours, tops, but I didn't sleep much on the plane.' He couldn't help it if he was a sucker for seat-back Nintendo games and multiple movie channels playing on a loop. 'And I've never been a morning person.'

'It's nearly two in the afternoon for us.'

'For you, maybe. Anyway, that would make it just about time for an afternoon snooze.' Ben folded his arms behind his head and indulged in a prolonged blink. Closed was definitely preferable to open.

'You can't just lie here moping.'

'I would have been quite happy sleeping.' Ben pulled the

heavy Egyptian cotton covers up to his nose and relished the weight of the down duvet on his weak body.

'Bull…it'd be good for you to get your blood pumping.'

'It'd be better for you. You're the one writing an article on the gym refurbishment. I might come along tomorrow, or I'll go for a run in the park later. I need more sleep.'

'Whatever.'

'One of the advantages of being single is autonomy. Or at least that was the idea…'

'Julia wasn't bossy.'

Ben smiled to himself. In some respects she and Ali had been way too similar. They always say girls pick men like their fathers, but did brothers pick women like their sisters? Right now, he hoped not. 'Besides I hate gyms. Too many mirrors. I want the before and after, not during. I mean, who looks good while they're exercising?'

'You'll have to look yourself in the eye eventually, and she's bound to have pulled herself back together by now—she's a tough cookie…'

He just wished she didn't have to hate him in the process.

'Far better that you were honest. The longer you'd left it, the harder it would have become—and if you'd strung her along I'd have disowned you. Plus, just for the record, there are far more single women of your age out there than men. Read any of the magazines on my bedside table if you don't believe me.'

'Hey, I'm not desperate.'

'I know.'

'Even if I said the "d" word out loud, which might mean that you think I am because I've said I'm not.'

'You are such an amateur shrink sometimes.'

'I'm just a little disheartened. She wasn't who I'd thought she was.'

'We've all done it.' Ali shuddered at the memories of dating pre-David. The drip-feeding of information at appropriate moments in an attempt to generate common ground before coming out with the more contentious, potentially deal-breaking stuff farther down the line. At seventeen she'd even reinvented herself sartorially in pursuit of Johnny's affections. But he had been very cute. Everyone in her year had wanted to date him.

Ben smiled. 'Are we talking ten-hole Doc Martens?'

Ali nodded sheepishly. Hormones had a lot to answer for.

'And the rockabilly quiff...?' He was enjoying this moment. She'd looked like a cross between Morrissey and the B52s.

She laughed nervously, willing the conversation to move on. 'It was an important experimental phase...'

'Turn-ups on your vintage 501s...bright red lipstick... Mum thought you were about to come out.'

'Yeah, yeah... All photographic evidence has been systematically destroyed. And I don't think I need to take this from the boy who wore eyeliner.'

'Once. I was twelve and I wanted to be a New Romantic.' Ben sighed, allowing his head to sink back into the pillow and making his next point to the ceiling. 'It would just be much easier if single people were required by law to carry a card stating their genuine age, profession, aspiration for children, preference for Coke over Pepsi, cats over dogs, *Friends* over *Frasier,* you know...'

'You need to get a real job. You've got far too much time to think.'

'A real job like yours, eh? O freelance journalist.'

'Just remember, it's your choice that you're on your own.'

Ben shrugged. Silence. Ali decided to ease off a little.

'...so you're not prepared to compromise. That's a positive not a negative.'

Ben nodded sagely. Even at the time there'd been a sense of relief. Julia had become a habit rather than a choice. And he'd been very fond of her. Fond. That said it all. Great-aunts were fond of their great-nieces; the British nation had been very fond of the Queen Mother. But the bottom line was he wanted it all. The whole mutual love and respect thing. The Paul and Linda. The Brad and Jen. Someone to grow old with. To have children with. Or nothing.

'But…' there was always a bloody but '…maybe I was just being male. Wanting the thing I didn't have just because… She was a great girl in lots of ways. Spent a bit too much time at the office…'

'She was ambitious.'

'So am I. I just don't feel the need to talk about my career trajectory incessantly. And at least I have an office to go to.'

'As do I.'

Ben scoffed as he folded his arms across his chest. 'I think you'll find yours is the spare room.'

'At least I have a spare room.'

Why did she always have to have a comeback? 'Anyway, people need television.'

Ali snorted. 'Only in the way I need four pairs of black boots. Anyway, it's not like you have a biological clock that's ticking—and you've still got all your hair. Relax, unwind, have a bit of fun…'

Ben nodded. Right now the random shag option was far more alluring than playing the relationship game. He didn't have the energy for false starts, thoughtful gifts and the whole wooing process if there wasn't long term potential. Lazy? Tired? Uninspired.

'She's out there somewhere, Benj. Maybe even at the gym.'

'Nice try, Al.'

Resting on his elbows, Ben eyed her suspiciously as she contorted herself through a number of stretches at the side of the bed. Women were definitely more supple than men, and Ali was always hyper when they were back in New York.

'OK, I'm ready. Are you coming or what?'

'Nope.'

'Fine.'

Ben knew from her tone that it absolutely wasn't, but he also knew she was his sister and by the time she'd sweated away over three hundred calories he'd be forgiven.

'I'll be about an hour. Why don't you get some breakfast sent up?'

'We can just grab coffee and a bagel.' Ben wasn't in the mood to spend forty dollars on tea and toast.

'Order whatever you like. I'll claim it.'

She knew him quite well.

'I don't want you whingeing about hunger pangs in a couple of hours—we've got a big shopping day ahead of us.' Ben wished that he could get a little more excited at the prospect. 'Now, shape up. This weekend is not all about you. Work aside, I need new clothes—and, having unpacked your bag, I know you do. Not least because we've barely made an impact on the walk-in wardrobe. I think this suite is bigger than your apartment in London.'

'Not difficult.'

'Stop being so antsy.'

'I'm tired. Blame it on sleep deprivation. You're the one who felt the need to set an alarm.'

Ali performed her most serious stretch while whistling 'New York, New York'. It was like watching some freaks' talent show.

'And no one asked you to unpack for me.' Maybe she was rechargeable. A couple of hours plugged into the mains and good as new. Now she was practically bouncing on the spot.

'It was a pleasure. Love you too.'

The door closed—and opened again almost immediately. What now?

'Hey, Daddy Warbucks, the *Times* and the *Journal*. I want you fully up to speed by the time I get back.'

The thud of broadsheet on carpet preceded the click of the room door and, relieved to finally be alone, Ben exhaled as he closed his eyes and fleetingly imagined himself on the treadmill. He could always go down and surprise her. Just a couple more seconds.

One of the things he loved most about living in England was the fact that everyone he knew talked about going to the gym whilst in the pub and, with the exception of January, they didn't quite get there. As long as you paid your membership and could theoretically go and work out instead of hitting a bar, you actually felt fitter. And anyway, he always walked up escalators. Well, if he wasn't carrying heavy bags...

Suddenly dimly aware that he was on the verge of his deepest sleep yet, Ben jerked awake. Sitting up far too fast, a wave of numbing pins and needles swept up his body as he stared at the alarm clock. It had only been a few minutes. Reaching for the remote he allowed himself a quick pre-shower television moment while his body came to terms with the fact that sleeping opportunities were over for the day.

He surfed fast and purposefully. If his career wasn't going to be spiritually rewarding or making a difference, it could at least be paying better. He needed to be thinking format. *Who Wants To Be A Millionaire?* He did. Such a simple idea. Just sadly not his.

Flicking between MTV and VH1, now he was awake he needed sustenance—even if the only growing he was doing these days was outwards. Leaning over, he tried the bedside drawer—Manhattan *Super Pages* and a pristine Holy Bible. In a single movement he rolled over to the other side of the bed. Nothing. Forcing himself into the vertical position, he padded across to the desk and checked the drawers.

Bingo. 1 x folder containing everything you would ever want to know about the hotel and its environs, including the extensive Room Service menu, and 1 x nondescript black hardback book. Moments later breakfast for two was on order and Ben was back in the horizontal position. But with the MTV channels on a simultaneous ad break, cartoons and infomercials on almost every channel that wasn't showing the news, and Ali's glossy magazines proving to be totally resistible, Ben opened the black book at a random page.

'If anyone calls from The Carlyle put them through immediately...'

Please. Mel mouthed the word silently as she rolled her eyes at no one in particular from her desk outside Sam's office.

'...and I need those file notes typed up as soon as you've got a moment.'

'Will do.'

Sam dialled the next number without even looking at the keypad.

'Good afternoon, Greenberg Brownstein. EJ Rutherford's office.'

'Hi, is she there?' Sam took another sip of her cranberry juice on the off chance that her nausea might be attributable to dehydration rather than the projection of what just might be in a no holds barred, worst-case scenario. Never before had she wanted to be able to turn back time. Where were Michael J. Fox and his customised DeLorean when she needed them?

'Who's calling?' Standard screening procedure and a success-related perk. When your firm charges you out at nearly four hundred pounds an hour you get a full-time secretary-shaped filter to allow you to select who you speak to.

'Sam Washington.'

She was through in a nanosecond.

'Hi, darling. How was NYC? I haven't been home for way too long.' EJ kicked her shoes off under her desk, rubbed her tired feet against her ten-denier encased calves and swivelled in her chair to face the window. Blue sky and cold golden sunshine mocked her from the other side of the enormous double-glazed pane that was designed never to open. There might as well have been bars on it. She deserved a break.

'Not bad.' Who was she kidding? Sam glanced around the sanctuary of her office. Two hundred and seventy-five square feet of personal space. Almost a direct reflection of the percentage of her life spent at work. Not to mention the millions she'd made for the partners. She definitely needed some sleep and a holiday. Unless she was having a quarter life crisis. In which case she was expecting to live one hundred and sixteen years… Maybe taking golf lessons wasn't such a stupid idea after all?

'Did you bring me a Tootsie Roll?' EJ Rutherford, top corporate lawyer, reduced to seven-year-old child complete with whiny voice at the prospect of her favourite candy.

'No.'

'What? Hey, you're kidding, right?'

'Sorry—I forgot. Mad rush at the airport. Plus I had Richard with me.' See, she could do normal. Just another day at the office. And the hotel hadn't called, so at this precise moment nothing was officially lost, merely missing in action.

EJ regrouped quickly and remained as optimistic as she could under the circumstances. 'Raisinets?' The silence spoke for itself. 'Reese's Pieces?'

'You can buy them here.'

'But they don't taste the same. Did you say Richard was with you?'

'They are exactly the same... Yup, he just turned up out of the blue for the meeting.'

'Jeez. That man has a nerve. You've got to hand it to him—he sure is persistent.'

'I don't have to hand him anything.'

'Hey, easy, tiger.'

'Sorry, it's been a long week.'

'So...' EJ sounded like a child bracing herself for disappointment. 'Did you bring me anything at all?'

Sam exhaled. This she could handle. 'I might have copy of *W* in my computer case...'

'I knew you wouldn't let me down.'

'...and a bag or two of Reese's.'

'Awesome. Yay. Thanks, darling. You're the best. I love presents.'

'They're one hundred and five per cent fat.'

'Just because you don't like peanut butter...'

It was a valid point.

'Anyway, they taste of home to me.'

'Give me a fruit & nut any day. You guys have a lot to learn about chocolate and biscuits. I mean, Chips Ahoy? What's that all about?'

'They're cookies.'

'You are so pedantic.'

'Look who's talking...' EJ trailed off, distracted by a man skilfully pasting a new twenty-four-sheet poster onto the advertising hoarding visible from her window. He was making it look very easy.

'Anyway, how's things? Good week?'

'Just another takeover at the office. Still, at least the weekend is looking pretty safe—although I'm still standing by for final instructions from an American fund on an acquisition. Fancy a bit of supper tomorrow? It feels like ages since we last actually saw each other.'

'Sounds like a plan.' The more distractions the better.

'Excellent.'

'Maybe we could squeeze a film in too?'

EJ watched the young man smooth the final sheet down with his low-tech broom, finally revealing the release date of the film his handiwork was promoting.

'How about *Taking Stock?*' Never underestimate the power of advertising. He wasn't exactly the Diet Coke man, but it was quite refreshing to see muscles, jeans and Timberlands...and a full head of hair—a pretty rare sight at Greenberg Brownstein, where, it would appear, the success of male employees was intrinsically linked to their being follically challenged.

'Taking Stock?'

'Yup.' EJ squinted at the billboard. '"Jim Stock, Wall Street whizz kid, goes missing"—and by the look of the ad campaign it's going to be big budget and totally unrealistic.'

'Perfect. Nothing I like more than a bit of global financial meltdown on a Saturday night.'

'Great, because it's finally happening. I'm losing touch with popular culture. We so need an extra day in the week. Just imagine—three-day weekends every week, only forty-five weeks a year... It'd be a hell of a lot more popular than the Euro. You sure you're Okay? You're very quiet. Unless, of course, you're just using me as filler while you go through your inbox...'

Sam took her finger off her mouse button. She'd only been skimming a few. Meanwhile the clock on her phone was silently baiting her. 13:36. 08:36 in Manhattan, and they'd promised they'd check first thing. Sam didn't care about interrupting the sleep of guests who'd paid over five hundred dollars for a night of luxury. Plus it was Friday; most of them were bound to be jogging around the reservoir or knee-deep in a breakfast meeting by now.

'Did it all go well?'

'I'm just tired.' Finally it would appear her physiology was starting to limit her once indefatigable attitude. One of her school reports had called her a human dynamo; now she needed a jump start. Sam rested her forehead on her fist and exhaled.

'What's with the yawning? Didn't you sleep at all?'

'Hmm?' To her annoyance, Sam was feeling worse since she'd got to the office.

'Sleep...on the plane?'

'A bit. Well, I pretended to so I didn't have to small-talk my way home, but I had a lot on my mind...' Her masochistic self wanted to confess, but EJ wasn't really listening. Sam didn't begrudge her. They were both experts in self-absorption—plus, since their law school days they'd had an unwritten rule that governed their friendship, outlawing negativity and insecurity. Together they perpetuated strength and success. And Sam hadn't granted this situation crisis status yet.

'I know what you mean, honey. What are we like—? Oh, my God!' EJ interrupted herself. 'I just have to tell you about last night.' EJ dropped her voice to an almost whisper. 'Let me tell you there is only one thing worse than a dinner party full of couples at our age, and that is a singles dinner party thrown charitably by a couple of cohabitees attempting to streamline their Christmas card list. I seriously thought about stabbing myself with a fork during the main course so I could pretend I was coming down with meningitis. Seventy per cent of the men were called Ed, only fifty per cent had hair, forty per cent had talked about their serious ex before dessert and, at a guess, one hundred per cent of them would like to screw a thirty-year-old lawyer, if not marry one.'

'Well, I'm safe for a few more weeks, then.'

'Why is it now that we've hit our thirties we're suddenly expected to be grateful for any male attention that comes our way? If it wasn't so fucking hilarious it'd make you want to cry. It's all about older men. Obviously it's better if they're not married, but…'

Sam's focus returned. 'Elizabeth-Jane—you're not, are you?'

'No…afraid not. Even though it was the best sex I've ever had.'

'La-la-la. Fingers in ears. Not listening.'

'Oh, yes, you are. Prude. Just because you haven't had sex in…'

'Hey, that's harsh.'

'Anyway, Nick's ancient history.'

'Just ancient.'

'He's only forty-eight…and I haven't seen or spoken to him in weeks…'

'Weeks? I thought it was January when you…' Conscience more stabbed than pricked, and Sam swallowed hard as her error dawned on her.

'Hey, a girl's got to live a little…'

She'd had nowhere else to turn. But now, thanks to the blank page and Bic biro approach to secret-keeping, it wasn't only *her* personal life currently out there on a pale blue feint line. Sam shook her head as her Friday feeling hit an all-time low. She envied EJ. Having a therapist was no stranger than having a hairdresser if you were American. And you couldn't accidentally leave a therapist in a desk drawer.

'I really better get on, honey. I need to sort some stuff out before my tele-con with the LA office. I promise I'll give you the rest of the story tomorrow. I'm planning to run Hyde Park first thing—call me if you're interested. Make sure you get a good night's sleep.'

Sam was miles away, torturing herself silently with details. Now the phone had gone quiet. Bugger. And she hadn't actually heard EJ say goodbye.

'Look forward to…' Sam stopped herself when the dialling tone cut in, confirming that she was talking to herself. Cupping her chin in her hands, she stared at her computer screen, seeing nothing except imaginary tabloid headlines. Despite her desire to come up with a proactive master plan, all roads currently led to Wait Patiently. Not something Sam Washington had been designed to do. Losing things coming a close second.

As if she'd been waiting for a silence, Mel popped her head round the door. Apparently privacy was an outmoded concept.

'Three file notes for you to proof, and I've brought you some tea. Thought you might need pepping up before your meeting.'

Sam was about to request a herbal alternative, but from the wafts of minty steam knew her secretary had anticipated well.

'Thanks. Meeting?'

'Your two o'clock. Fifth floor. Conference room 1. Just thought it might have slipped your mind, what with the not having been to bed thing. I mean, I know your seat practically turns into one, but I imagine it's not the same.'

'Right. Yes. I'll be there…thanks.' Sam picked up a pen and stared at the papers on her desk. She'd been counting on losing herself in a drafting but the words were just taunting her. As for a meeting…

'No problem.' Mel turned as she got to the door. 'Oh, and your mother rang. Please call her when you get a chance. She said it was fairly urgent.'

'Will do…'

Sam suppressed her irritation. Despite repeated briefings on the subject, her mother still hadn't grasped that phoning the office was best kept for emergencies and that organising Sunday lunch didn't deserve 'fairly urgent' classification.

'Oh and Mel?'

'Yup?'

'If The Carlyle Hotel call…'

'I know, I know. I'll put them straight through.'

'Right…'

Conversation closed.

Taking a sip of her tea, Sam brushed her hair, applied a little extra Touche Éclat, a fresh coat of powder, lipgloss and a generous squirt of perfume from the bottle she kept in her desk drawer. Restored to at least a superficial level of normality, she smoothed down her skirt as she got to her feet, and checked her appearance in the mirror. Perfect.

Insecurities filed away in an internal drawer somewhere, she strutted towards the lift. She loved the high-profile deals, and she was getting more and more of them. Youngest partner in the City. She dared to dream. As long as EJ didn't get there first.

Chapter Two

January 24th

Ben hesitated. Ali hadn't seen the funny side of him reading her journal, and that had been nearly twenty years ago. But there was a high probability that this one might contain more than high school crushes, exam angst and playground politics. Plus, if he didn't at least try to identify the author, how was he supposed to reunite the two in exchange for eternal gratitude? Perfect justification. He flicked back to the beginning.

If found please return to:
Flat 3,
68 Warwick Road,
Battersea,
London SW11 8HP

Damn. But breakfast wasn't due for another forty-five minutes, and he only needed to have a quick shower. After all, he was unpacked already.

Jan 1st
Hungover. Should never have gone to Sophie's dinner party. Food always fantastic—really must learn to cook properly—but midnight was a bit like watching the slow dance at the school disco. Bed at 4:00 a.m. Resolve to wake up next New Year's Day without having to apologise to liver, stomach and kidneys for immaturity. Brain seems to have developed pulse of its own. Just waiting for it to burst out of my forehead, *Alien* stylee.
NY Res:
1. a) Run/cycle round Battersea Park at least 3 x week
   b) Register for charity half-marathon. Would like to hit 30 at peak of physical fitness

Ben held his two-pack in. What was it with women and exercise? As far as he could make out they spent most of their schooldays avoiding physical education before devoting their late twenties to single-handedly combating the twin forces of evil—cellulite and gravity—determined to make amends.

2. Posture.
Stand and sit up straight.
Don't want to become hunchbacked old woman

He sat up a little straighter. Round shoulders were the curse of the comfort generation.

Smile while walking fast. Don't want to be old and fierce-looking with furrowed brow
3. No carbs. (January only) Fresh fruit x 5 daily. Espec. red peppers and tomatoes—antioxidants
4. Read one Penguin Classic every 2 months
5. Keep legs and bikini line hair-free even in depths of winter—remember am doing it for self
6. Be better friend, however busy at work. Owe Sophie and Mark at least five dinners—prob. more
7. Sort out nuclear winter in window boxes and try and keep them alive for more than two months at a time.

Replanting is cheating. Water might help. Think last batch of plants were dodgy. Water. Sun. Photosynthesis. How hard can it be?

8. a) Have great sex
   b) Have sex more than once
   c) Have sex more than once with the same person
   d) That person must be someone you have never had sex with before
9. Pilates or yoga? Research difference

Research difference? Ben scoffed. He was sure one was just the new-fangled version of the one before. It was all a gimmick. New millennium women were exhausting.

10. Streamline wardrobe. Be ruthless. Do not need another pair of black trousers, probably ever.
11. Buy anti-wrinkle cream. Is it too late once wrinkles have started to appear? Ask EJ. She seems to have inside track on new products
12. Buy night repair cream—why do repairs have to take place at night? Is it like roadworks? But no one has to dig anything up, do they?
13. Find tennis coach. Am too old to still have a crap serve
14. Try whisky again. May have grown into it now.

Ben grimaced sympathetically. He'd never understood the allure of cough medicine with ice or water, and despite David's repeated determination to make him a man, Southern Comfort was as close as he'd managed to get to the whole malt zone.

15. Exfoliate

Liver now feels like is trying to burrow its way out of my back cavity. Sure in desperation it has borrowed water from other vital organs. Can't rehydrate fast enough and have officially run out of soap operas, Australian, American and otherwise, to watch on apparently numerous digital television channels that I pay for. Hangovers definitely getting worse.

EJ says we have passed physical peak. Wish I'd known when I was reaching the summit. Should've had more random sexual encounters. Anyway, who says I need man to rescue me? Am perfectly happy. Wonder how Paul is? Oh, no. Usual downward hangover spiral and selective memory kicking in. Always wouldn't mind having boyfriend, however unsuitable, on days like today. And if alcohol is a depressant why did I feel so good last night? Lonely. No one has called. Not even Mum. Don't know why I bother to have answer-machine *and* call-waiting.

Ben shook his head. If she had just got off her toned arse and headed down to the pub for a couple of Bloody Marys with a buddy or two she'd have been feeling a lot better, he was sure of it.

Must call Sophie and Mark and say thank you. Not now. Probably still in bed. Not sure will make it out of house today. Maybe should add atrophy to list of skills to perfect this year.

All out of empathy, he flicked forward a handful of pages.

Jan 16th

Bad day. 1—Caught myself counting faint lines on forehead in lift mirror at 7:00 a.m. before remembering CCTV memo. 2—Richard called twice about having lunch to discuss my progress—more like *his* progress. 3—Departmental drinks tonight—decision to have onions in salad at lunch was wrong one. 4—Monster spot brewing on lipline, with roots in central nervous system and fast-track link to tear ducts. Have drenched in tea-tree oil and now whole office smells like aromatherapy zone. Have despatched Mel to buy industrial strength cover-up and air-freshener.

Ben yawned. Just reading her life was exhausting, but no wonder Adrian Mole and Bridget Jones were world-famous. It was mundanely addictive stuff, and without thinking he'd conjured up a mental picture of a black-trousered, ageing, hyperactive hunchback in need of chill-out, pilates and serve lessons.

Hope that someone laughs at early attempt to be witty before I lose will to live or they notice spot. Definitely should not have attempted pre-emptory squeeze. Lip must not swell. Are there genuinely confident people out there or are they just better at bluffing than the rest of us?

Sam sat in the conference room and watched the bubbles in her mineral water lose their battle to cling to the bottom of the glass before forcing herself to concentrate by diligently taking copious notes. Doing her utmost to avoid Richard's gaze, even though she could feel him observing her from the other side of the table, she channelled all her positive mental powers of retrieval to the other side of the Atlantic.

Jan 21st—Edinburgh
Freezing my tits off despite two fleeces and long sleeved T-shirt. Perfect skiing weather, only there's no snow and no piste. If I ever have hen weekend it will be somewhere hot and will not involve being hungover in hiking boots. Sunshine is glorious. Wind-chill is positively Scandinavian. Thank God Sophie has opted for London-based traditional drinks, dinner and nightclub approach. Hope Gemma not having some sort of travellers reunion on Designers Guild sofa and has remembered to feed George.

Hard to share after months alone, and probably impossible to ever find someone totally compatible post-Soph. Can't believe G caught me waxing legs in front of Dolly Parton documentary on Thursday night. Now probably thinks I am some bluegrass nut. And all because I couldn't face *Newsnight*. Miss the anonymity. And do miss topless cup of coffee first thing, pre-shower. Maybe am secretly some sort of naturist? Will actively discourage that tendency.

Deal should close next week. Hope EJ is still up for skiing. Can't believe she is still sleeping with NG after everything he's put her through. But apparently sex is awesome.

Ben stopped skimming. This was the Holy Grail of diary snooping.

Fact he is so well known has got to be recipe for disaster...not to mention the takeover. Have had serious chat and she's adamant he's got more to lose than she has. Therefore she's safe. She didn't even buckle at the *Hello!* spread. Perfect home, perfect children, perfect wife. But you can't just go shagging the other side. Even if he did make the first move, how could she ever prove it?

A surge of adrenaline powered up Ben's hard drive as he began to scour his archives. NG... NG...

Can't believe it's been on and off for 5 months.

Ben counted back on his fingers to August/September and added the details to his search. Still nothing.

She insists monogamy is flawed. I just don't want to see her get hurt. Of course if you never over-estimate a man then he'll never let you down, but she deserves so much more, and it's not like she needs to be checking in and out of hotels midweek, even if they are all five-star. She claims it's all on her terms, but how can it be when he dictates where and when? She says this is the future. I am still hoping for more. Seems impossible that is now six years since my last, okay my only serious relationship ended. Wanted period of being single, but not necessarily a lifetime. And what if that was the best I—

A knock, followed by—what was that?—the doorbell?

As he crash-landed back in his world, Ben's amusement at

the fact their room was large enough to merit a bell was only momentary as he heard a key slice into the lock.

'Coming…'

Momentarily forgetting the breakfast order, he wondered whether this could have been a set-up. The curse of a vivid imagination coupled with mild paranoia. One of the many side effects of being a true creative…along with lower than average salary, propensity towards messiness, predilection for alcohol and the inability to look truly smart even in a suit.

'I'll be with you in a second.' Stuffing the diary under his pillows, Ben strode across the fitted carpet to answer the door.

Disappointingly there was no sign of any food. Instead, a woman power-dressed in a black suit, who looked as if she had been made up enthusiastically by Picasso using a trowel, was waiting patiently, hands clasped to display her freshly manicured nails.

'I'm so sorry to bother you, sir…'

Ben loved the formality of hotels. Being a paying guest was a prostitution of sorts. Instant respect without having to earn it so long as you had a valid credit card number. Where else would a thirty-something producer for a mediocre television production company, dressed in his underwear, be addressed with such deference? Although somewhat disappointingly she had resisted the urge to bob a curtsey. It wasn't until he felt her gaze wander to his midriff and back that Ben realised he was only wearing boxer shorts. A cursory glance due south confirmed that nothing was gaping and everything was exactly where it was supposed to be, albeit shrinking rapidly.

'I can come back a little later if this is a bad time?' This time she looked him squarely and unblinkingly in the eye, the directness of her stare more than a little unnerving.

'Really, it's no problem. What can I help you with?' Ben folded his arms across his chest to remove the likelihood of his hands accidentally straying to his groin area for a morning scratch. It was either that or hands on hips, which would have looked even stranger and much camper, if not like a little teapot. He would have pulled on yesterday's jeans if he'd been able to see them. Obviously they were hanging in a wardrobe for the first time in their life. There were advantages to having an interfering older sister, but this wasn't one of them.

'It really shouldn't take a minute.'

'I was just getting up anyway…' To his relief, Ben spotted a bathrobe and belted it round him to reduce his increasing feeling of semi-nakedness. But now, with his underwear still on underneath, he might have appeared more decent but he felt like a cross between Hugh Hefner and Lily Savage.

She was still hesitating on the threshold.

'Really. Come in.' Taking a step to one side, and with a hospitable sweep of his arm, he finally persuaded her to enter the room and, shoulders back, she strode past him to the bedroom.

Retreating to the sitting room, Ben pulled back a curtain, flooding the room with light. It had been dark when they'd arrived, but now a patchwork of power stretched out below, the long green rectangle of Central Park a perfect contrast to the density of towers midtown that made the New York skyline one of the most distinctive in the world.

The sky was a perfect high-pressure blue, and as the sun reflected off cars and windows, with glimpses of handkerchief-sized stars and stripes blowing in the crosstown breeze over twenty floors below, it was as if the city was twinkling. Surveying the scene, he was overtaken by a sense of pride. He loved London—its quirkiness, its history, its architecture—but the British just couldn't do skyscrapers. Canary Wharf wasn't in the same league.

'I've just got to check a couple of drawers.'

'No problem.'

'The previous guest thinks she may have left something behind…'

'Really?' Ben silenced himself. Each word on the subject only deepened his deception. Picking up the *New York Times* he forced himself to sit down and act natural. He was an oxymoron in action. Maybe just a moron. And he might as well have been holding the *Times* upside down for all the information he was gleaning.

Ben watched and listened over the top of the paper, half expecting the book to fling itself into open view from its inadequate hiding place. But on Tuesday he'd be back in London—or he could hand it in to Reception later. It was a win-win situation.

Sam stared at the Post-It in the centre of her desk. Melanie's curvy writing filled the primrose-yellow. There had to be a logical explanation. But if she didn't have it and neither did the hotel…

Her chest was tight. Only a diary. Only a diary. Only a diary… It wasn't working. If anything, hysteria was tiptoeing a little closer. If she'd wanted to expose her soul to an audience she'd have been a talk-show host, not a lawyer. Yet now someone had the fast-track to her unencrypted inner sanctum and, worst of all, it wasn't only *her* privacy that had been invaded.

Sam shook her head vehemently and deliberately. She needed a calming influence. There was only one person for the job. She might have moved out in October to start a joint life with Mark in their little house on the Fulham prairie, but thankfully she was still at the end of the phone.

Sophie eyeballed the phone, daring it to ring. She'd only popped out for stamps, and she'd left return messages for Sam everywhere. Something was up. She couldn't remember the last time Sam had called her at home in the afternoon. All part of the not-needing-anyone-for-anything charade that she seemed to have successfully perpetuated with everyone who hadn't met her before she'd finally split up with Paul.

Double-checking she had all the photos and samples she needed for her meeting, Sophie made herself another coffee. As the kettle boiled she stared critically into the mirror, pawing at imperfections only she could see before standing back to allow a more soft-focus view and grimacing to tighten the skin of her neck in an attempt to exercise the muscles responsible for keeping her chin in place.

As Mark swept in to the sitting room, pinstriped from head to toe, newspaper tucked under his arm, a bunch of flowers wrapped in the usual pastel paper from the flower stall outside the tube station, Sophie gave her hair a quick flick and hoped he hadn't noticed her moment of gurning madness. She was never going to stop men in the street with her looks, but she'd always been attractive enough. And happy enough. It was just—well, what with all the planning for the wedding she couldn't help becoming a little more self-absorbed and self-conscious...

'Hello, you. Happy weekend. Smells gorgeous in here.' Mark presented Sophie with the bouquet and planted an enthusiastic kiss on her cheek before striding over to the oven and peering in. 'Mmm. Cottage pie. My favourite. You are clever. Lucky me. But only a small dish...' He looked up. 'So does this mean you're abandoning me again this evening?'

'Only for a few hours. And only for another woman.'

'Excellent.'

Sophie smiled. Mark's fantasies were as original as his taste in suits.

'She's just inherited four floors of Artex and woodchip in Richmond and needs serious help.'

'Sounds expensive.'

'Here's hoping.' Sophie walked over to her husband-to-be. His five-thirty shadow was giving him an atypically rugged appeal that she really quite liked. 'It's just an informal meeting—a chance for me to introduce myself and give her a few knee-jerk ideas—but at least this way I've still got the weekend to myself, and if she likes my recommendations it's potentially my biggest project yet. Apparently her husband's loaded.'

'And hopefully devastatingly unattractive.'

'Hideous, I believe. Anyway, there must be a good four hours of crucial sport for you to watch on cable until I get back.'

'Well, they're repeating the one-day cricket from India...'

Sophie pulled a face. She couldn't understand the point of a sport in which the quick version took a whole day to play. '…plus there'll be the weekend football and rugby previews, and of course essential tractor-pulling on Eurosport. But first I was planning on getting out of my uniform and having a little rest.' Mark filled a pint glass with water from the mixer tap, liberally showering himself in the process.

'Poor you. Have you had a horrible day?'

'Not too bad, but it's Friday so of course there was a large lunch to contend with.'

She should have known. His breath was far too minty for this time of the afternoon.

Mark grabbed at his love handles with a contradictory combination of pride and disgust. 'These must be worth a fortune. Pure sirloin, *frîtes* and Fleurie.' He gulped down his water, wiping his mouth on his forearm in the manner of a true nine-year-old. 'What time are you off, then?'

'Ought to be out of here in less than an hour, and I still have to change.'

'Don't go changing…'

It was one of their standard lines, and one that had proved very lucrative for both Billy Joel and Barry White, but it still made her smile.

Wrapping his arms around her curves, Mark pulled his fiancée in for a kiss. 'Don't suppose you want a quick lie-down too?'

Minutes later the phone rang, but Sophie didn't hear it.

Chapter Three

Ben sat himself down in a leather armchair identical to the one he had just vacated a few blocks east and, arranging the expanding collection of shopping bags at his feet, exchanged an empathetic smile with the men sitting on either side of him.

He'd done almost all his clothes-shopping in a couple of stores on Lexington straight after lunch, and yet this was their third branch of Banana Republic in two hours. Ali assured him this was their flagship, the mother ship, the Mecca, the ultimate collection, and until they opened a branch in London he'd just have to be patient. Reaching for the *GQ* magazine that he was using as a disguise, he settled into his seat and selected one of the most recent entries.

Wednesday March 21st

Furious. Richard turned up at hotel this morning all smiles for final meetings. Not even a call or e-mail first. Wanker. He claims he is relationship-building. Yadda-yadda-yadda. If he's waiting for me to screw up it's not going to happen.

Must keep calm. Home tomorrow. And, small consolation, did pick up killer DKNY trouser suit yesterday. Simple lines. Classic cut. Great fabric. Always feel unassailable in NYC. Energy levels infectious and people no ruder than in London. Need green card. Or American firm to sponsor me. Or American husband—note: George Clooney has previously shown a healthy degree of interest in English girls.

Nick still periodically chasing EJ. Am proud to report she is resisting and has no shortage of alternative offers. Own daily routine feeling bit flat by comparison. Busy enough socially, but is increasingly girlie nights and am often sole singleton at dinner parties, expected to entertain with tales of the City so they can relive their dating days vicariously. Less random new people. Need new project. Most exciting thing to happen to me last week was new series of *Friends* on E4. And never have time to watch whole series. Know I will end up buying DVD and filing it, unopened, along with others. Scene change would be good. And it's not like I'm going to give it all up and make jam.

Ben shook his head. These pseudo-feminists were their own worst enemies, believing they could eat men for breakfast when all they really wanted was a man to make it for them.

Sometimes I think I'd like to spend more time outside. Personal trainer? Landscape gardener?

Landscape gardener? He was supposed to be the creative one, yet in his regular life and career crises he only ever came up with the traditional bar owner/teacher/doctor options.

Or at least do something that feels more tangible. I have good job. Good salary. Qualifications. Prospects. But sometimes wonder if I am too sensible—own worst enemy—but then maybe grass is always greener in a landscaped garden. But haven't met any guys with long-term potential since I've been at 3L. Not that this is all about a man. Far from it.

'Yeah, right.' Ben stabbed the diary with his finger before turning the page. Apparently she wasn't the only one with problems. He was talking to a magazine.

Could retrain. Teaching is tempting. Salary is not. But increasingly feel would like to make a difference, however small.

Need gym session. Not sure fast walking in semi-heels to Bloomingdales and back counts as exercise. Now Richard has suggested exercising corporate Amex over cocktails with clients in Bemelmans Bar at 6.30. Could just be a little late. Woman's prerogative. Then again, probably not quite future partner prerogative. At least have new classic cocktail dress. Makes me feel fabulous, especially now upper arms are more toned. On the whole these NY boys are more attractive than their British counterparts, but sadly they rarely have any substance, any real spirit. As if their strength has been sapped by their sand-coloured Chinos.

Ben shook his head and looked down at his black round-neck jumper and Diesel jeans, irritated by her descent into cliché. Yup, all American men were dull and without style, and all British women only had sex in the missionary position. Maybe if she stepped out of the executive gene pool she'd have a bit more fun.

I think Bill likes me, though. Should make evening slightly less painful. And with a bit of a power flirt I imagine 'just call me Harvey' will be happy to agree to the fee proposal and recommended deal structure, just as long as Richard doesn't interfere. Cocktails not such bad idea after all. Bugger. Just seen time. Instead of scribbling could at least have done a session on the stepper.

Never had American man. Maybe this is where I've been going wrong…

★ ★ ★

He wasn't surprised there wasn't a queue. Like she knew anything about the real world, locked away in her ivory office block. Smug, supercilious…and single.

'Well, what do you think?' Ali strutted over in an all black outfit, a bundle of tags swinging from her belt loops.

'Hmm?' Ben gave his sister the once-over and, still fuming, must have accidentally frowned.

'What?'

'Nothing.' Ben did his utmost to minimise the machinations of a lawyer in crisis and focus on his sister as she sashayed along an imaginary catwalk in front of him before coming to an abrupt, less glamorous halt.

'Well, come on—spit it out. I didn't bring you along to be polite.'

'It's all lovely.'

'Fence-sitter. Now, let's start again. Trousers?'

Ben refocused. 'Aren't they the same as the ones you tried in the last place?'

Ali's subsequent sigh was tinged with exasperation. 'No, the waistband is totally different and there are no back pockets on these.'

'Of course.' Amateur error. How could he have missed the waistband/pocket detail?

'Well?'

'They're very nice. Great. Get them. How much?'

'Flattering?' Ali ignored the last question. How could you put a price on the perfect pair of black trousers?

'Yup. Very.' Ben tried not to stare at his sister's bottom. 'Seriously, I like the cut. Simple lines and, um, great fabric—classic.' Ali's eyes lit up. Ben knew he'd hit the jackpot. 'Yup, definitely classic.' Silently he thanked his anonymous tipster. When it came to women's fashion, she was good.

'Great. Thanks. Right, just a few more things to try and then we'll stop for a coffee.'

'What else do you need?'

'A couple of sweaters, maybe a spring coat, a bag, a belt…'

Ali paused. Ben was getting the idea.

'It's not like I've got a list…'

Of course. The hunter-gatherer try-it-all-before-deciding approach to a new wardrobe.

'…but I'll know them when I see them.'

'Whatever.'

'Thanks for being so patient.'

'No problem. Look, we're here now—take your time, try anything you like…'

Ali cocked her head and studied her brother for a moment before strutting back to her cubicle. What about the 'they do have shops in London' line he usually came out with? She'd get to the bottom of it just as soon as she'd found the perfect pair of jeans, and maybe a couple of sweaters…

Suddenly, clearing her social plate for her first night home was seeming less sensible. EJ was out, Sophie was with a prospective client, and Gemma was as likely to be home on a Friday night as Cherie Blair was to have a number one single. Yet Sam was lingering in the office, afraid to face up to both her conscience and her empty fridge.

For the twenty-first consecutive minute Sam stared out of her window, mesmerised by the moon rising over London. Perfectly round and almost whitely luminescent against an increasingly deep blue sky, it was the sort of scene you expected Elliot to cycle across with ET in his basket. And a timely reminder of the fact that the world was still doing its spinning thing while she remained powerless.

Sam swivelled back to face her desk and reached for another file-shaped dose of reality. Give her a complicated deal any day over the emotional stuff.

The writing was much messier now. And in a different pen.

Richard Blakely is a wanker.

Richard Blakely is an arrogant wanker.

Richard Blakely is an arrogant, misogynist wanker.

Richard Blakely is an arrogant, misogynist wanker who

wields his (not exactly enormous) sexuality like some sort of power tool.

Richard Blakely is a tool, an egomaniac, and my boss. Fucking marvellous.

A smudge. Her hand? A tear? Neat vodka?

How can this be happening? Tired of being an adult. Want someone else to take responsibility for me. To help. Am so tired.

'You're making me feel guilty, just sitting there. Why don't I meet you in that enormous shop you love and I hate?' Ali's voice came sailing out of the changing area.

'What?' Grumpy at the interruption, Ben tuned back in to his life just as Ali appeared with an armful of rejects and further requests for the assistant.

'The Virgin Megastore.'

'The last thing I need now is a virgin.'

'Benjamin…' The warning tone. 'Just go.'

Carefully he closed the magazine. 'What you still fail to understand is that you can never have too much music. Fashions come and go. The soundtrack of your life is ever-expanding.'

'Whatever.'

'It's true. Certain tracks are like milestones.'

'Yeah, yeah.'

'Which song did you have your first French kiss to?'

'Um, George Michael—"Careless Whisper".'

'1984.'

'You're a freak, do you know that?'

'And what were you wearing?'

'God knows.'

'See.'

'Please, be a music anorak with my blessing…just leave me out of it. But really you might as well go on ahead. You must be bored out of your mind.'

'Bored?'

'I know what I'm like when I'm on a mission. I've still got

a few more things I want to try here, and then I need to go to Barnes & Noble and Sephora.'

'Here you go, miss.' The assistant had returned with Phase 6 of the try-ons and another pseudo-genuine smile from her collection.

'Thanks...could you find me a belt too?'

'Sure.'

Ben rolled his eyes at the girl and she did her best not to reciprocate. Hey, the customer was always right. One belt selection coming right up.

'Okay, I admit it. There's no such thing as a selfless good deed.' Ali headed back behind the curtain. 'But you know how much I hate it when you insist on walking up and down every aisle, including the Country, World and Extreme Reggae departments. Maybe if we were married I'd find it endearing. Then again...'

'I'll go later...or tomorrow.' Ben tried to focus.

> Why is he even here tonight? Why can't he understand I am not now, nor *ever* will be, interested in him? Can't believe he actually suggested we have a fling. Correction, an affair. Jesus. Much worse. OK, I admit have been ignoring some signs, a few glances, a couple of compliments, but I never thought he meant anything until now.
>
> And to think he said it wouldn't change anything...

'Ha. Busted. Extreme Reggae. I invented a whole new musical genre and you didn't even notice.'

> ...that he actually suggested that fucking the boss, as he so delicately put it, might be exciting. That I'd be the perfect mistress. Mistress. He didn't even want a one-night stand. What is it with me? What is it that I exude that makes men want to sleep with me, yet date and marry someone else?

'Yup.' Ben selected a monosyllabic random response and hoped it fitted in with the general gist of Ali's conversation.

> God, I'm stupid to have let him come up here when he

said he just wanted to collect some papers. Honestly didn't think I was being naïve. I only went to the bathroom for a minute and then there he was, in my bed, his clothes abandoned in a pile on the floor. How can Richard think of me as some sort of emotionally detached sexual predator? Increasingly unsure whether I even have a romantic core any more. Think Paul may have packed it, along with my Crowded House CD, when we split up. Must repurchase.

Nodding sympathetically, he turned the page. Julia had squirrelled away quite a few of his old favourites, but it had seemed a bit petty to bring it up at the time.

Could it be that I've only got as far at 3L because Richard...? Know I am being ridiculous. Am bloody good at what I do. But suddenly everything feels sordid. Why does it always have to boil down to sex? Why can't it be more like school? End-of-year exams. Pointless rules. Regulation hockey socks. Gym knickers. But no sex. Well, not for me at any rate.

Ben's eyes darted along every line, taking in as much as he could in as short a time as possible. Ali was bound to interrupt again any minute.

At least I kept my cool. Didn't overreact. He apologised. Questionable sincerity. Claimed too much to drink. Got carried away. Should be carried away. Such a smooth operator. I never want to be a wife if this is what happens. Am adult. Can cope.

Still don't know how EJ managed to be so laid back (laid back!) about NG thing. If it gets out her life at GB is as good as over, and all for the sake of a few orgasms. Then again, when was the last time I even had one of those? Maybe he wanted her to be his in-house counsel. But now his wife is expecting a third. And he never pretended his marriage was in trouble.

And why would I leave one of London's top firms

when I can almost see my name on the headed paper? Guess it's just business as usual, then. I can do professional and so can he. I'm not the one with a wife and children. Sometimes the world is so disappointing. Wanted my life to be *St Elmo's Fire,* not *Carry On Up Against the Filing Cabinet.*

Ben laughed before attempting to segue into more of a cough when he realised there were other people listening.

Ali waltzed out in a different outfit.

'Hey. What about this?' Ali pulled the back of the top down, tightening it across her chest. 'Is the sweater too pink? Or not pink enough?'

Startled by her speedy return, Ben had barely enough time to tilt the magazine to his chest.

'Nice.'

'What?'

'The pants. I mean the trousers.' Twenty years of living in London and he was almost fluent in English.

'Get with it. They're the same.' Ali wasn't doing a great job of disguising her impatience. 'It's the top I want to know about.'

'Quite tight. Good colour on you.'

'It's supposed to be tight.'

'Then it's fine.'

'Fine? Just for the record "fine" and "nice" are not acceptable answers when clothes-shopping.'

'It's great. Splendid. Marvellous. Exquisite. Really, it suits you.'

'Not too tight?'

'No.'

'And not too big either?'

'No. Tight. Definitely tight.'

'Sexy tight?'

'I guess.'

'But not tarty tight?'

'No.'

'Nor shrunk-one-size-in-the-wash too tight.'

'No.'

'Which is a good point.' Ali twisted the seam until the care instructions were in her grasp. Dry Clean Only. But, fingering the wool, she was sure she could hand-wash it carefully. 'Do you think David will like it?' Ali was contorting her chest in the mirror and tilting her upper body through ninety degrees, presumably in case she ever needed to wear cashmere to a gymnastics meet.

'I'm sure he'll love it.'

'And it's not too pink?'

Too pink? Ben was confused. It was pink, definitely pink, but too pink? He was out of his depth.

'No.' He was a little hesitant.

'I think it's a great pink. Not too pale, not pastel or insipid, but not puce either…'

Phew. He'd clearly said the right thing.

'I'll take it. Shall I get it in black too?'

'Why not?' Ben's attention had been drawn back to the page.

'You don't think black's too harsh?'

'No…'

'Good. That's what I thought.'

'It's just a sweater.' It was a mumbled afterthought. Ali didn't appear to hear him. Which was a relief. But, slowly taking his eye off the page, he realised she hadn't retreated to her cubicle either. This didn't bode well.

'What are you reading about?'

'Um, nothing.'

'Ben?' Her hand was definitely on her hip. 'You never do reading unless there is absolutely nothing else to do. And it isn't even the hundred sexiest women in the galaxy issue.'

'I do read.'

'Since when? You skim.'

Much as he loved her, if there was one person who could wind him up instantaneously with a change in tone it was his sister.

'Everyone reads on the subway.'

'The tube.' Ali corrected her brother, making sure to pronounce it in perfect English as 'tyoob' and not 'toob'. 'Although I don't know how you'd know. You even bought a scooter because you hate public transport so much.'

Ben refused to rise to Ali's goading and, with a shrug of his shoulders, returned to his extract—or at least he would have done if she hadn't snatched the magazine. A few photocopied pages drifted lethargically to the floor.

Ali scanned a few lines as she fought Ben to gather them up, her gaze becoming stonier by the minute. 'Whose is this?'

'I don't know.' Ben was suddenly sheepish, despite the fact he'd definitely been an adult in his own right for a good thirteen years. 'I found it...well, I found the original...in a drawer in the room. This is just... I didn't want it to get damaged... I'm going to hand it in when we get back. Or post it. There was a London address.'

'There was?' Ali had turned a different colour, and if he was honest the sweater was now clashing a bit with her skin tone. A sort of raspberry ripple effect. Maybe it was too pink.

'Calm down. No harm done. It's not like it's yours or anything. And I'm just reading it, not auctioning the film rights.'

'I'm confiscating it.'

'You can't. It's not yours.'

'And it's not yours. Honestly, I thought you'd know better...'

'It was lost. Now it's not. I'm the good guy.' Probably not a great time to mention the management search earlier, or the multiple programme ideas that had been bubbling under since he'd started reading it this morning.

'Hardly. You're the creep who went to the copy shop.' Ali took the magazine and the pages and stuffed them into one of the bags he was guarding for her before taking it away.

'You were having a manicure...and I didn't want it to get thumbed.' Ben could see that neither was a winning argument.

'So, what? Now I have to check your pockets and I can't leave you on your own? We'll discuss this later.' Ali re-entered the changing area.

'How about I buy you the sweater?' Ben shouted after her.

'Jumper,' Ali corrected him.

'Just because you've got an English husband doesn't mean you have to let go of your American roots completely.'

'We've got an English father. And stop changing the subject. I'll accept the bribe, but don't think this is over yet. This is the only the beginning of that conversation.'

Somehow Ben had suspected that already. Plus, now he was bored.

Sam lay in the bath and watched the shadows flickering on the blue and green mosaic tiles. Her candles were failing to live up to their calming aromatherapy promise. Holding her breath, she allowed herself to slip under the hot water and, crossing her legs to remove her knees from the cold air of the bathroom, she cocooned herself in muted warmth. Bed beckoned. When the going got tough, the tough hibernated.

'Next, please.'

Ben shuffled a little closer to the till, clutching a tower of CDs to his chest. Mid-season sale. Not that he was sure which season they were mid at the moment, but he wasn't complaining. He needed coffee. He still had a good hour before he was due back uptown. And the more time Ali had to calm down the better. Women.

Leaving the store, he walked a couple of blocks east to Grand Central Station and ordered a coffee at Cipriani's. Absorbed by the swirling crowds on the main concourse below, he let his mind wander back to the diary. Having drained his cup, and ignoring the waiter's scowl at his failure to order a second, he found a pen and started scribbling on a napkin.

Chapter Four

Kicking the front door closed behind her, laden with shopping bags, Sam rustled her way along the corridor to the kitchen before her arms gave out. Her quads were smarting slightly after the intensity of her gym session, but thank God for endorphins. It was almost impossible to feel morose with your heart-rate at one hundred and sixty. Determined to keep her activity levels high, she switched the radio on for instant company and automatically re-boxed the CDs lying on the work-top while she searched for a station with a little less bass line and a few 'classic' tunes. Classic meaning old. Old enough for her to remember.

Having explored every possible plan of action on the running machine, she had come to the somewhat unsatisfactory, if definite conclusion that there was nothing she could do. According to calendar convention it was a new day, and so, for the time being, Captain Optimistic was back in town, having finally shaken off Assume-The-Worst Woman on the rowing machine.

As she restocked her cupboards Sam noticed a tell-tale slick of grease on the floor tiles. Obligingly, the Chinese take-away diva had left her foil containers out, and it appeared that the insatiable George had gone for self-service.

Roused from a warm corner of the flat by the crinkle of a supermarket carrier, he careered into the kitchen, anxious not to miss a potential feeding moment, and once in full view attempted to feign nonchalance but failed miserably thanks to the negative braking properties of claw and paw on terracotta. Having regained his composure, from the purr crescendo and surprisingly powerful shoves Sam was getting, he was claiming to be hungry. Not physiologically possible but he was one of the few who knew, contrary to popular myth, his owner had a slushy core.

Sam retched at the intense aroma burst of meat, offal and jelly as she opened a new can. Living on her own hadn't been a problem, but living on her own with a kitten? Cliché-tastic. Now Gemma was around. That had been Sophie's idea too. Breathing through her mouth, she put George's dish on the floor and carefully washed up the fork. According to the clock on the oven door it was nearly eleven-thirty, and there was no evidence that the Queen of Peking had even surfaced to make herself a cup of tea.

Sam flicked the kettle switch and turned the radio up in an attempt to mask her enthusiastic, if somewhat atonal sing-a-long. No more tiptoeing around in her own flat. Today had started hours ago.

Gemma appeared in the doorway almost exactly as the kettle boiled, bleary-eyed, her unruly hair even wilder than normal. And she seemed to be wearing a strappy top and pyjama shorts. Obviously the latest in naughty-but-nice-girl-next-door sleepwear, and much more Sarah Jessica Parker in dishevelled sexiness, Sam noted, than it would have been on her. Gem was a natural. The sort of girl who'd never sat at the side of the school hall at the end-of-term disco. Who'd never had to pretend that she didn't want to dance to 'The Power of Love' or the 'Lady in Red'. Boys had always sidled up to her on the off chance. They still did.

'Morning.' Gemma started rubbing her eyes in an attempt

to uncrust last night's mascara and restore the individual lash look.

'Only just… Look, do you think you could try not to leave food out? He's a cat—he's going to help himself. And he's definitely not designed to eat spring onions drenched in plum sauce.'

Sam had her head in the fridge and was in the process of jettisoning most of the salad drawer, which had apparently liquidised itself in its bags since last week. This had never happened when Sophie had lived there. Mark was a lucky man. Sophie was a rare find in the twenty-first century—perfect wife material. And Sam was speaking from experience. Having a flatmate who'd enjoyed cooking, worked irregular hours and often from home might not have been great for the phone bill, but it had been fantastic for leftovers and getting her washing done.

As she replaced the old bags with new ones, freshly shopped, she knew it would be as good for her nutrition as buying them was for her conscience if she actually ate the stuff—but she never seemed to have time to eat at home at the moment.

'Sorry. Chuck us the milk. I need tea.' Gemma might not get up until late, but she was always incredibly perky when she did finally surface.

Sam handed her the plastic container, simultaneously liberating a shrivelled courgette from a dark corner of the second shelf, and did her best not to appear fazed by the similarly dishevelled young man now standing in her kitchen. From his slicked-back hair it looked as if he had at least managed a shower. In fact, he smelt familiarly citrusy.

'Good shower?' Her tone was mordacious.

The bastard reeked of her Jo Malone bodywash. And the whole point of paying a mortgage was so that you didn't have to carry your towels and products in and out of the bathroom each morning.

'Yes, thanks.' His reply was hesitant. Small talk or sarcasm? His eyes darted to Gemma and back, hoping for a clue. Gemma, however, was concentrating on squeezing every last drip of caffeine into her cup.

'Well, hi. I'm Sam.' She faked a smile.

Now she'd sodding well have to change all the towels. She couldn't risk drying her face in his pubes, even if Jo Malone had given them the once-over. She swapped neurotic for civil. At least for the short term. Giving her hands a quick rinse with antibacterial wash, she dried them on a teatowel, absent-mindedly polishing the fridge door with it before re-hanging it over the handle on the matching stainless steel oven.

Finally Gemma looked up. She must have sensed the tension because she was actually taking her teabag to the kitchen bin, albeit leaving a trail of drips in her wake, only to realise that she'd filled the bin to capacity before bed. Pushing the teabag down with the spoon, she did create enough space for the lid to spring back—even if it had now become slightly stained in the process.

Sam pretended not to notice.

'Sorry—how rude of me.' Gemma gestured with the hand holding the teaspoon and Sam watched more tea hit the tiles. 'Toby, this is my landlady…'

Sam pulled a face. 'Landlady' sounded so curlers and pink nylon housecoat. Friend would have been better…or flatmate…

'Sam, this is Toby, and he's just going.'

Toby blushed, even more awkward than he had been moments earlier. Sam had to hand it to Gem. She was bucking every so-called trend and single-handedly proving that there were plenty of single men out there if only you weren't too dismissive at first sight. She hadn't even offered him any breakfast.

Sure enough, five minutes later Toby had been consigned to recent history and Gemma had set up camp by the toaster while Sam vigorously attacked the soon-to-be-much-whiter sink with a 'new and improved' product she had invested in less than an hour ago. They did have a cleaner, but she never really seemed to do very much. A bit of ironing, cushion-plumping, plant-overwatering and ornament-shuffling. Well worth the eight pounds an hour.

'That's looking great.' Gem stretched and yawned, revealing a naturally toned tummy. Sam subconsciously clenched her abs and winced as a searing hit of lactic acid reminded her that they'd been crunched enough already. 'Guess I better hit the shower in a minute…it's about time I started my day before you finish yours… Just out of interest, what time did today start Washington time?'

Sam ignored her. 'So, he was about twenty-four, was he?'

'Don't be ridiculous. At least twenty-six.' Gemma laughed.

Sam scrubbed resolutely. 'And you met him where?'

'Hey, Mum, what's up with you this morning?'

'Nothing.' It was too dismissive to be totally true.

'You just seem a bit—well, a bit on edge…' Gemma took a contemplative slurp of her tea and Sam reminded herself that, all things considered, she was just fine. What was it with everyone? Now even her moods were public property. 'You just don't approve…' Now Gemma was planting opinions.

'Hey, I'm just your landlady. It's none of my business who you see…'

Sam rinsed the scouring pad. It wasn't that she was unequivocally anti the one-night stand. There were certainly times when she wanted someone to snuggle up to. Someone who didn't purr or exhale meaty fish. But she'd also definitely been at her loneliest the morning after the night before. Gemma sipped her tea, safely staring into the middle distance, whilst the timer on the state-of-the-art toaster ticked like a time bomb behind her.

'Sorry, Gem, I've just got a lot on my mind. So, do you think you'll see him again?'

'Doubt it.' Gemma seemed relieved at Sam's overture to normality. 'Not bad in the sack, though…a huge improvement on Sean. He was an anticlimax—and I mean literally. Plus it saves me going to the gym later. All these women pumping iron when all they really need is a good shag…'

Sam felt herself redden and instinctively clenched her pelvic floor muscles, managing ten repetitions whilst wrestling the stuffed liner from the bin. It was one thing letting a room to a former classmate, but quite another when she had (a lot) more sex and telephone attention than you did. Plus, Gemma was only too quick to volunteer the details.

'Anyway, Toby's a Capricorn. Astrologically we couldn't be more wrong for each other…'

As far as Sam could remember, birth dates were definitely a second or third date question in her book. Unless in these days of heightened security she was asking to see a driving licence or passport for ID purposes.

'Then again, he saved me half a taxi fare home, he paid for the take-away, and—well, my granny always used to say you never know until you try…'

Sam was sure Gemma's grandmother had meant foodstuffs, not fellatio.

'Now, if he'd been a Sagittarius it could all have been very different…' Gem trailed off mid-sentence as she observed Mr Muscle's more glamorous sidekick hard at work. 'Stop. Please stop. I swear I was going to give the kitchen a bit of a tidy when I got up, but I should've known your first thing and mine are about four hours apart. Sorry.'

Her good intentions pre-empted Sam's well-worn washing-up mini-rant. While Sam would admit, if only to herself, that her intolerance of dirty dishes was possibly teetering on the brink of obsessive behaviour, she had to hand it to Gem. Unless she was a bloody award-winning actress, most things really didn't bother her. As for bringing a bloke back to the flat—to Gemma, having sex was like Sam having a swim. Just about making the effort. And, judging from the Pisa-esque tower of toast and Marmite that Gemma had just made herself, it had a similar effect on her appetite.

Sam wiped the crumbs off the work surface without even realising what she was doing, before grabbing an apple and following Gemma into the sitting room.

'How's your job going?' Anything. Sam would rather talk about anything than leave her mind to wander today. It kept trespassing into restricted areas. And Gemma was the perfect distraction. Just chatty enough to require concentration, just day-to-day enough to allow simultaneous magazine flick-through and general multi-tasking.

'I could do this one standing on my head, but it pays pretty well considering I spend most of my day sending personal e-mails around the world and surfing the net. In fact, I was checking out the Friends Reunited website this week…'

'You haven't got into all that, have you?'

'It's brilliant. Most of our year have registered, and it's great to see what they're all up to. Loads of them are married.'

'Mmm.' Sam didn't mind weddings. She just didn't view marriage in the glorious Technicolor of many of her peers. She had trouble visualising the bit at the altar. Or maybe it was visualising the person waiting for her at the end of the aisle that was her main stumbling block.

'Can't believe it'll be Sophie in a month… Anyway, between you and me I'm sort of hoping Dominic Pearson will get in touch. He was so damn sexy.'

'He was pre-pubescent.' Puffer Pearson had been smoking twenty-a-day in ten-packs from the age of fourteen and spent his early teens loitering behind his fringe at the bus stop, wearing a denim jacket over his blazer. Needless to say he and Gemma had often had to be prised apart at the bitter end of house parties. 'And it's all very well getting nostalgic, but life's all about moving forward.'

'But your schooldays are supposed to be the happiest of your life.'

'Don't believe the hype. I have no interest in re-establishing contact with people who spent their lives poking fun at me.'

Probably not the best time for Gemma to mention that she'd registered Sam on the site, then.

'They were just jealous. You were annoyingly good at everything.'

'I was asked to give up Art.' She'd liked to think she'd been more of an abstract artist. The Kandinsky of the Greenside

High School for Girls art department. So what if she couldn't sketch a still life of a vase or a feather? She probably could have pickled a sheep or a cow in formaldehyde quite successfully, and with the right palette she was sure she might even have been able to give Mark Rothko a run for his money.

'Fantastic. You're not perfect after all. I've found your Achilles' heel.'

'No need to look quite so delighted. See, this is the problem.'

Sam's mood had definitely shifted again. Gemma decided to return to non-controversial tales from the typing pool.

'Anyway, the agency are going to send me somewhere new. The first few days anywhere are always the most fun…that's when I get to save the day. Once I've mastered the software and company protocol, and lost a few incoming calls in the system, that is…'

Sam couldn't imagine anything worse than being a temp—except maybe having Gemma as her temp. Still, she had to hand it to her. Her positivity was apparently unassailable. Gemma was one of life's more buoyant passengers.

'But it's been keeping me in beer money since Australia, and something better will turn up—I'm sure of it. Only yesterday I met this woman at the bus stop…'

Gemma collected people as eclectically as some people collected fridge magnets.

'…she was a photographer—nothing *National Geographic* would be bidding for, just weddings and family portraits, but tasteful. No soft focus airbrush or fake fabric weave…'

Sam nodded, to acknowledge that she was still listening. She prodded her neck and rolled it through one hundred and eighty degrees, first in one direction and then back again. There was no mistaking the tension. She was going to have to relax. She added it to her mental 'to do' list for the afternoon, but even she could see that 'relax' wasn't something she'd be able to fit in to the five minutes between bill-paying, shower-head descaling and toenail painting.

'She used to be an investment banker. Just woke up one

morning and realised she wasn't living the life she wanted and so she changed everything...'

Maybe if she ditched toenail painting? It was March: still far too chilly to get her feet out.

'...downshifted. With no regrets. It really makes you think, and it just shows you never know what's round the corner if you keep your eyes open to possibilities...'

'Yup...alternatively you can just set yourself a goal and work towards it.' Sam started sorting the papers and magazines on the coffee table.

'That's all very well if you're as focused as you are, but most people don't have as many objectives, goals, strategies and back-up plans as a political party in an election campaign...nor do they get up at eight a.m. on a Saturday.'

Sam was sure there was a compliment in there somewhere, just fighting to get out.

'But for the rest of us it's good to see that life all works out in the end. She had a really good karma...'

The only karma Sam knew anything about had something to do with Culture Club in the early eighties. She kept it to herself.

'Anyway, things do happen for a reason. If I hadn't come back from Australia when I did, you and I wouldn't be living together.'

'Exactly.' It had been meant to be a joke. Sort of. Smiling in an attempt to soften her tone, Sam got to her feet. 'Another cup of tea?'

'I'd love one...'

Silently Sam thanked India for providing the British with bottomless cuppas. There appeared to be no limit to their restorative powers...and no teabags in the jar.

'Gemma Cousins...'

'Mmm?' From Sam's tone, Gemma could sense trouble. And she could take a pretty could swing at why.

'We seem to be out of tea.'

'Ah.' She did her best to be contrite. 'Not to worry. I'll just have an instant coffee, then.'

Sam muttered to herself as she let the cupboard door slam. Gemma clearly believed in teabag fairies, loo paper elves and waste disposal pixies, and her faith was always rewarded.

'Luckily I went shopping this morning.'

Gemma's voice wafted into the kitchen. 'Let me know how much I owe you…'

It was only for six months, and then once again she'd be able to wax her legs in front of the TV, pluck her bikini line while on the phone to her mother and go the loo in the middle of the night without getting dressed.

'You didn't get a paper, by any chance…?'

Sam delivered her still pristine copy of *The Times,* along with fresh tea, to the sofa, separating the main body of the paper from its weekend sections and sitting down with it in the armchair opposite.

'Thanks, love.'

George, having optimistically followed Sam to the kitchen and back again, just on the off-chance a roast chicken or spare salmon might inadvertently have fallen from the fridge when Sam was getting the milk, decided to sit with Gemma, and when he glanced across, apparently innocently, all smug purrs and green eyes, Sam narrowed hers to express her disdain. As he turned away Sam smiled victoriously before stopping herself. Who did she think she was? The cat whisperer?

Gemma was heading straight for her star signs in the magazine. Despite herself, Sam could feel herself listening to the general murmuring noises. Today's sounded quite affirmative.

'Hmm. Interesting. Do you want me to read out yours?'

Sam raised an eyebrow. 'Now, let me guess… *As the week begins, Saturn makes its way through Aries, popping in to Gemini and Scorpio on its way. Take care around the new moon on Thursday, when Pluto's activity means business matters may not turn out the way you planned. Beware of friends who try and tell you what's going to happen next. Shop thoroughly. Watch out for Capricorn rising and Venus wandering in and out every twenty-eight hours, when emotions may run high and someone close to you may not be who they seem…* How did I do?'

'You really shouldn't be so dismissive. It's a science. You'd be surprised how accurate this stuff can be. If you'd only let me draw up a personal chart for you… I just need your birth time and I can calculate your rising sign. You'd be amazed at—'

'Then I'd know which days to stay in bed and which ones to bother with? Honestly, Gem, for someone as intelligent as you are I can't believe you are so into this hocus-pocus, this planetary, may-the-force-be-with-you bollocks.'

'And I'm surprised that someone as intelligent as you can be so dismissive. I think you're scared. You don't want to think that things might be pre-ordained.'

Sam ignored her. She was doing her best to concentrate on an article about law reforms. Gemma, sensing the stalemate of the situation, tried to return to the chit-chat.

'What's that you're drinking?'

'Chamomile.'

'Yuk. It smells like wee.'

'Thanks.' For a holistic, feng shui kid, Gemma was surprisingly hostile to the idea of herbal teas.

'Well, it does.'

Sam put her paper down again. She was feeling like a rather irritable husband at the moment. All she wanted was a bit of quiet and a chance to catch up with the rest of the world.

'No one's asking you to drink it, but I'm trying to cut out caffeine at weekends for detox reasons and this is great for stiff joints and generally calming—allegedly.' Sam rustled the broadsheet and turned the page pointedly.

'Well, rather you than me…'

Clearly not pointedly enough.

'And you wouldn't have stiff joints if you didn't go to the gym so often. Plus there are lots of free radicals in real tea that are good for you.'

'And it's full of caffeine and tannin, dehydrating, cellulite-inducing and addictive.' Sam knew she was being crotchety. Let Gemma think it was Mars clashing with Mercury, or whatever fitted the picture best.

'And delicious.' Gemma took a big sip and Sam had to

admit, if only to herself, that it did smell good. And finally a moment of peace. Just a moment.

'Oh, before I forget—Soph called yesterday afternoon.'

Sam could have really used a chat with the most rational person she knew last night. When she and Mark got round to having them, their children would be sorted. As opposed to Gemma's, who'd clearly be caked in snot and felt pen at all times.

'Any message?'

Gemma looked up from the travel section and squinted as she tried to recall the moment. 'No. Just to call her, I think…'

'Anyone else?' Sam was joking.

'Your mum. I must have been on the phone at the time, but she left a message on the BT answer-phone thingy. She said she'd try your mobile.'

'So that'd be two messages, then?'

'Yup.'

Sam took a deep breath, doing her best to refocus on the world headlines and ignore the proximity of the accident waiting to happen opposite. The potential stain cocktail of English Breakfast tea, Marmite, cat and weekend newsprint on bespoke sofa was making her decidedly twitchy. She was just ascertaining that the world was still as flawed as it had been the day before, that there was still nothing she could single-handedly do about it and that no one famous or notorious had married or died, when the phone rang.

Sam leapt to her feet while George opened an eye, got up, performed a perfect three-hundred-and-sixty-degree turn and sat down again. Without even really taking her eye off the page she was reading, Gemma retrieved the portable phone from between two sofa cushions just at the point that Sam reached its empty charging base in the kitchen.

'Hello? Hi. How are you? Great. Just having breakfast. Yeah, she's here. How did last night go? Great. No? Some people are unbelievable. Definitely. Yup, I'd be up for that. Tomorrow? Not sure. Send me a text if you decide to. Fab.'

Gemma passed the phone over, ignoring Sam's muttering about keeping the phone charged between calls. 'It's Sophie.'

'Hi, Soph. Lovely to speak to you. It's been far too long.' Sam folded up the section of the paper she'd been reading and retreated to her room, determined to retain at least a semblance of a private life.

'You're the one who's been gallivanting across the Atlantic. Sorry I didn't get back to you last night. I left you a couple of messages, but then I had a job on and I only got home just before midnight—at which point I guessed you were asleep and Mark was determined to seduce me.'

'No problem. Did your meeting go well?'

'Yup. Really well. But to be honest anything will be an improvement on what she's inherited. It was her husband's father's house. A gorgeous Edwardian from the outside, but the interior is a tribute to the seventies. There's even a hanging basket chair.'

'You're kidding. Was he related to Alan Partridge?'

Sophie laughed. 'The before and afters are going to be incredible.'

'Well, congratulations. You really deserve a big project.'

'Thanks. I have to say I'm really excited. Mark's bored already. He's more interested in whether the husband is after me.'

'Is he?'

'Of course not. Haven't even met him.'

'But it's not like you've never met anyone through work before…'

'It only happened the once. And I'm marrying him now.'

Sophie ignored Sam's attempt to be playful. She'd asked far too many questions already. Definitely avoiding something. Textbook behaviour.

'So, my little jet-setter, is everything hunky-dory with you?'

'Yup. It's fine.'

'Really?'

'Yup.'

'So why did you call?'

'Well…fine-ish.'

'Sam…?'

This total understanding was why, at the tender age of seven,

Sam had handpicked Sophie to be the sister she'd never had. It was one of the best choices she'd ever made.

'Well, Gemma's driving me mad, Richard made a pass at me in New York and I've lost my diary.' There, she'd said it out loud now.

'No way?'

'Way.'

'Oh, my God. Where do you want to start?'

'I thought I'd left it at the hotel, but they've checked my room and nothing. Unless...'

Sam felt her pulse-rate double. Had she seen it since?

'What was in it?'

'Shit.'

'What?'

'I think Richard might have it.' Sam's stomach plummeted to her ankles. Her life was over.

'Are you sure?'

She took a deep breath. But she'd only been in the bathroom for a couple of minutes...

'What was in it?'

'The last three months of my life. Plenty of unprofessional whingeing. Potentially libellous statements. Quite a few personal titbits I'd rather not think about. And worst of all...' Sam's thoughts interrupted her flow. 'Yes, I definitely wrote in it after he left my room.' The relief was quite overwhelming.

'He was in your room?'

'Forget it. I shouldn't have said anything. Even to you.'

'Sam, for God's sake.' Sam knew she could trust Sophie implicitly. Yet telling her meant that it was no longer a possible figment of her imagination. 'And worst of all...?'

'Pardon?'

'You said "And worst of all..."'

'I did?' It wasn't her secret to tell. 'I have no idea what I was going to say.'

'So, did the entries include the night of that Valentine's dinner party?'

Silence.

'You didn't do anything wrong…'

'Being caught snogging the younger brother of the host in the coat pile wasn't my greatest moment. Maybe if my skirt hadn't been round my waist when Tim turned the light on…'

'And the wine-tasting?'

Perfect example of alcohol-impaired judgement. It had taken her nearly three weeks to shake Steve off completely. He hadn't outwardly displayed any signs of being a telephone stalker. Sometimes she wished Sophie's memory could be a little less effective.

'All the stuff about Richard?'

Sam felt her stomach tighten. 'Yup, and I was in a bit of state. One minute he was collecting documents—the next thing I knew he was under my duvet.'

Sophie squealed. 'And where were you?'

'In the bathroom.'

'Your life is so much more exciting than mine.'

'I'm not sure "exciting" is the word I'd use.'

'Anything else incriminating?'

'You could at least try and sound a bit less gleeful.'

'Sorry. And I'm not even remotely…it's just, well, there's a lot to take in.' Sophie racked her brains. 'Not…?'

'What?'

'The thing I'm not really supposed to know about.'

'Did I tell you?' Sam was almost relieved.

'About EJ? Don't worry. I haven't told a soul—nor will I.'

'It's in there.' Sam's tones were hushed. 'Well, most of it.'

'His name?'

'Initials only, I think. But there are probably enough clues. Of course now I can't really remember, and it's not like I can check.'

Sophie paused. 'And *your* name?'

'Just an address.'

'Well, that's something. Have you told her?'

'What's the point?'

'Well…'

'It's like I'd be confessing to her and asking for her forgiveness. And if I was her I'm not sure I'd be doing a lot of forgiving. Meanwhile she thinks I'm all jumpy because of the Richard malarkey.'

'Which you are. I know this probably sounds impossible, but try not to worry and think positive. Maybe someone will post it back when they find it. Anyway, who on earth would want to read a total stranger's diary?' The pause that ensued should have come with a 'mind the gap' warning. 'Well, fingers crossed it'll turn up in safe non-contentious hands.'

'Maybe.' Sam wasn't convinced.

'At least you lost it abroad.'

'And of course no one reads English in New York.'

'Hey, maybe it's just been thrown away. Maybe it's being pulped or dumped in a landfill site as we speak.'

'I hope so.' Sam could have kissed Sophie for her irrepressible optimism. And it certainly helped to have her rooting for her.

'And, face it, the bottom line is there is nothing you can do.'

'That's the worst part…' Sam sighed.

'Just for the record, I think you need to give EJ the heads-up…'

Sam had been wrestling with her morals all morning.

'I don't suppose you're free for lunch, are you? I need to sort out my shoes for the wedding once and for all.'

Sam couldn't help but smile. 'You've still got a month.'

'A month? I thought I had ages to get everything ready.'

'You did…' Sam hesitated. She must be the least enthusiastic maid of honour ever to have been appointed. Fawning over empire lines and bias cuts didn't come naturally to her, and she'd only accepted the role on condition that shot silk and baby pink did not feature in her outfit. But shoes she could do. And general sounding board duties. And lunch. Eating on her own at weekends was something that she did her best to avoid.

'I need something that doesn't scream Essex girl or dental nurse. I can't possibly do barefoot, and Adidas Bride of Hip-Hop isn't quite what my mother is expecting.'

'I was going to sort some stuff out here…'

'If Gemma's winding you up it'd do you good to get out.'

'I refuse to be driven out of my own flat.'

'Stop being so bloody melodramatic. That girl's got a heart of gold, and you know it's just that things simply don't occur to her. Come on. Just a couple of hours. Self-flagellation is so last season.'

Sam looked at her watch. 'Give me an hour and a half.'

'Brilliant. See you at Selfridges at two. I'll be the one in the shoe department in a strop.'

'And I'll be the one with an ulcer.'

Sitting on the edge of the Bethesda Fountain, waiting for Ali, Ben felt very cloak and dagger—or very jacket and diary. As he revelled in the surprisingly warm spring sunshine, he knew morally she was right. The only problem being that, NG or not, he wasn't quite sure he could go back to his life as it had been on Thursday.

Turning his back on the Angel of the Waters, he peered south through the dark arches of the arcade framing the vibrant colours of the park beyond. He spotted her long before she saw him. Shares in Kenneth Cole were going to be right up on Monday.

They'd scoured the collections like pros, and while the perfect white shoe was still eluding them Sophie had approved several other shopping diversions, and a cluster of high-quality paper carrier bags were physical evidence that Sam was feeling a bit better. Sam was incredibly grateful to Sophie. Which was good. Because this maid of honour was tiring slightly. Until they hit the new summer collection in Jigsaw, that was.

Sophie sighed. 'Are you nearly done?'

'Just one more suit to try.'

Poking her head round the door, Sophie observed the near identical suits neatly hanging all around Sam. She hadn't known there were so many variations on a theme.

'Any good ones?'

'A couple.'

'Not trying any bar-hopping gear?'

Sam raised an eyebrow at her best friend. 'What for?'

'Weekends?'

'I've got drawers stuffed full of jeans and jumpers, Soph, and I hardly ever get to wear them.'

'I was thinking more—you know—*party*.'

'You mean tarty. When on earth am I ever going to need a backless, frontless, strappy handkerchief top?'

'Every single girl should have a pulling top.'

'My days of nightclubs are over.'

'Bars?'

'I'm not doing the semi-naked look.'

'Fine. Well, I've had enough shopping for now. I refuse to stand in front of another in-store full-length mirror until after April the twenty-first. And I can't be a size sixteen bride.' Sophie paused as a wave of fear flashed across her face. 'Maybe that's why brides have their dresses made to measure?'

'Soph…'

'Well, just remind me never to shop in here again. Those jeans were allegedly a fourteen and I couldn't get them past my knees.'

Sophie's head disappeared as suddenly as it had arrived. And just as Sam's mobile started ringing. Having scattered the pile of her own clothes in order to locate her bag, she hesitated for a split second when she saw the number on the screen.

'At last. Finally.'

'Hi, Mum.'

'Honestly, I think it would be easier to get an audience with the Pope.'

'Sorry. I've been in New York all week, working on a deal.' Sam still liked the way that sounded. Travelling was exhausting, and far less glamorous than anyone based in one place would believe, but it certainly sounded good when relating to family and friends.

'Last thing I heard they did have phones in the States, and according to Michelle you were due in yesterday.'

'It's Melanie and, yes, I was back—but we were manic.'

Overly defensive as she now remembered that she'd forgotten to return her call, Sam glanced down at her state of semi-undress. 'Mum, can I call you back in a minute? This isn't a great time. In five minutes…yes, I will.' Sam was beginning to wonder what on earth had possessed her to press 'answer'. 'Look, I'm barely dressed… In a shop… In town, yes—Bond Street. With Soph. Not that expensive. Again this morning? No, I didn't get it. Please, just give me five, ten minutes… I realise… I'm sorry, but yesterday was one of my worst days in a while. I've lost my diary.'

And I've just discovered that my boss wants to sleep with me. She stopped at the diary tidbit. Sam didn't think her mother would appreciate the latter detail.

There, she'd admitted all was not well in the World of Sam Washington. Immediately she felt better.

'Oh, dear, darling. Don't you have it all on your computer these days, though? Can't you just beam it into a new one of those hand pilots?'

'Not my appointments diary. My real one—my journal. And it's Palm, not hand.'

'How sweet! I didn't know you were still writing one…'

'Usually only on bad days.'

'Where did you leave it?'

'If I knew it wouldn't be lost, would it?' Sam reined herself in. Hostility was not a fair trade for sympathy. 'I thought I'd left it in a drawer in my hotel room, but apparently it's not there now.'

'Did it have your address in it?'

'Yup.' Sophie and her mother's minds clearly worked in the same way.

'Then I'm sure it'll turn up. Listen, darling, the reason I'm calling—'

'I can't believe I've lost it. Everything was in there…and if it gets into the wrong hands…'

'Darling…' Helen was becoming increasingly exasperated. Sam had always been capable of incredible focus and self-centredness. Only-child syndrome. 'I know it's important to you, but it's not like you're Geri Halliwell or Prince William.'

Sam smiled despite herself. Only a devout *Daily Mail* reader could put those two in the same sentence.

'No one knows who you are and no one really cares—except us, of course.'

'It's not just me I'm worrying about—'

'Excuse me, madam, but are you going to be much longer? There's a queue out here.'

'Sorry—just give me one more minute. Mum, I promise I'll call you back.'

'Listen, your father's in hospital.'

Sam was silent as her emotions jostled for supremacy.

'I'm afraid it's serious. He's got a tumour in his liver and apparently it's a secondary one. They're going to operate on Monday, and then hopefully start chemotherapy, but apparently it's large enough to suggest it has probably already spread further. It seems to be a case of damage limitation rather than cure.'

Her mother must have spoken to a doctor. Either that or she had been to med school since their elderly neighbour had gone through breast cancer when she had explained everything in terms of zapping and lumps.

'They're running all sorts of tests, and he says he's been scanned to within an inch of his life. They're still trying to ascertain the primary site.'

'Right.'

'He's at the Royal Marsden. It's one of the best places he could possibly—'

'I'm incredibly busy at the moment.' Clearly denial had beaten the others hands down in the battle of her emotions.

'I know it's been a long time, but you just don't know… I mean at the moment they don't even know…'

'So now I'm supposed to sit at his bedside?'

'Don't be so stubborn. You remind me of him when you're like this.' Her mother pretty much had a doctorate in emotional blackmail. 'I went to visit yesterday. He's in there all by himself.'

'What about his teenage girlfriend? Isn't this her remit?'

Sophie glared at the fitting room assistant as she approached Sam's cubicle, where she was now standing guard, protecting what little privacy Sam still had.

'Honestly, darling, Susie must be in her forties now. It's been a long time. You can't have seen him in at least five years…'

'More like ten.'

'I know it's a shock…' Sam could hear her mother's voice faltering as she battled with tears.

It didn't take much to set her off at the best of times: an Andrex puppy, a wedding on television, Sam getting into Oxford, Sam leaving Oxford, Sam finishing law school. So, by rights, an ex-husband with cancer should have had her in floods. She was obviously focused on being strong for Sam's sake. And Sam was quite happy not to have to support her mother on this one.

'Simon is more of a father to me than Dad ever was.'

'Simon's not going anywhere. You know how much he loves you. But the fact is Robert is still your dad. I'm sure it would mean a lot to him if you just popped in.'

'I don't know how you can be so nice about it. We were there for him. And then he left us.'

'He left *me.* Twenty-three years ago…'

Sam could still feel the weight of the silence after the front door slammed. Still remember the sun coming through the sitting room window. The dust particles swirling around her. The smell of the warm musty air. The pattern on her white knee-length socks. The sound of his car starting and driving off. For a fraction of a second she was a six-year-old trapped in a twenty-nine-year-old body.

'It wasn't meant to be. I married again. I learned to let go. And you need to. Because of you we've always kept in touch. And he does love you.'

'Well, he's got a funny way of showing it.' Sam knew she didn't have the monopoly on divorced parents. Almost everyone she knew had gone through the parents-living-at-separate-addresses thing. But, selfishly, all she'd wanted was a nuclear family. And maybe a brother or sister. And maybe a dad at home for a little bit longer than six years. It wasn't that she hadn't got on with her life. She couldn't have been working any harder…

'You're the one who won't see him.'

'He can't just expect to have a daughter at his beck and call when it suits him.'

He'd never taken her to the zoo. She didn't even really agree with zoos any more. But she didn't have any of those memories. No trips to theme parks or burger bars, no camping holidays—not that these were necessarily indices of good parenting, but it would have at least showed willing. Everyone knew children were the worst sort of investment plan. At least eighteen years to mature and no sign of the capital invested. Not much appreciation either. No good for impatient people. Simon, though, had unquestioningly done it all. Sam wondered if she had thanked him enough.

'We managed perfectly well without him.'

'Exactly.'

'And you know if we'd stayed together none of us would have been happy.'

Deep down she did. And maybe if they hadn't had her they'd still be together. He hadn't exactly made a secret of the fact that he'd never really wanted children in the first place.

'Sam, sweetheart, you don't have to be all brave about this. I'll come with you, if you like.'

'Don't be ridiculous. Next you'll be suggesting I bake him some biscuits.'

'There's no point taking it out on me. I didn't want him to leave either.'

'I know. And I'm sorry, but I'm not going.'

'Please? Think about it… He's in Room 136. Maybe just call him…'

'I've really got to go now, or it'll be death by coat hanger for me.'

'You're bound to need a bit of time to let all this sink in. Love you, darling. I'll call again later.'

'Bye.'

Sam sat down and stared at the floor, seeing nothing. There was a tentative knock at the changing room door.

'Can I come in?'

'Give me a minute.'

Sophie gave her twenty seconds.

'Come on, you, let's get out of here. I need a coffee. A diet coffee, obviously.'

Sam regrouped and pulled on her pale blue v-neck, shopping forgotten. 'I'm ready.'

'It's Okay, love.' Sophie shifted her weight from foot to foot apologetically. 'To be honest—' she gestured at the saloon-style swing doors '—these changing rooms aren't exactly soundproof.'

Sure enough, several sympathetic glances from the fitting room queue followed them to the front of the shop.

'She still doesn't get it. Just because I have a phone with me doesn't mean I can chat for ages.'

'It's your dad, isn't it?'

Sam nodded, momentarily speechless.

Sophie shrugged. 'You've never exactly had a whispery voice, and there were only a couple of inches of plywood between us.'

'Cancer, apparently. Liver secondaries.'

'Oh, God.' Sophie paled visibly. 'I'm so sorry.'

'It's not like we're close. I haven't seen him in years.'

Sam couldn't have been any more matter of fact. This had to be it. First Richard, then her diary, now her father. Everyone knows these things come in threes. Come in threes? Now she was sounding like Gemma.

'Sam, come on—give yourself a break. Don't be so bloody stubborn.'

'Gemma didn't even tell me she'd called again this morning.'

'Do you want me to go with you?'

'I mean, how hard is it to write down a phone message?'

'Sam?'

'She must have to take messages at work all the time. If she's not going to bother, I'd rather she didn't answer the phone in the first place. Anyway—right—shoes. Where next? What do you think? King's Road? It's still only three-thirty. We've got plenty of time. Let's just get a cab. My shout.'

Sophie dragged her into the nearest Starbucks. 'It's totally acceptable to be upset. In fact, it's recommended. And you only have one father.'

'Actually, I have two. Look, I'll have a think and take a view. But today you, my friend, need white shoes, and it's my job not to leave your side until we complete our mission.'

'So I'll wear flip-flops. You're not going to get away with using my wedding or your work as an excuse to hide from the rest of your life—partnership race or no partnership race. What about going tonight?'

Silence. Sam's face was expressionless, and for a moment Sophie wondered whether she had crossed the invisible unconditional-support-versus-advice friendship divide.

'I'm seeing EJ.'

'She'll understand.'

'I haven't seen her for a couple of weeks and I really want to—'

'You're right. You should tell her.'

Sam didn't want to correct Sophie. But she'd only been going to say 'see a film'. One step at a time.

Sophie had her diary out. 'Well, Mark and I have a lunch tomorrow, but I could go with you first thing.'

'Thanks, Soph, but honestly there's no need. You've got quite enough on your plate as it is. And I will go. Soon. I just need a bit of time.'

'Don't leave it too long.'

'He'd better be on his best behaviour.'

'He's got cancer.'

'Which is why I'm going…'

Sophie reached over and gave her a half-hug. Not that it was really reciprocated, but it made her feel better for a start.

A doyenne of denial, Sam gathered her bags and got to her feet. 'Now, come on. King's Road or Knightsbridge? Your call.'

Chapter Five

108, 102, 96, 94, 88...Ben squeezed the brake and focused on the house numbers. Last week, safely on the other side of the Atlantic, this had seemed like a great idea: one knight, minus shining armour—well, more of a boy scout—doing a good deed for a damsel likely to be in distress. But at this precise moment he couldn't help thinking that a stamp would've been far simpler. Added to the fact that he wasn't sure whether he was there out of guilt, gratitude or just sheer curiosity.

Gemma flopped onto the sofa, cold bottle of lager in hand. The relief of pyjama bottom on sofa cushion was blissful. It had been a mundanely hard day in PAsville, most of the afternoon had been spent in Excel hell, and her eyes ached from sustained concentration. Fortunately Sam and EJ were checking out the latest influx of actors trying to make the transition from the big screen to the small stage, so the flat was hers for the evening.

Stretching out, she wondered how early she could go to bed without losing every self-respecting girl-about-town point. Almost all her friends with new babies were in bed by ten…and up at one, three and five. Surely she wasn't getting broody? Well, maybe a little. And it wasn't that she was short of male attention, but she'd always wanted to believe in The One, a sole soul mate, yet judging by the forest of wedding invitations on Sam's mantelpiece, it did seem to be more about timing. In which case she should probably be out strategically sipping cocktails or salsa dancing. She knew she wasn't going to meet anybody lying in front of the TV.

Ben took a look around as he slowed down. Aside from the roar of his Vespa—well, more angry wasp buzz—it was an eerily quiet road. And tidy. Window boxes added carefully thought-out finishing touches to newly painted windowsills and lovingly glossed front doors in muted blues, reds and greens. A smattering of estate agent boards signalled the transience of Battersea's young residents as they moved onwards and outwards in search of more affordable space and room to park the inevitable people carriers. Shiny scooters broke up the Audi TT, MG, VW and Peugeot party, and Ben added his to the nearest bay. Strolling towards his final destination, he peered into the front rooms. Ikea envy. His foot was still nowhere near the first rung of the property ladder.

As he reached the front door of number 68, a large three-storey Victorian semi, he ruffled his hair. He knew better than to complain about an unruly mop when most of his mates were desperately trying to hold on to theirs, but it was a constant challenge to persuade it to lie flat, especially when there had been a helmet involved. Licking his finger, he held it firmly on the most independent tuft.

Houston, he had a problem. He'd carried the diary three and a half thousand miles and now there were three bells.

Johnson.

Brooks.

Washington.

And a perfectly acceptable communal letterbox. But surely that would be cheating?

Uncharacteristically tense, Ben rechecked the package in his hand. A sweat broke out in the small of his back as he remembered his broken promise to Ali, and he flapped his T-shirt to try and cool himself down. Flat 3. He checked his watch. Nearly eight-fifteen.

Taking a logical guess, Ben pushed the top bell.

A crackle of static. 'Halloh…who is speaking, please, thank you?'

He seemed to have been connected to somewhere in central Europe. 'Hi. Is that flat 3?'

A child shrieked in the background. Maybe two. Ben shook his head. He should have known that British electricians installed bells in whatever order they fancied. Bob the Builder should really have been Bodge the Builder. If he ever turned up at all, that was.

'Heylow?'

His adult self compelled him to stay. 'Sorry to bother you. Wrong apartment.'

'No party here.'

'Wrong bell. Wrong flat. Sorry.' Ben wondered why he was shouting. Should have posted it. Should have posted it.

Without giving himself a nanosecond for second thoughts Ben went for the bottom buzzer and leaned in closer to the door. He couldn't hear a bell ringing anywhere. He pushed it again, for longer this time. Second time lucky? He was sure the letterbox was winking at him.

Startled from semi-consciousness, Gemma sat bolt upright. She definitely hadn't ordered any food yet, and a quick glance at the video clock confirmed it was far too early to be out for the count in pyjama bottoms. Leaping to her feet, she picked up the intercom handset while her heart made a supreme effort to pump enough blood to her brain to prevent her from passing out.

'Hello?' Gemma had tried her best not to sound dazed, confused or asleep. Listening to herself, she had failed on all three counts.

'Is that flat 3?'

A delay. To reveal or not to reveal the information? At least she had stopped seeing stars now.

'Hello? Are you still there?'

'Yes…' It was a tentative response.

'Hi. Sorry to disturb you. My name's Ben…'

Ben? Gemma didn't think she'd ever had or known a Ben. She'd heard of plenty: Hur, Johnson, Affleck… In which case she could be Gemma from the block…well, maybe with a serious amount of work, a bit of Juicy Couture, longer hair and industrial hair irons.

Two floors down, all Ben could hear was breathing. 'You don't know me, but I have a package for you. If you're flat 3, that is…'

Package for you. The three magic words every girl longs to hear. Open Sesame. 'I'll be right down.'

As she replaced the handset Gemma wondered whether she should be a bit more circumspect. It wasn't your prime-time delivery hour. But she was sure all the e-mails she'd received about female safety involved quiet car parks and Rohypnol.

As she peered down from the sitting room window she could just about make out a bloke on his own. No TNT or FedEx van, but he didn't look like an axe murderer. In fact from this distance he didn't look bad at all. As for a package…disappointingly it appeared to be no more than a big envelope. She was still staring when he looked up at the house, obviously searching for a sign of life. Ducking down out of sight, she scrambled to her room, grabbed her combat trousers and, pulling them on over her pyjama bottoms, practically flew down the stairs, releasing her hair from its scrunchie *en route*.

'Hello!' She was unnervingly cheery.

Ben just stared. She was somehow…could she be too messy? He wasn't usually messyist. Unless… Of course. This had to be Gemma. In which case, she was much more attractive than he'd imagined. He was thrown.

'Um, hi. I'm really sorry to interrupt your evening…' Now what was he going to do?

'No worries.' The honest truth. Gemma was face-to-face with a slightly nervous but definitely attractive man. Normally it took her months to meet one of this calibre, and that was after extensive searching, misspent evenings in bars and multiple cocktails. Never on her doorstep. Granted, if you were being pedantic, it wasn't *her* doorstep, exactly, but for the purposes of this moment it would do nicely.

All he had to do was feign ignorance. How would he know the author even had a flatmate when, as he had reminded himself repeatedly on the way over, he hadn't read it?

'This is for you. I mean, it's yours. I just thought I'd bring it over and drop it off as I was in the area.' Ben stopped himself. Suddenly this was a ridiculous situation.

'Thanks.' Curious, Gemma took the padded envelope from him, still wondering if she was being overly trusting. But she was sure letter bombs and anthrax were never hand-delivered, and he wasn't wearing enough layers to be a suicide bomber. Plus the vibe was definitely a good one. Classic Adidas, dark jeans, leather jacket, motorbike helmet under his arm and, if she wasn't mistaken, a hint of an American accent going on. All excellent. Her prayers had been answered. The brat pack had finally come to Battersea.

'Thanks.' She said it again and, at a loss as to what to do next, went with convention and closed the door, watching the moment slip through her fingers in slow motion.

'You're an idiot, Fisher. Idiot. Idiot. Idiot.' Ben walked back to his bike slowly, muttering to himself. He'd handed over the only reason he had for ever being there, and still had no idea who the mystery author, EJ or NG were. And now he was far more interested than he had been even two minutes ago.

Gemma leant against the inside of the front door, ripped open the package and flicked through the notebook. No wonder London's most organised woman had been so highly strung recently. And a diary was an excellent thing. More proof that, despite her attempts to hide it, Sam was human after all. Gem skimmed a couple of pages before forcing herself to close the book. A sporadic journal-keeper herself, she couldn't do this to a mate. Not to mention the fact that guys didn't just appear out of the ether for no reason. Fate was at large somewhere in all of this. She had to act fast.

Gemma opened the door again. He wasn't there. She didn't know why she was surprised. It was, after all, customary the world over to leave a premises when the door was closed in your face. Hearing the rev of a bike, tiredness forgotten, Gemma sprinted to the end of the path, wishing she hadn't taken her bra off in a comfort moment earlier and slowing just before she hit the pavement in an attempt to at least appear laid back.

Folding one arm under her breasts to counteract the effects of gravity, she flicked her hair and waved just as he turned to look at her. Or maybe he was just looking left; it was difficult to see. Lifting his visor, he killed the engine. Gemma was beside herself. Classic Vespa. Sky-blue and chrome. And he was a cutie.

'Everything Okay…?'

Gemma glanced down. Her breast support arm was still clutching the envelope.

'It is yours, isn't it?'

Gemma hesitated before rallying round. Why complicate things? 'Really—thanks. You're a star. It's a real relief.' She stopped herself. She didn't even know when or where she was supposed to have lost it. 'Erm, I don't suppose you want to go for a drink or something? I mean it's the least I can do. To say thank you.'

'What? Now?' Ben made a show of looking at his watch, as if to suggest he had an action-packed evening ahead of him as opposed to the flat-line of activity that was sure to herald his arrival home.

Gemma really wanted at least half an hour to get ready, but this week was a great time for Librans to embrace new opportunities. And he was here now. Why run the risk of him not coming back or giving her a wrong number?

'Yup. I just need to go and…' Gemma spared Ben the details. 'Why don't you come up for a second?' As long as she had two minutes to get changed and at least glance in a mirror.

'There are loads of places just round the corner.' Gemma had to stop wittering if she was to retain an ounce of sophistication. Looking down at her sports-socked feet on the pavement, and the millimetre of tartan flannel poking out from under her combats, she strongly suspected she was too late.

'Why not?' Ben was surprised to hear himself agreeing. 'I was going to meet a colleague of mine for a drink, but I can easily postpone it.' He smiled as he plucked a credible lie from the ether. He was the man.

He paced round the kitchen. Their kitchen. Her kitchen. Tonight was shaping up to be significantly more interesting than his average Thursday. He looked through the pile of letters on the table, being careful not to alter their order. G Cousins had opened hers. S Washington, on the other hand, hadn't.

Her disembodied voice sailed into the room. 'Feel free to use the phone if you need to cancel your mate.'

Startled, Ben dropped the envelopes back on the table. 'Sure. Thanks.'

'It should be in the charger on the side—by the fruit bowl.'

'Got it.' In the panic of the moment Ben had totally forgotten about the fully functioning mobile in his pocket, and the fact that he didn't actually have an arrangement to cancel. Barely thinking, he dialled the office number automatically.

'Hello? Small Screen Productions.'

Suddenly realising he was calling to cancel a non-existent appointment with an as yet unspecified colleague, he cut himself off.

Sensing someone behind him, Ben swivelled to find himself face to face with Gemma, her grin highlighted by a fresh coat of lipgloss, a waft of newly applied perfume swirling between them.

'Engaged. I'll try his direct line.' Ben dialled his home number, and as he waited for his answer-machine to kick in, pushed the handset closer to his ear to ensure that Gemma couldn't hear that the voice at the other end was his own. Rolling his eyes, he covered the mouthpiece. 'Voicemail.' He couldn't even pretend to leave a message without hamming it up. Finally the beep came and went.

'James, it's Ben. Sorry it's such short notice, but I'm going to have to cancel our beer tonight. Something's come up. See you tomorrow. Cheers. Nice one.' Nice one? He'd never said that before in his life. Ever. Suddenly, in the midst of his role play, he'd gone all Naked Chef.

Ben turned to Gemma 'Voicemail.'

So he'd said.

'We can leave it if you'd rather?'

'No, now's cool.'

'Great.' Gemma beamed at him.

'Hey, no problem... Um...' He had never needed a drink more in his life. His palms were actually sweaty. He rubbed them on the seat of his jeans. 'Sorry, I didn't catch your name earlier.'

'It's Sam.' The thought-process, all completed in a split second, started and finished with pretending the diary was her own but knowing it wasn't.

'Sam?' Ben was thrown. He could hardly challenge her on something as fundamental as her identity, even if he would have bet his house—if he'd had one—on this being Gemma.

'Yup...'

Gemma shook her head imperceptibly. Now what? *Oops, sorry, did I say Sam? I meant to say Gemma, and not only is the diary in question not my own, I've just told you that I am my flatmate. But don't worry, little boy, I'm perfectly safe to have a drink with...* Cue: throwing back of head, long cackle... Far too late now.

'Well, obviously it's Samantha, but that's always felt a bit flowery, a bit girlie.' Gemma applauded herself as she built her part. Maybe she should try a career in acting? At least she wouldn't have to wear a skirt and tights to work every day.

As Ben followed her down the stairs he wondered what on earth he was doing. What sort of girl invites a bloke out for a drink having met him for less than a minute? And, more to the point, what sort of guy would take her up on her offer?

★ ★ ★

The real Sam was so tired she almost felt drunk, and her body longed for the swaddled insulation from the outside world that only her 12-tog duck-down duvet could provide. Burying herself in work from dawn until way past dusk had been a largely effective, if somewhat unoriginal method of keeping her mind off the obvious, but actually sleeping at night was proving a tougher challenge. Two nights running she had woken at four, body thermostat racing between hot and cold, her muscles almost twitching with tension, hands firmly clenched as fists, and by the time she'd lulled herself back to sleep it had been almost time to get up. Last night she'd listened to practically every syllable of every lyric on her Jill Scott CD, hoping to trick herself into waking up hours later.

Pouring herself a glass of filtered water, Sam ate a brown banana and a handful of shrinking grapes at the sink before emptying a few biscuits into George's bowl in a childish attempt to generate some company. Nothing.

She still hadn't told EJ. But it had been a week now, and with each day that passed Sophie's optimism felt a little less misplaced. If anyone was up there and watching, she'd learnt her lesson. Heading towards her bedroom, she tilted her head ceilingwards and saluted the cornice in gratitude. Exhaustion was having a strange effect. And if she was feeling a bit lonely she probably just needed to buy some iron supplements and some St John's Wort. If she could just manage eight hours of uninterrupted sleep she'd be off to a flying start. Roll on the weekend.

Kicking off her shoes, she sat on the edge of her bed, pausing to summon enough energy to release herself from her suited prison and allowed herself to fall back onto the duvet. But instead of providing its usual unflinching support it was apparently stabbing her in the back. Instinctively she rolled away, her concern over crumpling her suit vanishing when she spotted the envelope responsible. Closing her eyes for a second in silent prayer to whichever higher power might have answered her general call for her help, Sam tentatively emptied the package.

It was definitely her day. Emotional U-turn underway, clutching the black notebook to her chest, she leapt to her feet as reprieve-generated energy started to surge through her veins, shortly pursued by acute concern as to how her diary had made it home.

Methodically she inspected the package. Standard Jiffy. Standard staples. And it had already been opened. No stamps, no frank. So unless Lady Luck was hand-delivering these days there'd been a major security breach. Make that insecurity. And Gemma must have been the final link. But how could she expect a five-star service when she was a confirmed agnostic ninety-nine per cent of the time? Sam punched an urgent text message into her phone and pressed send. Seconds later, somewhere else in the flat, Gemma's mobile beeped. Typical Cousins behaviour.

Opening the notebook, Sam flicked past every page, scouring it for clues. She wasn't sure what she was searching for. Fingerprints? Bus tickets? A business card? Traces of tabloid editor? For a moment she wished she'd trained in forensics. And then there it was, mid-February, a fragment of a hair. A dark one. Quite thick. Sam gingerly extracted it with her tweezers and held it up to the light.

Too fine to be pubic. A couple of inches long. And straight. Sam studied it from every angle. If only she could send it down to the lab for testing. Having said that, on closer inspection it looked remarkably like part of one her own. Plucking one from her hairbrush to compare and contrast, her analysis was complete in a matter of seconds. A perfect match. Damn.

Adrenaline was generating a multitude of presently unanswerable questions; there was no way she was going to be able to sleep now. 11:24. Sam dialled Sophie and hoped she was nearest the phone.

'Hello?'

Mark. Bugger. Her life had been much easier with a live-in best friend. He sounded distinctly as if he might have been asleep.

Unless they were having an intimate in bed moment. Sam concentrated on imagining him with as many clothes on as possible.

'Sorry to call so late. It's only me—Sam. Hope I'm not disturbing you.' A mere platitude. Obviously she was.

He yawned languidly. 'What time is it?'

'Eleven-fifteen.'

'Everything Okay?'

'Yup.'

'I take it you're after the lady of the house, but she's not here. She's left me.'

'She's what?' Sam dropped her diary onto the duvet.

Mark laughed. 'Just for the night. She's at her parents'. Now, go to sleep. Or at least let me. Some of us have to be up at five-forty-five.'

Forgetting that Sophie's parents lived in the part of Surrey with the weakest mobile phone signal in the Home Counties, and ruling out the jumping in the car option on grounds of over-the-top behaviour, Sam had to make do with leaving a message, and then, having tortured herself with a recap of the content, tried and failed to trick her body into winding down with a hot bubble bath and a Horlicks.

Belting herself into her bathrobe and clutching the notebook to her chest, she assumed the horizontal late-night television position on the sofa to await Gemma's return—or dawn, whichever came sooner.

'Hey, wake up.'

Sam was doing her best to clamber towards consciousness. Someone was shaking her gently. 'Come on.' And then, less gently. 'Bedtime. It's one o'clock. Come on, you. You'll feel much better in the morning if you make it to your own bed.'

'Why don't you just leave her? She'll be warm enough with a blanket.'

The unfamiliar male voice penetrated Sam's sleep bubble and, suddenly remembering that she couldn't recall actually going to bed, only then did she realise from the cold airflow on her apparently semi-naked torso that towelling belts were bloody useless. Instinctively stooping as she pulled her robe around her, and still clutching her diary, Sam stumbled towards her bedroom, her limbs inexplicably heavy, barely making the transition into consciousness and hardly registering the guy hovering awkwardly in the shadows by the door to the sitting room.

Falling into bed, she narrowed her eyes to minimise the pain of the luminous display from her stereo. But she had to take a peek. 1:08. On a school night. Sam pulled one of her pillows over her head. She had to sleep. Had to. Mentally she counted down the number of hours to her alarm going off and squeezed her eyes closed far too tightly. Now all she could see were red and gold stars in the darkness. She concentrated on breathing deeply. Moments later she was fast asleep.

Chapter Six

The whirr of a blender and the unbeatable aroma of fresh coffee teased Ben's senses. But he lived alone. An elaborate dream or… Easing himself into a more upright position, he surveyed an unfamiliar room: a battalion of bottles stationed on the dressing table, a stack of CDs precariously balanced to test the law of gravity, a map of Australia incongruously Blu-tacked to the wall between tastefully framed black and white photographs of New York, shelves cluttered with a haphazard collection of well-thumbed books. A quick glance to his left revealed a dark mess of curls on the pillow beside him and, toying with the silence, the faint sighs of a deep sleeper.

Gingerly he slid himself out of bed, pulling on his jeans and jumper as quickly and silently as he could. Only as he closed the bedroom door behind him did he dare to look at his watch. And then looked again. Everything seemed to be working perfectly. In which case it really was six forty-seven. Barefoot, he padded towards the bathroom. From the moment she'd ordered a pint of Guinness he'd known she definitely wasn't Sam, yet here he was. Having arrived safely at the basin, he ran a hand through his hair and checked his breath. Nasty. Momentarily dazzled by the array of toothpaste alternatives on offer, he squeezed a stripey one onto his finger. It was the best he could do under the circumstances.

'Morning.' Ben went for cheery as he entered the kitchen in search of his helmet, socks and shoes. During his teeth-wiping moment he'd decided there was no point in pretending he wasn't there.

Sam froze mid-sip as the unfamiliar baritone sliced through her pre-work calm. While outwardly she might have appeared unfazed by the intrusion, internally she was wrestling with the gaping bathrobe moment. She drained her smoothie before picking up her coffee mug and heading for the doorway. Time to escape.

'I'm Ben.'

Not fast enough. And it wasn't as if she could pretend she hadn't heard him.

'Morning.'

'Nice to meet you.' Strangely formal, given the time, location and his lack of footwear, Ben proffered a hand for shaking. Automatically she shook it firmly, as if it was perfectly standard to meet new people in her own kitchen before seven on a Friday morning. 'Any chance of a coffee? It smells fantastic.'

'Sure.' Sam nodded at a clean mug on the draining board. 'Help yourself. Don't mind me. I'm sure I won't be wanting that second cup anyway.'

'Thanks.' Ben started pouring and Sam watched incredulously as he helped himself to the remainder. 'Ah. I get it… Sorry—it's too far too early for me to detect sarcasm. I guess I should have left it?'

'Maybe.' This one was far too chatty, and unless the Monkees were having a style revival or the Playmobil look was the latest to hit the catwalks he needed a good haircut.

'Next time I'll be more careful.'

Next time. Sam wondered whether Gemma knew there was going to be one of those.

'So...' Ben grappled for inspiration. Clearly she wasn't going to be helping. 'How come you're up and about so early? Going somewhere nice?'

'Work.' No smile. No conversation. Just fact.

'What do you do?'

'Lawyer...attorney.'

'Hey, no need to translate on my account. I have an English father.'

Sam nodded, clearly determined not to give a millimetre. And to think he'd been almost excited about meeting her.

'What sort?'

'Female.' Pointedly Sam checked her watch, even though she already knew what time it was. 'Now running late.'

'Your speciality? Family, personal injury, employment, criminal...?'

'Corporate.' Although what the hell it had to do with him she had no idea.

A brief silence. Quite an awkward one. About a six if one was comfortable and ten was excruciating. The tiles were cold on Ben's feet. He pulled out a chair and sat down at the kitchen table, pulling his knees up to his chest and resting his feet on the edge of the seat. 'Please—don't let me keep you.'

'Too late for that. And now not only am I going to be late but I'm caffeine-deprived.'

Ben laughed. 'Well, at least it's Friday.'

'What do you do?'

'I'm in television.' He had nothing to lose but his self-respect.

'Really...?'

Only the way Sam said it he might as well have said he was HIV positive. She was still standing there, though, framed by the doorway...unless, of course, she was worried that he was going to run off with the mug. Carefully he raised it above his head, allowing him to peer at the base. Hand-painted in Thailand. Nope, it must be something else.

Bemused, Sam watched the display of mug agility before

continuing. 'Then surely you have at least three more hours before you have to be anywhere?'

A big smile from Ben. Not the defensive reaction she'd been expecting at all.

'True. I do play for a living. But I need time to go home, shower, exfoliate, shave—you know... Change my play clothes. Different jeans. A bit of media black. That sort of thing...'

He had all the signs of a professional man-boy slacker, and currently was far more relaxed in her kitchen than she was. But at least he wasn't going to use her shampoo and face towel. Exfoliate, though. Did boys really do that? Maybe he was gay and in denial.

'Anything I might have heard of?'

'Well, maybe if you had time to watch television.'

'What's that supposed to mean?'

Ben had no idea. Too much background knowledge. 'I just imagine...people like you...' Flailing verbally, he reined himself in.

Sam wondered why she was being so defensive. It was as if the more easygoing he was, involuntarily the more clipped she became.

'Look, I'd better get off. I really didn't mean to stay out last night. I just had a few drinks more than I meant to, and my scooter was here, so it seemed easier to stay than to get a cab and have to come back again today—especially when I'd been offered half a bed. I mean, who was I to say no?'

'People don't usually turn Gemma down.' Sam immediately regretted being catty, even if her flatmate's latest conquest was delaying her with idle chit-chat while she no doubt slept on oblivious. 'Please excuse me, but I don't have the time to entertain this morning.'

'Sure.' Ben smiled again. This time he couldn't help it. Gemma. His hunch had been correct. Something tickled his foot and Ben glanced at the grey cat now weaving a figure of eight on the floor in front of him, its tail unflinchingly perpendicular, aerialesque. Maybe it was a remote control cat?

Reaching down, Ben picked him up and was immediately rewarded as a pneumatic purr started up. Sam turned.

'So you've met George, then?'

'I have now.' Gently Ben turned him so that they were face to face. 'George—Ben—Ben—George.' Once firmly on lap, George contorted his body in order to present his favourite stroking areas. Ben obliged as he returned his focus to Sam. 'Not named after a certain Mr Clooney, by any chance?'

'No.' Sam heard herself snap a reply. 'George as in King, Best, Boy, the one I always wanted to be in *The Famous Five*...after all of them and none of them.'

Anxious not to provide her with a silence in which to escape, he locked in to her gaze and continued, clinically changing the subject. 'My apologies if I startled you last night...'

Damn. Sam flinched internally. He'd definitely seen her.

'...and again this morning. I only met Gemma yesterday, and just for the record—not that it's got anything to do with you—I'm not that easy. Although she can be pretty persuasive.' Ben smiled.

'She's had plenty of practice.' Sam silently scolded herself. Rules of the Sisterhood, #68. Always take the woman's side—even if she didn't know that their oven wasn't self-cleaning.

Ben spotted his helmet on the floor by the door and, putting George down, got up to retrieve it. 'Anyway, I'll leave you to it.' He took a big slurp of his coffee before, to Sam's horror, pouring the remaining half a cup, still steaming, down the drain. 'See—I'm housetrained and everything. Nice to meet you.'

'Shoes?'

'I think I abandoned them in the sitting room.'

She followed him. To escort him off the premises—yes, that was it.

'Lovely apartment. Very tasteful, for a lawyer...'

'Meaning what, exactly?' Unwittingly he had stumbled upon a raw nerve. Spending the majority of her life in an office hadn't really prepared her for the inside track on soft furnishings and nude colours. But Sophie's encyclopaedic back catalogue of lifestyle and home improvement magazines had been lifesaving, and Sam loved her place.

'And great sofa… It looks familiar…is it Designers Guild?'

'Impressive knowledge.' Probably her most prized possession, along with her Waring blender and Dualit toaster. She was a total sucker for design classics.

'If you ever get bored with it I know of a place in Shepherd's Bush that it would suit.'

'Very media.'

'What? Second-hand furniture?'

'Living in Shepherd's Bush.'

'I know…I know… Scooter, faded jeans, the Bush. I am a walking, talking stereotype.'

Despite herself, Sam almost smiled. Ben noted her second of relaxation and stole a glance at the bigger picture. Despite her immaculate appearance, her eyes looked tired. A give-away in an otherwise perfect disguise.

'So, where did you meet Gemma?' Suddenly Sam wanted to know. She and EJ were obviously hanging out in the wrong places.

'Actually, on your doorstep. I came over to drop off a package and we just got chatting.'

Gemma was definitely getting lazier. And then it clicked.

'So it was you?' Sam suddenly felt a little faint.

'Hmm? What?' Ben pretended to be tightening the laces on his trainers, despite the fact he couldn't even remember the last time he hadn't slipped his shoes on. Amateur delaying tactics. If Sam had been looking closely she'd have seen that he hadn't even managed to untie the double knot, welded together by months of wear, slops of beer and London grime.

Sam was overcome with an uncharacteristic wave of gratitude. 'Thanks. If you brought the…um…book round, thanks very much.' The wave came crashing down. Had he read it?

'Oh, so it was yours…?'

Sam nodded, inexplicably mute. If he'd thought it was Gemma's he couldn't have…

'I was going to post it, and then I thought—well, you know

what the post can be like. Plus my sister used to write one, and she would have freaked out if anyone had posted it anywhere. I guessed whoever was missing it would probably want it back sooner rather than later, with a minimal risk of it getting into the wrong hands.'

'Wrong hands?'

'Well, you know—figuratively speaking. I mean.' Ben silently congratulated himself on the speed of his recovery.

'Well, thanks, I appreciate having it back...'

1.He knew it was diary. 2.He had a sister. 3.He'd probably read it—but then again he'd just asked what she did for a living and had thought it was Gemma's so probably not. 4.Or he was lying. But, shabby chic aside, he seemed like a fairly up-front guy.

'Where did you find it?'

Ben stalled. Was this a test? 'It was in my hotel room—in a drawer.'

'In New York?'

'Yup. Even former New Yorkers stay in hotels when they visit.'

'You're from New York?'

'Originally—although I've been in London since I was eleven, so I'm more of a NY-LON these days...'

Sam hesitated. Had he just said he was an artificial fibre?

'And my parents are now living in Chipping Campden.'

Sam treated him to her wryest smile. 'Americans in the Cotswolds? How twee.' Her mute button needed servicing. She'd meant to think it. No volume intended.

'What?'

'Nothing.' Rapid subject change required. 'So, you were staying at The Carlyle?'

'Meaning...?'

'It's just...'

'Expensive?'

Sam blushed. 'Well, I'm not suggesting...'

'I could be an oil heir.'

'Except you just told me you were in TV.'

'Well, the two aren't mutually exclusive…' Ben smiled. 'My sister was given a comp. She was writing a piece on the refurbishment for a magazine.'

Sam nodded.

'I was actually looking for the Room Service menu and, boom, there it was.'

'I knew they didn't check properly.'

Sam was muttering to herself. She found herself doing it more and more as she got older. Living on her own hadn't helped. It was all part of the slippery slope to dementia. At this rate one day—hopefully not for at least another fifty years—she'd be feeding pigeons sliced bread from a carrier bag, wearing kneed tan tights and a brown coat with a hat that didn't match.

Ben got to his feet. 'Well, very nice to meet you…?' His tone was expectant.

'Sam…Sam Washington.'

'Well, Sam Washington, thanks for donating your second cup of coffee to a down and out stranded south of the river, and I hope I haven't made you too late…'

Sam looked at her watch. What the hell was she playing at? It was gone seven. 'Bugger.'

'But it looks like I have.'

'Real jobs start before ten. Look…' Sam needed to know. If he was in television that made him a pseudo-journalist, and his sister wrote articles. Why couldn't a doctor have found it? 'Did you read it?'

Drat and double drat. He couldn't believe he hadn't anticipated the direct question. And it was the most obvious one of all. 'Well, no…not really. I mean, I flicked through it.' Ben's ears reddened, but at least his nose wasn't growing.

'Only, it's just there's quite a lot of confidential information in there. Nothing that anyone else would be interested in *per se,* but…' Sam listened to herself attempting to sound unflustered. Where was she going with this? 'So…'

'Don't worry, I haven't sent a copy to the *News of the World* for serialisation.'

'Why would you say that?' Sam's mood hardened.

'Say what?'

'Why would you even think about sending it to a paper?' Sam tried to sound as dispassionate and hypothetical as possible. She still hadn't told EJ. A double knot formed in her stomach.

'That'd be my inappropriate sense of humour, then.'

'I'm so not even smiling.'

'I won't lie. I read a few entries. But I promise I'll still respect you in the morning.'

'Is that the humour thing again?'

'Afraid so.'

Ben hesitated at the door. 'Hey, at least it's back. Reunited with its owner and no harm done.' Not quite the hero's welcome he'd been anticipating. 'I don't suppose there's a reward?'

'One night's accommodation and half a cup of fresh coffee.' Sam's delivery was deadpan.

Ben laughed. 'Look, can I give you a lift anywhere?'

'On a motorbike?'

'I keep a spare helmet under the seat.'

'You must be joking.'

'It's by far the quickest and most painless way to get around London. And it really leaves you feeling all fired up.' Not that she seemed to have trouble with erudition first thing in the morning. He, on the other hand, was almost ready for another sleep.

'I don't think so.' Plus, he might be the worst driver in the world, she'd have to change, and her trouser suit had only just come back from the dry cleaners.

'Well, bye, then. And thank you.'

'It's a pleasure.' An automatic response.

'No, you're supposed to thank *me*.'

'Of course. Thank you.'

'No problem.' Grinning, Ben left a shaken and stirred lawyer in his wake. And Sam was still staring at her front door moments later, when Gemma rushed in.

'Have you seen Ben?'

'He's just left.'

'At ten past seven? I can't believe it. I just woke up and he was gone... You didn't speak to him, did you?'

'No, of course not...'

Gemma breathed a sigh of relief.

'He came into the kitchen, helped himself to my coffee, chatted incessantly about nothing in particular, but I didn't utter a word.'

'So you had a conversation?'

'Yes.'

'Bollocks.'

'What? So now I'm not supposed to speak in my own flat?'

'Did you introduce yourself?'

'Yes.'

'And did he say anything?'

'He said lots of things.'

'But anything... It's just—well, it's all a bit embarrassing, actually.'

'What is?'

'It doesn't matter.'

'What is it? Something is definitely—'

'I told him I was you.' Gemma squeezed her eyes shut. Pure four-year-old behaviour. If she couldn't see Sam, then maybe she wouldn't be in trouble.

'You did *what?*' It hadn't worked that well in her pre-school years either.

'Well, you see, he brought your diary back.'

'I know. But how did you—?'

'I answered the door.'

'I mean how did you know it was my diary?'

'I opened the package, saw it was a—well, your diary, and didn't know what to do next.'

'Say thank you? Close the door? Put it in my room? Call me?' Years of incense-burning and the occasional joint had clearly taken their toll on Gemma.

'I did all of that. Well, except for the last bit.'

'I was waiting up for you. For an explanation.'

'Sorry—I didn't think.'

'Clearly you had other things on your mind.'

'I was compelled to just—well, sort of... It's just he was cute and, well, here, and you weren't, and so I asked him out for a drink...as a thank you...' Gemma wondered if this was sounding as ludicrous out loud as it was in her head. 'And then when he introduced himself I said I was you. I wasn't thinking straight. Not that it really matters now. He wouldn't have known one way or another, only now you've gone and introduced yourself.'

'Not that it really matters? You can't just assume other people's identities in order to get good-looking guys to go out for a drink with you. It's fraud, a perversion of the truth, misrepresentation...' And how galling that clearly Gemma had managed more success with her identity in one evening than Sam had managed in months.

'So you thought he was good-looking, then?' It was an unprecedented moment of accord on the male of the species.

'What is the going rate of gratitude for the return of a diary these days?'

'Going rate?' Gemma hesitated. Her brain was still yawning and stretching. She needed a caffeine jump start; it was still very early. 'No, no, it wasn't like that at all. I wasn't trying to lure him into bed.'

'Of course not. I'm sure he had to fight his way in.'

'He only stayed because he'd drunk too much to drive, and he only stayed in my room because I couldn't find the spare duvet for the sofa bed and you weren't in any fit state to ask. You practically sleep-walked down the corridor.'

'Sophie borrowed it a couple of weeks ago.' Sam absent-mindedly scribbled 'duvet' on one of the many Post-It pads scattered around the flat and stuck the note on the wall by the phone, to remind her to call Soph later. 'I can't believe you told him you were me.'

Gemma at least had the decency to blush. 'It was just easier in the heat of the moment. If anything, I was trying to protect your privacy—otherwise I'm sure he'd have wanted to know what you were like.' That wasn't one hundred per cent true, or even fifty per cent, but Gemma had to admit it did sound good provided you didn't over-analyse it in any way. 'Hey, you're lucky that he found it. At least you've got it back. And you should have told me you'd lost it. No wonder you've been cranky…'

Lucky. Definitely not the word Sam would have used. If Ben hadn't been so helpful maybe she'd be one week less close to a stomach ulcer.

'So, do you think he read it?' Sam knew she could be her own worst enemy.

'How would I know?'

'Didn't you ask him?'

'We didn't spend the evening talking about you.'

'But he thought it was yours.'

'I've said sorry… I guess maybe he read a few pages. I mean, who wouldn't?'

Sam reminded herself that Gemma's intentions were probably better than their execution.

'Did you?'

'No, of course not.'

'Right.' Sam wondered if you could buy lie detectors in Dixons…or maybe by mail order from one of those Innovations catalogues?

'And apparently his sister lives down the road in Clapham, so he knows the area and it wasn't, like, miles out of his way.'

'So why didn't he stay with her last night, then?'

It was a good question, and Gemma was annoyed she hadn't thought of it. 'Well, I'm glad he didn't…it was weird, though. Nothing happened.'

'Nothing?' Sam braced herself for explicit details.

'Not even a kiss. Although I could've sworn he was being quite flirty at the bar.'

'Oh, no, don't tell me you've met the only man in London immune to your charms… Anyway, he was returning my property, so by rights he's mine.'

Gemma cocked an eyebrow. 'Yeah, right. As if you'd even entertain the idea of a television producer.'

'He's a producer?'

'You see, I knew he'd fall at your first CV hurdle.'

Maybe she was changing. Maybe this was the new, improved version of her former self—a Millennium edition. There were still a few glitches but she was trying to be more open-minded. At least internally, even if no one else had noticed. And she had been given a second chance. 'Look, kiss or no kiss, you're going to have to sort this mess out. This morning, preferably.'

Gemma flinched. This morning was very soon. Mind you, it was the perfect excuse to get in touch—if, of course, he was still interested after the 'Hi, I'm actually someone else' bit of the conversation. Gemma shook her head. Complicated already, and her fault entirely.

'I will. I promise. I just wasn't thinking and suddenly it all got a bit out of hand.'

'Right. Good.'

Gemma followed Sam to her bedroom and, leaning against the wall, watched as she applied the finishing touches to her face. 'Don't you think it's strange that we had a perfectly nice evening, very friendly, a few beers, good chat, a bit of banter and then he just went straight to sleep?'

'Maybe he's gay, maybe he's a virgin, maybe he was tired or maybe the new moon hadn't aligned itself with Venus in time?' Sam blotted her lips on a tissue.

Gemma was staring wistfully into the middle distance. 'Do you know, I'm not even sure what he is? Many conflicting traits—hard to place, really. Quite an interesting bloke. American mother, English father, one older sister who's married. Creative. Free-thinking. Thirty-one.'

'You mean you managed to find out his age and not his birth date? Oh, Gem, your standards really are slipping. No sex and no star sign? Really. You'll have to ask him next time.'

'If there is one of those.'

'He seemed to think he'd be back.'

'Really?' Gemma perked up. 'What did he say?'

'I'm sure he said something about another time. Oh, I don't know—maybe I was just imagining it.' Sam grabbed her bag and jacket. 'Look, just call him and clear up this misunderstanding. I take it you got a number?'

'He gave me his card. Although he hasn't even got my number.'

'But he knows where you live.'

'True. Although I think I would probably have given this one a call anyway.'

'Of course.'

'It is the twenty-first century.'

'How could I possibly forget?' She'd been there. Fireworks. Terrible hangover. Sam winced as she remembered the peer pressure to have the best night of your life on December thirty-first 1999. Rather like Finals, she was quite relieved it was something she would never have to experience again. 'Look, I realise I'm hardly the expert, but personally I think men like to do the chasing.'

'Yeah, well, don't be offended if I don't take notes.' Gemma smiled.

Sam knew she was supposed to laugh at herself at this point, but suddenly she couldn't.

'Look, I've really—'

'Got to go.' Gemma finished Sam's sentence for her as she glanced at the clock. Only Sam could be running late for anything at seven-twenty-three.

'Call him.'

The command lingered in the hallway as Sam slammed the front door behind her.

Chapter Seven

His eyes were closed. The room was quiet. No flashing lights or frenetic monitors. No team of nurses. Instead, a drip silently feeding him poison via the same circulatory system that had spread the disease in the first place.

Slowly Sam tuned into the rhythmic rising and falling of his chest, her breathing unconsciously synching itself to his. The lines on his forehead were deeper than she remembered. His face was bigger, or maybe his hair was smaller. Once as thick and dark as her own, it was now heavily flecked with grey, the silver concentrated around his small sideburns and the hairline at his neck, highlighting the stubble that pushed through his tired skin. His hands were resting on his chest. She spread hers out in the air above them. Same shape. Unmistakably genetically linked. She wanted to be angry. He was the one who'd wanted time on his own. Peace and quiet. Something a six-year-old needed practice with.

As she watched him sleep, deeply buried animated memories of her early childhood surfaced, dancing jerkily before her eyes like an ancient silent cine film. Riding on his back in the garden. A rectangle of vanilla ice-cream between two wafers. Learning to swim. A furtive can of Fanta before lunch, needing help with the ring-pull. Dancing to a Jackson Five LP. The occasional fifty pence piece in her piggy bank. And then, interspersed, the memories she had fought to suppress. Lying in bed listening to the muffled arguments behind closed doors. Peering between the banisters from the top of the stairs. Being shouted at for waking him before ten o'clock on a Sunday morning when she couldn't even tell the time—and it had been so much harder before the invention of the digital watch. She suspected he'd never really wanted a child. He'd never had another.

Suddenly and soundlessly he opened his eyes.

'Samantha? Is it you? They didn't say anything about these drugs having hallucinatory side-effects. Unless, of course, I'm dead already. Good Lord, I must be really ill if you're here…' He smiled weakly, the smile fading as he observed the resolute steeliness of his daughter at his bedside, her eyes failing to convey even a flicker of the emotion welling up inside her. 'Dying even.'

'Hi, Dad.' Out loud, the word sounded foreign. 'I'd have come sooner, but…'

'You don't have to make excuses. Despite your mother's optimism, I wasn't sure you'd come at all. You've made it perfectly clear how you feel about me.'

Clear as mud. She'd wanted to punish him for leaving them. For giving up. And yet here, now, twenty-three years later, she still wanted him not to have left. It had been far easier to pretend that he didn't exist.

Sam watched as he pulled himself up onto his elbows, a surfeit of skin on his ageing arms, the effort of the manoeuvre showing clearly on his face, his brand-new pyjamas gaping to reveal visible ribs and a sinewy torso, his breathing laboured. He watched her back. A stranger surveying his lost property with nostalgia and affection. And he smiled.

'No need to look so shocked.'

Sam nodded, the power of speech temporarily deserting her.

'Look, I know I look terrible, and these drugs are bloody awful, but apparently they managed to cut it out of my liver…'

Sam tried to relax her features. 'Oh, good.' It was good. But typical. A brush with death to stir up everyone's emotions and now he'd live to be one hundred and five.

'The bad news is they think they've found a primary site in my pancreas, and to be honest, between you and me, I don't think there's an awful lot they can do. Plus, apparently there's quite a high chance that it may already be in my lungs.'

Speechless, Sam shook her head as she silently succumbed to the rush of guilt at even thinking that he might be building his part. He was in hospital. Having chemotherapy.

'I should've known something was up sooner. I haven't been truly feeling myself for ages. I just thought I was tired, achey, getting older. I convinced myself it was just a virus. Then Susie told me she needed a lift to the doctor and when we got there, the appointment was for me. That woman is always right.'

'What about radiotherapy?' Sam's Ladybird knowledge of cancer was stepping up to the plate.

Robert shook his head. 'The cells are already detectable in too disparate an area. I must have been ill for years and I just didn't know a thing about it.'

'Transplant?'

'Well, maybe if the liver tumour had been the primary one…' Robert's eyes were suddenly glassy. 'Anyway, a week down the line and I've still got my hair. Not sure that I could carry off a baseball cap at my age. But I might have to. Or maybe I'll just be brave and go bald.'

'It's easier for men…I mean easier to be bald in public, not easier to have cancer…obviously.'

'I know.'

Sam had to hand it to him, his togetherness was impressive, if eerily familiar.

'How about you, Samantha? A beautiful young woman with the world at your feet… It really is good to see you.'

Despite herself, Sam felt a surge of something at the compliment.

'Is everything going well? You are finding time to eat between meetings, I take it? I know women these days think it's all about jutting hip bones, concave stomachs, fat-free diets and mandatory gym attendance, but, take it from me, men like something to hold on to.'

Sam didn't want to think about her father holding on to anybody.

'I'm good. And don't think you can do the concerned parent act twice a decade.' The statement was more malignant than anything that been cut out.

A flash of hurt in his eyes. She should have held back, but she couldn't just pretend this was all routine.

'Look, I can't stay for long. I've got a lunch, and I might have to head into the office later.'

'So you're still married to that firm. Life can really be a lot of fun if you allow it to and if you're not at the office on a Sunday… It is Sunday today, isn't it?' Robert tilted his wrist, the watch suddenly looking outsize as gravity ensured the bracelet kept the heavy face out of sight. With a flick of his wrist he got it. 'Yes, Sunday. Good. I'm not losing my marbles yet, then…'

'I have fun.' She was always out doing things. Although just for a moment Sam couldn't quite put her finger on when she'd last had a really good time. She rarely had moments of side-clutching, tear-inducing, breathless laughter any more. But who really did? Sitcoms and romantic comedies not included.

'Look at me. You never know what's around the corner. You've always been a tough cookie. Or at least pretended to be as far as I'm concerned. But I worry about you all on your own.'

Sam ignored him. She wasn't all on her own.

'So…'

'So.'

It was an awkward interaction. So much feeling just below the surface.

Sam checked her own watch. 'I'm afraid I can't stay.' She'd arranged it that way. 'I'll come again.'

'Well, thanks for popping in. Really, I appreciate it. And

when I get out of here, if I ever feel like eating again, let's get together for a meal. Maybe you'll let me buy you dinner.'

'Maybe.'

'I know you think I don't care, and I know your mum and Simon have looked after you, and they've done a terrific job, but you'll always be my little girl.'

He pursed his lips and instinctively Sam leant down far enough for him to kiss the top of her head. His smell was still strangely somehow familiar, and evoked an uninvited tide of emotion. As he fleetingly placed his hand on hers Sam fought back tears. This was much harder than she'd anticipated.

'You know what—it was the best thing I ever did.'

'What? Having a child and walking away?'

'You certainly know how to hit me where it hurts. I mean, look at you. A father couldn't help but be proud. You're beautiful, successful, in control of your life…'

'Screwed up…' Sam hadn't meant to say it out loud.

'Are you?'

'Well, probably no more than anyone else.' Sam tried to demote the comment to joke status. What was the point in being petulant now? She was cross with him, but despite everything she didn't hate him. Not even nearly.

'You really remind me of me when I was your age—although my hair was a little shorter and I never looked good in a skirt.' Robert smiled affectionately at his progeny. 'But there's no doubt about it, you're a true Washington. And, just think, I was only your age when you came along…'

He made her birth sound like a bus arriving unexpectedly.

'I was terrified. I didn't know who I was yet, or where I was going. But the one thing I've learned since, and learned the hard way, is that material success is one thing, but there's so much more to be gained from life if you share it.'

'Like a divorce lawyer, Soccer Sunday, undercover flatulence, never getting to drive on long journeys… I know, Dad. I lived with Paul for nearly three years.'

'From what your mum said, you were both far too young.'

He was right, of course. But Sam had been in a hurry to

prove to herself that she could have a more successful relationship than her parents.

'Look, your mum and I had the best intentions, but I soon realised that marriage didn't suit me. I admit, I got it wrong. She deserved better. And luckily she found it.'

Sam really hadn't planned on soul-searching before lunch—although, thinking about it, she should have realised that they weren't going to be talking home improvements and car engines. Her father had never been one to duck the issue. That was her department.

'Look, you really don't need to worry about me. I've got everything I could possibly need. A gorgeous flat, a great job, fantastic friends, a personal trainer, a tennis coach and probably the most intelligent cat in south-west London.' Sam laughed consciously in a concerted attempt to lighten the tone. But apparently Robert hadn't finished with her yet.

'Just remember, Samantha, wanting to be loved is not a weakness, and loving someone is one of the most fulfilling and rewarding things you can do. If it goes wrong you'll recover, but we need the highs and the lows in life. The contrasts are what drives us forward. It's not just about survival, and don't confuse being tough with being strong.'

'Are you sure you haven't got brain cancer?'

They both laughed. A shared moment. Sam forgetting her anger. And, just for a moment, forgetting that this was supposed to be difficult.

'You really are a chip off the old block, Samantha.'

'It's Sam, Dad. It has been for seventeen years.'

'Right—Sam.'

'Right. Well, bye, Dad. See you soon.' Such a normal sign-off for such an alien situation.

'I hope so. You take care. I do love you…'

Sam couldn't speak. Instead, half-nodding, she turned and walked to the door, straight to the stairwell and down to the exit. Her mind was an emotional kaleidoscope, memories drifting in and out of focus. A chip off the old block? Even if the old block was selfish, self-centred and unprepared to compromise? Since he'd left, sometimes consciously, sometimes not, she'd made every effort to be good, to be better. At first in the hope that he might come back, to make him proud, and then later on just to try and be the model citizen, as if to spite him. She was terrified of history repeating itself, but maybe the whole time she'd been fighting bad genes? Or maybe she just expected too much.

She couldn't stop walking. She hadn't seen her father in nine years. She hadn't spent twenty-four hours with him in seventeen. Robert had shattered her mother's hopes and dreams over twenty years ago, and she might have been married to Simon for fifteen but it wasn't the same. Not that she would ever have said, but Sam knew. Her father had been the love of her mother's life. In their hangover from the late sixties she'd fallen in love completely and forever. Only forever didn't work. And, exposed and vulnerable, she'd been left alone with Sam to recover.

Chapter Eight

'Where is she…?' Sophie checked her watch. The minute hand had barely moved since the last time, but the second hand was defiantly continuing to flinch its way round the dial.

Mark and EJ shrugged their shoulders as they fought over the business section of the Sunday paper. Their obvious lack of concern only focused her own.

'She doesn't know how to do fashionably late. She's always the first one to arrive.'

'Less stress. She's probably stuck in traffic. Knightsbridge is a nightmare today. I saw her last night and she was all set. In fact if anything she was in a much better mood. Mark, what's your take on interest rates at the moment?'

'She's had a lot on her plate.' Sophie leapt to her defence.

'Oh, I know.'

Oh, no, she didn't. From EJ's demeanour, Sophie was certain Sam hadn't told her everything.

'Do you think she's driven?'

'Sam? She's one of the most driven people I know.' Mark looked up to take full credit for his not so throwaway line.

'Good call.' EJ smiled at Mark.

'You can talk.' Sophie pretended to flick through the colour supplement in front of her, failing to retain any of the information on everything from thread veins to sarongs to life as a lesbian and the return of the perm.

'Darling, can we order? I'm starving.'

'I think we should give her a bit longer. And I think you'll find you had a bacon sandwich less than three hours ago.'

EJ looked at her phone. 'She's only twenty minutes late. I'll text her.'

Sam's phone vibrated and beeped simultaneously as she walked into the main dining area of her favourite brasserie. She'd barely started scanning for familiar faces when Sophie waved from their preferred table by the window. What was that saying about friends being the family you choose for yourself? She needed a dose of normality. All alone. She wasn't all alone.

'Hi, guys. Sorry I'm late.' Sam was as cheery as she could be. And only partly for the benefit of the assembled company. 'I decided to walk. It's gorgeous out there, almost summery.' Sitting down between Sophie and EJ, she was glad of the warmth of the company. A support sandwich. Just what the doctor ordered.

'Four days without rain and counting. Practically a heatwave.' EJ still couldn't get used to the random nature of the seasons UK-style. Nor could she understand how the British remained so upbeat when it was pretty much compulsory to have an umbrella in your handbag fifty-one weeks of the year and a summer wardrobe versatile enough to be able to cope with everything nature could throw at you—not necessarily in any logical order. No wonder they were sarcastic. It was in their nature. Literally.

'It's only March.' Sophie could always be counted on as a staunch defender of all things British.

'Actually—' Mark checked his watch '—it's April today. Happy wedding month.' Leaning across, he gave Sophie a kiss while EJ and Sam made childish retching noises, simultaneously stealing a glance at the happy couple.

'Just for the record, I don't think you get a whole month dedicated to you.' Sam glared at EJ. Sometimes tact was not her forte.

'Hey, if it's April maybe it's time to fire up the old BBQ.' Mark, true to his Y chromosome, liked nothing more than piling up charcoal and firelighters and cooking his food over coals that were just a little bit too hot, at the first sign of a cloudless sky.

'Maybe next weekend?'

'Great stuff, darling.'

'Summer will probably have been and gone by then.' EJ couldn't help it.

'So we'll eat inside.'

'That figures.' She never failed to be impressed at the innate optimism of the natural-born griller.

But Sophie was still preoccupied with Sam's opener. 'You walked? From Battersea? Was it sponsored? Or is this some sort of new power-strut your way to the perfect arse fad? Why couldn't you have driven, or got a cab like the rest of us? EJ, promise me you'll take her home.'

'Sure I will. It's a great afternoon for having the top down. Have you got your shades?'

'Of course.' Sam delved into her bag and produced the case as proof.

EJ nodded approvingly. 'Do I detect a little Prada in the house, darling?'

'Duty-free.'

'Who said transatlantic travel had to be gruelling?'

'I knew you'd approve.'

'Too right—and your arse is looking fabulous, by the way.'

Mark nodded almost imperceptibly, but Sophie noticed and made a mental note to ask Sam for some buttock-firming exercises. Three weeks and counting. Maybe she could hire a body double.

'Honestly, Sam, it's Sunday. Traditionally a day of rest.'

'Look, you lot, give me a break. I only walked from the hospital. I was going to get a taxi, but I really needed a few minutes to clear my head. I guess I should've called, but I didn't think you'd worry…'

'Worry? Us?' Sophie affected a laugh while shooting a silencing look at Mark and EJ, and poured Sam a large glass of wine in an attempt to make instant amends.

'If you were hungry you should have ordered.'

Luckily for Mark, his 'See?' was lost amongst the 'Hey, don't be silly' and 'There's no hurry' emanating from either side of him.

'How was he?' Sophie silently scolded herself for being insensitive. As for Mark, next time she'd bring him some biscuits, a carton of Ribena, and maybe a colouring book in case they had to wait for more than five minutes.

'Is it still all about him?' EJ looked up from the paper again. 'Was his teenage girlfriend there?'

Sophie glowered at EJ. That sort of attitude wasn't going to help anyone.

'No, he was alone. And he's in good spirits, considering they don't really seem to know the extent of the spread. You never really know with cancer, do you? Deep down he must be terrified.'

'I think your state of mind counts for a lot in these things. If he can just keep positive.'

'Darling, I'm not sure that's really the case.'

'It can't do any harm.' Sam decided to jump in and prevent a potential domestic. 'And it certainly makes it easier for visitors.' To be honest, Sam was with Mark on this one, but she knew Sophie well enough to know that dismissing her opinion out of hand would only cast a black cloud over the rest of the meal.

Mark grunted his agreement. Anything for a quiet life.

'And how are you feeling about it all?'

Sam was incredibly grateful to have at least one friend who really listened. In the absence of a significant other, it was a real comfort to know that there was someone out there who would drop everything for her if necessary.

'Lying there, he looked—well, he looked old. I mean, obviously, if I'm nearly thirty then he's nearly sixty, but it was more than that. Pained—vulnerable, maybe? But then I haven't seen him in—well, literally in years, and I think over time I'd probably built him up into someone much larger than life. Some sort of hybrid hero/biggest disappointment of my life. In some ways we really are total strangers. In others there's something eerily familiar. And he can still get under my skin in a matter of minutes. It's like he knows exactly which buttons to press.'

'Typical manipulative male behaviour.' EJ was always much tougher on her.

Sophie refused to be ruffled by EJ. 'You see? You can't fool me with all this don't-really-care stuff.'

'I shouldn't care. He doesn't deserve it. He doesn't know anything about who I really am. Then, just as I was leaving, he told me he loved me. Like if he just says it out loud everything will be Okay…'

Sophie nodded, encouraging Sam to continue.

'But then talking to him…it's something in his eyes.' Sam was fiddling with her cutlery. 'Despite everything… We even look alike… I don't know how I feel, to be honest…' It was a rare admission of fallibility.

'You just need to let everything settle. And just because he made a mistake doesn't mean he doesn't deserve another chance. So he's flawed. We all are.'

'Steady on, Soph. Stick to interior design, will you? You have to train to be a psychologist.' Sam smiled wryly but warmly at her oldest friend. 'And I'm starving.' Sam had never wanted food less, but she wanted to deflect some of the attention.

'Now you're talking.' Mark entered the fray. 'Shall I have steak frîtes, rack of lamb or fish pie?'

Sophie rolled her eyes through three hundred and sixty degrees. 'You always have the lamb when we come here, darling.'

'So maybe I should have steak for a change. But the lamb is bloody good. Then again, I haven't had any fish for ages….'

'You don't have to take all this on the chin, you know, Sam.'

Sophie shot a glance at EJ, who thankfully was nodding. Although maybe about the lamb…

'I think I'll go for the lamb.'

'No one's listening, sweetheart.'

'How about French beans?' EJ joined in and Sophie grinned at her.

'Fantastic idea.'

'And Dauphinoise potatoes instead of roasties.' As EJ completed Mark's order they all laughed. Despite a brief flirtation with a couple of alternatives, if Mark's menu fidelity was anything to go by, he and Sophie would be celebrating their golden wedding anniversary in just over fifty years. And probably with the lamb. Sam found the whole thing strangely touching. With so many of her peers struggling with the whole long-term relationship thing—the peaks, the troughs and their perceived loss of identity—it gave her hope. It gave them all hope.

'Seriously, guys, I'm fine. And, anyway, I don't have nearly enough time to have a nervous breakdown. I should probably pop into the office for a couple of hours later, it's my last chance to see the Warhol at Tate Modern, and I've got a reassessment at the gym before work tomorrow morning.'

'He made a mistake. He married the wrong person. I know you're doing your best—' Sophie hoped Sam would rise to the challenge '—but this is the sort of thing that makes you realise that life really is too short…and that time does its healing thing whether or not you want it to.'

EJ pulled a face behind the unit trusts. Since when had Sophie started being such an expert? This was Sunday lunch, not *Oprah*.

'Hmm?' Mark swapped business news for the sport. Maybe he should have gone to play golf after all. He wasn't sure if he could cope with all this sharing, caring stuff—and certainly not on an empty stomach. Despite Sam's green light, and his incisive decision-making, they still hadn't actually ordered yet.

Sam scanned the menu, willing something to tempt her appetite back from wherever it had gone.

'Do you think I'm selfish?' She'd meant to think it. Bloody

menu. Shellfish bisque sounded far too much like selfish bitch to a corporate lawyer in the midst of a self-questioning Sunday lunch crisis. She really had to get a grip. Today was not all about her.

'Nooo. No, of course not.'

The girls instinctively and automatically deflected the directness of the question while Mark started memorising football league tables. He couldn't wait for Sam to meet a nice bloke. Ideally, one with a Chelsea season ticket. Or EJ, for that matter. Sometimes he couldn't help feeling that there wasn't enough testosterone at these lunches.

'Well, you know what you want—you set your sights and you go for it. But I'd say that was focused, not selfish.' Thank God for EJ and her therapist.

Sophie was being more circumspect. 'Don't take this the wrong way, but you can be quite self-absorbed...'

While Sam had always appreciated her totally direct and honest approach, she had been hoping for more of a compliment.

'But not in a bad way.'

'Focused is better.' Sam wasn't convinced she'd heard of anyone being self-absorbed in a good way.

'But underneath it all you're a total softie. It's just that not many people know the real you. You don't let them anywhere near close enough, plus you're a cynical romantic—actually more of romantic cynic. Either way, that's a hard combo to please.'

'And we're all selfish to a degree. It's an essential blueprint for independent survival.' EJ, as ever, was ready to turn the tables on the condition. 'Look at the upside: we make good money, own our flats, drive our own cars, live our own lives and on our own terms...' It was pure Destiny's Child. Sophie was surprised she hadn't whooped at the end of it.

'I suppose sometimes I worry that I'm going to be alone. With the exception of you lot, most of the time I actually prefer my own company. And, between the four of us, I can't wait for Gemma to move out. Plus, I've never even felt remotely broody. Is that normal? Maybe I've got some sort of hormone deficiency? I mean, have you always known you wanted children, Soph?'

EJ studied Sam's face. She didn't look as if she'd been drinking. But maybe she'd stopped for a few vodka-tonics *en route*. Or maybe she'd contracted one of those virulent infections that routinely plagued hospitals these days. Normally it was, Do you think I should get highlights/kitten heels/a digital radio decoder…? Much more Sunday lunchtime than this.

'Definitely.' Sophie's eyes lit up and she and Mark exchanged an affectionate glance.

As Mark squeezed Sophie's hand Sam felt a stab of something unfamiliar. She needed food. Her blood sugar must have dropped to dangerously low levels for her to be feeling this emotional. Or maybe it was PMT.

EJ couldn't contain herself. 'I can't imagine anything worse. Sleepless nights, no time for yourself, non-stop screaming and eighteen years of being told you're not good enough whilst throwing hundreds of thousands of pounds of taxed income at a terminally ungrateful specimen.'

'But I bet you'd be a great parent.'

'Soph, don't start trying to convert the rest of us—and it takes two. I could set out to be the best parent in the world, but what if the guy I choose turns out to be a total loser, a wife-beater, a serial philanderer, married…?'

Sam studied her menu a little harder. She still hadn't told EJ. Meanwhile Sophie searched for a positive word, a syllable, anything…

'You can't control everything.'

'No, but I can try and limit the damage. I was a trophy child, basically born so my parents could tick "have child" off their list of things to do. Money might not have been an issue, and on paper I had the best of everything—the best schools, the best childcare and nannies who I adored and who adored me—

but then they left. There was no real continuity. Maybe if I'd been a boy it would have been different. But I don't think so.'

Sophie was amazed at the amount of emotional baggage EJ kept packed away.

'And then instead of rebelling, running away, stealing cash, flunking school and developing a habit, I was determined to get on with my life despite them—and, I guess, to spite them. They won't even speak to each other except through their counsel these days. It's pathetic. I was a valuable pawn. And now I'm not…'

A reverential silence had descended over the lunch table.

'Hey, I know I've got major issues.'

And Sam had thought *she* was angry—but the venom simply wasn't there. She squeezed EJ's hand supportively. This conversation was all her fault.

'Okay, well, that's enough of that. Mark's looking pained and I see my therapist on Mondays, so I might as well save it for her… Hey, did anyone see that article about tattoo removal in *Marie Claire?*'

Mark inwardly breathed a sigh of relief. This was much more like it. He loved women's brains. Therapy to tattoos in one sentence. No wonder male psychologists had been fascinated by female logic for years. Judging by that segue, they were never going to crack it.

Sam was still studying EJ with concern.

'Oh, come on, Sam. You know I'm addicted to glossies, and I readily admit I only bought this one for the free make-up bag—oh, and the interview with that hot singer turned actor Jake Jones. He's a fox.'

'Jake Jones? That can't be his real name.'

'I think it is. He's Welsh Texan, or something. I met him once at a party a few months ago. Ego all over the place but great eye candy.'

'EJ!'

'Nothing happened. I was there with someone else…'

Sam and EJ exchanged a look. Just as Sam had thought.

'But a girl's got to window shop.'

'Which would be fine if that was all you did.'

'Look, I need to have fun…we all do. We work hard and we play hard…'

Sam made herself a mental note to try harder in the second category.

A waiter reappeared and, pen poised over pad, waited. Mark looked as if he could have kissed him.

Chapter Nine

Disentangling her windswept hair from her lipgloss, Sam opened her front door feeling much more relaxed as EJ accelerated away, roof down, music blaring. She wasn't even disappointed to find that it wasn't double locked.

Popping her head round the sitting room door, Sam was surprised to discover the TV was dormant and the sofa deserted. In fact, she was already two-thirds of the way through a medicinal pint of water at the kitchen sink by the time Gemma appeared—and nearly drowned mid-gulp at the discovery that Ben was in tow. Forget temping. Gemma would have been far better off writing a guide to 'Always Getting the Man You Want Without Seeming Easy'. Less of a self-help, more of a help-yourself manual. And, looking at their crumpled appearance, she'd probably interrupted a research session.

'Good lunch?' Ben was disappointed to note that their second meeting in her kitchen was feeling just as awkward as the first.

'Great, thanks.' Was he really wearing a T-shirt with Love is the Message plastered across the front?

'So where to now? Gym or office?'

It was a cheap jibe from her flatmate, and bonhomie evaporating rapidly, Sam suppressed the suddenly overwhelming urge to retort that at least she had a job with responsibilities. Forcing a smile, she fought to cling to the feeling of serenity that had accompanied her home only minutes earlier, even if the face-pack-and-toenail-painting-in-tracksuit-bottoms option for the afternoon was clearly now out of the window.

'Neither. I've had far too much red wine, and I was seriously thinking of bonding with my new plasma television later…' Being a lawyer wasn't so bad sometimes. 'If there's room.' See—she could do chilled out and bitchy all at the same time. Multitasking was a speciality.

'Plenty of room.' Ben was quick off the mark. 'And you can top up your alcohol levels with us…'

Sam could have sworn this was her flat…

'Bit more red?'

'Why not?'

Incredulous, she watched Ben pour her a glass of her favourite everyday Australian Shiraz Cabernet, and battled with her inner Scrooge not to say anything about a six-pound bottle of wine.

'If you're sure I'm not interrupting anything…' Sam headed into the sitting room and settled into her armchair-for-one, leaving the sofa for the teenagers.

'Course not.' Ben was hot on her heels, personal space clearly not a concept he was familiar with. He and Gemma were clearly destined to have a long and happy life together.

'Have you just surfaced?' Sam couldn't remember ever spending an entire day languishing in bed without a temperature.

'We were up earlier. Ben went for a run while I made bacon sandwiches…'

Sam tried not to think about the state of the grill pan.

'And then we watched the end of a film.'

'Any good?'

'If you believe in things being meant to be, I guess.' Ben hesitated as he tried to recall the title. 'Pretty schmaltzy.'

Could it be that he didn't know he was sitting alongside south-west London's answer to Mystic Meg? Gemma obviously hadn't managed to ascertain the time of his birth, then. No wonder she was looking a bit stroppy. Or maybe that was because her landlady was in the house.

'Do you?' Sam deliberately avoided making eye contact with Gemma. Playtime.

'Sometimes I think I'd like to...'

'Really? I think if you want something in life you have to work for it.' Sam was limbering up.

'I don't think it's that black and white. You can't just sit around watching daytime TV, waiting for lightning to strike and your life to change. But, strangely, the older I get the more I think that things happen for a reason—that there are people in life you are meant to meet.'

'Me too.' Gemma was gushing. If Sam had been Ben she'd have retreated a few millimetres.

'And they all lived happily ever after? Very convenient.'

'Hey, no one said it was going to be easy. Fate merely supplies the raw materials... But the older I get the fussier I am, and the fewer new people I meet—so maybe it's getting more convenient to believe in serendipity. Bit like my grandfather suddenly getting religious just before he died. Sort of covering my bases just in case.'

'Or just another excuse for not taking responsibility for yourself. *Hey, I know, let's vest our destiny in a greater force which we are helpless to control and see what happens...* All I'm saying, Ben, is don't be surprised if it doesn't all work out the way you were hoping it would.'

Gemma decided to intervene while they were still in round one and move into a more hypothetical arena.

'Maybe it's partly the media's fault and we're all looking for something that doesn't exist? Maybe we're destined for disappointment?'

'I don't know, Gemma…' Ben seized the question before Sam could quash it.

Sam took a long sip of her wine. At least he knew her real name now.

'People like to use the media as a scapegoat for the world's problems, but I'd argue that—in television, at any rate—we're just reflecting society, not shaping it. Hope and aspiration motivates us all, and that's not cynicism—that's human nature.'

'Do you work for the Philosophy Channel?' Sam was curious, if more than a little sarcastic.

Ben shook his head. 'Nope, I'm currently at an independent production company—Small Screen Productions… They specialise in popular documentaries…'

Too much information. She was beginning to wish she hadn't asked.

'Which I guess comes under factual entertainment or edutainment.'

Sam scoffed. 'What is this? The "invent a compound noun" round?'

Ben laughed. Secretly Sam was impressed. Courage under fire and no overt sign that she'd unsettled him so far.

'Anything I might have seen?'

'The biggest project I worked on recently was an exposé of the glamour modelling industry. It was well received, and quite highly rated across the board.'

'Not *Storm in a D cup?*'

Ben wished he could disappear as Gemma chipped in with the detail he had deliberately excluded.

'And that was *your* idea?' Sam could feel her lip curling.

'Yup.' If he hadn't hit rock bottom in her estimation thus far, Ben knew he had now.

'Wow—I can't believe that.' Gemma was obviously impressed.

Sam could.

'Hey, it's not brain surgery…'

'More like cosmetic surgery.' Yet for some reason Sam's B cups were suddenly feeling rather inadequate. She pulled her shoulders back, surreptitiously glancing down at her front. Not quite enough room for a storm.

'So what? I concede that making television isn't exactly a calling, but at least I get to wear jeans to work. At fourteen I definitely wanted to be a surgeon. But the thought of another seven years' hard labour after A-levels was too much to bear. I was impatient to start earning in the real world and, face it, Doogie Howser aside, who looked good in a lab coat at sixteen? If I retrain now I'll be nearly forty by the time I qualify, so I'll just make do with a bit of voyeuristic *ER* action instead, while supplying people with programmes to help them escape their own lives.'

'What about all this reality TV?'

'It's still escapism for the people watching. It's not their lives under the microscope. And, as I mentioned earlier, for a lot of people TV is aspirational.'

'I don't know…' Sam didn't know why she was wading in to this discussion. Her three or four hours of television a week hardly made her an expert. 'It's not like everyone wanted to spend the eighties drilling for oil in shoulder pads.'

Ben laughed. 'Soap operas are different. That's about knowing on-screen families better than your own. Feeling part of a virtual community.' He thought back to his holiday reading. 'But I'd say you are more of a *Friends, The West Wing, Sex and the City* sort of girl.'

Sam shrugged. 'So you've seen my DVD collection? Your point is…?'

'You want five best friends, more power and great sex.'

Sam folded her arms defensively. Just sex would be fine. 'I think it's more about the realisation that camaraderie and trust are just as important as finding the so-called and much-debated One.'

While in theory Sam would have loved her life to be a little more Carrie, Miranda, Charlotte and Samantha, if she was totally honest the thought of a different man every night of the week, even every week, just made her feel one thing: tired.

'Rubbish.'

'Excuse me?'

'You'd be surprised how many women would like to think that they could be more predatory. I guess it's fair revenge for years—make that centuries—of bad dates and reprehensible male behaviour. But this new attitude—it's about being in control, being able to be feminine without being vulnerable or exploited…'

'Sounds like you've got it all sussed then.'

'But it's dishonest. I'd hazard a guess that most women would rather be in a steady, strong relationship, having great sex with someone who really loved or cared about them, than out on the town with nameless, faceless semi-strangers. It doesn't mean they don't have a side of them that would like to be more risqué—the ratings are testament to that—but it does mean that they're never going to settle for shoes that aren't Manolo Blahniks.'

On the day she and EJ had recklessly treated themselves to their first and as yet only pair, Sam could have climbed Everest in her three-inch heels.

She found herself taking mental notes.

Positives: non-smoker, SATC fan, articulate, thick dark hair, no sign of receding, would like to retrain as doctor, generally clean, nails unbitten, relaxed, funny, not married, not divorced, parents still married, older sister—Clapham, London based. Went for run on a Sunday morning.

Negatives: career path? Porn documentaries? Poseur potential—scooter, hair is very fifth Beatle, is wearing cords. Faded, admittedly, but pale blue needlecords. And trendy trainers. Maybe too relaxed—lack of ambition/general ambivalence. Probably takes recreational drugs. Probably goes clubbing. Probably listens to lots of guitar music by those bands that boys like with one name as their title. Rents. Shepherd's Bush. Sleeping with Gemma.

Pending: Small Screen Productions—check for Web site.

What was she doing? There might be a drought in the talent pool at the moment, but there were rules. And her judgement was bound to be way off today. Terminally ill estranged biological fathers and red wine at lunchtime had a lot to answer for.

'Earth to Miranda.' What did Gemma think she was playing at? But she had looked up. Bugger.

'Time out.' Ben's hands were in the *T* sign. 'They're all caricatures anyway. There's a bit of all of them in all of us.'

Sam added 'diplomat' to her list of positives.

'Anyone need a refill?' Sam tried to maintain her poise as she wondered where her bit of Carrie was—or Samantha, for that matter.

Two simultaneously relieved nods.

Darting to the kitchen for cover, Sam swapped her wine for a peppermint tea, and as the kettle boiled Ben appeared in the kitchen: to help? to stalk? to provoke? to chat?

'How about *Ally McBeal?* Irritating or identifiable?'

Sam sighed. She was tiring of the game now. 'If the general public genuinely think lawyers can make a decent living singing in the loo or talking to dancing babies—or indeed that everyone in the legal profession could also have been a model. That we have time to do fashionable, that we only work on one case at a time and that we have a bar downstairs to facilitate in-house coupling...let alone time for fooling around, it's no wonder they've canned it.'

'No singing at all?'

'None.'

'And no office romance?'

'Not at 3L. In fact not in the City, last time I looked. Someone has made the fatal mistake of telling men there is a surfeit of single women out there—as if their egos needed any encouragement.'

'Maybe you're giving off the wrong vibes.' Gemma had joined them and was currently teetering on the tightrope of diplomacy without a safety net. 'I mean, without realising or meaning to.' Double caveat. 'It's not like you'd ever admit that you need anyone else.'

Sam could feel herself bristling. 'It's not about need. And I'm not about to do helpless female either. All I'm saying is that it would just be refreshing to occasionally meet people who are interested in getting to know me rather than my mattress. Who want to just date and see. It's starting to feel like it's the men who are dying to settle down, get married and start having children in their early thirties. Getting to know someone becomes a timed challenge, and for some reason if you're a single female most men presume you must be gagging for sex, if not a husband. EJ has this all the time.'

Gemma glanced across at Ben to see if he was contemplating doing a runner from the Battersea branch of Feminists Anonymous, but to her relief he looked as if he'd be staying put for a bit longer.

'Who's EJ?'

'One of my best friends. We met at law school.'

'And you work together?'

'No, she's at Greenberg Brownstein. But the gene pool there is just as dodgy as it is at 3L.'

'Stop right there. Enough is enough.' Ben stood up and held his hand out in a pure Village People disco move. 'At least let me try and defend my race. Starting with me. Thirty-one. Not married. Not nearly married. Never been married. And, although I have high hopes, not actively looking for a bride…'

'Well, you're a rarity, then…or lying.'

Sometimes Gemma wished Sam was one of those girls without an opinion on everything.

'I don't think that I'm that unusual. Of course it may be that I've set my standards too high.'

She knew the feeling. 'Most people compromise.'

'You think?'

'Definitely. No one wants to be the last one picked for the team. But I'm not interested in being someone's spur of the moment, this-one'll-do decision.'

Ben was only too familiar with Sam's thoughts on the subject.

'But there are never any guarantees.' Gemma, caught in the crossfire, was doing her utmost to keep herself involved. 'And as we get older we've got less time—we have to take a few risks, follow our instincts. Ultimately over-analysing everything is just destructive—'

'True.' Ben interrupted her before turning back to Sam. 'But maybe you're going to all the wrong parties.'

'Maybe you just need to *go* to a few parties.'

If Gemma wasn't careful there was going to be a savage rent review in the next half an hour.

'Seriously, I know quite a few men in their thirties who are single and not rushing to settle down.'

'Gay?'

'Straight.'

'Divorced?'

'Bachelors.'

'American?'

'And just what is that supposed to mean?'

'Hey, I've got an idea…' Gemma waded in up to her neck in an attempt to salvage the afternoon.

'Really?' Sam couldn't have sounded any more dismissive.

Now all Gemma needed to do was come up with something—and pretty sharpish.

'Look, why don't we all go out for dinner next weekend?'

'Is his next documentary on threesomes?'

Stinging. Ben recoiled under his T-shirt.

It might have been a spur-of-the-moment suggestion, but Gemma was sticking to it. 'Seriously—why not? Me, you, Ben and a fourth. Ben, you select one of your single and suitables. What's the harm in that?'

Sam racked her brains for a party/play/heavy metal festival that she was definitely attending, or could at least book for next Friday or Saturday. She was pretty definitely free at the moment. Time to be honest. 'I hate blind dates. And I don't want anyone feeling sorry for me. I'm quite happy on my own.'

Ben was almost relieved. On the basis of the last half-hour he wasn't sure if he knew anyone who could take her on.

Gemma, however, wasn't done yet. 'Who said anything about a blind date? Just a relaxed dinner. If the worst comes to the worst we'll just drink a lot and you can do a runner after the main course.'

'I don't know...' Sometimes Sam longed for her early twenties, when everyone had just dated without thinking long term.

'The guy has to keep one foot on the floor at all times. Do we have a deal?'

Ben nodded despite himself. He was curious. Sam flirting was something he definitely wanted to see. He only wished he didn't have to supply the victim. Unless he could find a genuine contender. A real twenty-first-century gladiator.

Gemma stared at Sam, willing her to agree. In exchange she would never leave the washing up again, she'd bleach the shower tray, recatalogue the videos and polish the kitchen floor with her Calvin Klein vest at seven every morning. She needed to know where this Ben thing was going. And she wanted a proper date. Confirmation of their status.

Sam shook her head slowly. 'I don't think so. I mean, it's not like I'm a registered charity.'

'If you were you could have your own Christmas cards...'

Ben stopped himself. Sam's gaze could single-handedly have halted global warming in its tracks. Just because he could visualise a 'Save Sam Washington' logo. 'Giving lawyers a chance to live a normal life'...

'Your final answer?'

'No.'

A glimmer of hope. 'So you'll think about it?'

'No. My final answer is no.'

If Gemma had been twenty years younger she would have stamped her foot. And if Sam had thought she'd been irritating before, she hadn't seen anything yet. Time to dust down her *Monsters of Rock* CD.

Sam picked up her mug. 'I'm not trying to be deliberately obstructive, but I've got some big deals running at the moment, and...' She could have done with a pair of sunglasses to deflect the glare coming from Gemma. 'Well, maybe some other time.' As if. Maybe in another life.

She had only just reached her room when the phone rang, the shrill tone triggering a red-wine-in-the-afternoon head throb. There was only one thing worse than drinking too much during the day, and that was stopping the drinking part before it was time to pass out for the night. Gemma answered, silently fuming, and knocked on Sam's door before poking the hand holding the phone through the slimmest possible crack to avoid having to make eye contact.

Sam snatched the proffered phone before closing the door between them assertively. She could feel her irritability spreading with her headache. More drugs needed, and fast. But that meant going to the kitchen.

'Blimey, Sam, I can feel the atmosphere from across the river. Have you and Gemma had a row?'

'I don't want to go into it.'

'Suit yourself.' Sophie had learnt over the years to just let Sam volunteer information. Sophie didn't do arguments. Sit, listen and dissipate was much more her style.

'They're clearly sleeping together now. Probably on my sofa. And it doesn't even have removable covers.'

'Gemma's having sex? That's hardly news.'

'But by the looks of it this might be more than a one-night stand.'

'You didn't catch them *in flagrante delicto,* did you?'

'No...but they're all coupled up on the sofa—on my sofa—while I'm hiding in my room talking to you.'

'And you're sure you're not being over-sensitive about joining them?'

'How can you be over-sensitive? Either you're sensitive or you're not. Anyway, it's outrageous. The girl can't help but interfere.'

'Right.'

'And it's *my* flat.'

'Of course.' Sophie refused to feel guilty for suggesting Gemma moved in.

'Basically, Gemma and Ben...'

'Ben being her newest sex object?'

'Yup, the diary guy.'

'Oh, it's him? Interesting.'

'Bit full of himself, actually. Anyway, Gemma suggested that I go out for dinner with them and one carefully selected male other, but not a double date. Yeah, right. To prove that there is hope and that there are men out there with potential. Between you and me I think this is just some madcap plan of Gemma's to try and use me to persuade Ben to take her out for a meal rather than just banging her brains out here.'

'Sounds idyllic.'

'Well, you know what I mean.'

Sophie wasn't sure. She attempted a tentative summary. 'So they want you to go out for dinner?'

'Yup.'

'How ridiculous.' Sophie was handling it like a pro. 'As if you're not busy enough.' Reverse psychology had always been a winner with Sam.

'Exactly. I mean I suppose it might be tolerable, but I hate the whole concept of a blind date. It's not as if I couldn't find someone if I really wanted to.'

'Of course not.'

'It's just a question of applying myself.'

'Right.'

'And I'm not even trying to meet someone at the moment. First of all, I simply don't have the time. And secondly, just because I'm not prepared to start going to mixed circuit-training sessions or take up some hobby masquerading as something less obvious than a dating agency to meet people, that doesn't mean I need charity.'

'Agreed.'

'Even if inadvertently I live and work in a social vacuum and hardly ever meet anyone new.'

'Right.'

'But then I guess I have to eat anyway…'

'That's true. Of course, the whole evening might be horrific.'

'But how bad can it be? I can always hop into a taxi if it's a disaster…'

'You certainly can.'

'And it's not like I've got anything else planned at the moment.'

'No.'

'So I guess I'll go.'

'Okay.' Sophie smiled into the receiver. Gemma owed her one.

Chapter Ten

'How about Robin?'

'Too quiet.'

'Too quiet? He's a lovely guy.'

'Just because you have a thing for him.'

'I don't have a thing.'

'Well, you used to. Pre-David.'

'Don't be ridiculous.'

'Ali, a brother, rather like an elephant, never forgets.'

'Nothing happened.'

'That's more like it. Anyway, she'd destroy him before the main course.'

'Damian, then?'

Ben hesitated. 'Too opinionated.'

'David says every dinner party should have a Damian.'

'Not if there are only four of us.'

'Okay…let's see…' Ben could hear Ali flicking through her Filofax. 'Got it.'

'Go on.'

'Jim.'

'Jim?'

'Jim. Jim Bateman. Works with David. Usher at the wedding. Rowed for Oxford. Did an MBA at Stanford. Fiercely intelligent, yet almost self-deprecating—even though he is probably one of the most successful people I know. Oh, and not bad-looking. Fit. Funny. Recently re-singled.' Ali waited for a glimmer of recognition from Ben. 'In fact, on reflection, now I'm not sure why I married David...'

'No way. He sounds far too nice.'

'Too nice?'

'Yeah.' Ben closed the copy of *Hello!* magazine he was skimming and added it to the pile on his desk. Legitimate research. Sometimes he loved his job.

'R-i-i-ight. But you don't like this girl?'

'No. I told you. I don't even really know her that well.'

'But is she supposed to like this guy, or is he supposed to make her think that you are in fact much more her type?'

Ben paused.

'What's your motivation?'

'She's a friend of a friend—of someone I'm sort of dating—and, well, she's lost her faith in men.'

'You can't blame her.'

'What do you mean?'

'Well, against all the statistical odds I have so far suggested three totally available and eligible guys in their mid-thirties and you've dismissed them all out of hand. Plus, you're asking your sister to help—proving yet again that women are better at everything than men. Surely you must know some decent single guys?'

Ben glanced at the array of unsuitable men scattered around the open-plan office, all currently hunched over today's newspapers. 'There's a hell of a difference between having a Friday-night beer and expecting someone to chat intelligently, animatedly and humorously over dinner with a beautiful girl.'

'So now she's beautiful?'

'Well, potentially attractive. So is that really it from your little black book?'

'Almost. I know—how about Martin?'

'Too feral.'

'What?'

'He looks like a weasel, and I have to have standards. Martin would reflect badly on me.'

'And I thought it was girls who were superficial. Peter, then?'

'Too right wing.'

'This is a dinner, not a political rally, right?'

'But he's anti-everything, a bit sexist and terribly un-PC.'

'And lousy in bed.'

'You and Peter?' Ben didn't want to think about that one for more than a nanosecond. It was too late.

'I blame the Malibu promotional evening at college. I haven't been able to look a coconut in the eye since.'

'You never told me.'

'Giovanni?'

'Sounds Italian.'

'Benjamin…'

'Just an observation. How's his English?

'Perfect. How's your Italian?'

'Does he wear brown suede loafers, navy jeans and have a pastel sweater permanently knotted round his shoulders?'

'Do you only wear GAP chinos and sneakers? Don't tell me—too European…?'

'I didn't say that. I'm just not sure that she would… Well, is there anyone else?'

'How about you?'

'I'm going with Gemma.'

'Who's Gemma?'

'Sam's flatmate.'

'And you like Gemma?'

'I guess… I mean, it's nothing serious. Sam just needs—well, she deserves a bit of fun.'

'Don't even think about bullshitting me. I am your older, wiser sister. Who are these girls anyway? You've never mentioned a Gemma or a Sam before. What was it? Buy one, get one free?'

'I sort of met Sam when we were in New York, and I got to know Gemma through her.'

Ali could barely hide her excitement. 'Where was I?'

'Oh, I don't know—having your nails done, shopping, at the gym or somewhere.'

'And there I was, worrying about you moping over Julia. So Sam's over here now?'

'She lives here.'

'What does she do?'

'Lawyer.'

'And Gemma?'

'Is her flatmate.'

'Cosy.'

'Yeah.'

'Hang on. Benjamin Henry Rudolph Fisher—'

Ben hated it when she did this. Plus, it wasn't *his* fault his grandfather had shared his name with the world's most famous reindeer.

'What?'

'This isn't anything to do with that diary?'

'Of course not.'

'Swear?'

'Sure.'

'Swear on your collection of Christmas number ones?'

Silence.

'Ben?'

'Well, look, the thing is…'

'I *knew* it. I told you to post it. So whose diary is it?'

'Sam's…but I met Gemma first.'

'And I'm assuming neither of them have any idea that you actually read the entire thing from cover to cover?'

'Not exactly.'

'And you like Gemma?'

'Yeah… I guess. But nothing's really happened. She's just decided that we're an item.'

'Presumably you've perpetuated this by sleeping with her?'

'Only a few times. But she's not like that. She isn't a typical girl.'

'Of course not. Can men really be so dim?'

'Look, it's just four people having a bit of supper and a few drinks. Or hopefully it will be. Only three at the moment.'

'I'm trying to help.'

'Well, I've got to go. We've got a development meeting later and I need to finish off a couple of programme treatments.' Suddenly Ben was getting cold feet. Who was he to presume that he knew what Sam wanted, when he suspected she probably didn't even know the answer to that one herself?

'Excuse me, but you called me. And just because I work at home doesn't mean I've got hours to waste. Good luck with your search for the not too perfect man. Hang on, I know—what about Luke?'

Ben's enthusiasm rejoined him. 'Perfect. Shall I call him or will you?'

'Maybe you'd like me to do the invites and book a table as well?'

Ben smiled. Message received. 'Give me his number. Thanks, Ali. I owe you.'

'I know.'

Sisters. You can't live with them and you can't live with them. But Ben had to admit it was useful if they were in the same city. Forgetting his impending meeting, he focused on a different pitch before dialling Luke.

Chapter Eleven

Sam clicked the *Carpe Diem* icon on her screen, allocating the last three hours of work to her biggest client, and sat back, proudly watching her outbox empty. As she stretched her arms out to release the tension in her shoulders she looked at her watch. Just gone seven. Her thirty-sixth consecutive hour in the office and, despite forty minutes at the gym at lunchtime, a shower, change of underwear and fresh shirt, her sixth wind was on its last legs.

Pulling open her desk drawer, Sam retrieved her emergency Snickers and, placing it on her mouse mat, eyeballed the sugar rush intently before invoking extreme will power and replacing it out of sight. Letting the weight of her head rest entirely on her hands to give her neck a moment of respite, she slipped her shoes off and kicked her legs out under the desk. Not that anyone was ever going to notice whether she had cellulite or varicose veins if she continued to spend every waking moment in her office chair.

Ping.

Sam clicked on the new message.

From: Richard Blakely
To: Samantha Washington
Date: Thursday 5th April
Time: 19:03
Re: Thanks

Favour, please. Have told Jeff you are contact this evening if he or any of the Chicago team have any questions on the attached. Jeremy's birthday. Am at theatre with him, Charlotte and Annie. Will call and check-in at 10:30, or whenever it is the Lion King *goes to bed. Thanks for babysitting this one.*
R
—Partners meeting week after next. Should chat. Coffee Monday?

Her bed suddenly seemed a continent away.

'Fuck. Bollocks. Shit.'

Articulate or not, sometimes there was no better way to express yourself…

'Bad time?'

Except, of course, when you have a visitor.

Sam could feel tears of sheer frustration and exhaustion forming deep in her tear ducts, bone-dry from hours of continuous air-conditioning and VDU abuse, but blinked them away. Andrew Thorne, 3Ls' very own Casanova, stood framed in her doorway. Always a bad time.

'I should've knocked.'

'That is the tradition.' Prickling at the intrusion, Sam leant back in her chair.

'Sorry, but your door was ajar. I can't seem to get enough caffeine in this building, so I thought I'd shake off these shackles and head out on to the streets for some hard drugs.'

'You're going to Starbucks?'

'Yup.'

She was supposed to be going home. Running a bath. Going to sleep.

'Get me a double espresso…'

Her order was purely medicinal. A latte or a cappuccino might be misconstrued by her body as a hot milky bedtime drink, and she'd lost count of the number of cans of Diet Coke she'd drunk in the last twenty-four hours.

'And make sure it's the Sumatran roast rather than their standard blend.'

'Got it.'

'Thanks.'

She was just reaching for her wallet when another envelope icon pinged into the bottom right-hand corner of her screen. Her mobile beeped simultaneously as the forces of communication bombarded her from every angle.

'Who's a popular lawyer, then? Don't worry. My shout. You can get the next one.'

Sam went for the text message first.

B called. Belg/Thai/Ital on Sat? Let me know asap.
Assume you stuck in office? G x

Time to speak to someone who wasn't a lawyer, a client or an employee of 3L. Picking up the office phone, Sam dialled Gemma's number. It barely rang.

'Belgian?'

'So, you are alive?'

'Here all night yesterday, and not done yet.'

'You should've called.'

'I guess.' The light from her monitor was searing her retinas. Sam reached into her bag. She had no idea how people had managed before the invention of eye-drops and all-in-one face wipes.

'Well, at least I know you're not under a bus.'

'Sophie knew I was here.' Satisfied that this call wasn't going to require her undivided attention, Sam popped to her inbox.

'I'm not telepathic.'

She scanned the new message.

'Are you still there?'

But how could he possibly…?

'Sam?'

'Mmm.' At least this time her response was audible.

'You okay?'

'Mind if I get back to you on that?'

'You've lost me.'

Sam sighed wearily. 'Sometimes I wish I could lose me. Just for a couple of hours. I've done my shift, yet it would very much appear that, courtesy of the information super bloody highway, I've been caught in the world wide web.'

'Seriously, Sam, could I have a non-cryptic clue?'

'I've just had an e-mail from Paul.'

'As in *Paul* Paul?'

'Indeed.'

'He'd better not be suggesting anything for Saturday night…'

'He's not suggesting anything. He's getting married.' Her voice a monotone, Sam re-read the message as a detached hollowness engulfed her.

'He is?'

'The thing is, I just don't understand how he got an e-mail to me… Hang on… Gemma…?'

'How can this possibly have anything to do with me?'

'"*I couldn't believe it when I saw your name on Friends Reunited…*"'

An instructive silence.

'What the hell did you think you were doing?'

'It's Okay, I didn't give any personal details—just your name and your e-mail address for other subscribers…'

'Sounds pretty personal to me.'

'I was going to tell you, and then…' Then what? Sam had been in a permanently bad mood? They'd run out of tea bags? She'd wimped out? Luckily Sam interrupted before she had to take her pick of inadequate excuses.

'Please, Gem. Just stick to your own life.' She was too tired for an all-out scolding.

'I just thought… On reflection… Okay, I think maybe the first problem might be that I didn't really think at all…'

Gemma needn't have worried. Sam wasn't listening.

I really wanted you to hear this from me, and not a few months down the line as a rumour filtering through some rusty branch of our old grapevine.

'The internet really is an excellent accomplice for your average cowardly ex. If he'd wanted to tell me himself he could at least have called.'

'I didn't know you were still in touch.'

'We're not.' It was an excellent point.

'Well, then. And surely it's better to know he's getting married than not? Does he say who to?'

Sam scanned the message again. 'Nope. Honestly. Men are crap. At least I could have looked her up on Google or something....'

'And tortured yourself with the outcome...'

Maybe Paul had been hoping to provoke a reaction? Maybe this was his way of telling her it was her last chance? And maybe she needed to go home and get some sleep.

'I promise I'll take your name off tomorrow.'

'It's too late now.'

'I'm sorry.' It wasn't as if they'd ever been going to get back together.

'I'm fine,' Sam was telling herself. 'It was just a bit of a shock. I mean, suddenly here he is, years later, a landmine lurking in my inbox. So—Belgian...?'

To Gemma's surprise, Sam had snapped back to their original conversation.

'And I take it you haven't given my details to any other organisations?'

'Of course not...'

'Just checking.' Okay, she might have imagined marrying Paul once or twice in her early twenties, but not once since they'd split up—until, of course, irrationally, right now.

'We can go for Thai or Italian if you'd prefer.'

'Where?'

'I don't know.'

'Why don't you tell Ben...?'

Gemma interrupted, Sam's impertinence threatening to dent her karma. 'I'm not telling him what to do.'

'It's not going to be somewhere in Shepherd's Bush, is it?'

'Look, they—'

'They?'

'Ben and Luke.'

'Luke?'

'The guy you're having dinner with.'

'*I'm* having dinner with?'

'We're having dinner with.'

'I did say just dinner and not Last Supper?'

'You did.'

'Any more details?' Sam still couldn't believe she'd agreed to go.

'Not many. Friend of Ben's older sister. Been single for a while…' Gemma paused. 'Fit—ran the London Marathon last year…'

Sam had always meant to. And yet every year she hadn't quite got round to it.

'Into windsurfing…'

She couldn't help thinking fluorescent sunblock, blond highlights, wraparound shades… And only the last one wasn't deal-breaking.

'Works in the City.'

Which meant he was unlikely to own a camper van, goatie beard or ponytail. And he probably earned enough to travel to sunnier climes to practise…in which case he might even be tanned. See—she could do positive when pushed.

'Anyway, chill out. I think it's going to be somewhere central. I think Luke's based in Chelsea…'

Better still. If he had to keep a windsurfer in Chelsea he couldn't exactly be living in a box room.

'You're just going to have to go with the flow on this one.'

'Go with the flow?' Sam struggled to get her head round the concept. Gemma might as well have said 'take it up the arse'. Flow-going and arse-taking both being everyday *modus operandi* for some, just not her thing. 'And I'd like to point out, just for the record, that I'd been drinking when I agreed to this.'

'Stop trying to invoke some sort of legal disclaimer bollocks. It's just a meal out. It'll be fun… So, yes to Van Damme?'

'Hmm? What?'

Sam's other line was flashing. Someone who knew her direct line. Switchboard had gone home for the night. *Please don't be Chicago, please don't be Chicago…or Paul…* An image of him circa 1995 unkindly projected itself into her subconscious. She added three stone and removed all hair. Much better.

'Yes to Belgian?'

'Whatever. You let them know. I've got to take this other call.'

'Just make sure you're back by Saturday.'

'Hello—Sam Washington.'

'Hi, Sammy. God, you sound efficient.' Simon was the only person in the world allowed to call her Sammy, and that was because he'd been doing it since she was seven and a half. 'Have you got a minute?'

'I could probably spare you a couple. Thank goodness for you. I thought you were going to be Chicago…'

'I'm surprised you're still there. Isn't Thursday supposed to be the new Friday in social terms?'

'It's been a ridiculous couple of days. And actually I'm sort of going on a blind date on Saturday, so who needs Thursday-night barflies…?'

'Well, just as long as they're still paying you highly for your troubles.'

Sam paused. He hadn't picked up on the date carrot. Not that she was sure why she'd mentioned it—and anyway Simon never called her—not that she was surprised. After all, it would mean wrestling the phone out of… 'Is everything okay? Where's Mum? How's Mum?'

'She's not great.'

Sam felt her stomach lurch.

'It's Robert.'

And twist.

'Not good news, I'm afraid, and she's taking it all very badly.'

Sam could feel an unexpected tide of tears building and tried to retain her handle on the conversation, which was threatening to blur into a squall. It was only four days since she'd seen him, but it had been nine years before that. Stubborn. Focused. However you wanted to pitch it.

'When—? Did he...?'

'No. Oh, no. He's still alive.'

Sam exhaled. But it was too late. Her pulse was thumping and she was practically shivering.

'Sorry, love. I didn't mean to scare you.'

Emotional see-saw. Robert's speciality. Sam sat up straighter in an attempt to restore calm to her psyche. 'I'm all right.'

'But they've found more. Lungs too, I'm afraid.'

'But he didn't look—' Sam stopped herself. Pragmatist she might be, but oncologist she was not. 'He said...the scans didn't show...' Sam had lost the ability to complete a sentence on the subject.

'Who really knows how these things work...?'

Now Sam's temple was throbbing but, relaxing her grip on the receiver, she restored the blood flow, the pulse instantly abating. She wished she'd put more pound coins in the Cancer Research collection tins over the years. It probably wouldn't have made a difference, but at least she might have been feeling better. And surely she could have managed to send him the occasional birthday card...

'There's some debate now over whether it's even worth continuing with the treatment. They seem to be talking months. General consensus on the prognosis is eighteen at the most. I'm sorry to have to give you the bad news.'

'But I can't believe... I mean, I was there on Sunday, and he looked—well, he didn't look great, but—well, he didn't look like...months...' Sam shook her head, just in case there was some sort of short circuit going on in her ear area. And surely eighteen months was a year and a half. That already sounded better. Fractionally.

'I really didn't want to worry you while you were at work. But we've known since this morning, and your mother's just getting worse.'

'Let me speak to her.' A whole sentence. Sam silently congratulated herself on her powers of recovery.

'I'll pass you over. It's just that for once I think I might be the wrong person to help.'

There was suddenly a lot of static on the line, or snivelling, or something…

'Mum? Mum? Come on. You have to be strong.'

'Hi…darling.' It was a semi-whisper.

'Now, what happened?'

'It's just—I mean…' The sentence petered out.

'Mum, come on.'

'It's Daddy…'

Sam felt sick. She hadn't heard the D word spoken with that much affection since her underwear drawer had been stuffed with white vests and knee-high socks with doily patterns. Suddenly she felt like she had twenty-four years earlier, when her mum had told her that her dad was moving out for a bit. A bit of what? No one had said.

Sam waited patiently for the symphony of nose-blowing to end.

'He's home now. He wanted me to call in case you were thinking of visiting again at the weekend. Also, he keeps going on about arranging a time when you, he and I can get together for a meal. And he said we'd better make it sooner rather than later…' She was off again.

Sam remained strangely calm in the wake of her hysteria. A reminder of years gone by. And there was no point in both of them getting upset. Her mother gathered her emotions.

'Sorry, darling, it's just such a shock. I mean, one week he's ill and now it looks like he's never going to get better. Plus, I suppose it's also a wake-up call. It's like suddenly, we're next in line and there's still so much…' Her voice cracked. 'He was dying to get home. It's all wrong.'

Dying to get home.

'I'm sure we can organise dinner soon.' The last time Sam had eaten supper with her biological mother and father she'd thought that fish had fingers and crinkle oven chips were the epitome of *haute cuisine.* 'You could all come to mine. I'll buy something nice and foolproof. Maybe Dad would like to see my flat…?'

More tears. Patently being nice was the wrong way to go.

'Anyway, you know how stubborn he is. He might live for years. They have to be over-cautious when estimating a timescale so families don't get unrealistic hopes up.'

'Maybe you should invite Susie too?'

Sam wondered when her family had decided to go all nu-dysfunctional—although these were extenuating circumstances.

'Maybe.'

'I wish you were here, darling. I want to give you a hug.'

A hug would have been good. 'I'll try and take tomorrow off. Otherwise I'll do my best to pop over on Saturday. We could even drop in on Dad together.'

'That would be great. You are a funny one, Sam. Blowing hot and cold, pretending not to care, but underneath it all it's good to know your heart's in the right place…'

Praise. And Sam had no idea what to do with it.

'Mum, will you do me a favour?'

'Of course.'

'Make sure Simon doesn't feel like he's on the sidelines. In some ways he's the heart and soul of this family—'

'Jesus, sorry I was so long. Honestly, it would almost have been quicker to…' Andrew stopped himself. Ashen, grim-faced, but definitely Sam-shaped. This was obviously a bad moment. And bad, terrible as opposed to *Bad* Michael Jackson-stylee. He put the coffee and paper bag down as fast as he could, before beating a hasty retreat, pulling the door closed behind him.

'It's funny. From when you were very small you've always been so emotionally mature. When Simon first met you he said you were seven going on forty.'

Only, ironically, suddenly Sam felt twenty-nine going on six. 'I've got to go.'

'Hopefully see you tomorrow or Saturday. Just let us know. And be brave. We've all got to be. Lots of love from us.'

Hanging up, the silence in the office was palpable.

She hadn't felt part of an 'us' for years. And her mother had told her to be brave once before. But this little soldier needed to go on a refresher course. Instinctively Sam dialled Sophie. Voicemail. EJ—the same. Suddenly the world seemed like a very big place. This was the moment when most children rang their parents.

Beep-beep. Sam glanced at her mobile phone screen.

8:30 Sat. Beers & Belgian.
Camden. So sorry about
FRutd. Keep Sat afternoon
free if poss. Have girlie plan.
Gxx

And to add insult to injury she was going on a blind date with a City-based windsurfing apostle in forty-eight hours.

Shaking her head, Sam allowed herself to raise the sluice gates and liberate a rare stream of tears. They were still flowing silently down her cheeks when the caffeine fairy returned to check on her.

She knew the rules. Crying in front of a colleague: lose ten points. Do not pass Go. Do not collect £200. Yet she was currently providing Andrew with an office scoop. An exclusive. She was the weakest link. Goodbye.

'I'm sure I asked for the Costa Rican blend. They didn't make a mistake, surely? Oh, hang on, you said Sumatran…or did the Rocky Road offend your sensibilities?'

Rocky Road? So now she knew the meaning of getting her just deserts. Her emotions were doing their best to do a three-point turn, and while she was waiting for them to complete the manoeuvre Sam retrieved a box of tissues from her bottom drawer.

'I'm fine.' Adrenaline had proved to be the perfect energy-provider. 'How much do I owe you?'

'It's a gift.'

'My mother taught me never to accept sweets from strangers.' Sam blew her nose hard.

Andrew smiled. 'Hey, I'm not a stranger.'

'Not to most of the department.'

He cocked his head. The trademark cheeky grin. 'Don't believe everything you hear.'

'I try not to.'

'Look, I don't want to pry…' For once he was a banter-free zone.

'I'm better. Really.'

He seated himself in the chair on the other side of Sam's desk. 'You can tell me. Might do you good to talk about it.'

'It's nothing, really. I haven't been home for nearly thirty-seven hours, only it feels like thirty-seven years.' She'd never been great with sleep deprivation. She could still work, co-ordinate her limbs, even draft contracts with deadly accuracy—but her emotions were all over the shop.

'So, Britain's toughest chick is human after all?'

'Plus, my father is really ill.' Professional pride. She couldn't have him thinking she was just overtired. 'And my ex-boyfriend is getting married…' So? Sam dug her heel into the arch of her foot just firmly enough to teach herself a lesson. That had been a totally unnecessary confession—to completely the wrong person.

'Look, why don't you shut up shop and go home?'

'Can't. This is an international Mergers & Acquisitions department, not a greengrocer, and RB has left me in charge of one of his deals.'

'All night?'

'Well, until elevenish. He's at the theatre.'

'That's still more than three hours to go.'

Sam gave her nose a final blow and straightened her shirt. 'I'm fine.'

'So you keep saying.'

'Although I think the air-con might be giving me a bit of a cold.' Sam produced a bottle of pills from her bag.

'An overdose isn't going to solve anything.'

'Very funny. These are herbal. Echinacea will sort me out in no time.'

'I personally would prescribe a brandy or a whisky.'

'Well, I'm not sure I've got any to hand.' Sam returned to her drawer. 'Let me see—no, as I suspected, just Lemsip, Pepto-Bismol and Benylin, long-life milk to go with my Fruit & Fibre, nail polish remover...oh, and a carton of apple juice.'

'Luckily my office is more off-licence than chemist. You call Richard, I'll get you a real drink, and then I'm going to put you in a taxi and send you home.'

Sam drained the last sip of brandy and observed Andrew's distorted features through the side of her glass. He'd brought a bottle and they'd been drinking in her office for the last hour—forgetting that Chicago could call at any time, that she hadn't had dinner and that she hated brandy. But she felt better. Or at least divorced from reality. Same difference.

'Come on. Leave a message for RB, and then how about a quick bite to eat across the road?'

'Definitely not.' Food, bath, bed. Not noisy pub. No more alcohol. Not Andrew. Not now.

'Look, you can't just go straight home...'

'Just watch me.'

'Ten pounds says you don't have any decent food in the house.'

Sam paused. She definitely had bran flakes, and they were fortified with vitamins and iron.

'Come on—just a snack.'

'Who put you in charge?'

'I'm starving.'

'Aha, the not so hidden agenda.' Sam was warming to the suggestion.

a) She'd sleep much better if she had a balanced meal.

b) Tonight was not the night to teach herself to cook or,

c), indulge in the toast and chocolate spread cure-all—although toast did count as hot food.

'Look, far be it from me to stand between a girl and her personal crisis. Leave now. Go weep. But, believe me, life's much worse on an empty stomach.'

'I'll see you down there.' Sam picked up her phone and prayed Richard had remembered to switch his mobile off before taking his seat in the stalls.

Richard listened to the message one more time in the cab. Personal crisis, tomorrow off, and she sounded terrible. Concerned, he checked his watch. Probably not fair to call her now, but he might as well stop by the office. Then at least Jeremy and Charlotte would be tucked up in bed by the time he got home. He'd done quite enough parenting for one evening.

'So, moving on to the more trivial, tell me about Paul.'

The Judge & Jury was packed and noisy. But they'd found a table for two, even if Sam was having to lean in very close to hear what Andrew was saying, and food was thankfully on its way.

'Just an ex who's getting married.' Sam attempted a simple statement of fact divorced from any emotion.

'Serious ex?'

'Well, we lived together for almost three years—but more out of sheer geographical convenience than for any relationship reason.'

'Did you ever think you'd be Mrs Paul?'

'Me? Get married?' The subsequent laugh was far too shrill to be genuine. 'Well, maybe once, in my former life as a pseudo-domestic goddess.' Sam tried to do laid back. 'It would never have worked.'

'Who ended it?'

Sam skipped a beat as she weighed up the merits of telling the truth.

'It was a mutual thing...'

Andrew nodded.

'We were far too young…'

Soundbites from The Conversation were still etched in her mind. *She wasn't what he wanted.* Not it but her.

'He must have been mad.'

Sam's face must have registered surprise.

'Well, it's never mutual, is it? The impetus has to come from somewhere.'

'Impressive insight, Mr Thorne. Not that I ever let him see how upset I was.' Sam paused. 'Pathetic, I know.'

'He clearly didn't deserve you. You were out of his league.'

A compliment. And, as his gaze lingered for an unsettling moment too long, Sam had to remind herself who it was coming from.

'Most men seem to get completely the wrong idea about me.'

She should have gone straight home. Sympathy votes were not something she ever canvassed, and certainly not from Andrew Thorne.

'Those sharp edges need filing.'

'I refuse to do needy.'

'Your word, not mine. Look, I've been round the block a few times myself. I've been there, done that and got most of the T-shirts.'

'Round the block? You haven't had to leave the building.'

'Anyone would think I've slept with half the secretaries.'

'You haven't?'

'Of course not.'

Sam wasn't sure she believed him.

'Sure, I've slept with two or three—in two or three years, I might add—but I'm not the 3L love machine.'

'Oh.'

'You sound almost disappointed.'

'Definitely not disappointed.' Had she accidentally paid him a compliment? Her clear thought process was no longer working. 'Why don't you set the record straight?'

'What do you suggest? A round-robin e-mail? A full-page ad in a broadsheet? Or maybe just a little something on the kitchen noticeboard? Shelley's the one responsible for most of the rumours, and that's only after I refused to make love to her in the stationery storeroom.'

'Room? That's a cupboard…'

Andrew nodded.

'And, just for the record, I don't think you can make love in a storeroom.'

'Oh, believe me, I can…'

'Mr Slime in action.'

'Mr Slime?'

'Don't tell me you haven't heard that one before?'

'Can't say I have.'

Sam reddened. 'I'm surprised.'

'I'm not.' Andrew bet she had no idea what some of the others called *her* when she was locked away in her office.

Richard stood at the bar and ordered another whisky. All calm on the Chicago front, but he'd stopped by Sam's office and there were no clues. And, sadly, no Sam. Surveying the scene, he scanned the end-of-evening crowd. Some of the most expensive hangovers in London started here. And an animated Andrew Thorne was working his magic at his preferred corner table.

Richard watched him. The consummate professional on and off the pitch. One on one attention. Continuous eye contact. Drinks. Dinner. He craned his neck to get a look at tonight's target. A break from the blond tradition. Richard gripped his glass too tightly as he finally got a clear view. Downing his drink in one, he slammed the empty glass down on the bar and left.

Sam laughed. She'd gone through melancholy and self-indulgence, discovered perspective, and the combination of vodka, Grand Marnier, cranberries and lime on a brandy base was having a truly uplifting effect on her mood, her prior knowledge of Andrew's reputation apparently banished to a dark, distant corner of her memory. He was flirting and, to her surprise, with her cocktail specs on, she was definitely reciprocating. Yes, in today's *Just So-So* existence this bird, dearly beloved, had made it to the watering hole and her flirt was back. And, if a little rusty, it was apparently determined to learn a few new moves.

Chapter Twelve

Sam stood in the shower and washed herself again, before rinsing with extra cold water to tighten her pores and to try and focus her mind, which was already in the process of erasing this evening from her short-term memory and losing the details somewhere on her hard drive.

Her romantic projections of falling asleep in a bear hug had clearly failed to take into account the bit between getting home and going to sleep. Big mistake.

'So, you don't want to have sex, then?'

Shaking her head at the recollection as she stepped onto the bath mat, she felt a shiver grip her scalp and run down the full length of her spine. What on earth had happened to dating protocol? Apparently in New York you got dinner dates, a good-night kiss on the doorstep and, if you were lucky, a follow-up phone call. In London you got a double espresso, a slice of Rocky Road, a couple of cocktails and now Andrew was expecting to access all areas. Sam silently apologised to everyone who had burnt their bra on her behalf, but right now she was in favour of bringing back the 1950s, and at the present moment Prohibition seemed like quite a sensible idea too.

Having towelled herself dry, she wiped the condensation off the mirror and gave herself a disparaging look. Since when did she do what she was told?

A tentative knock at the door.

'Hey, Hot Stuff, you didn't tell me there was a shower plan...'

Sam froze. It was real. The man who had called her 'a legend in her own lingerie' only minutes earlier was back for more. She could almost see the funny side. No action for months, yet apparently she was iconic. Sam was curiously proud of her ability to reinvent herself whatever the situation required. She was a legend. And he was not.

'Are you okay in there?'

'Yup.'

Heading to the basin, she picked up her electric toothbrush, determined to remove all traces—even if the main source was still going to be a problem.

'I've brought you a glass of water. Thought you might be thirsty, you know...'

Who had given him the right to roam? As far as she was concerned, he sure as hell hadn't been issued with a licence to leave the bedroom. Sam watched as he tried the door handle, only to discover it was locked, and silently congratulated herself on being a details person.

'I'll leave it out here, then. Don't be too long. It's not even that late yet.'

Maybe she could sleep in the bath? It was far too early to pretend she had to get up and far too late to send him home. And she wished he would keep his voice down. She had no idea if Gemma was back.

Scanning the room for inspiration, it was very much a case of limited resources. One damp bathsheet, one dry hand towel, no clothes and no sodding bathrobe on the back of the bathroom door...wet towel it was. Careful to ensure all curves were covered, Sam mustered a confident swagger for her return to the boudoir. And there he was. Propped up in her bed on her Egyptian cotton pillowcases.

'Hey, I'd say I'm not the only one who's been misjudged at work…'

His grin was curdling her insides. And did he have to mention the office now?

He flung back the duvet for her. 'Now, what can I do for you?' The man was clearly an optimist.

Get up, get dressed, get a taxi… In the film of her life this scene was definitely on the cutting room floor. She should never have let him invite himself in for coffee. She should never have let him buy her a coffee. Plus, she needed some shut-eye. Maybe she had hallucinated this whole evening.

Sam took a deep breath. 'I think you should go.'

'What? And leave all this?'

She hadn't meant it to get to this stage. Correction. She'd wanted to see if she could make herself an attractive prospect and then suddenly he was all over her in the taxi, on her doorstep and in her bed. Kissing with confidence and she'd been enjoying the moment. Past tense.

'Plus—' a smirk from the man in her bed '—I'm naked under here...'

Not an irreversible condition. And Sam had left her sense of humour in the bathroom.

'Let me call you a cab. It's nearly three a.m. and I really need to get some sleep. I've got a difficult day tomorrow.'

'But Maida Vale is on the other side of London.'

'I can't believe you came back here then.'

'I can…' Andrew smiled as Sam's stomach flipped involuntarily—and not in a good way.

'You must have spiked my drink.'

'Hey, careful with those allegations.'

'But this is so not the sort of thing that I do.'

'A bit of fun was just what the love doctor prescribed.'

Her patience was running out, and his patient would have done too, if she hadn't been at home already.

Sensing imminent eviction, the doctor-on-call refined his

bedside manner. 'Look, I promise I'll do my best to behave.' As if to prove his point, he snuggled down into her bed. 'Night, sexy.' And turned over, feigning instant unconsciousness.

Sam scrabbled in the drawer under her bed for as much sleepwear as she could find. Tying a double knot in her draw-string pyjama bottoms, she selected a tight, long-sleeved T-shirt to tuck in and, face down, assumed the thinnest sleeping position she could manage at the very edge of the bed. She wasn't even on her side. Clamping her eyes shut, she pretended to be out cold.

Andrew slid over and snuggled up against her, a human radiator. His hand wandered down her back. His best was nowhere near good enough.

'You're not seriously keeping all that on?'

'Got to sleep. Got to.' Sam slurred her speech as she pretended to be well on her way to comatose and kicked out, apparently unconsciously, while trying not to smile as she felt her heel connect with his shin. He rolled away. But sleep was not forthcoming. She was far too hot, dehydrated, and ashamed as she drifted fitfully in and out of consciousness for what felt like mere minutes at a time while Andrew snored continuously beside her.

Maybe EJ was right. Maybe she was a prude. And maybe he really liked her. Or maybe she just wasn't destined to have a sex life. Images of Paul in a morning suit now plagued her sleep-deprived subconscious. The door to that chapter of her life was now finally, irrevocably closed, but her conscience was apparently set on peering round one last time. Resistance was futile. Listening out for the faint rumble of traffic and police sirens Sam willed the sun to rise.

Romance wasn't just dead, it was six feet under.

'Feeling better this morning?'

Sam's whole body tensed as she felt Andrew nuzzle up behind her and place his arm across her. Protectively/affectionately/obstructively? She couldn't tell and had no intention of finding out. Rolling away, she made it out of bed and onto her feet in a single movement. 'Just tired.'

She stole a glance. Naked Andrew was propped up on his elbows and, to add insult to injury, the bastard was even looking quite rested.

'Any chance of a coffee?'

It was a vicious coffee circle.

'Sure. I'll go and make some.' Preferably in another country. For once Sam really hoped Gemma was at home this morning. She didn't want to be alone.

'Perfect. I'll just grab a quick shower.'

To Sam's horror, Andrew flung back the duvet without any embarrassment whatsoever and unhurriedly picked her towel up from the floor, tucking it round him tightly while she tried not to look, meanwhile attempting to construct a sentence before the moment passed altogether. He was much paler and skinnier than she remembered.

'I know this is going to sound… Well, I don't want you to think—or at least I don't think anyone else needs to…'

'Don't worry.' Andrew walked over to her and pecked her on the forehead. 'I won't be sending a group e-mail round. I'm sort of hoping that you might call on me in a crisis moment again.'

'Right. Good.' Sam was itching to strip the bed, but knew she'd have to wait until he'd actually left the building.

'And no delaying me any further, you corporate minx.' As if. 'Some of us are actually going to the office today.'

Ben was standing by the coffee machine reading as Sam rushed in, flapping her T-shirt in a futile attempt to transfer enough cool air to her upper torso.

'Morning. Loosening yourself up for Saturday night? "You didn't tell me there was a shower plan."' He grinned playfully as she peered into the water chamber.

'Fuck off.' The one night they could have stayed at his…

'Full pot on its way.'

'Is that my bathrobe?'

'Yours? Oh, I thought it was a spare.'

'This isn't a hotel, you know.'

'Here, have it back, if you like.'

'Bit late now.'

Ben pulled at the belt and Sam held out both hands. 'No. Really.' She'd seen quite enough flesh for one morning.

'Take it.'

The last thing Sam needed was an extra layer, yet as Ben helped her into her robe she couldn't help noting that he was a far superior example of the male species than the one probably peeing on her toilet seat right now. Emotional freefall. One icy cold shower coming up just as soon as she could safely get into her bathroom—alone. This was the sort of moment that made her wish she hadn't given up on her diary. She hadn't written in it since New York, but today she wasn't sure who she was punishing more. It or her…and it was still early.

'Aren't you cold?' White T-shirt, wine-red boxer shorts and great legs. Sam tried not to stare as, thanks to her bathrobe, traces of his morning muskiness snaked into her respiratory system.

'No.' He didn't even look up.

She forced herself to refocus on his book.

'A Penguin Classic? Surely the self-appointed king of porn doesn't have a more literary side?'

'What?' Ben folded the corner of the page and closed the book before he noticed Sam watching him and smiled slowly. 'Hey, you didn't like what I did with the book just then, did you?'

Sam shrugged. 'It's your book.'

'Actually, it's yours. I found it on a shelf.'

'That's where books usually live.'

'So you don't mind if I borrow it?'

'No.' Sam sighed. A few bent corners were the least of her worries.

'Hey, aren't you going to be late for work…?'

As Ben twisted his torso to look at the clock on the oven Sam found herself wishing that his T-shirt was a little tighter. Her hormones clearly needed to go on a course. They were going to have to learn to be a bit more selective.

'It's just gone eight.'

'I'm not going in.'

'More important things to do, eh?' Ben voice was thick with innuendo.

'Hospital watch. My dad has just been given a revised life expectancy, my mother needs putting back together again, and although he'd never admit it my stepfather probably needs a hug.'

'Oh.' Damn. Ben wished he could rewind the moment. 'I'm so sorry to hear that. Look, sorry—I mean, I just didn't know.' Ben had never felt more acutely verbally clumsy.

'Hey. It's been a long week. And I'm sure I'll be feeling a bit less freaked out by tomorrow. I just need some decent sleep.'

'Just see how you go. If it's too much, we can always reschedule.'

'Oh, no, we absolutely definitely can't.' Gemma was up. 'And, Miss Washington, a quick question. If Ben is standing in here with you, who exactly is singing in our shower?'

Chapter Thirteen

'Feel the stretch along your spine and let your inner wind rise inside you…'

Sam had been meaning to try classical yoga for months, and she'd never been in more urgent need of some spiritual cleansing. Focusing on the middle distance, and concentrating hard to prevent her one-legged half-lotus from keeling over, plus determined to keep her inner wind from meeting its outer cousin, she breathed deeply to suppress a deep-seated neo-teenage giggle. She needed to locate her less self-conscious core, and fast.

'Breathe in…'

The room was very quiet, aside from the sound of twenty-five pairs of lungs filling against a faint background of music which sounded as if it had been recorded inside a whale's stomach and the light running of water across pebbles—the water feature—probably only there for emergencies on the off-chance that the aromatherapy burner burst into flames or to make all attendees wonder if they needed to pee. Disappointingly, no one was humming.

'Hold it…and exhale…'

Sam heard her mobile. A few audible tuts rose from the rank and file benders and stretchers as her polyphonic ringtone crescendoed.

'Could I remind you to ensure your phones are turned off before the class starts? All vestiges of the twenty-first century should be left at my door.'

Flushed, Sam slipped over to her bag to make amends and restore a more halcyon vibe, but not before her phone had beeped to signify receipt of a message and shatter a few more auras. She made her most solemnly apologetic face before stealing a glance at the ayurvedic pupils all around her as she joined the rest of the class, now on all fours, trying to keep her mind wide open. Irritatingly, to her left Gemma seemed to be fitting right in. And to think Sam had thought she'd be good at this. She'd have been far better jabbing the living daylights out of a punchbag at the gym, yet here she was balancing on one knee and one forearm in an attempt to punish Gemma for organising this evening. So much for a master plan.

Twenty minutes in and Sam was still waiting for her muscles to loosen up. She'd always been supple as a child, yet it would appear from the challenges her body was currently failing to meet that, since her teens, it had apparently acquired the innate flexibility of a Pringle crisp. Gemma, on the other hand, was apparently Little Miss Malleable.

'Feel the stretch. Good.'

Sam looked across just in time to see the resident guru complimenting Gemma. Competitively Sam pushed her leg a little higher and felt the muscle in her groin stretch a little too far, in the style of an elastic band.

'Relax and breathe. Feel your potential.'

At least this way she might end up in Casualty tonight. Although she strongly suspected that Gemma would bring the guests and the main course to A&E rather than cancel. And wasn't she supposed to be thinking of colours and auras and higher planes, not Andrew, Richard, her dad and the rapidly approaching Just Dinner situation? Only a massage and a manicure remained between her and her evening. In stark contrast, Gemma's excitement was unrestrained and currently being demonstrated by the fact that she was up, dressed, out of the house and about to do a shoulder stand at ten-fifteen on a Saturday morning.

'Good.'

In perhaps her proudest gymnastic moment since junior school, Sam was doing her first shoulder stand in nearly twenty years.

'Now, lower your legs over your head…'

Sam cracked her neck round to check with Gemma that she was hearing correctly. Why did these people always have to take it one step too far?

'Slowly, gently…keep breathing…feel your control. Slowly lowering now, towards the floor.' Her voice was almost hypnotic.

Sam had started lowering gently. Then gravity took over and her feet hit the floor behind her. Pinned to the floor by her own thighs. She refused to panic. Even if her chin was pushed up against her chest so firmly that she was having trouble breathing. Her spine was indeed stretched beautifully.

From somewhere to her left Gemma giggled, and Sam did her best to smile. Her knees were definitely getting in the way.

'Feel the releeeease. Good. And breathe. Now, slowly start bringing your legs back up…'

It was no good. Her legs were just too heavy. Her brain was begging, her thighs weren't listening and her calves weren't strong enough to go it alone. There was nothing for it. Sam rolled herself onto her side and unfolded herself manually before joining the others now curled up on their backs, growling, and made a mental note to tell Gemma that any mention of this part of the class this evening would result in instant eviction.

Well? What did you think? Gemma was striding, posture-perfect, in the direction of hell on earth—Oxford Street on a Saturday—while Sam was hoping that none of her muscles would seize up before they made it to their massage.

'I need a higher centre of gravity, but overall I think I do feel better. You, on the other hand, were fairly goddamn impressive.'

'Same time next week, then?'

'I'll have to see how work goes.'

'You can't expect to be brilliant on your first attempt.'

Oh, yes, she could. Sam's phone bleated several times as it rejoined its network. According to the screen she had missed four calls and a text message. And it had only been off for an hour.

GR8 night. Hpe UR
feeling bttr. Drink
2mrw pm?
;-) A

One stupid smily face sign and her mind was straight back from its higher plane. Delete.

Her mood was already spiralling downwards when she picked up her voice messages.

10:04
Sam—Richard. Just called you at work. Imagined you'd be at your desk catching up after day off. Need to talk to you about a couple of things. Call me later if you get a chance. Will be on mobile.

Day off? Whatever happened to compassionate leave? She could feel her stress levels soaring.

10:06
Apologies. Meant to say I hope everything is Okay re personal crisis etc. Have rescheduled Friday's meeting for Monday afternoon. Melanie has details. Speak soon.

She supposed an afterthought was better than nothing.

10:36
Sam, love, it's Mum. Thanks for yesterday. Hope tonight goes well. Speak soon. Maybe I'll call you tomorrow.

Sam knew she shouldn't have mentioned the dinner to her mother.

10:45
Sam, Richard again. Mobile reception isn't great here so call me at home on landline as soon as you can.

'Richard? Hi—Sam.'

'Sam.' Richard closed his study door at home. 'How's things?'

'Okay, thanks.'

Gemma paced up and down on the pavement, willing it to be nothing urgent.

'Only I ran into Andrew Thorne yesterday and he said you were in a bit of a state on Thursday night.'

Sam froze. Andrew and Richard chatting? About her? Yesterday? Not good at all.

'I was tired. He caught me at a bad moment.'

Sam could feel herself blushing, grateful that this conversation was happening remotely. 'I hope you didn't mind me leaving early. I just felt dreadful. The news was such a bolt from the blue and I needed to get home.'

'I asked you to wait for me to get back.' Richard's tone was a hard one.

'I know. I'm sorry. It won't happen again.'

Richard could still picture their cosy dinner.

'Sort of wish you'd felt you could come and talk to me about this.'

'You were at the theatre, otherwise of course I would have told you personally.' There was no 'of course' about it. But it hardly mattered now.

'Presumably your father was under the weather before Thursday?'

'Well, yes. But we didn't know the extent of it…and there are complicated family politics involved. Anyway, no harm done. And I promise I'll be back to my best on Monday.'

'Glad to hear it.'

'Did you want to discuss anything specific?'

'Is now not a good time?'

'I'm just on my way somewhere. But I can call you later if there's something you need to discuss.'

'I was hoping you could pop into the office and prepare a few things for our meeting on Monday.'

To Gemma's alarm Sam was checking her watch. 'I suppose I could spare a couple of hours—' Gemma shook her head assertively '—tomorrow.'

'Excellent. It's just the other side have come back. They're still not happy with the wording on that Exclusivity Agreement.'

'Couldn't one of the others have seen to it?'

'I thought it best you kept across it. And I guess you haven't finished marking up that Sale & Purchase Agreement…'

'Harvey's not expecting it until Thursday. They're still waiting for Investment Committee approval. And it's all in hand.'

'If you're sure you're happy with everything as it stands?'

'I am.' She had been. Only now, thanks to Richard, she was having doubts.

'So I'll see you first thing Monday?'

'First thing Monday. Have a good weekend.'

'How can you let him talk to you like that?'

'He's not usually so difficult.'

'Well, I wouldn't stand for it.'

'It's complicated, and I can't afford to piss him off at the moment.'

'But there's more to life than work.'

'Easy for you to say.'

Gemma raised her hands in mock surrender. 'I know I have the most inconsequential job in the world, but no one needs some big swinging dick flinging his ego around the office.'

'Thanks for that mental picture. Obviously it would help if I agreed to leap into bed with him.'

Gemma's eyes were like saucers.

'Oh, come on, Gem. I thought you knew.'

'How would I know? Well, that's even worse…'

Sam nodded. Relating her office status quo to a third party was hardly inspirational stuff.

'And what if he knows about Andrew?'

Sam hesitated before shaking her head. 'He's toying with me. He loves playing games. Plus, I specifically asked Andrew not to say anything.'

'You didn't?'

'Of course I did. And, anyway, we didn't sleep together.'

'Why not?'

'He only ended up at our place by accident.'

'By accident?'

'It's a long story.'

'We've got all afternoon.'

'What are you going to wear?' Gemma was in Sam's bedroom, despair creeping into her pre-dinner vodka moment. Kylie was in high spirits on the CD player and, office politics long forgotten, Sam was dancing around in black trousers, heels and her bra.

'Well, I thought I was wearing the black jacket—but then you gave me that look.' Yoga, massage, lunch, manicure. Sam couldn't understand why she didn't do the girlie pampering thing more often.

'Only because you looked like you were going to a meeting.' Gemma disappeared into Sam's drawers 'Don't you have any tight jeans? Any little tops, T-shirts that you don't wear to the gym?'

'I've got loads of clothes.'

Gemma kept rifling. Smart, smart, smart, work, smart, cocktail party, gymwear, outdoor girl, tomboy, smart.

'Not sure that I've got any tight jeans, though.' Step, step, twirl, shimmy, shimmy, wiggle, wiggle. Thanks to Ms Minogue and Mr Smirnoff, Sam was almost ready to go.

Watching Sam sashay over, Gemma wondered whether perhaps she'd been a bit liberal with her spirit measures. She'd wanted Sam relaxed, not paralytic. And her outfit still needed some work.

'Well, I've never seen so many variations on a black theme in my life.'

'Can't go wrong with black. Although I admit some of them are a bit more green-black and blue-black these days.'

'Look…' Gemma hesitated. 'Try not to take this the wrong way, but maybe I could lend you something?'

'I've got masses of stuff.' Sam waved a slightly tipsy arm at her wardrobe, all clothes hanging neatly by colour.

'But nothing that says "sexy woman who would like to meet a fun-loving guy".'

'I'm not interested in doing tarty…' Sam realised her error and attempted a U-turn. 'Not that I was suggesting—I just meant that I'd feel really uncomfortable in some of the stuff you wear. I'm just not confident enough, and I do think it's important to just be yourself on occasions like this.'

'Not confident enough? Now that's a first. And I'm not suggesting a personality overhaul. I just want you to look relaxed. This place we're going to doesn't have a Michelin star. It may not even have linen napkins. A tailored jacket will stand out far more than a faded sweatshirt. Come with me.'

'I'm not wearing a sweatshirt to dinner.'

'It was just a figure of speech.'

'You mean it was just for effect. A figure of speech is—'

Gemma waved a wire coat hanger at Sam in a threatening manner. 'Stop being so pedantic… How about this little number?'

Sam drained her glass, stalling for time. The top in question was red. Bright red. And not exactly capacious.

'I'm far too old for that.'

'You're twenty-nine.'

'Exactly.'

'In your twenties. At which point you are definitely not too old for any sort of top.'

'You're sounding remarkably like Sophie all of a sudden.'

'Well, then, maybe we're onto something.'

'But—'

'Look…' Gemma looked around for inspiration, her gaze

settling on the stereo. 'Kylie's in her thirties and she hardly wears anything.'

'But look at her body.' Sam grabbed the CD cover as evidence and waved it at Gemma.

'I'm hardly suggesting you dance around in a strategically cut sheet, but it's Saturday night. You dress like you're pushing forty all week—just let yourself go a bit.'

Pushing forty? That was harsh. 'I'm a lawyer.'

'Not at seven-forty-five on a Saturday night, you're not. You might as well not bother going to the gym if you're never going to expose any flesh.'

'I go for *me.*'

'I've even got a great little bag that will match. At least try it on.'

Reluctantly Sam took the item. 'I can't believe you're suggesting I wear half a top.' She disappeared behind the wardrobe door.

'You're impossible.'

'I'm beginning to think that might be my trademark. And thanks for listening earlier.'

'No worries. I genuinely believe that change is good. So, how's it looking?'

Sam observed her reflection in the full-length mirror.

'Well?' Gemma was rapidly losing her nerve. 'Okay, if you really want to wear the jacket then maybe you should…'

Sam nodded, bemused by her new incarnation. 'It's fine. This, Miss Cousins, will do nicely.' While she didn't exactly look like her normal self, she didn't look bad either—and if she was going to go through with this evening she might as well go in full costume.

Finally she was ready.

Chapter Fourteen

'So what's she like, then?'

Luke leant against the bar and checked out the Saturday-night crowd as Ben sipped his mango beer cautiously. Despite the fact it really did taste like mangoes and beer, contrary to his initial scepticism, it wasn't bad at all.

'Hmm?'

'The low-down on Sam. What do I need to know?' Luke drained his glass and to Ben's dismay ordered a round of something with the word 'cherry' in the title.

'What do you mean?' Stalling, Ben took a large gulp.

'Well, you're trying to do her a favour and you've known her for about ten minutes, so you either fancy her...'

'Don't be ridiculous.'

'...or you're doing this as a favour to a girl you do like, or, of course, you're selflessly trying to help me out. But as I know Ali much better than I know you I find that hard to believe.'

'Come on, that's not fair. Why can't I just be a nice guy who's helping a nice girl?'

'Because life doesn't work like that.'

'Well, it should.' Ben looked at his watch. He knew there were rules but they'd already been there twenty minutes and he really wasn't interested in walking any proverbial planks while he waited.

'So...Sam... The bluffer's guide...a potted history...' Luke was a man on a mission.

'Well...' Ben took a sip of his new beer and, wrinkling his nose, swallowed quickly. He'd never been able to understand the Cherry Coke thing. And cherry beer should have been illegal.

'Something...anything...'

'Well, she might seem like a bit of a cold fish at first—a bit aloof, disinterested sometimes...'

'Have you thought about a career in PR?'

'I'm just saying don't be deterred by your first impression, because underneath her shell—not that she'd acknowledge she has one of those—I think she's probably much more fun. She just needs to let herself go a bit. Which is where we come in.'

'Well, why don't you deal with Sam and I'll have your one?'

'It's just...' Ben thought about how best to pitch his response '...well, it's a bit complicated...'

'Just kidding, mate.' Heartily Luke slapped Ben on the back. 'But it was good to see you squirm. Ali warned me that there might be an ulterior motive, and I have to say I might be inclined to agree with her.'

Ben shook his head. 'Just a bit of wining and dining.' Ali was the end. Her mind was more suspicious than Elvis's had ever been.

'Consider me on board. Here to melt ice maidens to slush.' Not for the first time that evening, Ben wondered what on earth he thought he was playing at.

'Go gently. No flash-floods.'

'Roger, roger. May the best man win.'

Walking down the steps into the restaurant, Sam felt uncharacteristically self-conscious. And late. The light-headed feeling had vanished as they were getting out of the taxi, replaced by old-fashioned nerves. Plus, she was beginning to wish she'd had time to slip a black polo-neck into her bag in case of emergencies of an insecure nature.

Gemma was three paces ahead, and if Sam hadn't been wearing totally unsuitable shoes she would have been tempted to do a runner. But, then again, at least a basement restaurant meant no mobile phone signal, and if she was going to survive tonight she had to be grateful for the smallest of mercies.

'Gem, hang on. I'm just going to nip to the loo—I think I need more lippy.'

'If you're not at the bar in five minutes I'm coming to get you, and if you're not there I swear I'll spread peanut butter on your sofa cushions.'

'Honestly, I'll be very quick.'

'Okay. Good. And at least try to smile. Not only is it a universally recognised ice breaker, but you look amazing.'

As Sam strutted to the Ladies she focussed on maintaining her poise. She still couldn't quite believe she'd agreed to this, especially when there were so many films on at the cinema that she wanted to see.

'Hi, you.' Gemma sauntered over and planted a kiss on Ben's cheek. 'And you must be Luke.' Gemma smiled winningly. An excellent choice. This was going to be the perfect Saturday night. She could just feel it in her bones.

'Pleased to meet you.' Luke and Gemma exchanged pleasantries. So far so good.

'Is Sam on her way?'

'Just coming. She's in the Situation Room. Lipgloss emergency. Although there was a moment earlier when I thought she'd be at the office. But wait 'til you see her.' Gemma could have clapped her hands with raw excitement. In her eyes, not since the Pink Ladies had got their hands on Sandy D had a makeover been so successful. 'Here she comes…'

Ben scanned the room. Twice. And then he saw her. So much for a cold fish. She was practically smouldering.

'Hi guys. Great place. Luke, I presume? I'm Sam.' Inwardly

she felt sick; outwardly she was taking this all in her stride. 'Gem, what are you drinking? For some reason I'm feeling really dehydrated.' That was six sentences without a gap. Sam turned to face the bar and took a deep breath as subtly as she could, hoping that her nostrils weren't flaring visibly. Champion the Wonder Horse was never a good look on a first date/just dinner/whatever...

'Let me get these. What would you like?' Luke was in perfect gentleman mode. Ben was still staring.

'Don't worry, I've got it.'

'Really, it would be my pleasure.'

How could it be his pleasure when they had, as yet, only exchanged a couple of syllables? And now Gemma was giving her a look. Sam glanced down to check her top hadn't slipped. Nope. Different type of look, clearly.

'Oh, well, if you insist—thanks.' She shot Gemma a winning smile. See, she could relinquish control. Easy. 'Lime and soda, please.'

This time Gemma was almost incandescent.

'I mean, vodka, lime and soda.' Clearly Gemma didn't think her liver was working hard enough yet. 'And could you make sure that they use cordial and don't just put a wedge of lime in? Thanks.'

Gemma shook her head imperceptibly. Maybe Sam would like to offer to make it herself? How to come across as a high-maintenance woman in one drinks order. God only knows what that said about her bedroom manner.

'And I'll have a gin and tonic. Thanks.' Easy, classic and no margin for error.

'Mr Fisher? You ready for another one?'

'Could I just have a normal one?'

'How about a white beer—a Hoegaarden?'

Ben had been drinking beer for fifteen years and he'd managed perfectly well without one of those so far. 'How about a yellow one, like a Stella?'

'Peach is good...or honey?'

'Just a beer.'

'One Leffe coming up.'

'As long as it's never rubbed shoulders with a cherry.'

'So, Ben, how's work been?' Sam decided to take the initiative. She wasn't in the mood for pauses, pregnant or otherwise, plus she didn't want to be grilled herself.

'Good, actually. It looks like they might commission a pilot for one of my ideas.'

'A pilot?'

'Yup. TV-talk for a trial episode. Just to see if it works.'

'Oh, right.' Sam's *Top Gun* fantasy disappeared as quickly as it had arrived from the teenage archives of her mind.

Ben suddenly realised he needed to change the subject.

'What's it about?' Too late. Damn Gemma for being interested.

'Oh...well...' Ben took a quick sip. 'It's about sex in the workplace. People who sleep their way to the top...or not.' He laughed, moving the conversation on as swiftly as he could.

'And it was your idea?'

'Yup. Working title is *Sex, Lies & Sellotape.*'

'Clever.' Only the way Sam said it Ben found himself wanting to apologise. 'Your mind works in mysterious ways.'

Ben shrugged. She didn't need to know that Richard's New York moment had been the inspiration, or that they'd also loved his proposal to find 'The Real Ally McBeal'.

'Don't suppose you'd be interested in taking part, would you...?'

Sam could feel herself blushing, her décolletage well on its way to matching her top.

'I mean, that bloke on Thursday night...' Ben did his best to affect nonchalance. 'He was a colleague, wasn't he?'

'Well, technically—yes. Although nothing...well, not much—'

Ben interrupted her. He didn't want the details.

'And I gather that you're being pursued by your boss as well?'

That hadn't taken Gemma long.

'Just sounds like yet another excuse to talk about sex on television to me.' Sam folded her arms across her chest.

'We just reflect real life.'

'No, you give people something to gawp at. And I'll bet the only people who aren't laughing are the ones on the screen. It's not like you can claim anecdotes about who had who on the boardroom table are educational. What about the aspirational stuff? How about setting some higher standards?'

'So…'

To Gemma's relief and gratitude Luke arrived back laden with drinks before Sam could inflict any irrevocable damage on the evening

'Can I suggest we head to our table straight away? Sorry to sound like an old man, but I could really do with a seat.'

'Great idea.' While Sam's heels were great for making entrances and exits, they had definitely not been designed with prolonged periods of jostling for personal space in the bar area in mind. Plus, the probability of alcohol spillage on satin was too high to enable real relaxation. Sam clicked her way after Luke enthusiastically, Ben and Gemma bringing up the rear and hopefully not paying too much intention to hers. She really should have been doing squats every day.

Sam was laughing at Luke's anecdote. Not forcing a dutiful smile but actually laughing. Ben watched her flick her hair and wipe a tear from the corner of her eye. Tonight she was beautiful, sexy and surprisingly feminine…and regrettably she thought he was the new Larry Flynt.

'She scrubs up well, doesn't she?'

Ben, embarrassed at having been caught staring so blatantly, returned his focus to Gemma.

'Yup, maybe I should be thinking about finding you a job as a stylist…'

Gemma's eyes shone at the compliment. 'And thanks for finding Luke. This is just what Sam needed. She's had a terrible week.'

'Her dad. I know.'

'And… Well…no, it's not for me to say.'

'What?' Ben's imagination ran amok.

Gemma shook her head. It had taken nearly four months of flat-sharing to be admitted into Sam's inner circle of confidence. 'Anyway, cheers…' Gemma clinked her glass against Ben's. 'Here's to us.'

'Us?' Ben's throat felt a little narrower than normal as he took his next sip. Why did Ali always have to be right?

Pans piled high with empty mussel shells littered their table, and Sam was regretting going for the Thai option. Not only had her sauce contained enough chilli to make her cheeks red and her nose run, but it had also incorporated incisor-sized pieces of torn coriander leaf cunningly designed to stick both to and between her front teeth. She'd given them a quick once-over with her tongue, but she could've done with a mirror moment and maybe a bit of dental floss.

'So, you don't compete any more, then?' Sam blew her nose for what felt like the tenth time in as many minutes. Maybe there was an internal washer that needed replacing?

'No, I don't have the time. And, hey, let's face it, I'm not looking as good in a wetsuit these days—although my hair definitely takes less time to dry.' Luke ran a hand across the area where his hairline must once have been. 'I don't think I've raced since I was at university. But it's still great to have a hobby which gets me outdoors. I hate being stuck in an office all day. But I can't afford not to be. Mortgage won't pay itself.'

Sam nodded empathetically. 'Where did you study?' A dab at her top lip with her napkin followed by a sip of her mineral water. She must have been losing fluid far faster than she was taking any on.

'Gonville & Caius, Cambridge.'

Sam ticked an invisible box on her mental questionnaire.

'And they had a windsurf team?' She couldn't quite see fluorescent sails cutting up punts on the River Cam.

'No. Just a club. But we entered a few competitions and we

organised a great trip to the Caribbean. I think Oxford was there too.'

'Don't tell me. You got naked a lot and drank loads and…'

'Yup, that's the one… You weren't there, were you? I'm afraid I spent most of the time in a cloud of local beer and rum cocktails…'

'Nope, I was probably in the library.'

'Yeah, right.' Luke laughed and Sam joined in. But only because she knew it was true.

'But it's not just the Caribbean. Maui's good—Florida, Staines…'

'Staines?'

'Yup. Big up to the Windsurfing Massive…check it.'

Sam smiled. For some reason most guys thought they had an Ali G impression worth sharing, Luke included.

'It's close enough for an evening session if the weather's good. Hey, they do lessons for beginners, if you're interested. It's much easier to learn without waves, and with your dagger board down you're really quite stable…'

Ben checked in to their conversation.

'Dagger board? Sounds dangerous.'

Could that be flirtation from Camp Washington?

'It's totally exhilarating, and that feeling when the wind catches you…it's nothing short of addictive. You've definitely got the upper body strength. I'm sure you'd be a natural.'

Subconsciously Sam proudly tensed every muscle she owned.

Ben balked. Textbook compliment paying from Mr Luke. And Sam didn't even seem to have noticed.

'Well?'

Ben returned his focus to Gemma, who wasn't looking stunningly impressed by his amateur eavesdropping capabilities. He knew women could do two lots of listening at once—but, yet again, he was at the mercy of his genes.

'Sorry, Gem. I'm back with you now.' But his attendance was only momentary as Sam volunteered something unexpected.

'I white-water rafted once, at a place called Cripple Creek in Tennessee. It's on the Ocoee River, I think.'

'Hey, I know the area. Mostly Class III, IV and V. rapids.' Luke tried and failed to hide the admiration in his voice. 'The toughest course I've survived, though, was in Zimbabwe. Totally awesome.'

Ben resisted the urge to bang his head on the table. How was he supposed to know Sam liked water sports? She hadn't so much as been swimming since January. Maybe he could set fire to his napkin to interrupt them…

'I'll bet. I thought the whole experience was fantastic. I was even conned into buying a "Rafters do it Rapidly" mug in an adrenaline-high moment.'

'So, are you interested in going on Thursday? Shall I see if I can get tickets?'

'Hmm? Thursday?' Ben's attention span would have made a goldfish's look impressive.

'The Shepherd's Bush Empire.'

Gemma was on the verge of a sulk. Ben wasn't picking up on any of her suggestions, even when they involved locations a short walk from his front door. Luke was being far more attentive to Sam. Maybe she was barking up the wrong tree.

'Sounds great. I'd better check my schedule at work, though.' Ben wondered what he'd almost promised to see. An Iron Maiden tribute band? Rick Astley on his 'Never Ever Gonna Give Up' tour? He'd better check the Web site before getting back to her.

A mobile started ringing, stopping all four of them in their tracks until Luke stood up, clutching the winning phone. Sam wasn't impressed. So much for their underground location. Not deep or lead-lined enough. She checked her bag and made sure hers was switched off.

'Really sorry.' Luke directed his apology to Sam. 'But I have to take this.' As he strode off in the direction of the staircase Sam used the moment to stretch her spine, sitting up taller and gaining two inches of pure torso. At least her back hadn't seized up post-yoga. But her posture had never been more crucial than now, when wearing a top that revealed almost as much as it covered. Or at least that was how it felt to the girl who was never far from a long-sleeved shirt. A few hours in, though, she was definitely feeling less as if she'd swapped her burka for a bikini.

'So—' Ben seized his chance '—having a good time?'

'Not bad. But mention a wedding bell, even in a jokey fashion, and you'll wish you'd never been born.' Not a glimmer of a smile. He'd bet she was a black belt at something.

Ben glanced across the table for support. 'Gem, I think your flatmate is trying to intimidate me.'

'Why should you get special treatment? Excuse me for a minute.' Gemma needed to give herself a pep talk. So far, so disappointing.

'So….' Sam suddenly felt nervous.

'What a coincidence that you've both been rafting.'

'Have you been listening in?'

'Just to check you were getting on, and only during one of Gemma's longer sentences. Don't take this the wrong way, but I wouldn't have thought you'd be into that sort of thing.'

'You can't judge a girl by her day job.'

'Anyway, I'm glad you're having a good evening. It's not like I had a database of hundreds to choose from. I'm not really a dating service.'

'More of a delivery one. And just for the record I've only done it once. Along with abseiling—for charity—and water-skiing—for thinner thighs.'

'I ski. Both water and snow. And I have been known to surf.'

'Really?' Sam didn't remember asking but, deserted, they were going to have to talk about something.

'Yup—internet, wind and waves. I didn't know you were such an outdoor sportswoman. Although I did notice your blades at the flat.'

'Blades?'

'In-line skates.'

'Oh, those. The most expensive doorstops in Battersea. EJ and I were really into that for…' Sam puffed out her cheeks and exhaled as she mentally counted the number of times they'd actually driven to the park to have a go. 'We must have been at least six or seven times.'

Ben whistled. 'That's quite an addiction you've developed there, skater girl...'

'It just ended up being incredibly frustrating. I just wasn't as good at it in reality as I was in my head.'

The story of Ben's life.

'But never say never, and I'll try anything once. I've even been horse-riding a couple of times—both occasions were abroad, and I think the horses involved are probably still in traction.'

Ben laughed. For someone who rarely did it out loud, Sam was very good at self-deprecation.

Encouraged by his reaction, Sam continued. 'Let's just say my legs were strong enough to prevent me from falling off, but despite the fact that I own a pair of pearl earrings that's about it when it comes to horsemanship—although I did read those Enid Blyton books when I was growing up and I always wanted to win a rosette for dressage.'

'I bet you'd be great after a couple of lessons. As for the skating, I can give you a hand, if you like.'

Sam laughed. 'I think those days are over now. Although I bet you're annoyingly good...and I'd take a guess that you've owned at least one skateboard in your past.'

Ben nodded. 'Wasted youth.'

But he was grinning at her. Something she was finding quite unsettling. Plus, thanks to Gemma, she was feeling decidedly naked.

'So, would you say Luke was your type, then...?'

'This is your first official warning, Mr Fisher.'

'Just asking...'

'I thought this was Just Dinner.'

'It is.'

'And I was Just Testing. Off the record—not really. But, having said that, he's succeeding in making me laugh—no mean feat at the moment, I can tell you. So, who can say?'

'What happened?'

'I suppose he just said something funny…'

'That's not what I meant and you know it… Well, as long as it's providing you with a little light relief. I gather you've had a pretty tough week?'

'Make that fortnight.'

'Well, it's always good to get out. Human beings aren't designed to operate in a vacuum. And what with your diary going missing, your dad and Andrew and Richard's advances I'd say you've had your quota of drama.'

Sam stiffened. 'I never told you my boss was called Richard.'

Ben felt a sweat break out. Own goal.

'Yeah, you did—earlier on. Or maybe it was last weekend?'

'I'm positive I didn't.' They both knew she was far too careful. 'Unless Gemma…?'

'Maybe that was it.'

'Or maybe it was something you read?'

Ben didn't know where to look. Feeling Sam staring, he addressed his beer glass.

'Well, maybe I picked his name up unconsciously when I flicked through. And I do have a pretty photographic memory. Useful for exams. Not so useful at moments like this.'

'Quite useful for programme ideas, I'll bet.'

'What?' As he looked up she caught his eye, and held on to it.

'You must think I'm stupid.'

Ben shook his head. 'Far from it.'

'Come on.'

'Look, sex in the workplace is a pretty common phenomenon. A very high percentage of people meet their partners through work. And my proposal plans to look at the more serious side too—sexual harassment, bullying, blackmail, that sort of thing. I've been developing the idea for a while. I know you think I make dodgy semi-pornographic documentaries, but—'

'Hey, Fisher.' Luke was back and Gemma was right behind him. 'I should have known you'd lower the tone. Sorry, Sam. Inexcusable rudeness, but I hope you'll forgive me.'

'I'll see what I can do.'

'Has this boy been bothering you?'

'Not really. He seems pretty harmless.'

'Well, I hate to be the one to do this, but I'm going to have to make a move.'

'Now, that's what I call foreplay, Luke. No wonder you're single.'

Suddenly the males were verbally jostling for supremacy, and Sam was first prize.

Luke reddened. 'That's not what I meant. It's just that I've got an early start tomorrow.'

Sam glanced at her watch, concerned at how it could possibly be eleven-thirty when it had only been nine o'clock about ten minutes ago. 'Actually, I'd better be off too. I might have to go into the office tomorrow.'

Luke nodded as he put a handful of notes on the table. 'That should cover our meal.'

'Our meal?'

'Certainly. Always like to unsettle the sassy lawyer by paying.' Sam wasn't sure about the wad of cash. Who carried that many notes around with them these days? Plus she had been hoping to see who he banked with.

'Well, thank you. If you're sure.' Sam smiled as Luke bent down and kissed her on the cheek.

'My pleasure. Great evening. Thanks, Ben. Give my love to Ali.'

'Will do.'

'And great to meet you, Gemma. If you want to come down to the club and have a lesson you're welcome any time. You've got my card.'

Sam did an aural double take. Quick work by the Gemster. Clearly her forcefield of attraction was up and running again. Although she was sure there were rules about hitting on your flatmate's date. Not that she was on a date, exactly, but alcohol had blurred the boundaries.

'Are you heading south?' Luke was at Sam's chair, easing it backwards for her.

'Yup, Battersea.'

'We could share a taxi?'

Sam hesitated. 'No, really—I'll sort myself out.'

Polite but firm. Ben smiled to himself. Once a control freak, always a control freak.

'Go on. It'll be a nightmare trying to find two round here at this time of night, and I promise I'll behave.'

Sam smiled grimly. 'I'm afraid I've heard that line far too recently.'

'You'll be dropping me off first…'

'True...okay... But I'll only agree if you let me pay.'

'Right, boss. From now on you're in charge.'

'Thanks, you two. Gem, you were right—this was just what I needed. And, Ben, thanks for inviting this chap along.'

Sam punched Luke's arm playfully, and he punched her straight back. And much harder. Sam rubbed her shoulder. 'I take it you don't have any sisters?'

Luke looked confused. 'Two brothers—why?'

'I thought as much. Come on, then.'

As Ben watched Luke escort Sam from the restaurant area he could feel a strange mood descending.

Gemma leant in and said conspiratorially, 'Ten quid says they kiss in the taxi but don't sleep together tonight.'

Ben didn't want to play.

Chapter Fifteen

'You needn't bother with Knightsbridge. If you just cut through Eaton Square that would be great, and then we can hang a left at Sloane Square.'

'Right you are, love.'

Luke watched Sam as she directed the driver to his door.

'I've had a great evening.'

'Yup, me too… Then first right.'

'He's done his Knowledge. Just relax.'

'I am relaxed.'

'Could have fooled me.'

Luke rested his arm on Sam's shoulder.

'Okay, not so relaxed now.'

'Just wondering if you'd mind if I kissed you?'

'I thought you had an early start.'

When Luke laughed his whole frame shook. The rumble of mirth almost had a Father Christmas *ho ho ho* quality to it and, Sam imagined, was possibly the reason he was still single. Definitely potential grounds for divorce after a few years of marriage.

'You don't miss a trick.'

Sam thought back to Thursday. 'Not any more.'

'Just one kiss...'

Sam was still considering his offer when Luke leant in and, taking the initiative, kissed her gently.

Sam couldn't help but see the funny side. No interest on her part, yet apparently all the fish in the sea were heading in her direction—and she hadn't changed her bait or her perfume. Luke, however, was doing a better job at persuading her to try the dish of the day than Andrew had. Strong lips, but not pushy. Patiently lingering, waiting for her to reciprocate, and just when she didn't think she was going to she did. Just like that. Apparently her heart was not tuned in to her head at the moment—or at least that was its story and it was sticking to it.

Luke pulled back, grinning. 'Thanks.'

Far too polite.

'No problem. My pleasure.'

'Excellent...'

Sam was going to have to pick her platitudes more carefully.

'I will confess to being a bit circumspect when Ben called. I mean, I'm not a great fan of the set-up situation. But I didn't have anything else on...and it was fun. Or at least I had fun.'

A Chelsea-dwelling Cambridge graduate who used 'circumspect' in casual conversation and was willing to admit that he'd had a Saturday night free. Luke was clocking up points as quickly as their cabbie was making money on their fare. Sam smiled. Maybe Ben was right. Maybe she needed to get out more. She clearly wasn't meeting the right people in the office.

'Hey, don't think I can't see you smiling to yourself.'

'So what? One kiss...'

Luke leaned over again. Sam kept it brief.

'Two kisses and now I'm not allowed to smile without it being down to you? Where does the male ego end?'

'Ooh, I love it when you talk dirty.'

A deal-breaking siren screamed through Sam's subconscious, but she allowed one more kiss to linger a little before hitting him with the bad news. She sat back in the seat and ran her fingers through her hair nervously before pulling her coat closed, signifying the end of the innings. 'I really am going to drop you off now…'

'Shame. But it's your call. Can't say I'm not disappointed, but I can tell you're a woman who knows what she wants.'

'You can?' Maybe he could tell her what it was she wanted, because right now she wasn't sure.

'Of course. And I can't think of anything worse than trying to persuade someone they're interested when they're not.'

'I didn't say I wasn't interested.' What? Was she becoming some sort of slut now?

'Well, that's a start at least.'

'But I didn't say I was either.'

'I think I'm still with you. So what you're saying is you haven't got a clue…'

'I guess.'

'Ben was so wrong about you.'

'What do you mean?'

Luke back-pedalled mentally. 'Nothing.'

'Whereabouts on Cheyne Walk mate?'

'Just drop me anywhere. I can walk the last bit.'

Luke went for a hat-trick as Sam closed her eyes, sat back and thought of England…and, to her surprise, America.

Chapter Sixteen

The flat was still quiet as Gemma let herself back in and scattered the Sunday papers on the table. She'd always been more bounce-back than bunny-boiler, and he'd said all the right things. That it was him, not her. That she was sexy, attractive and deserved someone who was one hundred per cent focused on her, which she did, and he wasn't. He had, however, missed out the line about this probably being the biggest mistake of his life. Because it wasn't.

Ten-fifteen and still no sign of a human sounding-board. In the interim George was doing his best, his mechanical purring a comfort as he carefully selected his supplement of choice before taking a pew.

Gemma boiled the kettle for her third cup of tea, watching the sheets of rain blowing against the kitchen window. It was a grey day. Elephant grey. No lighter patches. No promise of a sunny interval. But she couldn't help but smile at the strains of Ol' Blue Eyes now emanating from Sam's bedroom. Someone had obviously sprung out of bed on the right side.

Sam was having a big band morning. She'd woken with the

melodies building in her head, and now Frank Sinatra was singing his heart out on her CD-player and, as she quick-stepped her way to the mixer tap, she allowed herself to join in. Luke had been the perfect antidote to Andrew, yet sleeping alone had never felt so good. Now she was taking an empowered shower. As the steam rose up from the tray she massaged her scalp vigorously. Despite her slight hangover she was feeling calmer than she had in days. A new perspective was unfolding. And she was enjoying the view.

'Morning, Gem.' Ol' Greenie-Brown Eyes entered the kitchen and, resisting the urge to tap dance her way to the fridge, flicked the kettle switch and grabbed a mug, her actions choreographed to an imaginary beat. 'What are you doing here?'

'I live here.'

'Indeed you do. I meant, this is a rare pre-noon sighting of the Cousins species on a Sunday. Dressed and apparently having visited the paper shop. Must check yesterday's weather forecasts for references to a blue moon.'

'Yeah, yeah.'

'Anyway, thanks for yesterday. Clearly I need to go out and drink lots more often. And stop thinking that I'm the only person in the world with issues. Can I persuade you to join me in a bit of cooked breakfast? And what about Ben? Do you think I could tempt him out of bed with a bacon sandwich?'

'From W12?'

'Have you just got back, then?'

'Nope. I just woke up early and couldn't sleep.'

The Rat Pack's latest addition stopped in her tracks. 'But everything's Okay?'

'Not exactly…'

Concerned and expectant, Sam turned to face Gemma—who was only too ready to share.

'We've called it a day.'

'You've what?'

'Me and Ben.'

'Why? And when?'

'Last night. After you'd left.'

'What happened?'

'There's someone else.'

'But how can you be sure he'll be any nicer?'

'Not me. Him.'

'Oh.' Sometimes Sam thought she should carry a government health warning for insensitivity. She sat down at the table. The big band petered out. 'Gem, that's terrible. I'm sorry. I just—for some reason…I thought you meant you.'

Gemma shrugged her shoulders, pretending to be engrossed in one of the broadsheets. Sam knew she was faking it because it was the editorials page and even she didn't really read those.

'It's no big deal, really. As usual I'd just brought my high hopes to the situation. You'd have thought I'd have learnt by now.'

'Hey, this isn't like you. And far better to be an optimist than to be like me, with my one hundred and one reasons why every man is totally unsuitable before I've even given them a chance to open their mouth.'

Gemma smiled. 'I'm fine—really. Just a little bit disappointed… Anyway, enough of all that...'

Sam was impressed; Gemma's little black cloud moments didn't last long.

'Where's Luke?

'Surf's up, man.'

'So he didn't stay?'

'Of course not.'

'Er, sorry…it's not like you never bring people home.'

'That was a blip.'

'And nothing happened in the taxi?'

'Not really. I mean, a quick kiss but no big deal—and it's not like I need my life to be any more emotionally action packed.'

'I thought he was great.'

'He's all yours.'

'And it looked like you were getting on terrifically.'

'He was nice enough. But never forget I am a pro. I can do

interested. And, whether it's chess or canyoning, I can bluff with the best of them.'

'So not just a pretty face?'

'And at least he was a gentleman. I have to confess I am disappointed by Ben. Someone else...'

'Well, it's not like we had anything serious going on. It's more of an ego dent. Superficial damage.'

'I don't have time for any of this. Two men in a week and I've wasted more time worrying about how I feel and what to wear than I have to spare. So if you fancy a bit of windsurfing be my guest. Luke's all yours, dagger board *et al.*'

'Ooh, look at you with your flashy jargon. Shame you didn't like him.'

'He was perfectly entertaining for one evening, but—well, he's just not my type. And I sort of told him.'

'You didn't?'

'What's the point in pretending?'

'You really are the ultimate dating pragmatist. How can you possibly know after a couple of hours?'

'They say you know after thirty seconds.'

'And what's your type anyway?'

Sam hesitated. Brilliant. She was waiting for someone and she didn't even know who. 'I guess I'll know when I know.'

'How about you try the one hundred and one reasons, or even just the ten reasons, why it might be fun, or at least not an unmitigated disaster, if you did see Luke again.'

Sam hesitated. How about the fact that she'd been thinking about Ben and not Luke when she'd woken up this morning?

'Very funny. But, back to you. I really can't believe Ben had his eye on someone else. I mean, what on earth was he doing, asking you out for dinner if he wasn't interested?'

'He didn't actually ask me out, if we're going to be accurate about it.'

'Don't you dare try and defend him. And, thinking about it now, there was a moment when I thought that maybe he was being a bit flirtatious with me.'

'Was there, now...?'

Sam interrupted Gemma before she could go any further. 'I was thinking about it in the shower. I reckon he was just being friendly, but maybe I should have mentioned it to you last night? Shows how out of practice I am…I just don't talk to that many single men—well, men at all—these days.'

Gemma was hoping to interject just as soon as Sam paused for breath. Which surely had to be soon.

'So, you see, Ben has proved to be another example of why I shouldn't be allowed anywhere near a member of the opposite sex with a drink inside me. This is the girl, after all, who thought Andrew was genuinely concerned about her personal welfare and then…' Sam shuddered. 'I so should have seen it coming. Right, that's it. From now on I am going to keep my eye firmly on the ball—on their balls—whatever… It's just so disappointing. I can't believe Ben, of all people, has turned out to be another charlatan. Clearly my dating dial needs recalibrating. Sometimes I think Sophie is lucky to be out of all of this. Not that Mark has ever been my type, but you know what I mean…'

Gemma seized the pause in the polemic. 'Your dial is in perfect shape…'

'How can you say that? After what you've just… This whole situation really reminds me of Jim. He's still the only guy post-Paul who even got close. Wooed me with intent and passion, yet just at the point I dared to project into the future by more than twenty-four hours he told me that there was something missing. It wasn't a question of blowing hot and cold—it was more a case of all four seasons in one date.'

'Will you just shut up and listen to me for one whole minute?'

Sam was shocked into silence at the firmness of Gemma's tone.

'Ben's not interested in me because he's interested in someone else. And it's not like he coerced me into sleeping with him. At least he was honest.'

'Give the guy a medal.' Gemma shook her head. So much for a minute. Sam had barely managed to spare her ten seconds.

'Jesus, Gemma, he took you for a ride. You're entitled to be angry. I've got a great tape EJ made me somewhere. Alanis Morissette, Kelis, Meredith Brooks. Perfect for man-hating moments like this.'

'You and EJ really are two of a kind sometimes. And before you dig yourself in any further, he's not interested in me because—'

'I think it's in the car.' Sam grabbed her keys from the bowl by the phone. 'I'll go and get it. Really, it's just what you need.'

'Because he's interested in you.'

Sam stopped mid-stride.

'It all makes sense and I really should have seen it. I mean, he was delivering your diary.'

System error. Sam was speechless as her mind drew a blank before rebooting. First Richard, then Andrew, then Luke, now Ben. Clearly she was transmitting some powerful pheromones at the moment.

'Don't be ridiculous.' Faced with a difficult situation Sam went on the offensive. Trademark Washington tactics.

'It's not ridiculous.'

'Well, he's hardly my type.'

'Drop the shopping list. So he doesn't earn a six-figure salary? You don't need to be all coy for my benefit.'

'I'm not being coy. And you're not fine. Nor would I expect you to be.'

'I will be in twenty-four hours or so…and if you're honest I think you secretly quite like him. Isn't there a little something—a niggle, anything—that makes you think that maybe… just maybe…?'

Sam shook her head. 'Why can't I just be allowed to be in a good mood? Why does it have to be man-related? This isn't the nineteenth century, you know. My happiness is not dependent on the attentions of a man…'

Gemma had forgotten that she shared a flat with Germaine Greer's understudy. 'Of course it's not. I was just saying that—'

'Maybe it was the yoga?'

'And maybe it was just having a few drinks, a bit of a flirt and checking out of your day to day worries and forgetting about everything else for a few hours.'

'That may have been a factor…'

'Admit it. You're just like everyone else.'

Sam didn't want to deal with any of this now. There was only one way to handle a morning like this. Time for emergency rations.

'Hello?' Ben answered the phone without taking his eyes off his laptop screen. Not that anything was going on in his creative department this morning.

'Ben. You're up. Great.'

His heart sank a millimetre. 'Morning, Ali.' It was far too early for a post-mortem.

'Well…come on. How did it go?'

'Far too well.'

'Too well? What do you mean?'

'They left together.'

'Result for Lukey. I'd better give him a call. Or maybe it's still too early? I'm great at this, don't you think?'

'Hey, Cupid's friend. They left together. That's all.'

'Just because someone got out of bed on the wrong side. Sometimes you are absolutely infuriating.'

'I'm a brother. It's genetic.'

'I'll call you later.'

Ben grunted a goodbye. He wasn't even that hungover. There was a faint fruity edge to the stale beer taste in his mouth, but only one real thought in his head.

Logging onto his e-mail, he created a new message.

Dear Sam,
Hope this week is less stressful than the last one. Hope you enjoyed yourself last night. Hope to catch up soon.
Ben

Pathetic. Three hopes. Shades of desperation.

Love Ben

Too much.

Ben xx

Too effeminate.
Bx

Better.

B

Ben

Back to square one.

But according to girlie rules Gemma should have told Sam first thing. And if he wanted something to happen he had to be proactive. Take a risk. Not that there was anything risky about the text of this particular missive. And, while this might be an open path of communication, it was one she could quite easily ignore. Maybe a call would be better? Ben rubbed his eyes. Seven and a half million people in London and these two shared a front door and a landline.

Pushing his chair back from the table, Ben went to make himself a sandwich. It was a Fisher family tradition. When all else fails eat, and then eat some more.

He stared at the assortment of random ingredients in his fridge. He could, of course, get Sam's work number from directory enquiries… *Did taramasalata go with tomatoes? Or honey-roast ham?* No chance of a direct line, though, until tomorrow at any rate. *And surely cucumber went with everything? Or a gherkin?* And then what was he going to say? *Cheese was always good.* But he'd only found her e-mail address from a group message that Gemma had forwarded to him. *How did you know when humus was bad if the deli didn't have sell-by dates?* Maybe it would be better if he called her at work? More mature. Up-front and personal. *Excellent, an ice-cold lager.* But then if he called at a bad time he might as well have not called at all, and voicemail was a whole new deal altogether. *Quick pork pie to keep him going.*

There was, of course, the old-fashioned letter or card approach. Maybe he should leave it a couple of days? Too many options. And he could just grill some bacon.

His Scooby Snack teetering on a plate, Ben sat down with the papers. He had just managed to wrap his mouth around it when the phone rang again. He left it to the answer-machine.

'Hello, brother of mine. You're probably showering, or of course just ignoring me, but thought you might like to know that I have tracked Luke down and they are in Devon.'

Death by sandwich. It was the only option.

'Just kidding. He's in Devon. Bit of kissing action in the cab, but *c'est tout.* Oh, well. You can't win 'em all. He's got no idea if anything else will happen, but he thought they were both lovely and he had a great evening, so full points to you and bonus points for me. Have a good day. Do try and get out of the flat. It's gorgeous out there. David and I are just off for a run on the common. Speak to you soon.'

Despite the number of people making their fortune telling you otherwise, you really couldn't plan life if you tried. Ben flopped into his armchair and reached for the remote. He was giving himself the day off.

Sam was sure she could almost feel her arteries hardening. She'd ingested a third thigh's worth of saturated fat in the last hour, and the second round of Nutella toast had just been plain greedy. But it was brunch. And it had served its purpose. Gemma had perked up, due in no small way to Madonna's *Immaculate Collection,* which was providing enough girl power for the two of them. Beached on the sofa, the papers strewn all over the floor, Gemma was now conducting a tabloid survey of her stars while Sam absorbed summer fashion tips and film reviews, simultaneously psyching herself up for the news sections of the broadsheets.

'Well, according to Veronica Bertelhold this is a big week for air signs...and Gerald George says that a certain new dynamism is going to characterise my week, an interesting situation may reveal itself in terms of my work and career but that I shouldn't say yes to anything definite without careful consideration.'

'Gerald George? Isn't he the sex-change one? From Geraldine to Gerald…'

'What's that got to do with anything?'

'I wasn't casting aspersions as far as his predictive powers go, or indeed any aspersions. I was just making conversation. Or trying to.'

Time to lighten up. Mentally, if not physically. Sam undid the top button of her jeans and hid the evidence of her swollen waistline under a magazine. She was sure it would go down again in a minute.

'Anyway, Sara West says "Home and personal life continue to be of real importance this week."'

'Well, she's covered all her bases, then.'

Gemma ignored her. 'And that "light romance is linked to work or scheduled appointments, such as trips to doctor, dentist or aromatherapist."'

'How about the boiler man? He's coming on Thursday, I think. No, actually, I think it's the week after.'

'And that I have to be careful how I get my message across to people over the next seven days as it'll either work for or against me.'

'For or against? Genius… You know what? I think these astrologers just count on the fact that you're only going to read your own star sign. I bet there's a whole battery of stock phrases that they just rotate through the sun signs every week.'

'Sun signs? Careful, Sam, you're beginning to sound like a bit of an expert.'

'Hey, I'm a fast learner.'

'Well, I always read my rising sign too, for a more individual picture.' Gemma swapped supplements. 'Right, let's see what Ella van de Mooster has got for me…she's normally quite accurate.'

'And what is she? A jazz-singing Dutch cow?'

Gemma ignored Sam, continuing to read extracts aloud. 'Good time for me to do something for somebody else…and, yes, excellent—she suggests that I may be in for a hint of passion. I just love the fact that my ruling planet is Venus.'

'What's mine?'

'Mars, of course.'

'A chocolate ruling planet. Fantastic luck.'

'Bananarama sang a song about mine.'

'See? I knew you had a sense of humour in there somewhere—even today. Now, come on then, what about me?'

'You?'

'Yup. Samantha von Georgecat. Come on, Gemma van de Flatsharer, do your worst. Sock it to me. Aries. Star of the month, I think you'll find.'

Gemma gave in and laughed. 'It's the week after next, isn't it? Eighteenth?'

'Thirtieth.'

'I meant the date.'

'Listen, I am one of the few people I know to have absolutely no hang-ups about turning thirty.'

'Course not.'

'Seriously. I've felt about thirty years old since I was twelve. Frankly, it'll be a relief to be finally taken seriously.'

'Aah, yes.'

'"Aah yes"? Your crystal ball gone cloudy? And I thought those hoop earrings were just a fashion item.'

Gemma rustled the magazine in an attempt to create a sense of gravitas. '"You have all the power you need this week."'

'More power? Excellent. Will increase resistance on circuit equipment at gym. Duly noted.'

'"Personal life becomes an area of real importance. Your focus is powerful, as is your need to get ahead..." Well, that's hardly news to me.'

Gemma picked up the next paper and Sam re-immersed herself in the *Sunday Times* 'Culture' section. Only two of their must-see films. Two of the plays. Three of the current paperback bestsellers. And one featured exhibition. Her standards were slipping. Hopefully life would ease up after Sophie's wedding. Thirteen days and counting.

'Yeah, yeah…good time for new beginnings and—yes! Sam, listen to this…'

Sam peered over her paper.

'"Love affairs that have been on hold may suddenly ignite…be careful to find out who is your friend and who is your lover. Throw caution to the wind and see where it takes you. Be sure not to judge people on their first appearances—you never know when they might become important to you…"'

'Your point being?'

'Well, just think—'

'Don't even say it.'

'You do quite like him.'

Sam hurled a cushion at Gemma. 'Any more of that and I'm going to the office.'

'You're going anyway.'

'Well, I'll go sooner.' Unless, of course, Richard was going to spontaneously combust with ardour in her office… This was the trouble with horoscopes. However tenuous the link, suddenly you ended up trying to shoehorn your life to fit into the prediction.

'Suit yourself.' But Gemma knew she'd been listening. And it had only been a teensy bit of poetic licence. Sometimes fate needed a helpful shove in the right direction.

Chapter Seventeen

Aries
If it's your birthday today:
Don't be afraid to do something different. This could be the key to your future success. You now have the potential to step into a new era, and a profound set of aspects gives you the ability to overcome any remaining obstacles. The initial effort required may seem daunting, but the rewards will far outweigh the trials in the long term. Listen to your head and to your heart. Provided you harness your enthusiasm with a little realism there'll be no stopping you…

Sam took a slurp of her latte and nibbled on her almond croissant as she flicked back to a news article in Melanie's copy of the *Evening Standard,* annoyed that Gemma's influence was permeating her routine.

Croissant aside, it didn't really feel like her birthday. No fanfare. No fuss. Just another Wednesday at the office and not a day of the week renowned for its party status. But it was ages since she and Sophie had indulged in a one-on-one, fast-talking catch-up session, and she was looking forward to a reminder of the good old days—old soul-mates on the town. Sam downed the rest of her coffee. Stomach lining was underway. She didn't want to end up nodding off before the interval because she'd had a cocktail on an empty stomach; nor did she intend to develop a hangover before the final curtain. But she had Nurofen and water in her bag just in case.

Her home number flashed up on her phone. Leaning back in her executive chair, she braced herself for a chorus of 'Happy Birthday'.

'Sam?

'Gem.'

'Sorry to bother you at work.'

'No problem.' She hadn't been blown away by the birthday vibe so far.

'Um, look, I just wanted to check it would be okay if I had someone to stay over tonight. I've got a mate who's only in London for a couple of days and I haven't seen her since Australia. I'll put her on the sofa bed if it's all right with you.'

'Fine.' She'd obviously forgotten. Although Sam was sure she'd written it on the kitchen calendar.

'Great. You're a star. Thanks.'

Melanie popped her head round the door as Sam hung up. 'Sophie's waiting for you in Reception.'

Sam checked her watch. Six o'clock exactly. Plenty of time for a drink or three first.

'Have a great evening. Celebrate in style.'

'Thanks. Do you want to come and have a quick drink with us?' Under the desk, Sam crossed her fingers and toes. Manners were a curse at times.

'No can do. Rushing off to the theatre for a bit of *cultcha* myself. See you in the morning.'

As the lift doors opened on the ground floor Sam allowed herself to feel a little birthdayish. Hugging gently, so as to avoid crushing outfits or allowing any freshly applied make up to transfer itself to an unwelcome or dry clean only surface, she felt their newly applied perfumes jostle for nasal supremacy before settling for a fusion of sorts. Scents and sensibility.

'Wow, Soph! But surely there are rules about looking better than the birthday girl on her big day?'

'Well, I could hardly turn up in jeans.'

Sam felt awkward as Sophie scrutinised her work outfit.

'Do you always look this great when you're at the office? And your eyebrows are different…or are they?'

Sam blushed. 'I had them threaded at lunchtime. Present to myself, along with a massage.' Whoever said retail therapy wasn't effective was shopping in the wrong places.

'Well, they're fab.'

Sam beamed. She always felt better once she had Sophie's wholehearted approval, whether it concerned men, careers, soft furnishings or indeed eyebrows.

'Maybe I can squeeze in a visit before Saturday. Can't have you upstaging me down the aisle. Frankly I'm amazed you don't have a trail of men following you everywhere just in case you drop something. I mean, that skirt isn't exactly knee-length. And it's a gorgeous suit. Reassuringly expensive, I hope?'

'This old thing?' It was one of Sam's favourites, but she couldn't help but make some self-deprecatory gesture. After all, Sophie had known her in her tomboy, make-up-heels-and-skirts-are-for-tarts-and-drag-queens heyday.

'EJ's obviously a good sartorial influence on you, and I don't know how you do it but you don't look a day over twenty-nine. Mark sends his love and apologies. He had a corporate golf day or I'm sure he'd be with us.'

Sam was quite pleased he was ensconced at the nineteenth hole. An evening with her oldest friend on her oldest day so far. Doing something different could start tomorrow.

Sitting on a suede banquette, Sam absorbed the minimalist modern grandeur which characterised the bar area at the Trafalgar as Sophie ordered a round of vodka martinis. Instant uplift of mood caused by an unadulterated alcohol injection with no mixers to get in the way.

Sipping together, they surveyed the scene. Most of the clientele were customised to the hilt. Nips and tucks. Sunglasses designed to repel UVA, UVB and F-YOU rays, and to tone down the glare from bleached teeth, bleached hair and St Tropez tans. But the aesthetically pleasing bar staff were omnipresent, and as Sam rotated her glance every few seconds Sophie interrupted her window shopping.

'So, have you had a good day?'

'Not bad. And, hey, I walked out at six—which can only be a good sign.'

'Richard behaving?'

'Pretty much. To be honest, it's been pretty quiet. We're just waiting to see what happens with share prices before our clients decide whether to go ahead, and the deal bible is all ready from the last time they got cold feet.'

Sophie nodded politely. Sam might as well have been speaking Japanese for all the sense she was making.

'And—' Sophie attempted to feign indifference '—have you heard anything from anyone?'

'From…?' Sam shook her head in defeat. 'What's she said?'

'Who?'

'The little matchmaker girl.'

'Not much.'

'Soph…'

'Just that there's a guy who likes you, who you don't hate.'

'Did she mention that she liked him first?'

'No…'

'Or that they went on a couple of dates?'

'No…'

'Or that they were sleeping together?'

'No.'

'Interesting.'

'So how does that work, then?'

'He was, or should I say is, the guy who found my diary.'

'Really? Ben?'

'Yup.'

'Perfect.' Sophie clapped her hands with excitement.

'Hardly. I really think I've had quite enough misguided interest of late.'

'I'm just wondering whether the fact that I'm clearly the last to know about this chap means that maybe she's on to something…' From where Sophie was sitting a few blotches had appeared on Sam's neck. Tell-tale signs that not even state of-the-art light-reflective foundation and powder could mask. 'So you haven't heard from him at all?'

'Well, I did get an e-mail about a week ago. All of four lines and it didn't really say anything.'

'Maybe he's waiting for a sign that you're interested—alive, even.'

'To be honest I don't have the time or the energy.'

'Just occasionally you are going to have let people through your emotional firewall.'

'Look…' Sam paused. This was not the time to get tetchy. 'I don't know what Gemma has implied, but he was just being friendly.'

'So why not just be friendly back?'

'But if I reply now it'll look like I've been saving the message and am still thinking about it over a week later.'

'He was probably just testing the water, you know.'

'Maybe. Although EJ thought he was probably just keeping his options open—you know, in case nothing better came along.'

'And you believed her?'

'It's certainly a valid hypothesis.'

'Will you stop only calling people who are going to tell you what you want to hear? Seriously, when was the last time you liked someone? Really liked someone?'

'Does Ewan McGregor in *Moulin Rouge* count?'

'No. The fact is there hasn't even been a blip of male interest on your screen in months.'

Sam racked her brains for evidence to the contrary. Her

search engine was far less effective than Google. Ten seconds so far and still searching…

But her time was up as far as Sophie was concerned.

'You see. I rest my case.'

'Rest your case? What are you talking about? It's not as if I haven't had some male attention lately.'

'Hardly quality encounters.'

'But, Ben?'

'At least he has a glimmer of potential. According to Gemma, maybe more.'

Sam hesitated as she tried to come up with a strategy to divert this ambush.

'I'm afraid I'm going to have to hurry you. Procrastination and delay. All the usual signs. Hey, no need for the face. I'm not going to tell anyone if you admit it. And you know you always meet someone when you least expect it.'

'But surely that theory doesn't apply when he's going out with your flatmate?'

'Just admit it. You like him.'

'He's infuriatingly laid back…'

'Right.'

'His sense of humour is way off target. He seems to specialise in seedy documentaries. His hair is ridiculously long. He's had unauthorised access to my innermost thoughts and he's been sleeping with Gemma.'

'But…?'

'But?'

'There's definitely a but.'

Sam paused. 'Well, he's got kind eyes, a nice smile, emotional intelligence…and a good butt.' She laughed at her own joke in an attempt to lighten the tone.

This was all excellent. When Sam described people as 'intelligent' it was a sure sign that she fancied them.

'You could at least explore the potential before he meets someone who will reply to his e-mails. You're forgetting that I know more about you than most people. I even know about your double album of love songs…'

And Sam was sure that she'd always hidden that one—or at least stored it back to front. Damn.

'...and the fact that your favourite films all happen to have a boy-meets-girl theme.'

'I think it's time you had a Diet Coke and a cold shower. This is definitely a case of impending nuptials. Last time they looked, the world wasn't heart-shaped.'

Sophie didn't even smile. Very bad sign. 'Convincing as your defensive propaganda may be, if you're hoping to be swept off your feet, even for an afternoon, by a knight on a white charger—which, FYI, in the twenty-first century doesn't mean you have to stay at home, bake and do the washing up—then you're going to have to reveal a chink in your own armour. The whole joy of dating is that it's a trial period, and if you don't like the end product you just send them back. No twenty-eight-day clause, and you don't even have to keep the receipt. Life's messy.'

'Says she who's about to get married.' A shiver raced up Sam's spine. 'I really admire your faith. I still don't quite understand how you're not scared of putting all your trust in someone who might just leave one day, delivering you back to square one...'

'That's where you go wrong.'

Wrong? Sam was never wrong. Well, rarely...

'You are never back to square one. And don't think that it was all hearts and flowers from the moment I met Mark.'

'What do you mean?'

'Well, how can I put this? There was a slight overlap.'

Sam furrowed her brow. 'I thought he was the brother of a client?'

'Make that boyfriend...'

'You stole someone else's guy?'

Unruffled, Sophie continued.

'By the time I finished the job they'd split up and he'd asked me out.'

'Why didn't you tell me before?'

'I think you'll find the answer to that question in your reaction. I was merely a catalyst. Plus, it's not exactly the how-we-met story you want to be relating to your children and grandchildren on your anniversaries. Speaking of which—' Sophie rummaged in her bag '—happy birthday.'

'What's this? My reward for sitting through the annual lecture?'

'Something like that.'

'Well, I really hope we're still sipping cocktails together in thirty years' time.'

Sophie knew that was the closest to gushing that Sam could do after a mere half a martini. 'That's what friends are for…'

'Are you singing?'

'Don't be daft? Me? Sing?'

'Just thought I was hearing a little Dionne Warwick there…'

'That's your problem.'

Sam blushed. Time to file a few old favourite CDs in her knicker drawer. Easy access in emergency moments, but less fuel for ritual humiliation. 'Soph, you really shouldn't have.' Sam had carefully opened the paper and was now fondling a Liberty box on her lap. And it was definitely jewellery sized. 'The tickets would have been enough.'

'I know. Well, go on then. Open it.'

Sam giggled. She couldn't help it. And it was part nerves. Sophie usually had impeccable taste, but what if it was a cat brooch to go with George? At her age it might as well be a Toby Pimlico T-shirt with Spinster on it. The pressure of reacting in real time with the donor in full view was acute.

Sam peeked into the purple box and, taking the plunge, unwrapped the tissue paper in a flourish before planting a kiss on her best friend's cheek.

'Fab, Soph—this is brilliant. You are a star.' Sam fiddled with the bracelet, its chunky asymmetrical polished pink stones doing a good job as New Age worry beads. Lisa Kudrow meets Liza Minelli. And very stylish, even if the tightening device owed a lot in its design to the noose.

'It's rose quartz. For love…'

Sam raised a perfectly threaded eyebrow challengingly.

'Or just for pink, in fact. You can change it if you don't like it. I nearly got you a Lapis one, but I thought you had enough self-confidence. Or at least other people think you do, even if I know you are bluffing some of the time.'

'Love or no love, it's great. I like it. I really like it.'

'As opposed to all the other presents that you were just being polite about? I just thought, you know—not sure that it really goes with a double-cuff shirt, but the colour really suits your skin tone.' Sophie was babbling. 'I've kept the receipt just in case. It was only when Gemma said she thought it was fab that I started to worry.'

'It's perfect.'

Sam was admiring her wrist from every possible angle as she raised her glass to her lips.

'It's great that Gem's seeing this Luke chap the weekend after next, isn't it?'

The icy vodka caught in Sam's throat. 'Is she?'

'I could have sworn you lived at the same address. Although maybe I've got it wrong. You know what I'm like…'

Sam did, and Sophie never made mistakes on this sort of thing.

'Anyway, it's no big deal. Not really a date, as far as I can work out. Going off sailing, is it? Apparently you told her she was welcome to him.'

'I think you'll find it's windsurfing.'

'Whatever.'

'And he's all hers.'

'I'm not sure that there's anything going on.'

'Yet…' *In vodka veritas.* The Romans clearly hadn't been big cocktail drinkers, but the premise was the same.

'Just think—it could be like a partner swap…'

Sam wasn't even going to qualify that with a reply.

Sophie could take a hint. 'And how's your dad doing?'

'Well, he's not going to get better, but he seems to be coming to terms with it all. He says he doesn't feel worse, but who knows what his cells are up to? And I would say he's looking weaker. Not that I've been monitoring his decline for very long. I still can't really get my head round the fact that there's nothing they can do. In this day and age you expect there to be a prescription for everything. Or some sort of treatment or transplant.'

Sophie nodded.

'But he did call this morning.' Sam looked at her watch. Seven-ten. 'Hey, we'd better go. Doesn't the play start at seven-thirty?'

'It's only a few minutes' walk. And according to my watch it's only five past...'

Of course. Sam always set her watch a few minutes fast. She hated being late.

'Anyway, I'm just going to nip to the loo here. I can't face the queue for three cubicles for three hundred people at the theatre.'

7:20—Sam shifts her weight from foot to foot as Sophie dries her hands finger by finger and applies moisturiser, apparently in slow motion, whilst inspecting her cuticles.

7:21—Sophie meticulously reapplies powder and lipgloss while Sam's cardiac activity augments and she starts to taste acid at the back of her throat.

7:22—Sophie decides which of the available perfumes to use.

7:23—Still deciding. Sam suppresses a scream of frustration and wonders whether the slight acid taste might be representative of a nascent stomach ulcer.

7:24—Finally out of the Ladies. Sam can almost see the pavement when Sophie branches off into the main restaurant, claiming to recognise one of the diners and promising to 'only be a minute'. As if they had a spare one of those.

Sam wished she had her own ticket. But, racking her brains, she couldn't remember a moment when Sophie had actually missed anything altogether. Scanning the dining room she couldn't see her anywhere. Sam took a deep breath. She knew she had to relax; it just wasn't always that easy. 7:26. Real time.

As she wandered forward she was intercepted by a cute waiter. Cute? Martinis were marvellous…

'Can I help you?'

'I'm looking for my friend. She just came in, but now I can't see her.'

'Her name?'

'Sophie Simpson. It's just we need to be at the theatre, like, five minutes ago. So if you could just press "pause" on today—just for ten minutes or so—that would really help.'

'Well, I think she might be round the corner. I'm not sure I can help with the other thing, though.' He grinned at Sam.

'Great. Thanks.'

7:27—Sam walked as quickly as she could without running. Plays probably never actually started until seven-thirty-five. But her head was definitely sounding the minute bell. And she always liked a chance to people watch and flick through the programme before the curtain went up.

And then there she was. There they were. A table of strangely familiar faces. Nine pairs of eyes, bright with expectation.

'Happy Birthday!'

To Sam's relief just a verbal chorus, not the full *a cappella* version.

'Thanks—' Sam took the welcome in her stride. No one seemed surprised to see her at all. 'Soph, I don't want to be a bore, but …' Sam tapped her watch face '—we're going to miss the start of the play.'

'Sam, you dope, we're not going. What do you think this lot are doing here?'

'But what about the tickets? They're like gold dust.'

'There are no tickets.'

'No tickets…? Oh…'

To the relief of the assembled company her brain finally caught up and her grin switched from sheepish to soaring.

Sophie was beaming. Phase 1 was complete. The legal eagle had landed. X had made it to Y and she hadn't suspected a thing. Sam's face was a picture, and as Mark put his arm around her waist Sophie could have walked on water. Life was good. If only she had more time she would definitely have volunteered to do a couple of mornings a week at Oxfam, but it was that or Pilates and, well, she had to keep in some sort of shape. Maybe when they got back from the Maldives…

'Thank you so much.' Overwhelmed by the moment, Sam felt her eyes sparkling with a cocktail of emotion and elation.

'Hey, I'm merely an accomplice—an apprentice, in fact. This was all Gemma's idea.'

Sam turned to her flatmate.

'You?'

Gemma grinned. 'It's no coincidence that we haven't run into each other in the last couple of days. I knew you'd guess something was going on. I mean, it's not like you really trust me to start with.'

Sam felt lousy. 'I do…'

'Come on, you won't even let me use your laptop when you're not at home.'

The birthday girl blushed with embarrassment. 'And I thought you'd forgotten. I can't believe I had no idea. I'm clearly going to have to keep a closer eye on you, you little…' Sam hugged her hard. 'Gem, thank you so much—and I'm sorry if I'm a nightmare to live with.'

'Look, you bailed me out when I had nowhere else to go, and I know you like your own space.'

'Well, maybe I will have to review my initial judgement. I really am overwhelmed right now.'

'I'm glad.'

'And I've never been very good at sharing.'

'Hey, I was teasing. Really. And you can stop hugging me now.'

'What?'

'It's just what with all that kickboxing, the gym and the excitement…I've always found my ribcage to be quite an asset…'

'Oops, sorry.'

'Anyway, it was a team effort. Sophie made a lot of the calls.'

'Oi, less of the self-deprecation. Please just accept the compliment.'

'Look who's talking.'

'Well, it's my birthday and today I'm always right.'

'And every other day…?' The heckle got a laugh from the assembled crowd.

No longer blinded by sheer adrenaline, Sam drank in the scene.

'Mum!'

'My little girl. Thirty. It makes me want to cry.'

'Everything makes you want to cry. If anything, it should make *me* want to cry.'

'And does it?'

'No.'

'Then don't deny me the moment. Plus, if you're thirty then I can't be forty any more. Damn.'

Helen hugged her daughter and Sam hugged her back. Mother and daughter. Equal height and stature—only a few lines, a couple of stone and twenty-eight years between them.

Helen pulled back to inspect her progeny. 'I can see a few potential tears in there, young lady. There's still hope for you.'

'I'm in shock. I can't believe you were all plotting this behind my back.' Slowly she made her way around the table. 'I should have known Sophie wouldn't be able to afford those tickets.'

'Hey, Sammy—so, how does it feel?'

'Like Wednesday.' Sam kissed her stepfather. 'And you're supposed to be in Leeds.' EJ was next, and Sam hugged her hard. 'Or at least that's where you said you had to be…'

'One hundred per cent fabrication. False information. Not a grain of truth. Not even a kernel.' There were so many smiles around the table now that collectively they could have been used for a toothpaste commercial.

'I can't believe I fell for it. And there I was, almost feeling sorry for myself—I mean, only momentarily. It's only a birthday after all…'

'Bullshit. With all due respect, of course. Although you did sound quite disappointed at one stage.'

'As if.' Sam's tone couldn't have been any lighter at the discovery of this total conspiracy. 'Work comes first…you don't have to tell me.'

Not so much a tissue of lies, more of a patchwork bedspread. And planned to perfection by Gemma, of all people. Guilt was hovering in the wings.

'And, hey—it's just a day, right? No big deal.' A familiar sentiment, but a different voice. Sam followed EJ's gaze to the man formerly known as Dad. Like father like daughter. His eyes were bright but he was definitely frailer.

'Only you don't really mean that, do you?'

'Hey, it's no great shakes. And if we're drinking to anyone it should be to your mother. She's the one who got the stretch marks and sleepless nights.'

Helen blushed.

Sam took a glass from the table. 'To Mum. After all, what did I do? I just turned up.'

'Bloody good month early too. She never forgave me for not having painted the nursery in time. Beginning of the end, that was.'

'Robert…' There it was—slightly softer, but the tone Sam remembered from all those years ago.

'All right, I'm willing to concede that maybe the fact that I was totally incapable of being faithful might also have had something to do with it.'

Everyone laughed. Almost everyone.

'Susie—come on. I was far too young to be married. Not in physical years, in emotional ones…'

It was obviously a well-worn line.

'And that was then. I got better with age. As for you, darling—' he turned to the birthday girl '—I'm sorry I made things so hard for you.'

Sam wasn't sure that he got off scot-free with one line of public apology, but she was definitely pleased he was there.

'And for years I thought it was my fault, because I couldn't be quiet enough.'

'You didn't know the meaning of the word.'

'Robert.' This time both Simon and Helen were quick to react.

For a split second Sam didn't know whether to laugh or to cry, but she bent down and kissed her father hello. Ageing was making her more generous spirited. Or maybe it was the Absolut. 'Are you sure it's okay for you to be here?'

'Well, I was invited, if that's what you mean.'

Sam pursed her lips.

'I can be dying anywhere I like. And, do you know? I haven't seen you on your birthday since your eighteenth.'

Sam didn't allow herself to think about the fact he might not be around for her thirty-first.

'Anyway, which one of these studs is your boyfriend?'

'I'm definitely old enough to send you home now.'

'Mr Washington—I'm Mark…' Ever the gentleman, he proffered a hand for shaking.

'Pleased to meet you.'

'Obviously I thought you were on a golf day.' Sam butted in.

'I'm with Sophie.'

'Who, I take it, is the girl you've had your arm around since she got here?'

Laughs all round. Except for Sam. It would appear that even parents estranged until recently could be embarrassing.

'And I'm Luke.'

'Mr Luke, we meet again.' Sam pecked him on the cheek.

'Happy birthday.'

'Thanks.'

'Is this him?'

'Dad!' Sam was really pleased they hadn't slept together. She didn't think she'd be able to lie to her father.

'So he's here with…?'

Sometimes mothers needed to be a tad more perceptive.

Sam paused in case Gemma wanted to answer this one. Apparently not.

'Well, I imagine he's probably here to balance the boy-girl numbers, and probably to try and persuade Gemma to buy a wetsuit—or at least hire one.'

Gemma laughed. Luke didn't.

'Hey, I'm just teasing.' Sam smiled gaily at her previous dinner date and gave his arm what she hoped was more of a reassuring squeeze than a Chinese burn. Time to move the conversation on.

'So, Gem, where's your Aussie mate? You should have brought her. I wouldn't have minded.'

Gem giggled. And Sam realised. Only too late to avoid facing embarrassment head-on. 'Aaah…not over here at all?'

'Late for something, Soph?'

'Pardon?'

'If you check your watch one more time…'

'That's the trouble with these agencies…' EJ grinned.

'No way—you wouldn't…'

'The senior partnergram was quite a tricky one to get hold of.'

'I suppose you think that's funny.'

'Everyone else is laughing.'

Sam did her best to join in, despite the fact that out of the corner of her eye she had spotted a small fire breaking out on a tray near the kitchen. On closer inspection it would appear that Gemma was determined to embarrass her at every turn. Singing in restaurants wasn't something she'd ever enjoyed.

Happy Birthday to you
Happy Birthday to you
Happy Birthday dear Saaam
Happy Birthday to youuuuu.

Relieved that the composer had only come up with the one verse, and holding a hand out to indicate to the assembled party in general—and to Simon specifically—that a chorus of 'For She's a Jolly Good Fellow' would really be too much of a good thing, Sam blew out all bar two of her candles on her first attempt, without singeing any wisps of hair or spitting obviously onto any part of the cake. And then, as the smoke rose like a cloud of wishes towards the ceiling, she saw him.

'Hey, you,' Ben unzipped his leather jacket before bending down to kiss her cheek, his face cold. 'Happy birthday. Sorry I'm so late, but I've been on a shoot all day.'

A hush had descended, and as Ben did his best to smile at everyone he really wanted a quiet word with Gemma. The message she'd left had definitely said 'a quick birthday beer'.

Sam was doing her best to take this all in her stride. Four lines of electronic communication stood between them and their last meeting, and suddenly he was kissing her hello, calling her 'you' in a familiar way and, moreover, was apparently here just for her. Along with her all, her best mates and all her parents. Which meant that he'd be meeting her dad, for starters, and a furtive glance to her left revealed her mother's mouth was somewhere between ajar and gaping.

Attempting at least semi-privacy, Ben squatted down by Sam's chair. 'Sorry—I had no idea this was going to be so formal.'

'Well, you're talking to the girl who thought she was going to the theatre tonight.' Sophie, Gemma and EJ appeared to be in a conspiratorial huddle. EJ too? She'd be speaking to them later.

'Gemma just invited me to come along for a drink. I mean, if I'd known it was like a sit-down meal I'd have changed or shaved or something…and tried not to be so late.' Not the warmest welcome he'd ever received. In fact, positively tepid. 'Plus, I've been filming in a smoky bar for the last three hours. I must reek of cigarettes, and it's boiling in here…' He started pulling his jumper over his head. 'Or maybe it's freezing outside.'

'Stop right there.' Sam was hissing at him. 'What is that T-shirt?'

Ben glanced at his chest. 'Oh, no.' Parental Advisory. Explicit Content.

'Nice choice.'

Ben shook his head in disbelief. Of all the T-shirts in his life he couldn't believe this was the one he'd selected in the dark that morning.

'So I'm not exactly wearing my best "meet the parents" shirt... Don't worry. I'll just be hot.' Ben started putting his jumper back on again while Sam watched him closely. Plain navy blue. Thank goodness.Not a FCUK logo in sight.

'Samantha...perhaps you'd be so kind as to introduce your latest guest?'

Sam raised her eyes heavenwards as Ben smiled sympathetically. Parents he could do. Daughter was evidently much trickier.

'You'll have to excuse him. He's terminally ill and, it would appear, terminally gauche.'

Ben stood up, a pool of sweat forming in the small of his back thanks to his extra layer. 'Mr Washington, I presume?'

'Indeed.'

'Ben—Benjamin Fisher, sir. I'm a friend of your daughter.'

'That much I can see.'

'Dad...' Sam looked around for support. 'Please can someone take that glass of wine away from him. Should he even be drinking?'

'I'm only sipping, darling. You really should have been a headmistress.'

Her birthday. Her evening. Not funny.

To Sam's horror, Robert beckoned Ben over. 'Why don't you come and have a chat with me?'

'On my way, sir.'

'Please—Robert is quite formal enough.'

Sam desperately avoided catching her mother's eye as the group watched Ben's progress round the table. Slowly the ambient conversation, which had temporarily ceased in the hope of catching a soundbite from the new arrival and the birthday girl, returned to normal levels.

Pushing back her chair assertively, Sam got to her feet.

'Simpson, Cousins...a quick word, please—in my office. Rutherford, I'll deal with you later.'

Sophie and Gemma followed Sam to the loo.

'I take it this was all part of the master plan?'

'Master plan?'

'The lecture, the bracelet, the dinner… Poor guy didn't even know what he was letting himself in for.'

'Did you hear that Gem? "Poor guy." She definitely cares.'

'Hello—I'm standing right here.'

'Well, darling, what can I say?'

Her mother had invited herself to the summit.

'Not your usual type…'

Sam couldn't remember having a type. The line-up was far too sporadic.

'And a biker…'

The best moment of the evening so far. For the first time in thirty years Sam had managed to shock her mother. What was more, she was pleased. She shook her head. How emotionally stunted was that?

'Hardly, Mum. He just rides a scooter.'

'He just needs a haircut.' For some reason Sophie felt qualified to join this conversation.

Helen nodded. 'Maybe that's it…but your dad seems to like him. They're getting on like a house on fire.'

'Well, that's all settled, then. A Saturday in June okay for everyone?'

'No need to get all defensive, darling.'

'He's a friend. That's all. Gemma knows him much better than I do.'

Sam beamed at her flatmate. Let her deal with her mum. That would teach her. 'I'm going back out there. Someone's got to keep an eye on things.'

'Rose quartz—for love…'

'Soph, I'd hate to see you trip up on Saturday…'

Sam watched Ben refill her glass. This evening had been a veritable festival of unexpected twists and turns, and this was definitely the strangest element of all.

'I'm sorry I didn't reply to your e-mail.'

'I should have called. I was going to, and then... Look, I know we haven't exactly got off to a great start, but how about we call a birthday truce?'

'I'd rather have a birthday present.'

'Oh...'

Sam bit her tongue ten seconds too late. Half an hour ago she hadn't been sure if she'd ever hear from him again and now she wanted a gift? But, thanks to Gem, Sam's expectations had been raised to unrealistic levels. Plus, she was a formerly quite spoilt only child with an overactive imagination, a spanking new love bracelet and at least one bottle of red wine inside her. Not forgetting the martini.

'Well, I'll have to see what I can do. I've still got a couple of hours.'

Sam met Ben's gaze head-on, and for a moment she was captivated. Forcing herself to look away, she started playing with a spare dessert spoon. It had been much easier a couple of weeks ago. Add alcohol and emotion, stir gently, and this always happened. Reluctant to look up, in case she was just as absorbed as she had been a moment earlier, she could feel him watching her. And there was only so much you could do with a spoon.

'It's a bit weird, this, don't you think?' Sam congratulated herself for coming up with a question. Conversation. It's what's you need if you want to be an ice-breaker. Oh, yeah.

'Definitely... But good weird, I think.'

Sam nodded and they both paused to take tactical sips of their drinks, Sam finishing first. Damn, she couldn't even drink demurely.

'So, have you had a good ten days?' Ten days? Oh, no. Now she was definitely coming across as someone who cared. And, moreover, someone who counted. Although actually it was eleven days. Unless that meant he thought she could only count up to ten...

'Yeah, I guess. Busy at work. And last weekend I had the urge to get out of London so I went to see my parents in Gloucestershire. Not very rock and roll, I'm afraid. How about you?'

'Oh, not bad.' Sam was determined not to be whingeing about work every time they met. 'And we all survived Sophie's hen night, which is something—although there are definitely some things that should definitely not be made out of chocolate.' Someone had definitely spiked her drink. Topic change needed. 'So, how are you about the whole Luke thing?' Sam felt like a helpless spectator as she watched herself lurch from conversational bad to worse. She really hoped someone had bought her a return ticket.

'The Luke thing?' Ben wasn't sure if he wanted to know what she meant.

Sam nodded. If she wasn't actually speaking, surely she couldn't be actively spoiling things?

'Well, I guess I wasn't expecting to see him when I walked in.'

'You didn't know he was coming?'

'No one mentioned it.'

'Gemma probably thought you'd be a bit put out…'

'I am a bit surprised he didn't call to tell me himself.'

'You haven't got a clue what I'm talking about, have you?'

He smiled apologetically. 'Nope.'

'I think Gemma's going to have a go at windsurfing and—well, at Luke…' Sam wasn't sure why she was trying to soften the blow. It wasn't as if he was nine years old and hadn't been picked for the football team.

Ben shrugged his shoulders. 'Why would I mind? I mean, good for her, I guess.' Secretly he was delighted. Not only did he get to walk away guilt-free, but he'd kind of suspected that Gemma'd be the sort of girl who owned a voodoo kit. 'I suppose I was just surprised that you two didn't…well, you know…'

Sam shook her head. 'It was a fun evening, but we never really had much in common.'

Ben felt himself relax. So much for Ali's self-congratulation. 'Except your mutual deep love of white-water rafting.'

'There was that.' Sam smiled.

'So, I guess we're both single, then…'

EJ's voice cut across the table.

'Soph, a slice of chocolate cake is the least of your worries… I mean, what about the vowing to sleep with the same man for the rest of your life thing?'

'Watch it, EJ.'

'Sorry, Mark, but—really.'

'I'm just full. Not bulimic.'

'Leave her.'

Sam turned back to Ben, anxious to know what came next in the sentence, but he was chatting to Gemma now. The moment was over. As, it would appear from the movement of the parental contingent, was her party.

'Right, darling, we're off.'

'Thanks for coming, Dad.'

'My pleasure. And I hope you don't mind—and I don't want you going all independent feisty feminist on me—but I've got this. I owe you a couple of dinners, and besides, I've got inheritance tax to think about dodging now.'

'You old romantic.'

'Scratch the surface and you'll be surprised.'

'We can all chip in, Dad. There really is no need.'

'How dull would life be if it was always about need?'

'Are you sure you're sure?'

Robert nodded.

'Then, thanks very much. Really.'

'It really is my pleasure. I am very happy to be able to be here with you. Lovely friends you've got yourself.'

'I know.' Sam swallowed hard to keep her emotions at bay.

'And I hope I'll be seeing you soon.'

'I'm sure you will.'

'I'd say we've been abandoned.'

Sam nodded. Stitched up again. It was becoming a pattern. And, rudimentary button maintenance aside, she'd never been any good at sewing.

'So, when exactly did Gemma invite you?'

'Last week.'

'Last week?'

'Yup, hence my appalling levels of crapness about actually calling you.'

'Didn't you think it was strange?'

'That you'd want to see me again?'

'That your ex-girlfriend invited you to her flatmate's birthday party?'

'I don't think she made girlfriend status.'

Right answer.

'You smooth talker, you.'

Ben wasn't sure if she was joking or not, and right now he couldn't afford to take any chances.

'Well, I guess this is a little extraordinary—but then pretty much everything about meeting you has been.'

Sam was feeling atypically relaxed and comfortable. Or at least that was the justification she was giving herself for asking the next question.

'So, come on—did you read it?'

'Pardon?' Ben stalled. He'd heard all seven words perfectly. Observing Sam attempt nonchalance, yet fiddling with her napkin, her eyes wide, willing the answer to be no, he did what anyone in his position would have done. Leaning in, he kissed her.

Sam recoiled, but only for a moment before her mind emptied of everything. The here and now replacing the past and the future. The tension melting into something much deeper and more exciting. It might just have been her birthday cake, but he tasted delicious.

Ben pulled back first while, flustered, Sam tried to work out which way up she was. Much better than expected. A moment's delay and then she was determined to regain her composure completely. 'I knew they'd hire a kissogram.'

'Well, I have to supplement my income somehow.' Ben pushed Sam's hair back behind her ear, stroking her cheek with his hand in the process. If she wasn't mistaken his fingers were trembling, or maybe it was her cheek, or maybe the Bakerloo line had a tunnel directly underneath them.

'Well…'

'Well.'

Sam felt as if this was a test. The grown-up equivalent of the ones she'd spent her early teens completing in *Blue Jeans, Mizz* and *Jackie.* And then redoing or demanding a recount when she got an answer she didn't like.

Today's topic: How Uptight Are You?

You have spent the evening chatting to a guy who, despite your first impressions to the contrary, you really quite like. The place closes and you don't have his number, do you:
a) say thank you and disappear into the night without a trace, hoping he'll call in the not too distant future and that you find a black cab before you've walked half the way home?
b) brazenly suggest he comes back to your place—and not worry about the fact you can't remember whether you have shaved your armpits today or that you don't think you have any condoms, except perhaps for a spearmint one which was once given to you as a joke and is probably out of date?
c) follow b) but stop at a late-night garage to buy condoms and/or disposable razor?
d) call a cab and give him your number?
e) call a cab and hope he asks for your number?
f) whip out your PalmPilot and try and get a definite date confirmed for a follow-up evening?
g) suggest you go on for drinks somewhere else, even though you don't want, or have room for, another millilitre of liquid or time for a liver transplant and have to work the following day?
h) leave it up to him to decide what to do next?

'Suppose we'd better go. It looks like they're trying to close up.'

Gemma would pick b); Sophie would pick a)—proving yet

again that men can find your number when they want to. f) was so clearly the wrong thing to do, but somehow appealed to Sam if she was being honest…h) was a cop-out in some ways and a winner in others…

'Yup.' Sam nodded and drained her water glass, spinning out their departure. She didn't really want the evening to end. And she was about to fail the test. On the basis of her inertia she was clearly going to come out as '0–5 points: Mother Superior. Get real or get a cat'. And she never failed at anything.

Chapter Eighteen

Gemma moved in mysterious ways. If you can be blatant and mysterious at the same time.

Welcome to your dirty thirties.
Staying at Luke's tonight.
Speak tomorrow. G x

Sam deleted the text message and returned her phone to her bag.

b) f) b) h) b) a) h) h) b)…

Ben put his arm round her as he waited for the cloakroom attendant to retrieve his helmet and rucksack. Pretending not to notice, he was delighted when Sam rested her head against his neck. Probably just tired. And very drunk. Nice, though.

'So, what would the birthday girl like to do now?' He checked his watch. 'I reckon there are twenty-four minutes of your birthday left.'

'What do you suggest?'

'How about my place?' Sam pulled back to check out his expression. Cheeky grin. And total eye contact. She could feel herself slipping and, refocusing on her lapel, flicked an imaginary piece of lint off her jacket.

'I don't think so.'

'Oh.' Ben didn't know why he felt despondent; he hadn't been expecting her to agree. 'Look, I know you must be feeling a bit weird about the whole Gemma angle, and I know I handled everything really badly, but can I—would you mind if I called you?'

Sam nodded and then shook her head accordingly, before deciding to verbalise her response just to be sure there was no confusion. 'Of course not.' Plus, he had just scored very highly in the chivalry round.

As they exchanged mobile numbers she felt awkward. This was definitely the wrong end to this evening. b) b) b)...

'Hey, it's funny, I used to think you could plan...' Sam hiccuped. Oh, no, this was not good.

'Come on, let's get you into a cab.'

'Don't think I'll be falling for that ruse again...ever.'

'Just for you. I've got my bike.'

'Oh.' So much for a birthday flirtation. 'But you've been drinking.'

'Actually, I haven't.'

And he'd still kissed her.

'Well, how about that lift, then?' Sam surprised herself with the direct approach, her hiccups apparently vanishing as fast as her subtlety. Judging by Ben's bemused expression, she wasn't the only one who thought it out of character.

'What? Now?'

'Has there ever been a better time?'

'You'll freeze in that skirt.'

'Am I going to have to ask twice?'

Ben grinned and shook his head. 'You're just pissed.'

'I concede that I have consumed an excessive amount of alcohol, but I also promise that if you don't give take me home in the next five minutes I will never kiss you again.'

Ben took Sam's hand. 'In that case you leave me absolutely no choice. Your rusty steed awaits.'

As the cool night air of London whipped through her totally inadequate scooter apparel, her helmet muffled the sounds of midnight in the capital. When they reached Chelsea Bridge Ben slowed down for the benefit of his pillion, and Sam's eyes widened as she drank in the majestic sweep of magical lights on the Chelsea and Albert Bridges, twinkling in the inky black Thames. Gripping the weathered leather of Ben's jacket a little tighter, she nodded to herself in affirmation of her decision and knew three people who would definitely approve.

As yet unaware of the majority ruling in his favour, her knight on his pale blue charger, visor down, rode on.

Sweaty and elated Sam listened to Ben brushing his teeth. Frenetic sex. Not an outcome she could have predicted this morning, or even this afternoon, or even before eleven-thirty-six p.m. And if it hadn't been for Gemma leading by example she'd definitely be concerned that she was in real danger of becoming the loosest woman in Battersea. Not that it felt bad at all. Quite the reverse.

Muscles that she'd forgotten she even owned smarting, rolling over, she grinned into her pillow and inhaled deeply. Aware of the sheets almost tickling her now acutely sensitive naked body, Sam leant over the edge of the bed in search of a T-shirt before changing her mind and stretching out, languid and content, her post-coital state giving her an innate confidence that five years of gym membership had failed to achieve. Third time lucky or three strikes and out? At this precise moment she honestly didn't care.

As Ben slid into bed behind her Sam was engulfed by a silent sigh of contentment. Turning and pressing herself against the soft dark hair of his chest, she reached for his mouth again, and as his hands ran down her spine and pulled her firmly against him she emptied her mind of everything else. He was infuriatingly sexy. Birthdays were definitely making a comeback.

Chapter Nineteen

'Good morning.'

Sam opened her eyes and stretched out under the duvet. 'It definitely is.' No sign of a hangover either.

'I've made you coffee.'

An apparition. A better-looking version of Ben was standing next to her bed with a steaming mug in his hand.

'Great morning.'

She was finding his pillow hair strangely attractive, and the infamous T-shirt was much more crumpled than she remembered. And far more appropriate now.

Ben could feel her giving him the once-over as he bent down to put her coffee on the bedside table.

'Okay, okay—I'm just going to have a shower.'

She continued to observe her specimen intently as he absent-mindedly slipped his hand up his T-shirt to scratch his stomach.

'Be my guest. Help yourself to anything you need.'

'Any chance you might want to join me?' Squatting down beside her, grinning cheekily, Ben raised his eyebrows suggestively.

'Are you sure I'm awake? Have we met?' She hadn't said no.

Ben shook his head. 'I should've known better than to take advantage of you when you'd had so much to drink.'

He was so close she could feel his breath on her face and it was minty. He'd clearly been to the bathroom already.

'Excuse me, but *I* was definitely taking advantage of *you.*'

Ben leant across and kissed her, and Sam felt a ripple of excitement pass through her body.

'Fine with me. However you want to play it.'

'What time is it anyway?'

'Seven a.m.'

'Ugh.'

'Excuse me? This is far more your end of the day than mine.'

'What is this? A new leaf? I thought you were Mr Duvet?'

'I can't have you being late on my account.'

'I can't believe I forgot to set an alarm.' Unprecedented. She must have been very drunk, or distracted, or both.

'Luckily you have me *in loco* alarm clock.'

Sam laughed before taking a much needed sip of her coffee. 'Go on, then. Go and warm the shower up for me.'

Ben grinned. 'Being thirty really suits you.'

'I have to say so far I'm finding it very liberating.' Sam yawned. 'And exhausting.' There was a twinkle in her eye. And as Ben's lips brushed hers she had to confess, if only to herself, work seemed very overrated. For once Sam Washington was feeling cool. She only hoped no one was going to come in and blow her cover.

'Hang on a minute...' Standing up, Ben crossed the room and rummaged in his backpack.

What now? Easing herself into a more upright position, Sam noted that her head was feeling decidedly light. No doubt about it. A hangover was definitely creeping in.

'I forgot to give you this yesterday.'

Malaise forgotten, Sam sat up, clutching the duvet to her chest as Ben proffered an envelope. As a long-neglected muscle twinged in her inner thigh Sam smiled to herself. She was literally not fit to have a love-life. Maybe Gemma had a point.

Regular yoga was probably quite a good idea. Or indeed regular sex. Often as opposed to average.

'Thank you.' Blushing mentally, she hoped this had nothing to do with her petulant demand for a present at the restaurant—and indeed, that he had selectively forgotten that moment altogether. Not her best side.

Ripping it open, Sam extracted a black and white photographic image of the New York skyline and, inside the card, a voucher for a full body massage and evening membership at The Sanctuary.

Dear Sam
To help you get away from it all, if only for a couple of hours.
Happy Birthday
Love Ben

'Hey, it's just a token gift.' He studied her face. Nothing. And now silence.

Nice writing, no spelling mistakes, no strange sloping or smudging. She was touched. And very few people managed to surprise her.

Ben watched as, slowly, an expression started to form. It was looking promising.

'Fantastic. Thank you. Just what I need.'

Relief washed over him. She was grinning. His fault. And he was feeling good, James Brown-style. 'I just thought it might encourage you to give yourself a bit of a break.'

Had he given her a mini-break? Bridget Jones rushed into full focus and Sam dismissed her.

'I'm sure it will. Now, get in the shower before you delay me any further. I'll be right behind you.'

'No, I think you'll find that'll be me.'

Sam double-locked her front door at eight-fifteen, practically whistling. The sky was blue, Katrina & the Waves were 'Walking on Sunshine' and currently number one on her mental play-list. The promise of summer hung in the air—which was good, because she hadn't had time to blow-dry her hair.

By the time she was standing handbag to handbag with the rest of the professional herd on the platform at Clapham Junction, clouds of doubt were starting to gather.

Why couldn't she let herself take one day, or even one hour, at a time?

As she contorted herself in order to squeeze into a non-existent space in the train carriage, being careful not to make direct eye contact with any of the people she was actually touching, it was already feeling like the wrong thing to have done. Yet if she closed her eyes she could still feel his morning shadow on her cheek.

Just before her conscience presented her with a library image of Gemma's face.

Sam dismissed it. After all she had been yesterday's chief orchestrator. Sam heard her phone beep twice in the depths of her bag but, arms pinned to her increasingly sweaty sides she was helpless to do anything about it until she got to Waterloo.

Texting, texting, one, two, three.
Gorgeous morning, morning
gorgeous. Will call you later. Bx

Sam's smile was back *in situ.* Pursing her lips to force a expression more befitting a commuter, she realised she probably looked as if she was doing those exercises they recommend for a non-surgical facelift.

A second double beep, and this time Sam was quick on the draw.

Hey Birthday Girl… Any news? Soph x

Shortly followed one from Gemma.

Is it the morning after the night before?
Call me later.

So now the white witches were gathering. One at her Le Creuset cauldron, the other ready to read her text runes. But they were going to have to wait.

'Morning, Sam.'

'Morning, Mel. Did you have a good evening?'

'Yes, thanks.' Melanie was puzzled. Something was wrong with this picture. Maybe Sam had a less evil twin. Or at least a more interested one. 'How about yours?'

'Fab.'

'What was it you were seeing?'

'It was a hoax. Surprise dinner thing. In fact, have we got the number of a good florist?' Sophie and Gemma had just earned themselves a lifetime supply of Washington loyalty points and a bouquet.

'Do you want me to request anything specific?'

'If you get me a couple of numbers I'll sort it all out. In fact, don't worry. I'll call Directory Enquiries.'

'Are you sure?' Mel resisted the urge to ask her if she even knew the number.

'Of course. So, what's new here this morning?'

'EJ called first thing. She said it wasn't urgent…'

Sam could feel herself smiling. Trust EJ to favour the direct approach.

'…and Richard's rung a couple of times already. Between you and me I think he's in one of those pick-a-fight moods.'

Sam shrugged her shoulders.

'He's always like this the day before he goes away.'

She was never sure if it was his fear that he might lose his iron grip over his employees, the projected insecurity that they might manage too well without him or just the prospect of too much time with his nearest and dearest.

'Bring it on.' Sam breezed into her office, only to reappear seconds later. 'First things first—do you want a coffee?'

'Do I want a coffee?' Melanie sounded as if she was speaking English as a foreign language.

'Don't say it like I've never made you one before.'

Melanie's look said it all.

'Well, don't worry, I'm not about to break the habit of a lifetime.'

Mel cocked her head, confused.

'I'm going to buy you one. Latte?'

'Great.'

'And a pain au chocolat?'

'If you're sure.'

'Hey, why not? It's Thursday, after all. Any preference for brand or blend?'

'Pardon?'

'Costa, Café Nero, Starbucks or the little Italian?' They had four different shops in a hundred-metre radius from their revolving doors. Lawyers drank a lot of coffee.

As Sam headed to the lift bank Melanie sat at her desk and waited. At least it looked as if today was going to be different.

'Oi, Golden Bollocks.'

It was probably only an affectionate greeting from his desk neighbour, and there was no way James could know about last night, but Ben caught himself glancing south all the same.

'Morning.'

'It would appear to the uninitiated that this is your year, my son.'

Again, surely a coincidence. As for the 'my son', Ben must have been at least five years his senior. To the untrained, slightly tired ear, James was sounding a bit Michael Caine this morning. 'What are you talking about?

'Greg Grant wants to see you. In his office. For a quick word. Pronto. If you know what I'm saying.' James tapped the side of his nose in a manner Ben imagined he thought enigmatic but was in fact moronic. But at least it was Greg who wanted to see him. It was a well-known fact that the only quick word that Jonathan knew was P45.

'Any idea what about?'

James shook his head. Message delivered, he had re-immersed himself in one of the sleazier tabloids.

Ben didn't allow himself time to hypothesise. Most of his personal calls were in the EU, and he never forwarded porn to the rest of the team. Maybe that was where he'd been going wrong. Dumping his bag on his desk, he headed for the corner office.

'Erm…Sam. Sorry to bother you.' Melanie popped her head round the door.

'No problem.' Sam looked up, her good mood continuing to power her day. 'I thought I told you to head off fifteen minutes ago?'

'Oh, I just had a few loose ends that needed tying up.' And a few e-mails to send. Sam had been so productive today that Mel was way behind on personal stuff. She had friends who thought she was ignoring them. 'And just as well I stayed. I've got a gentleman out here for you. A Ben Fisher? He says he's come to collect you.'

'Does he, now?' Sam rummaged for her powder compact and squinted into the inadequate mirror. Even at arm's length she couldn't quite get her whole face in. She snapped it shut. What on earth was she doing? Mel's smirk was poorly disguised and Sam couldn't blame her. 'Send him in.'

Sam stole a glance at the clock on her computer screen. 18:15. What was he playing at?

'Hey, cool office. Is this all yours?'

Ben strolled towards her desk, turning three hundred and sixty degrees *en route,* a temporary security pass clipped incongruously to his leather jacket and flapping in the gust generated by his tornado of activity. He managed, however, to arrive at his final destination no less disoriented than when he had arrived, whereas Sam conversely was suddenly feeling a bit dizzy.

He planted a kiss on her lips. 'You must be seriously important…I had no idea.' Not entirely true. 'And this building is so grown-up. I think they thought I was a courier.' But behind his jovial exterior he was nervous. He wasn't quite sure how she was going to take this.

Striding across her office, Sam closed her door firmly and smiled to herself as she heard Mel's not very subtle sigh of disappointment as all eavesdropping opportunities were brought to a definitive end.

'Well, this is a surprise. Clearly I'm simply irresistible.' Sam wished she'd just thought it. Especially as Ben had spectacularly failed to react. From now on she was sticking to playing the straight one. No frills and no flirting.

'Sorry, I should probably have called first, but there's something I have to tell you.' Too direct? But he had to get this over with. He couldn't risk backing out now.

Sam stopped in her tracks.

'Should I be worried?' Suddenly she was feeling fourteen again. When, exactly, was she going to learn that boys were nothing but trouble?

'Any chance of a drink?'

'I don't know if anyone has mentioned it, but this is a law firm. There is, however, a pub just across the…'

'Just a glass of water or something?'

Dialling Mel's extension, she fought the concern creeping in.

'Diet Coke okay for you?'

Ben nodded. 'Actually, leave it. I'm fine.' He had to tell her now.

Sam replaced the receiver expectantly. 'Well, the good news is I've been promoted.'

'Great stuff. Congratulations. Hey, I might even have been able to stretch to ice and lemon for that.' Ben wasn't even smiling. 'Hey, surely that's good news?'

'It is…' Sam's relief was only minimal. Clearly the bad news was yet to come.

'Well, it's only a pilot, and I'm only series-producing this one idea for the US cable network in question, and the series might not even be commissioned, in which case I imagine I'll be back to where I am now. I mean, a lot of these things sound like a good idea on paper but are impossible to make in reality…'

'Is it a programme on pessimism?'

'What?'

'So far, so negative.'

'It's just—well, I don't want you to get the wrong idea.' Maybe dating a lawyer was going to be a mistake.

'What do you mean?'

He was still looking very earnest.

'And what's the bad news?'

'It's—well it's the subject matter.'

'Hey, how bad can it be? And, as you now know, I'm not as square as I look.'

Sam imagined her fingers in the crossed position. Please let it not be another sex one. Please let it be something she could proudly tell Sophie and Gemma about. No fetishes, no fisting…

'Well…'

'And by the way, this is when you're supposed to say that I don't look square.'

'Square?'

'That I don't look like a dork.' Sam had watched enough frat-pack movies in her time to know the jargon.

'You don't look square.' He needed to stay focused.

'No—like you mean it.'

'You don't look…' Ben interrupted himself; his afternoon was becoming more farcical by the second. 'Sam, this idea—well, I came up with it after I'd found—it was just, you know, sort of…well, it wasn't triggered by anything specific—just, I guess…I, well, I flicked through and it got me thinking…'

Sam was silent. Expectant.

'The working title—well, the title we're toying with at the moment—is *In Search of the Real Ally McBeal*.' Ben stopped and watched Sam's face carefully, waiting for a clue, a hint at the scale of the imminent explosion.

Sam couldn't have been any more relieved. In her at times crippling imagination he had definitely been building up to The ABC of STD. If this was the bad news, everything was going to be fine.

'So it's all about lawyers?' She knew she was jumping the gun a little, but she didn't think for a moment that her mother would be satisfied with "documentary-maker", nor did she want to bring up *Storm in a D Cup.* This was much better.

'Yes.'

Ben wished he could be party to her thought processes.

'As per our discussion with Gemma at my place?'

'Yup.' A sign. Anything would do. A smile would have been a start. Instead her demeanour was a serious one. Contemplative? Cross? It was difficult to tell.

'I doubt you'll get permission to film anyone at work. Breach of client confidentiality, for one thing. Plus no firm is going to want to take you on a tour of their offices—think about the security risks.'

'It's more about them as a whole person. Work is only a small part of that.'

'Depends on the lawyer. So...' Suddenly the penny dropped. 'A-ha, so you're all flustered because I came up with the idea?'

'Well...'

'Don't worry, you can have it. My pleasure. Intellectual Property has really never been my thing.'

'You came up with the idea?' Wrong penny. Wrong slot.

'That afternoon. When I was telling you that wasn't how lawyers lived their lives. That Ally McBeal was a fantasy world.'

It would have been easy enough to go along with, but Ben's guilt complex was ever expanding.

'Not exactly.'

Sam looked surprised. She was sure she'd been spot-on.

'In a way I guess it was your idea, but not in the way you're thinking. It was flicking through the diary, then meeting you. This might sound a bit hackneyed, but it's like you were the inspiration.'

'Hey, didn't Chicago write a song about that?' Sam clamped her mouth shut as the tune built powerfully in her head. But it was too late. There it was, apparently on the tip of her tongue. Soft-rock suicide.

Ben was surprised at the diversion. Not least because Sam was the last person he'd have expected to have an encyclopaedic knowledge of the mid-eighties power ballad. And he could definitely pull American rank on this in a crisis. Peter Cetera had been a far bigger star on the other side of the pond. But to Sam's utmost relief, he decided not to dwell on the moment. After all, admitting he knew the names of individual band members would make him less of an accomplice and more of an anorak. Instead, Ben decided to capitalise on a rare sheepish moment in Sam land. 'So you're not....you don't mind, then?'

'Why would I mind? I mean, if anything, I guess I should be flattered. It's not like you're saying *I'm* the real Ally McBeal. I mean, that girl has more hang-ups than...than...' Sam racked her brains for a germane example.

'No, of course not.' Sometimes he was glad that people were capable of incredible self-centredness. He'd guessed her reaction all wrong.

'And...'

Ben could detect a quiver of panic in Sam's voice

'...I mean, you're not going to suggest you film me?'

'Don't be ridiculous...' Obviously she would have been perfect, but he was an ideas person and he couldn't think of a worse one.

'Well, then.'

Relief all round.

'Although if you can think of anyone who might be interested that would help.'

'I'll just put a notice on the board, shall I?'

'That would be great.'

'It's never going to happen.'

'Of course.' Ben smiled. He still had a lot to learn.

Sam sat back in her chair and studied his face. 'I can't believe you were worried about telling me. Am I really that scary?'

'Terrifying.'

'I hope you're joking...'

'Look, I didn't want you to get the wrong idea. I don't know—I guess I was worried that it might come across badly...that you might think I... And just at the point where things are starting to…have started to…' Ben stopped himself. Sam seemed remarkably unfazed. 'Anyway, enough about me. How's your day going?'

'Pretty average so far.'

'Really?' Ben grinned mischievously. 'Well, may I suggest we get out of the building, then?'

'Maybe you'll let me buy you dinner…?'

Ben paused as Sam berated herself. Less than twenty-fours since their first kiss. But he was the one that had turned up in her office. This was his fault. Living in a blame culture was useful at times.

'You know—to say congratulations.'

'You could *cook* me dinner…'

'I don't do cooking. Nigella and Jamie have quite enough supporters. And, plus, it saves me from being exploited down the line. I'm very good at dialling, though. And booking. And I've got *Zagat's* in my drawer.'

'Alternatively, we could go back to mine?'

'Shepherd's Bush?'

'Well, there are no sheep, no shepherds, no bushes—but there are a couple of trees and—I think this might seal it—a very good Indian takeaway.'

'You, my friend, have a deal.'

Standing at the window of his fifth-floor corner office, Richard watched the scene on the pavement below. The figures might only seem ten centimetres tall from his vantage point, but it was definitely Sam hitching her skirt up to almost indecent levels before mounting the back of a scooter. Petulantly, he dialled her extension.

Down on the third floor Melanie stared at the number flashing up on her screen and wished she'd left when Sam had told her to. She only managed to ignore three ring cycles. Pavlov had obviously had a secretary as well as a dog.

'Sam Washington's office.'

'Good evening, Melanie, is she there?'

'I'm afraid not. She's in a meeting. Can I take a message?'

'Just ask her to come up and see me when she's done.'

A beat of hesitation. Richard watched the scooter disappear round the corner.

'It's off-site. And she's off tomorrow. Wedding leave.'

'Wedding leave?'

'Her best friend's getting married on Saturday.'

'So she's incommunicado until when?'

Melanie didn't like his tone of voice.

'Monday. Obviously I can get a message to her if you need to speak to her before your holiday.'

'Please try.'

'What is it concerning?'

Richard paused.

'Is it urgent?

'I guess it could wait.'

'I'll tell her you called.'

'If you could.'

Melanie deliberately dialled Sam's home number and waited for the beep. With a bit of luck Richard would be at high altitude by the time she picked it up.

Chapter Twenty

Sam spotted Sophie looking for her from the midst of her 'Boogie Wonderland' and, hips still swinging, side-stepped her way to the edge of the dance floor. Apparently at seven p.m. she was still on official duty.

'I trust everything is to your satisfaction, m'lady?' Sam bobbed a mock curtsey. 'No second thoughts that I need to be worrying about…?'

As Sophie smiled, Sam couldn't help noticing that she was radiating a glow that had nothing to do with her make-up or her three last-minute tanning sessions.

'Will you come upstairs? I just need to go and freshen up.'

Sam took a step back. 'Honestly, you look perfect.'

'Just a quick touch-up before the evening guests arrive.'

Sam surveyed the room. 'You know more people than this?'

Sophie nodded. 'Only a few work people to come. And Ben, of course.'

'Because I obviously couldn't have managed today without knowing he was arriving later… Anyway, forget meeting the right man. I'm going to have to make about a hundred more friends before I can even contemplate having one of these receptions.'

'Rubbish. And I just thought you might not want to dance with my dad all evening.'

'He's quite a mover, you know. I think your mother is quite grateful that she's being spared.'

'So call Ben and tell him not to come. I just thought it would be more fun for you.'

'Hey, today is *your* day. Far be it from me to exercise an opinion.'

'You see—you do want him to be here. And, don't take this the wrong way, but I haven't seen you looking this relaxed in years.'

'I love the way you put that down to one person in particular and not to the fact that today is nearly over.'

'I think you'll find three dates in four days speaks for itself.'

'Excuse me, one dinner set-up, one celebration of his promotion and one best friend's wedding. And, don't take this the wrong way, but to be honest I'm just relieved to have got to this point of today without treading on your train, swearing in front of any of the little bridesmaids or spilling gravy on my red silk dress. I'm still not sure what sort of message inviting Ben to a wedding this soon projects—although I guess I should be grateful that at least he wasn't watching me walk up the aisle earlier.'

'Just shut up and come upstairs.'

'I only hope Mr Butler puts that suggestion to you a fraction more romantically later on.'

Sam linked arms with Sophie and escorted her to the honeymoon suite.

'Ah, bliss—that is so much better.'

To Sam's dismay, Sophie was lying on her back on the marital bed.

'I think I forgot to eat, the champagne has gone straight to my head and these shoes are giving me backache. Are you sure I can't wear jeans for the next bit?'

'No way, Soph. First of all it'll shatter the illusion that this isn't just another day in a dress and heels for you, secondly white jeans are very eight seasons ago, and thirdly you need to get back downstairs and do a bit more circulating.' Sam checked the time. 'And sharpish.'

Sophie sat herself up. 'Mark wouldn't mind. He probably won't even notice what I'm wearing.'

'I think he might notice if you take that corset off.'

'It's hilarious, isn't it?'

'It's gorgeous. I'm just jealous. I couldn't have a cleavage like that unless they managed to harness the excess flesh from my bottom and thighs.'

Sophie laughed. 'Sometimes you are just quite simply ridiculous.'

'And funny?'

'Considering your day job…'

Sam frowned.

Sophie smiled contentedly. 'I'm so lucky. Mrs Butler, eh? I can't believe it.'

'He really is exceptional, Soph, and even to the more cynical observer you two are very good together. Oh, and while I remember, I thought you said Mark couldn't dance? Or was that like when you said you hadn't done any revision before that history exam in the fourth year?'

'We've been practising. We've even had a couple of lessons.'

'Mark agreed to that?' Sam laughed at the thought of a sequinned former *Come Dancing* champion choreographing a routine in their sitting room.

'He was really into it, actually.'

And Sam had thought she knew every single detail about today. She could even list the cheese selection from memory.

'I can't believe you didn't tell me.'

Sophie shrugged. 'I suppose we didn't need any extra pressure. Mark was nervous enough.'

'Well, you couldn't tell…'

Sam bet Sophie hadn't noticed the collective sigh emanating from the cluster of single women at table ten, dabbing their eye-liner and hoping that one day they too would find a handsome, wealthy man who loved dancing.

'And you wouldn't make a speech without practising, so what's the difference?'

Sam couldn't have agreed more. Forget Olivia Newton-John and John Travolta, Jennifer Grey and Patrick Swayze, Sam wanted a first dance routine that people would remember. Obviously she was still having trouble visualising an aisle moment, but the dancing bit could be fun.

'My feet are killing me.' It was the nearest Sophie had come to wailing all day. 'I only slipped my shoes off under the table for a moment, and I honestly thought I wasn't going to be able to get them back on again. I might give them a quick soak…'

Shoes abandoned, and trying to keep the weight off the pads of her feet, Sophie made it to the *en suite* bathroom on her heels without pulling a calf muscle.

Her voice echoed as she continued. 'It's been a perfect day, though, don't you think?'

Sam followed her in and resisted the urge to laugh at Sophie, dress hitched up, stockings on the floor, dunking a perfectly pedicured foot in the basin. Shortly followed by the other one. Why she hadn't just put an inch of water in the bath, or taken the dress off first, Sam didn't know. Still, as Sophie kept reminding everyone, it was her day.

'Absolutely.' If she was being brutally honest, she'd have liked a smidgen more time to herself and a bit less carrying this and fetching that, but on balance she was enjoying being a handmaiden a lot more than she'd thought she would, and Sophie's euphoria was almost catching.

'And I couldn't have done it all without you.'

'Course you could. You've been across all the plans from day one. I mean, what have I done…apart from a bit of shopping?'

A bit of sitting at the hairdresser, at the manicurist, choosing a honeymoon wardrobe, various fittings, organising the hen, organising the post-hen debrief dinner—well, that was about it. All in a few months' work.

'Why don't you put your trainers on for the next couple of hours? I mean, your dress pretty much goes down to the floor anyway. Just promise me, no moonwalking or scissor kicks.'

'Yay. Great plan.' Sophie punched the air with pure joy.

Sam managed to stop Sophie adding sports socks to the ensemble, but as she watched her tying her shoes she wished she had a camera.

'Hey, too late to be a runaway bride.'

Sophie smiled. 'The only running I'll be doing is over to Mark. I do love him so much.'

Sam buried the teenage instinct to fake vomiting noises. 'Well, that's a relief.'

Sophie hugged her best friend. 'I love you too, you know.'

'Hey, that's quite enough of that.'

'I do. And nothing is going to change.'

'Your signature is.'

'I'm being serious.'

'I know, and you know—well…' Sam hugged Sophie back. 'I love you too.'

'Even if you sound like you're being forced to say it.'

'I do?'

'Yup.'

'Oh.'

'We'd better get downstairs…' Sam smiled serenely. This hadn't been her idea. 'Only, I've just realised Masie and Nick might have arrived, and they literally don't know anyone but me.'

'Masie and who? They sound like pre-school TV presenters.'

'My clients with the house in Richmond. I haven't met him yet, but she's great, and I thought it would be a nice gesture to ask them along. They've been so good about working round today. They probably won't stay long, if they make it at all. She's pretty pregnant. Not that you can tell. One of those women with stomach muscles to die for. Still, if I could afford a personal trainer… I think she must have been quite well-known in her heyday. She had a big hit…I think she might even have had a number one…about ten years ago. But you know how crap I am about music.'

'Make that popular culture in general.'

'Hang on…um…could it have been called "Lifting Your Love"?'

Sam's jaw slackened. 'No way, Soph. Tell me you're not restyling Masie Gabriel's house?'

'No, that isn't her.'

'Well, she was Masie Munroe in her singing days. But then she got married.'

'Bloody hell, Sam. Very impressive. And since when did you have an encyclopaedic knowledge of chart-toppers?'

'Since EJ had an affair with this one's husband.'

'With Nick Gabriel? Shit. I didn't realise that was his… No way. And Masie's so adorable.' Sophie's face fell. 'But, thinking about it now, he does seem to spend a lot of his time away on business.'

'Or at least that's what he tells her. See you down there.'

The disco inferno was still in full finger-pointing swing, and, scanning the dance floor Sam couldn't see EJ anywhere—although she spotted Gemma spectating from the periphery, apparently mesmerised by the display of tail feathers of all ages being shaken to Missy Elliot.

'Hi, Gem…have you—?'

'It's no wonder the birth rate is down, if you think about it…'

'What?' If there was one time she could have done without the world according to an inebriated Ms Cousins…

'Well, of all the mammals on the planet, we do have the most bizarre courting rituals. Dancing to attract a mate when most of these men wouldn't know natural rhythm if it walked up and slapped them in the face. The women, on the whole, are much more competent. Weird, isn't it?'

'Not really. We were making up dance routines, singing into our hairbrushes and pretending to be the Kids From Fame while they were all building ramps for their skateboards and

BMX bikes and learning to ride in a straight line without holding the handle bars.'

Gemma paused as she waited for the information to filter through her champagne and white wine haze.

'Do you always have an answer for everything?'

Sam nodded. 'Apparently so. Look, Gem, I promise I'm not being rude, but have you seen EJ? It's just I need to give her a message quite urgently.'

'She's just gone to the bar for another round of drinks. But, Sam…?'

She'd vanished. But if Sam's hypothesis was correct then how come she, for one, could dance *and* cycle without holding the handlebars? She didn't want to be the one to tell her, but her theory needed work.

Ben checked his coat at the cloakroom and entered the reception alone. It was packed, the noise levels and lights from the dance floor making finding a familiar face more difficult than it should have been. Feeling slightly awkward in his suit and still-slippery leather-soled shoes, he headed in the direction of the bar. At least with a drink in his hand he'd be able to wander, or glide, amongst the guests with at least a semblance of a sense of purpose.

'Two vodka-tonics.'

EJ drummed her fingers on the bar in time to the well-known dance anthem as she waited for her drinks.

'Elizabeth-Jane—well, this is a surprise.'

If there was one person in the galaxy that she hadn't been expecting to run into today, it was the man standing next to her—and, regrettably, the effects of his physical proximity were just as powerful as ever.

Sam observed the collision from the other side of the room and quickened her pace, the combination of heels and guests preventing her from breaking into a light jog.

* * *

'Nick. What are you—?'

'You're looking fantastic.' The directness of his gaze was disarming. And, while his moral code might have been more than a little shabby, sartorially and physically he was looking as effortlessly stylish as always.

'Thanks.' EJ was practically speechless.

'Darling—over here.' Nick beckoned and EJ followed his gaze, waiting for her first glimpse. 'Can you believe the coincidence? This is Elizabeth-Jane Rutherford, one of the lawyers who worked on the Real Records takeover. Well, technically we were on opposite sides, but we spent several evenings going over contracts and I have to say she's pretty impressive.' Nick smiled and EJ did her best to follow suit, wishing she'd ordered a double. 'Elizabeth-Jane, this is Masie—my wife.'

'Great to meet you.' EJ shook her hand perfunctorily. 'So, how do you know Mark and Sophie…?' Totally unprepared for this moment, she did her best to focus on Masie. Nick's shirt was tie-less, and EJ was finding it hard to stop her eyes searching the small inverted triangle of exposed chest.

'Sophie's just working on some space that used to be Nick's father's.'

'Oh, right.'

Nick was determined to stay in the conversation. 'It's a great place. He hadn't done a thing to it in twenty-five years but Sophie's had some great ideas. She's very talented.'

EJ nodded. 'I know. You wouldn't catch me at any old wedding.'

Masie intervened. 'Not that my husband knows much about interior design. He hasn't even met Sophie yet, but she very kindly asked us along and I'm dying to meet Mark. She can't talk about him enough.'

EJ smiled. 'He's a lovely guy. Can I get you both a drink?' Unorthodox offer, perhaps, but if she was going to weather this moment she needed to keep herself busy.

'No, no—let me get these.' Nick was brandishing a twenty-pound note.

'Thanks.' It was the least he could do. 'In return, let me see if I can spot Mark for you.' EJ turned and scanned the room for a trace of the bride or groom. She had never wanted to see Mark more.

'So, tell me, how are things at Greenberg Brownstein?'

Masie rolled her eyes. 'Do you always have to talk about work? She's off duty and so are you.'

'Believe me, this girl is never off duty.'

EJ knew better, yet his words sliced through her defences. He should have come with a hazard warning. She could feel every fibre of his shirt on her arm as they leant over the bar side by side, elbow to elbow, conscience to conscience.

Approaching the crash site with caution, Sam was intercepted at the last moment by a good-looking man in a suit.

'Sam—wow, look at you. A vision in red.'

Sam did a double-take as someone sounding remarkably like Ben put his hands on her waist and swung her round to face him.

'Hey. My God, what have you done?'

'No good?' Ben wondered whether he had overdone it. But he'd been meaning to clean up his act for ages.

'Very good.' Sam murmured her approval as she absorbed the new look and ran a hand over the back of his freshly exposed neck, before raking her fingers up into his newly trimmed hair. 'Welcome to the twenty-first century Mr Fisher. Much more man than boy. A suit and proper shoes… steady…you'll have an identity crisis.'

'Hey, the suit is only for the next few hours. If I wore this to work people would think I had an interview…in a bank or something. I feel like I'm back at school.'

'On a Saturday?'

'Detention.'

'You wish…'

Sam laughed before she remembered she was mid-mission.

Ben planted a kiss on her lips and a fraction of a second later Sam tried to walk through it.

'Hey, what's the hurry? It's me, your date for this evening. And I want to dance.'

'Really sorry—won't be a minute. Emergency on Planet EJ. Gemma's over there, if you want to go and warm up with a few disco moves.'

Ben was left watching as Sam and Sophie converged on EJ and the bar. Sophie was going to get there first. He edged a little closer to the action.

'Sophie!'

'Masie, so glad you could make it. I really didn't expect to see you.' A fleeting glance over her shoulder during the air kiss exchange, but no sign of a Mr Gabriel anywhere. Phew.

'Congratulations. Fabulous dress. You look divine. And I love the Adidas touch. Very street.'

Sophie blushed. 'Just for dancing. Thanks so much for stopping by.'

'Hey, I wouldn't have missed it. Where's your husband, then?'

'My husband?' Sophie giggled. 'Of course—I've got one of those now. Mark's definitely around here somewhere.' She surveyed the room speedily but couldn't spot him. 'So, did you bring Nick?'

'Yup. Miracle of miracles, he was in town, without a meeting or a conference call.'

'Fabulous.' In which case, where was he…?

'But of course he's just run into someone he knows. A lawyer from the takeover or something.'

Too late. 'Really? It really is an amazingly small world sometimes.'

'He's just over there.' Sophie followed Masie's extended finger just in time to see Sam approaching apace. 'The one with grey hair—sorry, he prefers it if I say silver.'

Ben stood and stared. Masie Munroe. Ten years on she was still as striking, and pregnant again. Like the majority of his peers at university, he'd lusted over her debut appearance on *Top of The Pops:* that dress, that video. And, like most men of his age, he had indulged in an extra pint on the Sunday the pictures of her perfect wedding made the papers.

It had been such a disappointment: a rising star marrying an older man who happened to be the boss of her record company, when so many men of her own age were desperate to show her the meaning of love. But Nick Gabriel was no bore. A musical alchemist who'd made fund-raising cool, a sound businessman, entrepreneur and philanthropist—frustratingly, he had all the qualities of a superhero, yet worked and played hard while juggling his family life. It was enough to make the average under-achiever a little green around the gills. His autobiography *Charity Begins at Home* was still nudging the best-seller lists five years after publication as millions around the globe hoped to glean a few tips.

Sam had given up trying to catch EJ's eye and had decided to opt for the less subtle, barge-in-on-the-conversation approach.

'Where have you been? I've been looking for you for ages.'

EJ resisted the urge to kiss her incoming rescuer, even if Sam's opener had been a little wooden in its delivery. Nick caused her self-control to self-destruct, and this was definitely not the time or the place to be caught flirting with somebody else's guy.

'Just getting some drinks in.'

'Well, you might be sorted, but Gemma's dying of thirst. I think the Lambada was the final straw.'

'Gemma's drink…of course…she must think I've forgotten all about her.'

'Which you have.'

Nick smiled as EJ shook her head. 'The Lambada? How retro.'

Damn, Sam should've known better than to bring up musical references with the man responsible for a large chunk of the Top 40.

'Anyway, sorry, but you'll have to excuse us.' Sam glared at EJ who, now she had a bodyguard, was apparently in no hurry to leave.

'Nick, have you met Sam Washington?'

'I don't think I've had the pleasure.'

'Well I've heard a great deal about you.' It was Sam's most saccharine tone, it's syrupy consistency almost concealing the venom perfectly.

'She's the best deal at 3L at the moment.'

'I bet she is. Although rumour has it you can't beat Greenberg Brownstein for client care.'

Sam took EJ by the arm and started to guide her out of the shark-infested waters.

'Well, great to see you again…maybe we can have a dance later.'

'Maybe.'

Nick fixed his gaze on EJ and watched as she disappeared into the semi-darkness. With Sam clamped to her side, she didn't dare look back.

Ben had no idea what do with his surplus energy. Could it possibly have been Nick Gabriel and EJ? But surely no one would cheat on Masie Munroe? How the mighty liked to shoot themselves in the foot. Unless, of course, he had got completely the wrong end of the stick. Maybe Sam would give him the low-down. And perhaps there *was* no low-down. But there was plenty of time for speculation later. Far more importantly, as self-appointed world ambassador for all thirty-something male music fans, he was going to have to go and say hello to Masie. Maybe he could interest her in a return to the small screen? Or at least a soft drink…

Chapter Twenty-One

'So you're definitely feeling better about it all now...?'

Sam paused, allowing EJ to vent her latest stream of consciousness, then continued.

'...but sometimes logic just doesn't apply. Well, good. Glad to hear it. Yup, so far surprisingly so good—although if he plays her album to me one more time I might have to think about moving on... Anyway, he took me on a proper date on Wednesday evening, and I have to admit—well, I don't have to but I will, to you at any rate—that it was surprisingly good. You know, he's not really the person you first think he is...'

'Isn't he?' The voice was a new one.

Sam swivelled in her chair. And stopped.

Richard was in her office unannounced, Melanie hot on his heels, flapping her arms apologetically.

'EJ, I have to go. I'll call you later.'

Sam replaced the receiver and pulled her chair in, sitting up properly before ripping the top page of doodles off her pad and binning it, slam-dunk, basketball-style, into the bin in the corner. It went straight it, not even touching the sides. Yes. An imaginary crowd roared.

'Mr Blakely, what can I do for you?' She was feeling playful.

'Sorry to interrupt...I just got bored with talking to your voicemail so I thought I'd come in person... Oh, and, Melanie—white, no sugar, if there's a fresh pot.'

Sam looked at the phone base on her desk. Sure enough a light was flashing, but she worked far too many hours a week to feel bad about being caught on a personal call—especially when, as usual, she was at her desk when most of London were just leaving the house. Ben included.

'Anyway, good to see you smiling again.'

She waited for him to take the initiative. He was obviously there for a reason.

'Your dad better?'

'He's got cancer, not flu.' Sam was determined not to be ruffled by his arrogance. 'Good break? Weather must have been good.' Richard was unfashionably tanned.

'The weather was excellent.'

'I haven't had a holiday for months.'

'You of all people should've read the small print when you signed.' Richard settled into the armchair opposite Sam's desk just as Mel reappeared with his coffee.

Despite Richard's apparently ebullient mood, he'd already succeeded in bringing her down from cloud nine. About cloud seven at the moment. And she still didn't know exactly what he was doing in her office.

'I've got some news...'

Sam sat up to attention.

'...news that I wanted you to hear in person, and directly from me.'

Somewhere in her gut, a tiny seed of excitement was on the verge of germination.

'Annie and I are separating.'

Her internal fanfare faded. Was she supposed to congratulate him? She didn't do matrimonial disputes or shagging the boss, so she couldn't really see what it had to with her. Or she didn't want to.

'I'm sorry to hear that.' Her response was pure protocol. And she *was* sorry. The last thing she needed or wanted was for Richard to return to the open market.

'I know it's not exactly a surprise, and I'm only too aware that I've probably bent your ear on the subject one time too many. I actually wanted to talk to you about this before I left, but I couldn't get hold of you.'

'Didn't it make your holiday difficult?' Mentally Sam kicked herself. That definitely counted as taking an interest—something she really didn't want him to think she was doing.

'She didn't know about this until we got back yesterday morning. I didn't see any point in ruining the whole week for everybody.'

He was unbelievable.

'And Jeremy and Charlotte?'

'We're going to tell them at the weekend. Kids are far tougher than you think—plus, most of their friends are in the same boat.'

Sam felt a lump form in her throat.

'So, I was wondering if you and I could maybe have lunch?'

'Lunch?'

'I just thought that maybe we had a few things to discuss.'

'Such as?'

'Us.'

'Just like that?' Something in Sam snapped. 'You separate—correction—you are separating, and now we're supposed to be lunching?'

'This really isn't so out of the blue. You know I've always had a very soft spot for you.'

'I don't mix business and pleasure.'

'You don't?'

'No.'

'In which case how would you explain spending time with Andrew Thorne?'

Sam bristled. 'One evening.' She jotted AT on her Post-It pad. She'd deal with him later. 'I'm going to pretend we're not having this conversation. Was there anything else?'

'I had a long conversation with Philip first thing this morning.'

Concerns over the state of Richard's ring finger paled into insignificance with the next item on this morning's agenda. Philip Lucas. Senior Senior Partner. Grandson of *the* Philip

Lucas who had gone into partnership with Mssrs Lex and Lawton and was now the only person in the entire firm who had a direct genealogical link to the founders. Sam's corporate pulse pulse quickened.

'And we're making Sarah Watson partner this year.'

Going down… Cloud five, cloud four, cloud three…

'It's the name of the game, I'm afraid. Sarah's been with us for ten years. She was the obvious choice.'

Sam nodded, her lips tight, her expression blank.

Cloud two, cloud one…Hades.

'I know you'll be disappointed. But you've had an excellent year and it has been noted. I'm sure there'll be other opportunities.'

Sarah Watson. Surely not the image that 3L wanted to project in the market place. Unless, of course, the look they were going for was washed out and humourless. Plus, Sam's own case record was impeccable. Nothing had ever been too much trouble. Weekends. Late nights. Early mornings. Bank holidays. She had given them her twenties and they'd given her…? Well, aside from a salary that had enabled her to buy a flat and a car. Anger, indignation and old-fashioned disappointment crept ever closer to the surface. She didn't believe she'd lost out fair and square for a second.

'Thank you for taking the time to let me know personally.' Not a hint of a fissure in her speaking voice. 'Was there anything else? It's just that really I should be getting on.'

Suddenly she had a lot to get through. There was emotional regrouping, general ranting and raving and confidence repair for starters, followed by anger management, general fury, bitterness and an advanced life's-not-fair seminar—all to pack in before lunch. However, for the moment she was still HRH, Her Majesty Sam Washington, Queen of Control. What was it people said? Search for the positive in every situation. She wondered if there was a time limit.

'Not really. Just keep your diary flexible. A few complications seem to have cropped up in New York. I take it you don't have any concrete plans for the weekend at this stage?'

This stage being Friday. And, while her plans might not be concrete, they weren't plasticine either.

'I can work round them if necessary.' Sam was careful not to let any of her emotions show. 'Just let me know.' She was determined not to concede a point in this round.

'Maybe we should have lunch anyway—to discuss all the changes.'

'Well if I've got to get up to speed on New York, it's probably best to leave it until I'm back.'

He couldn't have it every way. Sam eyed the glass of water on her desk. People drowned in ponds and puddles, but she didn't think she'd read about anyone who'd drowned in a glass of water. Work was the one thing that she'd always managed according to plan. Not being made up to partner was simply outside her current field of vision.

She couldn't get him out of her office fast enough. She sat at her desk, mood transformed, a monumental area of low pressure hanging over her desk with not even the lightest breeze to drive it forward. 9:04. The day stretched ahead of her menacingly. She needed a holiday starting in approximately ten minutes' time. Instead nine hours of hard labour beckoned.

'I really appreciate you coming to meet me, Gem. First of all you're the only person I know who gets a proper lunch hour, and secondly I just really needed to get all this off my chest.'

'Hey, I'm glad you called.'

'I think I'm going to leave. You were right.'

'I was right? Have we had this conversation before?'

'No one has the right to talk to me like that…'

Gemma hesitated.

'Don't worry, I'm not about to hold you responsible for anything.'

Relieved, she nodded.

'But I've put my heart and soul into that firm, and I don't intend to waste years of my life waiting for a promotion. And I'm not going to sleep with Richard. Not ever. Enough is enough. Time for a change. And to think I always thought I'd got to where I am on merit alone.'

'Come on, it's always going to be the complete package that

they go for. It might not be politically correct, but thinking anything else is naïve.'

'So now I'm naïve as well?' Sam took a sip of her wine. Alcohol at lunchtime. That was how bad it was. But with Gemma there at least she wasn't drinking on her own. 'I should have known Andrew would open his mouth.'

'Andrew…? Of course. So much for your alleged Sahara Desert of a sex-life. You've had a bit of a purple patch recently.'

Sam cringed. She'd done her best to block the evening out, but she must have forgotten to empty her deleted items. 'And the thing is, if Richard bloody knows, everyone else at the office must too.' Sam shook her head. 'Still, I laughed it off as far as he was concerned.'

'Which probably wound him up even more.'

'Well, I was hardly going to apologise. It's got nothing to do with him. And I should have had nothing to do with Andrew.'

'Dominant male syndrome. Maybe Richard will eat Andrew.'

Sam couldn't help but laugh at the thought of the laws of the jungle being instigated at 3L. 'I don't think that would solve the problem. For some reason Richard just has it in his head that I could be interested in having long horizontal lunches in hotels and he can't see why it wouldn't appeal to me. Now, let me think. Aside from the fact that I don't find him physically attractive, that there's no chemistry from where I'm sitting, that he's a dick and, of course—yes—that he's got two children and a wife.'

'Didn't you say they were separating?' Gemma was doing her best to keep up.

'Which only makes it all worse. I can't just lie back and think of my career path. This has suddenly become a real mess.'

'Now you know how the rest of us feel. But so a couple of things have come up? It's not all doom and gloom…'

Sam waited for Gemma to give her a reminder, or better still a summary, of any reasons for her to be cheerful.

'Oh, come on. There's Ben, for a start.'

'We've only been dating for, like, ten minutes.'

'I'm choosing to ignore that little aside. And so what if your perfect plan is looking a little off target today? You wouldn't have got to where you are if you weren't incredibly good at what you do. And incredibly conscientious. Speaking as your mere flatmate, you're quite intimidating and inspirational all at the same time. I've never come across anyone as determined as you are.'

'Don't be ridiculous.' Sam had never been very good with compliments.

'You just need to hang on to your perspective. It may not feel like it today, but this is only one little setback. And I know 3L are one of the best, but you could always get a job at a different firm—either in London, or even abroad. You might be able to get a secondment in-house somewhere, or a transfer to an affiliate office...although they might have to be subject to Richard's approval, which could prove interesting...but maybe this is just symptomatic of the bigger picture. Maybe it's time for a change.'

'In-house or an affiliate? Don't take this the wrong way, Gem, but have you just been pretending to temp while secretly practising somewhere? Unless of course your real name is... Sarah Watson.'

'Enough, Miss Marple. I just went out with a hot-shot lawyer when I was in Sydney.'

'And what happened?'

'The firm came first and I've never been interested in being a corporate widow...'

But Gemma wasn't about to be side-tracked.

'Bummer that Richard's trying to sabotage your weekends. Maybe you should speak to some of your clients when you're next in New York about job opportunities?'

'It would be very unprofessional.'

Gemma sighed. Sam was apparently determined to be negative, and jump-starting her was proving to be quite tiring.

'But you love it out there, and there are ways of putting feelers out without announcing you are actually planning to move.'

Sam nodded. While it pained her slightly to admit it, Gemma was right. Again.

'Any firm would be lucky to have you.'

'I don't know—it's very competitive…' Sam suppressed a wave of fear, but not before Gemma's seismic insight had detected a wobble.

'It'll all work out—you'll see. It's like that maxim… Do one thing every day that scares you.'

'Every day?'

'Well, how about once every thirty years?'

Sam nodded. 'I guess it's just the shock. I've been working towards partnership since I started law school and now I can't even remember why.'

'Because you wanted to be the best.'

'But why did I equate that with being happy?'

It was a critical moment. Despair was edging in and Gemma was determined to halt its spread.

'Hey, this is no time to quit at the first hurdle, and don't believe the hype. These companies make you think it's impossible to get other, better jobs merely so you feel flattered into selling your soul to them. It's madness. You're probably one of the best at what you do. Along with EJ, of course.'

'Right.'

Gemma could feel them turning a corner.

'Therefore you are a commodity.'

Sam nodded.

'And I'll bet you're worth a lot on the open market…'

'You're right. And you're suspiciously good at this, Gem.'

They were on the home straight.

'Just don't shoot from the hip on this one.'

'This is me, Sam, you're talking to.'

Gemma observed the transformation in Sam's attitude. If her sense of humour was back then so was her perspective. Gemma's job was done. Sam was ready to roll. And she was free to go away for the weekend.

Sam strode back to 3L imbued with a new sense of purpose. Gemma giving her career advice. Sam was beginning to see the funny side of her day.

Knocking and entering his office simultaneously, Sam closed

the door behind her, ignoring the attempted intervention of his secretary. Andrew looked up from his monitor.

'Hey, Miss W. How's it all going? It's been far too long…'

Sam leant across Andrew's desk. 'You're pathetic.' She spat the words out.

'Oh, so this isn't a social call, then? Shame.' He was remarkably cool.

'I should've known you wouldn't be able to keep your mouth shut.' Poor choice of words. Sam flinched as her memory treated her to a flashback.

Andrew stood up, visibly perplexed. 'You can't just barge in here flinging allegations around. I promise I didn't say a thing. You have my word.'

'How does Richard know, then?'

Andrew shook his head. 'I honestly have no idea. He hasn't said anything to me, nor has he arranged for me to be sent to Siberia for a client conference.'

'Well, who else could possibly know?'

'Just hang on a second and calm down, will you?'

'So you didn't say—you haven't said anything? To anyone?'

'Not a word. I ran into Richard the day after and mentioned that I'd heard your father was very ill. That's it.'

'Sure?'

'Of course I'm sure. Anyway—' Andrew left his desk '—isn't it about time we had another coffee?'

Sam walked out.

Andrew sat down, finishing the conversation on his own. 'I guess I'll take that as a no, then.'

Melanie wasn't at her desk, and as Sam stormed into her office, throwing her coat on to the couch, she suddenly realised that the door had been ajar. As she entered Richard swung round in her desk chair. All very Bond villain-stylee. The only thing missing was a fluffy white cat on his lap.

'Good lunch?'

'Get out of my office.' Sam really wasn't in the mood for this. She was a commodity, after all.

'I'm sorry?'

'Now.' Sam didn't raise her voice but there was no mistaking her tone.

'I think you're forgetting the firm hierarchy.'

'Believe me, at this current moment nothing could be closer to my heart.'

'Sit down. I think we should start this conversation again…'

Defiant, Sam folded her arms across her chest and, standing in the centre of her office, just waited. Something was different about Richard's demeanour, even if she couldn't quite ascertain what it was.

'I just wanted to apologise for the…'

He was flushed. That was it. Sam approached her desk and leant in to confront him.

'You've been drinking, haven't you?'

'I'm not the only one.'

'Didn't realise I had to ask permission to go out for lunch. I needed to regroup.'

'I knew you were upset. And I shouldn't have told you the way I did. It was unprofessional. I was cross.'

'You were cross?'

'Well, all you do is throw everything back in my face.'

'What on earth are you talking about?'

'You mean *who* am I talking about?'

'Who? What?'

'Andrew Thorne.'

Sam sighed. 'Not him again. I'm just trying to do my job here.'

'I saw you two in the Judge & Jury and it didn't look like much of a personal crisis to me.'

'We were just having dinner.'

Richard narrowed his eyes almost imperceptibly. 'I don't like being made a fool of.'

'You're doing a pretty good job all by yourself.'

'I've been under a lot of pressure. Things have been tough at home—my marriage is over.'

'Don't you dare pretend that has anything to do with me.'

'But what about—?'

'What? You promise to leave your wife and now I'm supposed to fall at your feet? Has it never occurred to you that maybe, from where I'm standing, there is no spark?' Sam stopped herself as soon as she could. Apparently she hadn't taken off her holster before entering her office after all. And getting fired wasn't going to solve anything.

'But you fancied Andrew...'

'Actually, I didn't. He caught me at a vulnerable moment. It could probably just as easily have been you. But the way you're acting right now, I'm glad it wasn't. At least he has some dignity left.'

'So something did happen?' Sam could have kicked herself. She'd been played. 'I just thought you would have been more careful.' Richard walked round her desk and put his hands on her waist.

'What the hell do you think you're doing? Take your hands off me now. This isn't your own personal fiefdom...'

Richard stepped back a couple of paces.

'Believe me, you've just taken inter-office relations one step too far.'

'And exactly what is that supposed to mean?'

Sam wasn't sure. Luckily she had a surfeit of adrenaline on board, which was thinking much further ahead and forging a path through this emotional quagmire. She was only too happy to follow in its wake.

'I've got a deal I'd like to discuss with you.'

'There's no need for that tone.'

'I think there is. I've had enough of this.'

'Meaning?'

'Do I have to spell it out? My hotel room in New York. My office in London. You have absolutely no respect for my personal boundaries. My position here has become untenable.'

'You're far too sensible to resign.'

Sam's eyes were fiery. 'How dare you presume that you know what I think?'

'Come on, you're upset. Since when did Sam Washington let anything or anyone stand in her way?'

Richard attempted to take her arm and Sam wrenched it away. Conciliation was no longer on her agenda.

'Come on, it's been a hell of a day. Let's just let the dust settle and then how about that dinner?'

'I can't believe you're still not listening to me. I've had enough. Look, either you organise a transfer for me to join our affiliate office in New York or you are being recommended to a friend of mine for a documentary on sex in the workplace.'

'That's a big threat for a little girl.'

'A little girl…?' Sam was incandescent.

'You couldn't prove a thing.'

Richard sat back in the chair, his hands folded smugly behind his head.

'There's no written evidence—not even an e-mail. I'm not stupid.'

His audacity was breathtaking.

'It's my word against yours.'

'And who do you think they're going to take more seriously?'

'This is trial by television, don't forget. Do you really think the other partners will even hesitate for a moment if the reputation of this company is on the line?'

Richard sat up as his career teetered into view.

'You wouldn't dare.' He couldn't be one hundred per cent sure. Women were impossible to read when they were angry.

'This is just a job, Richard. I can get another one. Allegations of sexual harassment are much harder to shake.'

'Look, I can understand that you're disappointed the appointment didn't go your way—'

'This isn't just about the bloody partnership.'

'Well, good, because don't think you're going to get anywhere by bursting into tears on me or bluffing about some television programme.' Richard stopped. Something in her eyes was hard.

'You can't afford to risk it. You've got far too much to lose.'

Richard paused for reflection.

'You seriously want to go to New York?'

Sam nodded. 'It's time for a change.'

'And what about your new boyfriend?'

'It was a one-night stand.' There, she'd said it now.

'Not Andrew. The one with the motorbike.'

'Are you having me followed? Your story is looking more interesting by the minute…'

'I just saw you leave…'

'I'm not interested in what you think you saw. Just make the appropriate calls and get back to me. Soonest.' Sam turned on her heel.

'Where are you going now?'

'To see Sarah Watson.'

'What for?' Sam was delighted to see that for the first time Richard looked genuinely concerned.

'To congratulate her, of course.'

'But she—'

Flinging open her office door, Sam was relieved to see Melanie was back. She wasn't sure how much longer she could keep this up on her own.

'Melanie, call Sarah Watson and tell her I'm on my way round to see her.'

'Certainly.'

'And try and make sure Richard isn't here when I get back.'

'He hasn't called to say he's on his way down.'

'I think you'll find he's just leaving.'

'Come in.'

They'd worked in the same building for six years and yet Sam had never been into Sarah's office before. She barely knew her. And she'd barely considered her an arch rival. Mistake number one. EJ had always said to watch out for the quiet ones.

'Sarah? Hi—Sam Washington.'

'Hi, Sam.' Sarah put the lid back on her fountain pen and closed the file on her desk.

'I just wanted to pop by and congratulate you.' Sam had to admit that Sarah looked a little less dull than she remembered.

Sarah nodded graciously. 'I appreciate you coming round. So he's finally told you?'

'This morning.'

'Well, I'm sure it must be hard for you, and I'm very glad that you've stopped by. I didn't want there to be any hard feelings between us.'

'It was a bit of a shock, I'll be honest.'

'I'm not surprised. It's never going to be an easy time. And I still can't believe it, after all these years.'

Neither could Sam.

'We still haven't got round to getting a ring yet. I can't quite decide on what I want. It's a big decision.'

'Ring?' Sam did her best to take this latest nugget of information in her stride. At this rate Richard was going to need an entire series dedicated to his exploits.

Sarah noted Sam's confusion. 'Paul did call you?'

'Paul?' Sam did her best to put two and two together. So far she was consistently getting seven.

'You see, he didn't realise you were at 3L too until you replied to his e-mail...and I had no idea that you were the significant ex until he told me.'

'Oh.' Sam's brain was doing its best to decode the message.

'He hasn't called you, has he?'

Sam shook her head. 'No.' She was never, ever drinking at lunchtime again. Her articulacy had deserted her.

'Typical. Honestly, men are so crap at this sort of thing.'

Sam wondered whether the eye-roll was for her benefit.

'I told him to phone you before we ran into each other.'

'I had no idea...' Sam was suddenly very aware of today slipping through her fingers.

This time it was Sarah's turn to look confused. 'In which case you came by to say...?'

Sam got to her feet and prepared to leave.

'Richard popped in to see me this morning. This is clearly your month. You're not only being made a wife, you're being made a partner.'

Sam was surprisingly calm as she closed the door behind her, despite the fact that Sarah Watson had clearly hi-jacked her life. Pastures new beckoned. Her old patch had just become a little too overgrown.

Chapter Twenty-Two

Ben stifled another yawn. Only Greg Grant could schedule a production meeting for last thing on a Friday, expect full attendance and then overrun by forty-five minutes—forty-eight at last count. Sam was bound to have arrived by now. And, judging by the content of her last e-mail, she'd had quite a day. Fidgeting in his seat, he willed Greg to wrap it up.

Sam sat alone in the deserted open-plan office, eerily quiet bar the high-pitched electric hum of the monitors and the intermittent whirring of the air-conditioning fans. She stared at the mess on Ben's desk: a veritable soup of used Post-Its, pen lids, press releases, chewing gum wrappers and other assorted debris. Sitting on her hands, she resisted the urge to give it a quick tidy. It was a mess. Or, for those of an artistic persuasion, a creative milieu.

Having scoured almost every paragraph of the evening paper, she had nothing she could or should be doing. Adrenaline rush in remission, delivering Richard an ultimatum now felt like one of the most foolhardy things she had ever done. Which, frankly, didn't make her life sound very exciting. But she certainly wasn't going to have her life dictated by some power-crazed, under-sexed corporate partner. She could do mature. And if the partners were determined to be myopic in their outlook, she was going global.

Sam stretched her arms up towards the ceiling and enjoyed the ladder of release as her spine responded. Her moment of clarity was swiftly followed by one of impatience. Plus, she hadn't been to the gym all week and it was still early. Picking up a pen, she rummaged on Ben's desk in search of a blank piece of paper.

Nothing.

Pulling open his top drawer, she was greeted by an extensive collection of plastic cutlery, sandwich bar serviettes and sugar and salt sachets. Continuing her search, it wasn't until she reached the bottom drawer that there was any real potential. Flicking through the suspended files, boredom and workout temporarily forgotten, Sam glanced over her shoulder before rapidly walking her fingers through his personal folders, stationery requirements on hold.

Finally she came across a wedge of A4, yet, tugging at a sheet, felt it resist. Extricating the file from its surroundings, she discovered it was secured by a criss-cross of elastic bands. Prising a few pages apart, she managed to peer into the ream to assess its suitability for note-making—but as the all too familiar script blurred into a screen of tears she closed her eyes, willing the bundle to be an apparition. When she looked again it was still there, in all its photocopied glory, and, folded into the elastic band at the back, printouts from the 3L website. Her own stilted photograph alongside Richard's.

Hands trembling, Sam attempted a deep breath and tried to dredge some rationale up from somewhere. But all logic had apparently left town for the weekend. Clearly away on a short break with positivity. A wave of nausea threatened to topple Sam as her day re-routed itself for a third time: destination doldrums.

Keeping the manuscript, but returning its green suspension folder disguise, Sam slammed the drawer closed and, angrily wiping her eyes, stared at the incontrovertible evidence on the desk. She only had a moment before the distant rumble of a rapidly approaching production team on the verge of Friday freedom broke the silence. Slipping the bundle into her leather briefcase, Sam was still refastening the buckles when Ben came bounding over, his wide smile and warm eyes so effectively concealing his secret.

She really should have checked her calendar. Next year on National Disappointment Day she was going to stay at home.

'Time for drinks. To short-term memory loss and to your next move. And, while I'm not sure about you running off without me, I think it's only right that we celebrate our state of flux. And then I'm going to take you back to my lair…'

Not even a glimmer of a smile.

'Or we could go back to yours, if you prefer…?' Reminding himself that he hadn't been trapped at a strange desk for the last forty-five minutes, he downgraded from Friday de-mob euphoria to a calmer version.

'I'm so sorry. Obviously if I'd known this was going to happen I'd have suggested we meet somewhere you could have had a drink at the very least while you were waiting.'

'I had some water.' As she wiped her now clammy hands on her skirt she did her best to feign normality. Part of her wanted to fling her briefcase at him and submit the contents as Exhibit A.

'Well, I think we can do better than that.' Ben leant in to give her a quick kiss on the lips, ignoring the general wolf whistles and jeers of his colleagues who, faced with a new member of the opposite sex in the office, were reduced to a collective mental age of fifteen. 'Hey, are you okay?'

Sam wasn't. Blood was rushing through her veins and yet she felt frozen, as if she was watching the world through her eyes from the other side of the room, strangely divorced from reality. She had to go. Only she wasn't sure if her legs were still working. There was only one way to find out. She could barely look at him.

Ben berated himself for not noticing her ashen complexion twenty seconds earlier.

'What is it?'

'Mum just called. It's Dad.'

Sam broke with her non-religious roots and sent a silent prayer, a special dispensation, to apologise for lying about something as serious this. More pressingly, there was apparently a problem with her data-processing stream. She'd crashed. And IT support was busy tonight. Well, the branches that weren't honeymooning in the Maldives or windsurfing for the weekend. Retouching base with her senses, Sam noted that she was still gripping a pen in her hand.

'I was about to leave you a note.'

'Well, I'm glad that I caught you. Can I give you a lift anywhere?'

Sam shook her head as she got up.

'Cab…I'll just…better…need to go.'

Ben chased after her. 'What's happened? Are you going to the hospital?'

'Please—I just need to…'

'Hang on…Sam…'

Head down, she marched on. She didn't want to precipitate a scene.

'Stop.' Ben grabbed her arm.

'Let go of me.' Sam wrestled from his grip.

'Calm down.' Ben was upset. He couldn't have been any gentler. 'You're going the wrong way. The lifts are over there.'

Great, so now she couldn't even flounce out without assistance.

'Do you want me to call Gemma?'

Sam shook her head. 'She's away.'

'Do you want me to come with you? Just, you know, for moral support or to distract you from the taste of the dusty instant coffee. I don't need to come in or anything.'

'No.' Definitely not. 'No, thanks.'

Ben put her in the lift. His concern and kindness was threatening to weaken Sam's resolve. Reminding herself why she was leaving, she clutched her briefcase to her side. Or she would have done if she was holding it. Fuck.

'Call me if you need anything. That's anything—whether it's transport or food or a drink or a shoulder. I'm around all weekend.' Ben stopped himself. He didn't want to come across as too cloying.

Sam stepped out of the lift and Ben thought he'd made a little progress when she started to retrace her steps. 'My briefcase. I left it...'

'I'll get it. Wait there.'

Sam watched him sprint off and wondered if she should do a runner. She could hardly rugby tackle him to the floor in a moment of supposed spontaneous unbridled passion to prevent him from getting to his desk now. Sam shook her head as she read an advert on the noticeboard. Or pretended to.

He was back in moments. 'Here you go. You probably don't need to go to the gym. I'd be in much better shape if I had to carry this everywhere with me.'

Of course he hadn't looked. She was the flipping spy.

'Just something that needs sorting out over the weekend.' Sam exhaled inaudibly as she was reunited with her bag. Right—dramatic departure from Small Screen Productions take two, and...running up...and action...

'Well, good luck. Hope everything's okay. Maybe speak later?'

Sam nodded.

'And promise me you won't worry about that work?'

'I won't.'

'Or Richard? Or the rest of it?'

Sam nodded.

'What a day you've had...'

The ironies of life. He had no idea.

'But it'll all sort itself out, you'll see. I'll call you later.'

'Great.'

She didn't mean to encourage him; she just wanted to get out of there.

Ben watched the lift doors close, separating him from Sam and his rapidly dissipating Friday feeling. He knew it was way too early in their dating situation—if you could even call it that yet—to expect to be automatically involved in her family problems. But she was in quite a state. And for the first time in as long as he could remember he really wanted to be able to help.

'Oi, Casanova, lost your Midas touch? One kiss and she's gone. Me and the guys will be propping up the usual bar, if you fancy joining us later. Assuming that was your evening leaving early.' James pressed the button to call the lift as Ben put his hands in his pockets and started ambling back to his desk.

'She's gone to visit her dad.'

'Course she has. See you down there.'

'Have a good weekend.'

Ben shouted over his shoulder to avoid eye contact. He wasn't going drinking. His flat needed spring cleaning, and his screenplay was never going to progress from hobby status if he only tinkered with it once a month. Plus, he wanted to be able to hear his phone. He might even assemble his tummy-roll bar. He hadn't exactly been overwhelmed when Ali had given it to him for Christmas. Especially as he'd asked for *The Godfather* trilogy on DVD. It was still flat-packed in its box. And now it was nearly May.

Chapter Twenty-Three

Sam rummaged for her ringing mobile, currently missing in action along with the TV remote control in the folds of her duvet. The warm pile of cat on her stomach was more comforting than any hot water bottle.

'Hello?'

'Sam? Thank God. Are you still in bed?'

Bleary-eyed, Sam studied the debris surrounding her sofa island. EJ was sounding very awake.

'Not exactly.'

'It's twelve-thirty.'

'It is?'

'Oh, no. I haven't interrupted anything, have I?'

'Hardly.'

'Do I detect a little trouble in the love-nest?'

'Not even a love twig at the moment.'

'So you're at home?'

'Yup.'

'Then get up and let me in. I'll be there in two minutes.'

'What's wrong?'

'I think I may be about to have a few regrets.'

'What?'

Too late. Sam hauled herself to her feet and padded to the door.

'Jesus, Sam, this looks like a scene from *Apocalypse Yesterday…*'

Embarrassed, she followed EJ's gaze as it lurched from pizza box to salsa jar to Coke can, to Ben & Jerry's tub, to wine bottle—all empty.

'Did you sleep on the sofa?'

Sam nodded. 'Don't worry. It was justified. It was a truly shitty day. And you'll be pleased to know that I have the morning-after-the-night-before headache to prove it.'

'Why didn't you call me?' EJ opened the blinds and lifted the sash windows. 'When will you learn that you have to phone for help? And, just for the record, Expressly Pizza doesn't count.'

'Sometimes I think it's good to wallow.'

'Well, whatever it is, I can pretty confidently state that my crisis is bigger than yours.'

'Can you, now?' Sam folded her arms. The challenge was on. Not that she was competitive or anything. 'Go for it.'

'Nick left me a message yesterday…'

Sam nodded. Men were bad for your health. It was official.

'I ignored it, obviously…'

'Good girl.'

'But then half an hour ago I got a call from his lawyers.'

'And?'

'Not good.' EJ frowned. 'The Sunday tabloids are running a story on him tomorrow.'

'Just on him?'

EJ shook her head slowly. 'Nope. As I think you predicted would happen, many months ago, someone has finally sold a story on his infidelities.'

Sam's eyes widened. 'How many are we talking?'

'No idea. And what's worse is…' To Sam's admiration EJ was

projecting calm resignation. There wasn't even a hint of hysteria. '…I don't even know if that makes it worse or better.'

'Depends who the others are.'

'I know you never approved of my behaviour over Nick.'

'I never said…'

'You didn't have to. But I really do appreciate you being here for me. And not just today.' EJ shook her head, a wry smile insinuating that she couldn't believe it was all really happening. 'I can't see the senior partners being too impressed. You were so right. And to think I thought I could handle everything. I mean, who the hell do I think I am?'

Sam was shocked at EJ's submission. She was the one person Sam expected to retain control at all times. Yet now it was over to her, and for once she wasn't sure she was up to the challenge. 'You knew there was always going to be a risk.'

EJ nodded. 'But I didn't really think it through. Silly prick must have made a huge error of judgement somewhere down the line. I bet he was caught with some teenage wannabe.'

Sam's focus was returning. 'I bloody well hope so.'

'Sorry, honey? You lost me there.'

'And I had so been hoping that today was going to be an improvement on yesterday…' Sam covered her eyes with her hands and shook her head. 'Look, promise me you won't freak out—' she knew it was a lot to ask '—but there's something you should know.'

'Go on.'

'The thing is…stay there.'

Puzzled, EJ watched as Sam rushed out of the room and returned moments later clutching her briefcase.

'What is the matter with you today?'

'Your problem.' Sam took a deep breath before continuing solemnly. 'I think *I* might be your problem.'

EJ sighed. 'I knew what I was doing. I just picked the wrong man.'

'No, *I* did. And you picked the wrong friend. I'm so sorry.' Sam could feel every breath becoming shallower. 'When Ben saw you and Nick chatting at Sophie's wedding he must have had all the evidence he needed. I can't believe I thought this would all blow over.'

'Hello? What's with the cryptic chit-chat? You lost me about a minute ago.'

'He's been using me to get this story.' Sam was muttering to herself.

'Stop right there, conspiracy woman. You're a corporate lawyer. Just how much imagination do you think you have?'

Sam retrieved her bag and, opening it, handed EJ the copy. 'It's all in there—read it.'

'Look, I don't know if you were listening two minutes ago, but I've got an impending state of emergency on my hands and you're suggesting I read something? This really isn't the time.'

'I think you should take a look.'

'What is it?'

'My diary. He must have copied it before he brought it back. I should have listened to Sophie. She's always bloody right.'

'Brought it…? Why do I feel I have been left out of the loop here?'

Freshly showered, Sam topped up EJ's mug of tea. There were pages strewn everywhere.

'See?'

EJ looked up. 'I can't believe you didn't tell me.'

'I'm so sorry.'

'Not that I could have done anything, really…'

Sam was sitting on the floor now, her shoulders slumped in defeat.

'Look, enough with the big eyes. Don't worry.'

'How can you say that?'

'What is up with you today?'

Sam shrugged. 'I'm not sure any more.'

'Honey. Hand on heart, we're fine. I'm hardly going to stop talking to you or anything.'

Sam nodded.

'I put you in a very difficult situation.'

'But I've let you down. I can't believe this is all my fault.'

'Despite your determination to assume full culpability, if—and I mean if—Ben is somehow behind this, it still doesn't explain how he would have known there were other women…'

'That's his job, isn't it?'

'According to you he's only known for a week, and you've been pretty discreet in here.'

Sam proffered another handful of pages. 'Don't forget he's had this since the end of March.'

'But Nick has lots of enemies. I mean, even if Ben had worked this out, what's his motivation?'

'Money? A story like this must be worth quite a bit.'

EJ wasn't convinced. 'I just don't see it. But we could speculate for hours. There's only one way to get to the bottom of this. You're not going to like it, but you need to call him.'

'Are you out of your mind?'

'Why not?'

Sam inspected the lines on the palm of her hand. 'I'm not speaking to him.'

'Did you two have a fight?'

'Hello? He photocopied my diary…'

'So he can use a photocopier? Big deal.'

'It's a huge deal.' For a moment Sam wondered if she was being unreasonable. It was only a moment.

'And what did he have to say for himself?'

'Nothing.'

'But you have spoken to him about this…Sam?'

Sam moved on to a detailed study of her nail-beds. 'I didn't know what to say. I told him there was a Dad-related emergency and left.'

'You can't spend your life avoiding confrontation.'

'I'd managed until yesterday.'

'Sam…'

'I know.' Her voice was a small one. The drama queen within was departing, stage left. 'It was just an instinctive reaction. I was shocked.'

'When did all this happen?'

'Last night.'

'So you ran away?'

'I walked. I needed time to think.'

EJ shook her head. 'And he didn't come over and see you?'

'He thought I was with Dad.'

'It didn't occur to him that the diary thing might have upset you?'

Maybe Ben wasn't so astute after all. And in the absence of her own problems maybe she would have been giving Sam a bit more sympathy. But there'd be plenty of time for that later.

'He doesn't know I know.'

'Come again?'

'He wasn't in the room when I found it.'

'Where was it?'

'In the bottom drawer of his desk.'

'And where exactly was he when you were going through his desk drawers? Napping? Cooking dinner?'

'In a meeting. I was bored.'

'In a meeting…?' EJ's voice crescendoed. 'You went through his desk drawers at work? In his office?'

Sam had to admit that out loud it didn't sound very good. Now, thanks to EJ, she'd gone from victim to errant schoolgirl in under five minutes.

'I was just looking for some paper.'

'A likely story, your honour.'

Now EJ was shaking her head. And Sam hated letting other people down. It was so much harder than just disappointing herself. But she definitely had a case, even if EJ was refusing to acknowledge it at the moment.

'I was, and then I saw a bundle…'

'Blank paper often coming in bundle form, of course… You stole this.'

'It's *my* diary.' Sam's defences had reappeared at Fort Knox levels.

'He found a diary. He read it. I mean, who wouldn't?'

'I wouldn't.'

'Of course not. St Sam of Battersea, guardian of all privacy, model citizen. Well, I hate to disappoint you but I definitely would have.'

'You would?'

'Of course—and I probably wouldn't admit it either. In fact, good news: despite his taste in T-shirts, Ben is in fact normal.'

'It's just I can't help feeling now that ever since I met him he's been manipulating me.'

'Do you really think he'd go to all this trouble if he wasn't genuinely interested?'

'Maybe it's like some social experiment. Maybe I'm just research?'

'That is such baloney. He probably can't even spell anthropologist. He's just a guy who read about a girl, liked what he read, and followed her to London to find out more.'

'And took a copy in case he forgot.'

'Be negative, if you like.'

'Well he didn't "follow me" to London. He lives here. And if he hadn't stolen my diary in the first place—'

'You lost it. He found it. He brought it back.'

'I've never felt so violated and exposed.'

'Then you absolutely, positively should not be writing a diary. Or you should be burning the pages on a daily basis.'

'Too late now. And now look what I've done. Look at *your* mess.'

'I knew I was taking a risk when I got involved with Nick…'

'And to think I had the audacity to question your judgement of character.'

'There's really no need to get hysterical.'

'Don't you at least want to hit me or something?'

'Carry on with this self-flagellation and I might just be tempted.' EJ looked Sam in the eye. 'Will you just stop with the guilt? I just can't get my head round what I was thinking.'

'You weren't. You were having great sex.'

'Even so, it's interesting…I mean, why didn't I listen to you…?' EJ walked to the window and watched the people coming and going on the pavement below, their weekends intact. 'It's almost as if I'm addicted to the risk involved. You're not like that.'

'Hey, we're fighters. This will all sort itself out.'

'Maybe I just want to relinquish control. Maybe that's what all this was about. My therapist would probably say—'

'You need to stay calm. We need to sit tight and wait and see.'

EJ smiled. 'Nerves of steel.'

'It's what we were trained to do.'

'We're lawyers, not samurai.'

'And it looks like we might both be unemployed by Monday…'

EJ spun round just in time to catch Sam's return to the crisis position.

'I told you—yesterday was appalling.'

Ben was worried. It was more than twenty-four hours and he still hadn't heard a thing. Nor had she responded telephonically, electronically or textually to any of his attempts to get in touch. If she was in the middle of a family crisis she wouldn't be calling for help. And he knew not to take that personally. He'd been fortunate enough to read the manual. But he couldn't help feeling that it was definitely one of those occasions when no news was not good news. He decided to put his research skills to the test.

'Good evening—Royal Marsden.'

Ben assumed his best-spoken, best-educated and most authoritative voice.

'Ah, hello, I don't know if you can help me, but I'm trying to find out whether you have a Mr Robert Washington with you at the moment.' In his head he was sounding scarily like his father.

'Can you hold for a moment? Thank you.'

Ben surfed his muted music channels as Vivaldi's *Four Seasons* gushed through the handset.

'Hello? Robert Washington.' The voice was weary but familiar.

Ben froze. Robert was very much admitted, very much alive, very much disturbed, and now very much waiting for him to say something. He resisted the overwhelming urge to hang up and decided to bite the bullet.

'Hello, sir.' Alone in his flat, Ben turned the TV off and got to his feet.

'Who is this?'

'Ben—Ben Fisher.'

'Who?'

Hanging up would have been much easier.

'I'm sorry to bother you. I didn't actually ask to be put through…' He was pacing.

'Do I know you? You'd better not be trying to sell me anything.'

'We met briefly at Sam's birthday dinner.' This was a nightmare. Well an eveningmare, painfully real-time and not over yet.

A pause.

'The surfer?'

'No.'

Maybe they could be accidentally cut off?

'The late arrival?'

Ben was glad he'd made such a favourable impression.

'Yup. Look, I'm terribly sorry to bother you. I didn't actually want to speak to you…'

'So you said earlier. Top tip, though—if you don't want to speak to people always best not to call them.'

A semblance of a joke from Robert. Ben was far too on edge to smile, let alone laugh. How on earth was he going to explain this moment to Sam?

'Um, I was just calling to see if you were…' This was useless. 'How are you?'

'Well, I'm here, so I think we can all safely assume that I'm not so good…'

Ben couldn't believe this. He was never put through to people when his life depended on it, and yet now…

'But room service isn't bad—although if I'm dying I don't quite see why I have to have all these tests…'

'There may be something more they can do. I think you have to explore every avenue. For everyone's sake.'

A grunt. He was sure Robert didn't give a toss about his opinion on the matter. Fathers never really liked their daughters' suitors at the best of times. Least of all, Ben suspected, when they were calling them in hospital and telling them what to do.

'Sorry, I'll get to the point. This is probably going to sound a little strange, but you haven't seen your daughter since last weekend, have you?'

A throaty chuckle and a cough from Robert's end. It sounded as if he was enjoying this. 'Is my daughter giving you the runaround?'

'No. Well—maybe… Apparently so. She said she was coming to see you last night and I was concerned that something terrible had happened. But you haven't seen her all weekend?'

'No…'

Ben's worry was rapidly mutating to anger and humiliation. Not a winning combination.

'Or rather, she may have come to see me last night but I was at the cinema.'

'Well, I'm very sorry to bother you. Really. I'd better let you get on.'

'Yup, well, I've got quite a busy evening ahead of me, as you can imagine.'

'Okay—rephrase that. I'd better get on.' Ben looked around his flat.

'Ben?'

'Yes, sir?'

'Robert will do nicely. Rob or Bert, on the other hand, are likely to end with instant dialling tone.'

'Right—got it, si…Robert.'

'Excellent. Now, for God's sake don't tell Sam I've said this, or my life expectancy may be reduced even further, and I honestly promise I don't know what she's playing at, but she's not as tough as she'd like you to think she is.'

'I know, and I'm not. I mean, she's not…' It was too complicated. Ben decided to quit while he was ahead. 'Anyway, I'm sorry to have bothered you, and please don't worry. It looks like a case of crossed wires.'

'Or misinformation.'

'A misunderstanding.' Ben wasn't sure why he was standing up for Sam.

'Well, what do I know? But it's Saturday night and you're on the phone to me while she's clearly somewhere else…'

A good point, if perhaps a little too blunt for this evening's state of mind.

'And I take it we didn't have this conversation?'

'Well, if you don't mind—it would probably be easiest for me. I am hoping to pin her down eventually.' Ben slapped his forehead. Pin her down? To her father? It wasn't even worth thinking about.

'Ben who?'

'Fisher.'

'No, Ben who?'

'Oh, I get it. Good one.'

Hanging up, Ben found himself standing face to face with his wine rack. It was a sign. One bottle, one glass, one man and one DVD-player. *Escape from Reality.* In a sitting room near you…now.

Chapter Twenty-Four

Sam watched as a stream of black cabs delivered culturally sated passengers to Waterloo in time for their last trains. Sitting in EJ's car, she was feeling very *Thelma & Louise.* Except it was raining, the roof was firmly in place, she didn't have a gun and, most disappointingly of all, there was no trace of Brad Pitt on the back seat.

Continuing her people-watching via the rearview mirror, EJ finally came into view, clutching a pile of first edition newsprint which she thrust at her passenger before accelerating away. Sam started leafing through the papers—sleaziest first—reading titbits aloud. Kiss and tell was big business.

'*"YOU'VE BEEN NICKED…Charity record boss gets caught with his pants down."*'

EJ swerved as she tried to see if there was a photo.

'Don't worry. Just some blonde. You know—big tits, big lips, the usual clichés. I thought he'd be more discerning.'

'You thought…'

'Look, you just concentrate on the driving thing. There'll

be plenty of time to pore over these articles syllable by syllable when we get back to yours. And we've got a good eight to ten hours before most of the UK will be reading all about it. That's more than enough time for us to plot our route.'

'I keep telling you, we're not running away…'

'Shame. I could do with a holiday—and life's so much easier when you're sun-kissed.'

'Well, I'm glad to see you've perked up since this morning. I guess if one of us can remain positive at all times that's a start… Hey, this is no time to go all quiet on me. What have you found…? Sam?'

EJ stole a glance. Sam's currently grim expression wasn't doing wonders for her confidence levels.

'Sam? Right—that's it. I'm pulling over now….' A cacophony of horns as EJ took the most direct route to the kerb.

'*"ANGEL GABRIEL FALLS FROM GRACE. Real Records boss Nick Gabriel is exposed as the latest love-rat in the public eye. Today his pregnant wife Masie and their two other children are staying with family while we bring you the story he must have hoped would never get out. We talk to THREE WOMEN about their STEAMY encounters with the man who has always claimed to put his FAMILY first. Full story and pictures on pages 2,3,4,5,9 & 10…*" Well, I guess at least they've got three pages of other news.'

'And no one's asked me for my side of the story…which must be good, right?'

'Right.' Sam scanned the pages for a mention. 'And it looks like you're not named in this one.'

Relieved, EJ pulled off and rejoined the main stream of traffic.

'Plus, I think we may have the source. Some muso with an axe to grind.' Sam smiled as she was proved right. 'I knew it. *"Jake Jones, a former Real Records artist, speaking to us yesterday from his London base, revealed that…"*'

EJ slammed on the brakes as she realised the light ahead was red. 'Jake Jones?'

'Oh, Lord, don't tell me you know him too?'

EJ shook her head. 'Not really.'

'Not really?'

'Well, not in the Biblical sense. But Nick is so going to regret dropping him from the label after the merger. No golden goodbye and no talent. The boy is bound to be bitter.'

'Well, according to this paper…"*his girlfriend, soap star Courtney Craven, is amongst those Nick Gabriel has tried to take advantage of on his meteoric rise to the top.*"'

'Who the fuck is Courtney Craven? What is this? Dating by alliteration?'

'Sounds like a match made in a PR department—I don't think I've ever seen so much make-up…and that's on both of them.'

'I'd heard a rumour that Jake was gay…and Nick never mentioned a Courtney. Scrap that last comment. I know—I know it was a stupid thing to say. Just ignore it. Attribute it to stress. Anything you like.'

Sam nodded as she continued reading. In her opinion EJ deserved a special award for rationale in the face of adversity. 'And guess what? Mr Jones doesn't have a record deal at the moment…'

'I'm sure the last article I read said he was lined up for some teen movie.'

'Was. But not anymore, according to this feature.'

'Well, that would explain all this. So, let's see this Courtney bimbo-tart-bitch, then…' EJ leaned across for a better look at the pictures.

A Mini Cooper screeched past them on the inside, an extreme bassline vibrating their chassis as well as its own.

'EJ—road now. Papers later.'

'What is it with everyone tonight?' Accelerating past the Mini at the next lights, EJ cast a smug smile to her left while Sam pretended not to have noticed. Satisfied she was once again queen of the road, EJ was ready for more.

'What's next…?'

Sam shook her head as subconsciously she checked her seat belt was firmly fastened. 'No way. No more tabloids until we get home.'

Chapter Twenty-Five

'Thanks for staying over.'

'The very least I could do.' Sam felt like a breakfast TV host as she plucked another paper from the array on the table. She'd never been so up to date on current affairs.

'I just can't believe my luck. I promise I'll be a good girl from now on.'

'Don't make promises you can't keep.'

'Nope, this is the new me. I'm going to take a leaf out of your book.'

'The one where I threaten my boss, or the one where I fall for the guy with a photocopying fetish?'

'See—I knew you'd be able to laugh about this… Is that your phone ringing?'

Sam's heart-rate doubled as she saw the name on the screen.

'Dad? Hello? Daddy…are you okay?'

'Fine, darling, fine.'

EJ smiled to herself. Of course he was fine. Dead people didn't use mobile phones.

'Where are you?'

'My South Ken base.'

Of course. It was today. Sam hadn't forgotten. She just hadn't remembered yet. 'And the tests?'

'Are due to be happening tomorrow.' Robert coughed.

'What's that?'

'A cough.'

'Are you sure that's all?'

'Yes.'

'Will you mention it to the oncologist?'

'Will you try and be a bit less bossy? So, how's life?'

'Good.'

'Sure? You sound a bit stressed out.'

'You, on the other hand, are sounding very chirpy.' Sam said it almost accusatorily.

'That's good, though, isn't it?'

'If I knew you better I'd say you were up to something.'

'Me? How ridiculous. Although I did just want to let you know that I had a phone call from your Ben chap last night.'

'What?'

'Now, you didn't hear it from me but—'

'He called you?'

'The thing is, I'm definitely not supposed to tell you I've spoken to him. But he did sound a bit worried. So if you've decided, in your infinite wisdom and experience, that he's too nice, or too clingy, or whatever it is that you women don't want today, then please do the decent thing and tell him. I know I'm hardly one to dole out relationship advice, and I know you'd probably rather learn from your own mistakes, so feel free to ignore me—but I just thought I'd let you know.'

'What the hell did he want?'

'Keep calm, darling...no wonder he suggested I didn't say anything.'

'He rang you and then told you not to tell me?' Sam tried not to sound hysterical.

'Actually, that might have been my idea. I can't remember. Anyway, he wasn't asking me for your hand in marriage...'

'I should bloody well hope not.'

'You didn't use me as an excuse to stand him up, by any chance?'

'Of course not. As if I would.' Automatic denial.

'And you're not trying to give him the runaround?'

'Well, I may have told a little white lie. But I didn't think you'd mind.'

'I don't. But in future if you want your story to be watertight it would be better if you told me first. Well, I'd better go. Don't want this mobile phone to go and give me cancer or anything…'

Robert laughed, and Sam might have joined in if she wasn't trying to digest this latest installment in her new soap opera existence.

'Just thought you should be up to date.'

No sooner had Sam rejoined EJ at the kitchen table than her mobile rang again. Sam inspected the screen and, blood simmering, pressed answer. At the other end Ben nearly choked on his sip of coffee. He'd been expecting voicemail again.

'Yes?'

It wasn't the friendliest of openers, but at least she was in one piece.

'Hey, stranger. Where've you been? You haven't returned any of my calls. Not even a text. And I really didn't have you down as that sort of person.'

'Well, maybe you don't know me as well as you think you do.'

'What's that supposed to mean?' Ben hadn't been expecting a fight. Yet one sentence and he was on the ropes. 'Why did you lie to me?'

'Why did *I* lie to *you?*' Sam had lost control of her volume settings. Even she could hear herself screeching. She made amends. A headache was the last thing she needed right now.

'I happen to have it on good authority that your father is alive and well—or at least not any worse. Where were you last night?'

'In.' Her tone was pure acid.

'You're doing it again.' In this mood, he couldn't even remember why he'd wanted to speak to her—now or indeed ever. 'Unless you've spent the weekend moving, you're not answering your home phone.'

'There's no need to be so hostile.'

'I was worried. And now I'm just confused. I don't do games. If you don't want to see me again, just tell me.'

'I don't want to see you again.'

'What?' Kindergarten error. He'd handed her a loaded gun.

'Nothing.' Now she couldn't even follow through. Sam was disgusted with herself.

'I don't understand what's going on.'

'Who the hell do you think you are?'

This wasn't going the way Ben had envisaged at all.

'I'm not trying to keep tabs on you, but when you rushed off on Friday I was really worried about you, about Robert… You looked terrible when you left, and then you didn't return any of my calls. Yet it turns out everything's fine. Everything, that is, except you and me, and I just don't get it…'

'How dare you call him?'

He should have known better. Blood was thicker than water, and Robert's blood was clearly thicker than his own.

'I didn't actually want to speak to him…'

'What? You just thought you'd call the hospital and check he was still alive?'

Well, if you put it that way it didn't sound very nice. But she wasn't far off.

'I was simply—'

'Checking my story? Fact-checking is a bit of a speciality, is it not?'

Ben was baffled. Lesson 2. Never presume you think you know someone after a few weeks, even if you have read their diary. This was the rawest of hostility. She hadn't even apologised, and their horns were now firmly locked. Ben decided to retreat a couple of paces. Verbally at least.

'Sam, you're going to have to help me out, here. I have no idea what's going on in your head at this precise moment.'

'Difficult without the pass notes, is it?'

'Go easy for a minute, will you? I'm just a straightforward sort of guy, and I think I'm owed at least some sort of explanation. You're obviously still not going to tell me where you went on Friday…'.

'I went home.' Sam was tired of lying. She was also tired of this conversation. And so, it appeared, was her phone. The network intervened. Three beeps and he was gone. And this was one occasion when she wouldn't be complaining to her service provider.

'You went ho—?'

Ben stared at his phone in disbelief. Wednesday night: her place, her instigation. Thursday night: his place, mutual decision. Friday morning: cup of tea in bed, toast, e-mail exchange, evening plans…and then?

Time for breakfast and the papers. He needed a dose of escapism, and fast.

'I mean, the resolution on this one is appalling. It could be your mother, for all you can see.'

EJ was still poring over a few grainy photos claiming to be definitive proof that Nick had even paid for sex in the past. '*"The Real Deal"*, my arse. I mean, who even comes up with these headlines?'

'People like Ben. But at least it looks like you've weathered this particular storm.'

'Shhh. Don't tempt fate. There might be more women waiting to be tempted out of the woodwork if the price is right. The press love a bandwagon.'

'But no one has called to offer you money or check facts. When? How often? Favourite techniques…'

'That's quite enough of that, thank you…and, hey, more to the point…'

Sam looked up.

'This means Ben is in the clear.'

'Hardly.' Returning to her paper, Sam didn't miss a beat. 'Oh, my God. Have you seen Courtney's glamour photo in the

World on Sunday? And she says she hasn't had surgery. If those are real, I'm a virgin...'

Ben crunched through his bowl of cereal whilst skimming the pictures on page five. Nick with Masie on their wedding day.

The fairy tale comes true. Nick was said to have stated that he'd never been happier to sign an artist twice.

A PR shot. Nick and Pete with their artists, a circle round today's troublemaker.

Happy families? Empire building with former Real boss and founder Pete Kohn. Pete kept a non-executive seat on the board but Jake Jones is out...and the former golden boy of pop isn't going quietly...

Across London, EJ was fuming at the same piece. 'It's not Nick's fault that Jake's sales were based largely on his pecs. Real Records. Real music. He had to go.'

'Whose side are you on?'

'Mine. But for someone with negligible talent Jake's ego is quite incredible.'

'And you've met him?'

'Just a couple of times at industry parties with Nick.'

'But for some reason you can't have been on his hit-list.'

'As far as he was concerned I was just a lawyer working on the deal.'

Sam raised an eyebrow...

'Well, as far as everyone was concerned...'

...and cleared her throat...

'...apart from you...'

Ben was reading and re-reading. So much for journalistic instinct. No mention of EJ at all. Thank goodness he'd thought twice about running his hypothesis past Sam. Not that things were looking too promising on that front at all this morning. Maybe if he went over to see her in person…? And maybe she was just too high maintenance? What about someone wanting to be with him? Why should he do all the running? In fact, running wasn't such a bad idea…and then he really needed to pop to the office.

Chapter Twenty-Six

Dialling Sam's flat, Ben double-checked his drawer as the blood drained from his face. *Come on, pick up.*

This was his fault. No one else was to blame. There wasn't even a scapegoat on the horizon.

'Hello?'

'Gemma?'

'Ben.'

'Is Sam there?'

'Very well, thanks—and, yes, yesterday was great fun.'

'Sorry, it's just quite urgent.'

'She's not here.'

'Are you sure?'

'Am I sure?'

'I mean, she's not just standing there asking you to say she's out?'

'No. I presumed she was with you.'

'No chance of that.'

'What's going on?'

'There's probably a bounty on my head by now.'

'What have you done?'

'On Friday she came to meet me…' Ben stopped himself. The semantics were irrelevant. 'She found a photocopy of her diary in my desk at work.'

'You had a copy?'

'I know how it looks.'

'You idiot…'

Ben nodded. 'Yup.'

'Look, I'll get her to call you.'

'You can try. She hung up on me earlier. But I didn't know why at that point. I really do need to see her. Can I come over and wait there?'

'I have no idea when she—'

'Thanks—you're a star.'

Ali's squeal would probably have reached Soho from Clapham even without the amplification of a phone.

'I can't believe you are so stupid.'

'Honest to God, I'd forgotten I still had it.'

'Yeah, right. She's going to believe that for, like, no seconds… Who told you in New York you were going to wind up in a mess over this one?'

'Yeah, well, no need to sound so smug. This isn't an "I told you so" moment. It's more "fuck me, what the hell do I do next?" I meant to shred it.'

'You'll be lucky if she doesn't shred you.'

'Seriously, what can I do?'

'Leave the country?'

'I take it David married you for your innate optimism and encouragement in the face of adversity?'

'Well, I'm not sure you're going to be able to wriggle your way out of this one.'

'That's what I love about you. One hundred per cent sympathy.'

'You brought this on yourself.'

Chapter Twenty-Seven

'Hello?'

'In here.'

Wearily Sam headed to the kitchen, to find Gemma at the sink.

'You've tidied up...'

'Well, someone had to. Didn't want Health and Safety coming round. I've never seen anything like it.'

'That's not true.'

'Well, not from you. Coffee? Tea?'

'I'll make a pot. I'd hate to interrupt the moment.'

Gemma was even wearing Marigolds, pretty incongruous with combats and trainers. A truly twenty-first-century urban goddess. Subconsciously, Sam rubbed her eyes to check she wasn't hallucinating.

'Oh, and by the way, there were a couple of messages on the machine from Ben on Friday night...'

She'd meant to delete them. But that would have meant leaving the sofa.

'Has your dad taken a turn for the worse?'

'No.'

'Only it sounded like…'

'How was your weekend?'

'Great.'

'Great? Gossip, please.'

'Later. And only when you stop trying to change the subject.'

Sam faced Gemma. No more secrets.

'Ben made a copy of my diary.'

'Hmm? Sorry, didn't catch that. That kettle is bloody noisy. It's like having a Harrier Jump Jet on the worktop.'

'Ben photocopied my diary before he brought it back that day.'

'No?'

Sam's nod was laden with gravitas. Finally someone was taking this as seriously as she was.

'I was totally floored when I found it on Friday evening. Not that he knows I've got it. We're not really speaking at the moment.'

'He says you hung up on him.'

'I did no such— Hang on, when did you speak to him?'

'Hello, Sam.' A familiar figure appeared in the doorway.

'Ben?' Sam wasn't sure who deserved her death stare first.

Gemma shrugged. 'Sorry, he insisted on waiting for you. And, just for the record, he does know.'

'Sam, I'm so sorry.' Contrite was his new middle name. 'But you should have been honest with me. I had no idea what was wrong.'

Sam turned her attention to Gemma. 'Do you think you could, like, go and tidy your room or something?'

'I'm cleaning the kitchen.'

'I know, and I'm glad, but now is not a good time.'

'Spoilsport.'

'Why don't we go out?' Ben couldn't help feeling that being in public would only be a good thing.

'"We" aren't going anywhere.'

'I'm sure you've been winding yourself up all weekend—

not that I can blame you—but truthfully, I swear on my life, until last week I'd almost forgotten about it. I hadn't meant to keep it...'

'You're going to have to do better than that. And to think you even had the audacity to tell me that you hadn't read it.'

'I definitely admitted to flicking through it, and the second time you asked me I definitely kissed you.'

Not since they'd found the *Titanic* had a salvage operation been so delicately poised.

'Well, you didn't say that you had either.'

'Maybe not in so many words, and I have to say, judging by your reaction, I can't help feeling that perhaps my gut reaction was the right one. I admit it now. I read it. But does it really have to matter?'

'You even fucking photocopied it. And left it in your office. Of course it matters. And I take it you've seen today's papers?'

'Surely you didn't think I was going to—' Ben was shocked 'Is that really what you think of me?'

'Come on—do me a favour... *Sex, Lies & Sellotape,* the "Real Ally McBeal"...inspired by...based on...'

Ben sat down at the kitchen table and motioned for Sam to sit opposite him. 'Sam, listen to me. Over a month ago I found a diary in a drawer. An anonymous diary. I didn't know my life was going to change when I met you. And I only copied it because I didn't want to damage the original. My sister used to write one. I know how important they are.'

'Don't think for a minute that you can sweet talk your way out of this one...' His life had changed since he met her? Sam shook her head. Focus. 'How many copies did you make?'

'Just the one.'

'For all I know it's coming out in paperback next month: *Diary of a Confused Thirty-Nothing.* Hey, it could be quite a moneyspinner. After all—and luckily for EJ—someone got to the heart of the Nick Gabriel story before you got a chance to.'

Ben paused, the childish satisfaction that his hunch had been vindicated totally negated by the situation unfolding before him.

'You're not listening to me.' Ben paused to collect himself. Shouting definitely wasn't going to help. Resuming his explanation in more dulcet tones, he made sure he spoke slowly, hopefully giving Sam enough time to absorb what he was saying. 'I did not steal your diary. You lost it. And I found it. A chain of events that, despite your current mood, I wouldn't want to change. Because the bottom line is, you and I would never have met any other way. And if you put yourself through hell this weekend I'm very sorry. I would've been here on Friday evening if you'd told me what was going on, but it's taken me until three hours ago to work this out.'

Very secretly Sam was impressed that he'd turned up even when he'd known she was at her worst. At least he was a man of action. Brave...or stupid.

'Ali told me to post it back the day I found it...'

'You should have done.'

'Everyone knows that younger brothers don't listen to their older sisters.'

'It would have been the decent thing to do.'

'But I was intrigued. I wanted to meet you.'

'Because you read the diary?'

A rhetorical question? Either way, he decided to ignore it. He was in a deep enough hole already, and for all the shovelling he was doing he didn't seem to be any closer to the surface.

'Look, most women you know might go for this sort of romantic bollocks, but I'd think a lot more of you if you could be honest and admit you were just being nosy. I mean, you even went out with Gemma.'

'I heard that.'

Sam reddened as Gemma reappeared at exactly the wrong moment.

'Sorry, Gem. That came out wrong. You know what I meant...'

'Don't worry. I lied too. Off to my room now. Urgent appointment with my nail file and the Top 40.'

'The fact is, regardless of the details, I trusted you, Ben. And you let me down. Big time.'

'Really, I don't think it needs to be as bad as it looks.'

Sam wasn't listening. She was far too immersed in composing her next sentence.

'It's just not fair. I get to the stage where I think I like you—well, *know* I like you—well, at least I've decided to give it a go—or should I say *had* decided—and it turns out you've been lying to me the whole time…'

Ben resisted the urge for a whoop. Even a mini one. She liked him too.

'Thanks so much for being like everyone else. I should have known better. I do know better. I let my guard down and, boom, as you should know from your background reading, as per usual it all goes wrong.'

'If you'll just give me a second—if I'm allowed to be honest…'

'Well, there's a first time for everything.'

'Look, I admit this situation is all my fault—but, please, at least give me a chance to try and make it up to you.'

Sam simply stared at him.

'I mean, you're bound to be angry.'

'Livid, maybe. Furious, definitely. But, more than that, I'm disappointed.'

Ben was beginning to get the picture, and it wasn't his best angle. 'But deep down you know I'm not a bad guy…'

Silence. New tactic required.

'Anyway, what on earth did you think you were doing, snooping in my personal stuff?'

Sam looked away.

'So it's not like you're perfect either, is it?'

'I was looking for paper.'

'Don't treat me like the village idiot. You were rifling through my personal folders.'

'I was bored.'

'Well, I was bored in New York when I found your notebook. And I didn't know who you were. I could have left it there. I could have thrown it away…'

'You could have handed it in at Reception.'

'And let them all read it…?'

Sam was silent.

'Do you really think none of them would even have taken a look? You're lucky I found it.'

'I know. I mean, you even made sure you had a spare in case you lost the original. Jesus, Ben, don't push your luck.'

Sam pushed her chair back from the table, its legs scraping the tiles noisily. She'd had quite enough for one afternoon. And this was her kitchen.

'This is pointless. Please, just go.'

'Anything else that you helped yourself too? Should I be checking my bank accounts?'

'Don't be ridiculous. I'm not like that.'

'Exactly.'

'What?' Sam wheeled. She must have missed something.

'If we are going to give ourselves a fair chance we have to trust each other.'

'We? What are you? The eternal optimist? I did trust you. And now I don't. And, thinking back to that first morning here, I'm sure you mentioned the *News of the World*.' Sam was talking half to herself. 'You see, I should have known…'

'It was an unfortunate turn of phrase.'

'Very unfortunate.'

'Hey, EJ still hasn't been implicated, and don't think the papers wouldn't like to hear about another one.'

'You wouldn't…?'

'No, I wouldn't. Not everyone has a price, Sam. Life is all about following hunches, taking chances, trusting your own instincts. And the older we get the more our instincts have been honed.'

'So?'

'So, let's take a chance. Start again. No more secrets. No more surprises.'

'Start again? We've only been out a few times.'

'But come on—admit it. It felt right somehow. Like the beginning of something with potential. We'd be mad to let one misunderstanding get in the way.'

'So now this is a mere misunderstanding? And, call me old-fashioned, but I can't help thinking people ought to get to know each other gradually. Yet you had a starter pack.'

'Old-fashioned. Oh, come on, Sam. At our age it's impossible to start a relationship from scratch. Everyone has emotional baggage, whether it's visible or not, and since when has Samantha Washington been afraid of pressure?'

Sam sighed. What was it with everyone and baggage? She could cope with a bit of hand luggage, just not the five-piece matching set.

'Thanks for your concern, but I don't need rescuing. I was doing pretty damn well before you sauntered along.'

'Who said anything about rescuing anyone? But we either have to deal with this and move forward or we might as well give up now…'

Ben's mouth was suddenly dry. Precipitating a decision had not been part of his game plan at all.

'We'd be good together. We just haven't given ourselves a chance. I mean, what about kismet?'

'Maybe Gemma is more your type after all.'

Silence. She really must have been in her room.

'Don't pretend that you haven't thought the same thing.'

'But what do I really know about you?'

'Ask me anything you like. Shoot…'

Give her due diligence and a hostile takeover any day over this. Her head felt as if it was going to explode. She needed a time-out.

'I just… Look, maybe it shouldn't be so hard.' Sam was thinking aloud. 'I want it to be perfect, and now it's like it can't be.'

Ben sighed. 'Why does if feels like you are constantly searching for a reason why we can't work?'

'I'm just saying maybe we can't start again.'

'Or maybe it suits you better to believe that life has dealt you another shitty hand. The bottom line remains that I can't un-tell myself the things I read, so if that's a deal-breaker I guess that's the end of our road.'

Sam hesitated—but, to Ben's dismay, not for very long.

'Well, I guess you'd better go, then.'

'But what about Wednesday night? And Thursday night?'

'Even lawyers make mistakes.'

'I don't want to go.'

'With respect, I just asked you to leave.'

'Then, with respect, I will. Go on, do risk aversion, be on your own. Probably suits you better.'

'I'm just a realist.'

'I don't think I've ever met someone who is so scared.'

Sam was floored. No one had ever called her a coward before.

'Use the diary thing to play the victim if you like. But it doesn't suit you…'

Ben got up. Sam couldn't move.

'And I deserve better. I really had the highest hopes. More fool me. Maybe I should stick to what I know.'

Sam slumped onto the sofa and slowly counted to ten. At three she heard the front door slam, at seven Gemma's opened, and by nine and a half she was no less emotionally disoriented than she had been at one. The Bangles had got it all wrong. Sundays were manic. Mondays were fine. Or at least they'd used to be. Sam sighed and closed her eyes. She hated Sunday evenings.

Chapter Twenty-Eight

Sam reverse-parked before applying what must have been her fourth coat of lipgloss in a transparent attempt to delay leaving her vehicle. She'd never been very good at apologising, but now seemed as good a moment as any to try and improve her skill set. And tomorrow she was on her way.

Ben stood at the bar, a Mojito in each hand, surrounded by bantering colleagues. In an ideal, less stubborn world, he'd be hoping she'd send him an e-mail once she'd calmed down. He was old enough to know better. Despite his attempts to drink positive, never before had a happy hour failed to live up to its promise so spectacularly. Ben downed one of the cocktails, crunching the ice with the mint, before starting on the next. He was only sorry the buy-one-get-one-free offer didn't apply to women. At least that way he'd stand more of a chance. And where was Ali anyway? He still hadn't seen her post-Sam. Eight days and counting. On second thought, maybe still way too soon. He really didn't need to be reminded how foolish he'd been. He'd worked that out all by himself.

* * *

Sam leant on the bell again. For once she'd managed to be fashionably late and he, of course, was fashionably out. But she'd wanted it to be a surprise. And, more to the point, she didn't want to give him an opportunity to tell her not to bother. She could just leave the package. But she was here now. Walking down the front steps, she returned to her car.

'What the hell are you doing?' Ali waited at the front door.

'Shhhh.' Ben peered into the parked car. The driver's window was partially steamed up, and maybe it was a rum-fuelled apparition, but, no, it was definitely her, and she was out cold. Ben tapped on the window with his front door key.

Startled, Sam sat up suddenly and nearly broke a rib as the seat belt pinned her back into her seat. She fumbled for the door handle. Nothing. She was trapped.

Ben pointed at the door lock, depressed almost out of sight.

Sam released it, and herself. So much for surveillance. No wonder detectives always had a cup of coffee to hand. A convoy of thieves in black and white striped T-shirts could have walked past her bonnet with the Crown Jewels in carrier bags and she wouldn't have noticed. She'd been fast asleep. She did her best to disentangle herself with a semblance of finesse and, finally opening the door, feigned awake.

'I take it you were waiting for me?' He was unfeasibly pleased to see her, although some of that was probably down to the cocktails.

'Yup. I wanted to see you.'

'You did?'

'I think this is yours.' Sam stepped to one side to avoid the jet-stream of alcohol fumes emanating from his mouth, and proffered a familiar, now dog-eared bundle. 'And, well, I owe you an apology.'

Ben allowed a little of his negativity to dissipate, but held on to a thin layer for self-protective purposes. She hadn't flung herself into his arms yet. Although he was hoping that the *eau de* ethanol-with-a-hint-of-stale-smoke might have had something to do with that. Searching his jacket pocket, he found a stick of chewing gum and slipped it into his mouth as surreptitiously as possible for someone who had spent the evening downing several cocktails too many.

'Is that her?' A disembodied voice joined them on the pavement.

'Her?' Sam squinted at the source. 'Who is that?' Her stomach knotted. He was pissed and he'd brought a girl home. Great. Typical male recovery underway.

'Ali—Sam. Sam—Ali.'

And Sam had thought she could do trust. She had a long way to go. 'Come on, I brought this for you.'

Ben didn't even want to touch it. 'Please, it's rightfully yours. I should never have…'

'But I don't want…'

'Then please get rid of it. I never want to see it again.'

Sam nodded. She knew the feeling. 'Well, then, I'd better…'

'Will you come in? Just for a coffee, for a chat—I mean, if you're not rushing off?'

'I'd better get… Well, what time is it?' She had to pack. But it was all ready in piles, plus she'd just had a nap.

'Eleven-forty-five.' The speaking clock had been replaced by the speaking sister. 'Ben, toss me the keys. I need to pee and I need to order myself a cab. It's getting late.'

'It's getting late…' Sam repeated the last sentence.

Ali disappeared into the flat.

'I guess I could give her a lift home. She lives in Clapham, doesn't she?'

'Well remembered.' Ben was doing his best to be upbeat. After all, she was there, even if it didn't sound as if she was going to be staying.

But Sam noted the disappointment in his eyes. 'Oh, why not? One for the road.' As if she needed a caffeine fix for the twenty-five-minute road trip ahead of her.

★ ★ ★

'Right, Benj, I'm off. I'll grab a minicab from the firm opposite.'

'If you don't mind waiting while I have a quick drink I'll give you a lift back.'

'Are you crazy?'

'I live in Battersea. It's right around the corner.'

'Well, aside from the fact that I don't think Ben will ever speak to me again if I agree, I think you two need to talk to each other…don't you?'

Sam nodded submissively. Ali was even bossier than she was. No wonder Ben wasn't intimidated by her. He'd grown up with the more advanced version. Important insight #1.

'Good to meet you though. I've heard a lot about you, but—just so you know—I haven't read a thing. My apologies. I thought I'd trained him better… Idiot…' Ali poked her brother as she made her way to the door.

Sam grinned. Ben had never wanted to be an only child more.

'I'll walk you down.'

'Escort me off the premises, you mean…'

'Something like that.'

Sam heard the door to the flat click closed, but the windows were open and she could hear everything.

'Thanks, Ali. Great start.'

'You're both going to have to see the funny side of this eventually if it's going to work out.'

Ben nodded.

'Hey, I've had three more years to suss this stuff out.'

'Night.'

'Night. And hang in there.'

'I'm trying.'

'I know.'

'Text me when you get in.'

'I'm thirty-four.'

'Just do it, or I'll phone and David will wake up.'

'Message received. And one last tip from me: listen. You've said your piece.'

'I could have said it better.'

'Let her go first. You don't want to make a fool of yourself.'

'It's way too late for that.'

'Call me if you need to talk tomorrow.'

'Thanks.'

Ben embraced his littler big sister.

'Love you.'

'Love you too.'

'Text me.'

'Stop nagging.'

'Makes a nice change.'

One floor up, pretending to be immersed in an old magazine, Sam was moved at the warmth of their exchange. She wanted an ally. Or an Ali. Sophie was as good as they got and, updated this morning, post-Maldives, she seemed to be on Ben's side too. Well, at least leaning on his side of the fence at the moment.

'Hi.'

'Hi…'

Sam leapt to her feet as he re-entered the room. She probably should have remained sitting, but she knew she would find the next bit easier if she could wave her arms around a bit.

'I just wanted to say I'm sorry. I overreacted.'

'No, you—'

'Please, don't interrupt. I don't do humble pie very often.'

Ben nodded. His lips were sealed.

'I've been thinking about what you said, and I know I have a lot of room for improvement. But, just for the record, you should never have taken a copy.'

'I know.' Ben shook his head.

'But, then again, there's no harm done. Well, nothing that time won't heal.'

Ben walked over to Sam who was pacing a catwalk into his carpet, and hugged her, stopping her in her tracks. Sam continued talking to his shoulder. It was much easier not having to make eye contact.

'Just so you know, I've decided to go to New York. 3L are

in the process of organising my transfer to our affiliate office, and in the interim I'm going to tie up a few things with my biggest clients and take a holiday. I just wanted to tell you face-to-face—or face-to-shoulder—as opposed to sending you an e-mail. I didn't want you to think I was doing a runner.'

'I appreciate it.' She was going away.

'I'm no coward.'

'I know. You just needed a little nudge.'

Sam stepped back, and just as Ben wondered whether he'd blown it again she smiled.

'Not just a pretty face, are you, Mr Fisher?' His eyes were warm and reassuring.

Ben shrugged. She was cracking; he could feel it 'So, can I ask…?'

'Fire away.' Today she was ready for anything.

'Where does that leave us?'

Well not everything.

'Us?'

Ben's heart sank. This wasn't sounding promising.

She took his hand in hers. 'The thing is, I'm really not the right person to be getting into a relationship now. I mean, look at the state of me.' She let go.

Ben stared. He couldn't see anything wrong. Maybe her trousers were a bit crumpled, but surely that was because they were linen, and because she'd been asleep? He couldn't help feeling that slowly but surely Sam was pulling the rug from under his feet. Metaphorically, of course. In two years Ben hadn't quite got round to getting a rug. It was still on his list of things to do. Along with buying a dishwasher and a few more pictures.

'I'm doing my best but internally I still have a lot of stuff I need to sort out—issues, back-issues, you know the kind of thing. My gut instinct was to trust you and yet I couldn't give you the benefit of the doubt. I think I probably just need some time. Maybe I've been on my own for too long. I don't know.' She didn't.

'Take as long as you like, but let's at least try to do this together. There are no guarantees, but don't close the door on me yet. We've barely started getting to know each other.'

Sam listened. He made it sound so easy. 'I don't think we can.'

'I promise you won't regret it. You can even call my sister for a character reference…'

Sam shook her head, but her expression was a soft one.

'Or my mum. And I've got a copy of my CV around here somewhere. Three A levels, a BA in Broadcast Journalism…'

Sam laughed. 'Sounds like an excuse to watch television for three years.'

'Well, that was definitely part of it.' Ben started rummaging through some papers on his coffee table.

'Ben—stop. This isn't about you. You were right. You do deserve better. It's me that's not ready.'

'I'm not sure that anyone ever is.'

'I need a change. Fresh perspective.'

'Don't you think sometimes life presents an opportunity for a reason? Granted, usually at an incredibly bad time—like when you're married to someone else—in fact there's a statistic that says—' Ben interrupted himself. This was no time for tangential factoids on infidelity. 'I think, well, maybe this is one of them…'

'But I'm no use to anyone unless I sort myself out first.' Sam stopped herself. She was starting to sound like a bad self-help manual. 'And what with Dad and everything it's been a ridiculous month.'

'How is he?'

'Stubborn. I have to get it from somewhere. Although I am letting him pay my hotel bill for the first two weeks while I get myself settled.'

'So he's happy you're going?'

'He thinks some time away would be good for me. He insisted. I told him I could wait, you know, until…' Sam didn't want to think about it. 'But he's e-mail literate, and they do have phones, and I'm only a few hours away.'

'By plane…'

Sam was set to continue, but he silenced her with his eyes.

'And we—I mean, it hasn't all been bad.' Ben cast his line.

'I know.'

A nibble. Too bad. Not that he really approved of fishing for compliments. 'Sam?'

'Yes.'

'I respect what you're trying to do.'

'But…?'

'What do you mean?'

'I can feel a "but" coming…'

'It's just that sometimes you can't map everything out. Life's not a big flip-chart.'

'I have to do this my way.'

Ben nodded. Her mind was made up. 'I do understand. Or at least I'll try to.'

'Thank you.'

'And I do appreciate the personal explanation.'

Sam nodded.

'The thing is…'

Ben's tone had changed.

'…will you stay tonight? Just…no pressure…but I'd really like it if you'd stay.'

Sam hesitated for a split second—or at least Ben thought she did.

'I can't. It wouldn't be right. And, as you know, it wouldn't be me.'

He did.

Unexpectedly—well, from where he was standing, at least—and without warning she took his face in her hands and gave him a kiss. He felt every millisecond of her lips on his.

As she pulled back, her eyes were glassy. 'Thank you for being honest with me. You're a brave man. I needed it. And, I know you know this already, but I had a great time.'

To his utter dismay, it looked as if she was definitely on her way out.

'So is that it? You just disappear…?'

Sam nodded. 'It's for the best.'

* * *

It wasn't until he heard her car start that he fell back into his battered leather armchair, his insides hollow. His phone beeped and for a split second his heart leapt. Then he remembered.

Home. xx

Well, at least one of the women in his life was obedient.

Ben hauled himself to his feet and turned on the radio. Late-night love songs filled the flat for as long as it took Ben to locate his remote control and the 'seek' button. What were single people supposed to listen to after midnight? Eventually he found a station in the midst of an eighties session. Classic hits. That sounded more like him. Music from a bygone era, when life was simpler. When they'd all believed they were invincible. That they were going to change the world and never make a mistake.

Wandering into the kitchen for water, he washed his face under the mixer tap and listened as the DJ announced the next track from yesteryear.

'Taking you back to 1985, here's a man who's still having hits nearly twenty years later. It's Gordon Sumner, Sting to his friends, with a track from the *Dream of the Blue Turtles* album. "If You Love Somebody Set Them Free".'

Drying his face on his T-shirt before pulling his clothes off, Ben got into bed and turned off the lights. He was getting the message.

Chapter Twenty-Nine

'Honestly Sam, that's the last time I go on a honeymoon if this is what happens.'

'I'm sure Mark would be delighted to know you're not planning another one just yet, and anyway I think it's awesome, Soph.'

'It's not that I don't approve, Sam, but selfishly I'm gutted.'

'At least you've got a husband. I've just got…'

Sam stopped staring out of the window and rejoined the discussion on her next step. 'A flat, a cat and a car. And I'm not going for ever.'

'You don't know that. You could meet a handsome man across a crowded Starbucks/at a news-stand/waiting for a cab/on the Staten Island ferry…'

'What would I be doing on the Staten Island ferry?'

'Or maybe the office will have a softball team. You can get one of those gloves and everything. And men look so good in those two-tone baseball T-shirts. Think Rob Lowe in *About Last Night*.'

Sophie giggled. 'Just think Rob Lowe, period.'

'Mrs Butler, may I remind you that, although it hasn't been long, you're now married, as is he. As for you, Ms Cousins, you are incorrigible, indefatigable and insane.'

'And I'd just like to point out she hasn't met any men like that here.' At least EJ was still on her side. And, for once, the quietest of them all.

'But there's something about New York.' Gemma's eyes were shining.

'Says she who is living in London.' The London-based New Yorker had spoken.

Their debate on her future fading into background noise, Sam glanced to her right in a Shepherd's Bushwardly direction as they sped along the Hammersmith flyover. If Sophie noticed she didn't say anything. She should have got a cab. She hated goodbyes. And, thanks to two sickies and a freelancer, she was going to be facing three at once.

EJ had barely said a thing since Kensington. Sam turned and put her hand on her knee. 'You know I feel terrible that I'm deserting you.'

'I'll survive, honey. And with my arch rival in New York at least I can take the London legal scene by the balls. Anyway, as soon as you get settled I'm coming over to stay.'

'We all are.'

'I just hope the apartment I find is big enough, Gem.'

'Oh, so now you don't want me to visit?'

'Of course I do. Now, is there anything else I need to tell you?'

'I'm sure it's all in the house file.'

'You didn't make her a folder?'

'I've always had one, Soph. And, Gem, you will let George sleep on your bed?'

'If there's room…'

Gemma giggled. Sam did her best to join in.

'And—'

'Yes, I know—no sub-letting to randoms I meet at bus stops, however nice they first appear.'

'I was going to say that in emergencies Sophie has a spare set of keys…as does EJ…'

'Stop worrying about everything.'

'But you will call if anything crops up?'

'Of course…'

EJ interrupted them. 'Hey, Sam, I've just had a great idea.'

Sam turned to face EJ, her eyes bright with expectation. 'Go on?'

'How about we run the NY Marathon together in November?'

'Top suggestion.' Not quite the one Sam had been hoping for, but pretty good all the same.

Gem and Sophie exchanged a glance suggesting that 'top' was not the adjective they'd have employed on this occasion. Nor, indeed, at any point on a twenty-six-mile run.

'I've been wanting to since I was a kid, but I've never had anyone to do it with.'

'It'll certainly give my fitness regime a focus.'

'Because you don't have any of that normally?'

'Shut up, Gem.'

Sam returned her attention to EJ.

'And if you're finding the training too hard on your own over here, you could always come and spend a bit more time in New York…'

'You'll be so fine when you get there, and I'll be over soon to visit anyway. So, do we have a deal?'

'Deal.'

Sophie turned to watch the high five happening in her car. 'You two are quite mad.'

'Road, Soph.'

'I'm watching. Hey, Gem, we can go out and cheer…and hold water bottles and sponges and everything.'

'And maybe shop a little bit…?'

'Of course.'

'I was sort of hoping to see you all before November.'

'I thought you were coming back in the summer, to see your dad?'

Sam nodded. 'I only hope he's going to be okay.'

'He's not going to be any worse than if you were here…'

Bless Sophie for her common sense.

'And you can get back overnight if you need to. Come on, Sam, you need this change—and it's not like he's begged you to stay.'

'Quite the reverse.'

'Well, then.'

'And you can't just sit here and wait for him to die. I know the doctors don't see it this way but, he could live for years.'

'And then again...'

'It might happen...'

'It just feels like there's always a catch. A little black cloud, something unresolved.'

'That's adult life.'

'This is all so exciting, Sam. This could be a whole new you.'

'I'm still going to be a lawyer, Gem.' But underneath her low-key veneer and departure day worries lurked a pretty excited woman.

'Hello, 3L?'

'Hi, Melanie? It's Ben Fisher.'

'Ben Fisher?'

'I came in a couple of weeks ago.' Still nothing. 'The moped and jeans guy?'

'Oh, yes.'

'Is she there?' Ben gazed into the middle distance. Emotional limbo seemed to have affected his ability to do anything other than sit at his desk and read the papers. Mid-afternoon and he had nothing to show for today except a completed quick crossword—and he'd cheated.

'She's left.'

Ben squinted at the clock on his phone. 'At four p.m.?'

'Left, left. For New York.'

'Already?'

'She's flying tonight.'

'Tonight?' He hadn't stood a chance. But he had to hand it

to her. When Sam Washington made a decision she bloody well got on with it. Impressive, intimidating, inspiring and imminently departing the UK. Damn.

'When was the last time you spoke to her?'

'Last night…'

Why hadn't she told him? Because it was none of his business any more. Her choice. His reality.

'But you know what she's like…'

Melanie nodded. At least now she knew not to take it personally. Communication was clearly not Sam's forte. Difficult enough if you were her secretary, but far tougher if you were the love interest. Or hoping to be.

Goodbyes over, Sam leant back in her seat as she waited for the plane to push back from the gate, and despite the recent rollercoaster of emotion she felt fresh, imbued with a sense of alertness she'd almost forgotten she could possess. It was a proper adult moment. Hers. And one of infinite possibility.

As the setting sun cast its golden glow on the Tarmac the seat-back television played footage of a plane gliding majestically through an azure sky. But today was about more than transportation. On the drive to the airport she'd realised she'd only moved forty miles due east in the last thirty years. Yet today she was heading west. Ready to discover a new city with the comforts that only a suitcase and an *en suite* bathroom can bring, the learning curve of her twenties finally consigned to the past along with her backpack and sleeping bag. And for the next seven hours she was off life's radar. Incommunicado. She couldn't wait.

Fucking Piccadilly Line. This was no time for signal problems. Racing into Terminal Four, Ben stared at the television listing departures. Top of the screen. He didn't have long. Last call.

He sprinted to the main departure gate, only to be redirected, and, jogging to the BA enquiries desk—unsure of its specific location due to the distinctly unhelpful and intransigent nature of same passport and boarding card official—Ben was already succumbing to a sinking feeling. And a stitch. This never happened in films. And there wasn't even a barrier for him to vault. As for that corridor with the big windows, enabling him to run the length of five football pitches while the plane in question started to taxi into the distance in clear sight of him and all the viewers at home, there wasn't even a sign for it.

Instead he was trapped in departure hell. Queues upon queues stretched between makeshift barriers, a plethora of trolleys laden with luggage swarmed around him as, it appeared, people were intent on wheeling themselves to their final destinations. Doing his utmost to side-step the flocks of travellers in fleeces and comfortable shoes, he finally arrived at the desk in question. Yet, while the sense of energy surrounding him was undeniable, he had apparently stumbled into a pocket of inertia. A queue of three. One counter. One employee. No hurry. Eight long minutes later, he finally got to speak to a real person.

'Good evening sir, how can I help you?'

'HasBA179forJFKactuallyleftyet?' Ben's pent-up frustration and urgency was apparently manifesting itself in the speed of his sentence delivery. He paused for breath. 'Only I have an urgent parcel for one of the passengers and I wondered if I could get it to her before the flight departed.'

'Which flight did you say it was?'

Ben was sure the woman was speaking deliberately slowly. No wonder they didn't let passengers pack sharp items in their hand luggage.

'BA 179.'

Ben did his best to remain cheery, despite the fact that a ninety-year-old woman could have entered the information into the computer more quickly.

'To?'

'To New York—JFK.'

'To J-F-K from L-H-R.' She spoke as she typed the codes into a console in front of her. Slowly, deliberately and carefully, so as not to make any mistakes or chip her very red and very long nails.

'I think you're too late, but hang on and I'll check with the dispatcher at the gate for you…' Finally she picked up a phone.

'Sean? It's Faye. Is 179 closed? Right… Right… Only I've got a passenger here…'

'I'm not a passenger.'

Faye put her hand over the receiver. 'I'm sorry? Did you say you're not a passenger?'

'That's correct. As I said when I arrived at this desk—' keep calm, be polite, this was no time to alienate perhaps the last person who could help him today '—I simply want to get an envelope to one of the passengers already on board the flight.'

'So you don't have your own ticket?'

'No.'

'Well, I'm afraid we can't let you through, then.'

'I don't expect to be let through, I just wondered if someone could give this—' Ben thrust the envelope at her '—to someone on board, or whether it's too late.' His patience was wearing as thin as her lip pencil.

'What is it?'

'Documents. She's a lawyer and she needs to have these with her.'

'And you are…?'

'A colleague.' This was proving difficult enough without bringing in elements of the truth.

'You don't look much like a lawyer.'

'It's dress-down Tuesday.'

'Well, as you can see from the screens, I'm afraid the flight is closed.'

'But has it actually left?'

'Yes.' Faye's patronising nod was reminiscent of a 1950s children's television presenter. 'It pushed back five minutes ago. Should be taking off—' Faye consulted her screen and her watch '—right about now. You'll have to courier the documents. They shouldn't be there that long after the passenger. You can probably still get them on a later flight tonight.'

'Thanks.'

Fed Ex would have been great, if he knew where she was staying, but New York was hardly a one-hotel town. Despondent, Ben made his way back to the tube station. Proactivity was overrated. He had tried and he had failed. Probably worse than not having tried at all. He should have listened to Sting. But then again, he was the man who'd also told people to let their souls be their pilots…and to put messages in bottles. Life could be very confusing.

Chapter Thirty

Sam jogged anti-clockwise around the reservoir in Central Park and, breathing heavily, drank in the view while the other runners stared resolutely into the back of the person in front, apparently unaffected by or unaware of the dramatic skyline surrounding them. She couldn't believe she'd ever be able to take it in her stride. Plus, it was a perfect high-pressure morning. The air temperature in the park was still cool enough to be refreshing, and the hum of traffic on Fifth Avenue was almost entirely masked by the immediate crunch of regular footfall on gravel.

Gemma was right. Relocating, not running away. New challenges. New faces. New bloody York. And no plans for the day. Her credit cards hadn't had a decent workout in months, and in about twenty minutes she'd have finished hers for the day.

'Oh, good.' Robert sat up a little straighter. 'I do like it when you call. Usually means something is going to happen, one way or another.'

'You know I wouldn't be calling you unless it was an emergency…'

Ben could have kicked himself. For some reason telephone conversations with Robert brought out the gauche in him.

'I mean, I wouldn't want to be disturbing you or anything…'

'Yes, yes—get on with it.'

'How are you doing?'

'Well.' Robert sighed. 'My best. Not sure for once that it's good enough, but we'll see.'

Ben paused. They'd only spoken a few times, but this whiff of negativity was a first.

'Anyway, come on. This little soap opera keeps me going. What's she done now? In fact, I'm not even sure she's speaking to you.'

'She came to see me on Monday night.'

'Well, that's something.' Robert didn't sound overwhelmingly encouraging.

'I know I screwed up.'

'Don't be too hard on yourself. Life's a bitch sometimes. Believe me, I know.'

'And now she's gone to New York.'

'About bloody time. That girl has spent thirty years being far too responsible about everyone and everything but herself. She should have thrown her life up in the air and watched to see where it landed a long time ago. And some of that, regretably, I fear is my fault.'

'Um, I don't suppose you know where she's staying, do you?'

'Like I'm going to tell you.'

'I only want to send her a letter. I was up half the night writing it on Monday, and I wanted to give it to her before she left.'

'Well, you're a day late.'

'I know. But she mentioned to me that you were very generously sponsoring her first couple of weeks.'

'Just until she gets settled.'

'I only need her address. That's all.'

'This letter…it's not going to upset her again, is it?'

'I sincerely hope not.'

'Only, I don't think you've got too many lives left.' Robert laughed, a dry rasping, breathless laugh. 'Look…'

His breathing was laboured today, and Ben felt angry on his behalf. That his body had started to let him down when his mind was still razor-sharp. Not that Robert was the sort to complain.

'…I like you, but I'm not the one you're trying to impress. Just take a tip from an old softie at heart. Girls like the personal touch.'

'Exactly—which is why I thought a handwritten letter would be a good idea.'

'And I thought you were supposed to be creative. Anyway, she's staying at the Hudson.'

Ben smiled into the receiver. The Hudson was hardly an ashram, but then Sam was new to this self-exploration lark. And it was difficult to be intrepid with an iMac.

'Thank you so much.'

'My pleasure. Best of luck, and I hope you find what you're looking for.'

Laden with carrier bags, Sam strutted up Fifth Avenue, humming to herself. Pausing for a breath, she turned to face downtown, taking in the view as the still faint blue corners of the sky faded into orange and then to blackness. Night was falling from street level upwards. And Ol' Blue Eyes could forget Chicago, *this* was her kind of town. She didn't have a meeting with the office until Friday, but tomorrow she and the fund boys were having a proper covert lunch. With poached lawyer on the menu. A bath and beauty sleep were the only things that stood between her and her potential.

Ben's mobile rang as he got out of the cab. 'Yup?'

'Sorry to call so late.'

'Gemma?'

'Thanks so much for the message, and I'm sorry I didn't get back to you sooner.'

'No problem. They're in urgent need of a production secretary, so I'm sure they'll be in touch.'

'Wow.'

'Now, don't get over-excited. It's pretty mundane. I just wanted to make sure you had the heads-up for when they call.'

'I'll be the best one they've ever had.'

'I'm sure you will. Just view it as a stepping stone to bigger things. They don't pay nearly as well as the City.'

'Sure beats mail-merge.'

'I'm afraid you'll be booking a lot of cabs and ordering stationery, but you should get some other opportunities if you keep your ears open and don't mind doing a few extra hours.'

'Thanks again. I owe you.'

'It's cool. And don't worry about the other thing. It's all under control.' Well, kind of. 'Control' not being the right word for it at all.

'But why did you want to know where she's staying?'

Ben looked up at the understated entrance. It had all made sense when he'd put the phone down.

'Oh, well—you know. I just wanted to send her something.'

'Missing her already?'

'Hey, less sarcasm, if you don't mind. As it happens, she doesn't want to have anything to do with me at the moment.'

'Again?' Gemma wondered whether Sophie or EJ had been updated. 'You didn't have any more skeletons in the cupboard, did you? You hadn't written the screenplay or anything?'

'Don't be ridiculous.'

Ben didn't know why he was laughing. It was no more ridiculous than flying across the Atlantic on a whim. He'd never got on a plane without a suitcase before. And his life was so not big budget enough. Credit cards were a dangerous invention. He had felt excited all the way over. Only now, *in situ,* he realised he hadn't thought this through at all. Hollywood had a lot to answer for. There was never any hanging around in films. Days took minutes.

'I thought she apologised?'

'She did.'

'And?'

'And I wanted to try and put it all behind us.'

'Right…'

'But she says she needs her own space…and if she's in New York and I'm in London obviously she's going to have plenty of that.'

'Space is the last thing she needs.'

A convoy of police cars and fire trucks hared down Ninth Avenue. He waited for the sirens to fade into the distance.

'Ben?'

'I'm still here.'

'Still where?'

Ben paused. Only for a fraction of a second, but it was all she needed.

'You're there, aren't you?'

'The thing is…' Ben still couldn't believe that this morning he'd been at work in London.

Gemma squealed. 'Fanfuckingtastic. Just wait until I tell Soph. You're a one, Ben Fisher. She doesn't deserve you.'

'She does. She just hasn't realised yet. Although who says I've earned a second chance…?'

'This is by far the most exciting thing to have happened in years.'

Ben was definitely feeling buoyed by Gemma's unrefined excitement. He was glad she'd called.

'Have you found her yet?'

'I've only just got here. Hey, calm down.' Her energy was infectious. Suddenly this seemed like a great plan. 'I just figured, a guy's got to try. And, worst case scenario, I'll have a couple of days to pound the streets in Nike's latest technology.'

'Eleven out of ten for effort.'

'Thanks.'

'And good luck. Hey, you're like that song.'

'What song?'

'You know—that girl at the piano—sort of Natalie Imbruglia meets Bruce Hornsby and the Range. The one that said she'd walk a thousand miles to see you tonight.'

'If you say so.'

'Come on. You know who I mean.'

'A thousand miles? I thought that was a couple of Scottish blokes?'

'The Proclaimers? No, I'm sure that was ten thousand miles. And I thought you knew your pop?'

'I do. And I'm positive they walked five hundred miles and then five hundred more.'

'So, this is the same sort of sentiment...'

'And the same distance?' Ben was more confused now than he had ever been.

'It's almost a sign.'

Ben sighed. It must have been a girl thing. Or at least a Gemma thing. 'What is this, the "you too can walk your way to true love" hypothesis? And I haven't walked anywhere yet.'

'Stop confusing the issue. I'm trying to remember her name.'

'Do you even know how far a thousand miles is? I mean, I'm wearing trainers and there's no way...'

'Vanessa Carlton—I knew it would come to me eventually. No thanks to you, I might add.' Gemma sighed. No one had ever spontaneously boarded a plane for her. 'And if Sam doesn't come round, feel free to call me...'

Silence.

'Obviously I'm joking—just in case the sarcasm got lost on its way to or from the satellite...'

A laugh. Good.

'I have to confess, Gem, I'm feeling quite nervous. But maybe that's just about my credit card bill. Not being funny, but I'd better get off this phone.'

'Well, fingers crossed.'

'Gemma...?'

'Yup.'

'I know I probably don't have to say this, but you won't tell her I'm here, will you?'

'Course not.'

'Promise me. No sneaky calls. Accidental e-mails. No subtle hints.'

'As if I would.'

'Please. Just let me try and do this my way. Too many people have been involved from the start.'

Gemma sighed. She knew he was right. 'I'll give you twenty-four hours.'

'Forty-eight.'

'Thirty-six.'

'Done.'

'This is so exciting.'

'Not a word.'

'I'll do my best.'

'You'd better.'

Stepping into the minimalist entrance hall from 58th Street, Ben boarded the anonymous escalator and hoped it was going to take him to the lobby.

Having smothered herself in every available complimentary product, bar the shaving balm and applied a face pack, Sam was watching TV in bed, her new clothes de-tagged and ready for next-day action in the wardrobe. She hadn't been this relaxed in months. The remote control was all hers and Room Service was on its way. *Vanity Fair*, *In Style* and *Elle* jostled for attention on her duvet. Bliss. She wasn't sure she had the time or energy for a job any more.

A rap on the door. Dinner time. And so what if it was still early? She was sure the staff at this hotel had seen it all. At least she hadn't ordered hand-picked papaya, a nose job or narcotics. She was, however, resplendent in full purifying face mask.

To Sam's disappointment there was no food yet. Just a hotel employee and a very boring brown A4 envelope. Work. Work. Work. Some holiday. Flinging it on the bed, she headed for the bathroom to rinse her face before her pores got too relaxed.

Ben walked on, his hands in his pockets. As each block gave way to the next he became increasingly numb to his situation.

Mission accomplished. But Gemma's vicarious excitement had long disappeared into the ether, along with his optimism, and with each block he doubted Sam more.

Craving instant company, he hailed a cab and a few bumpy minutes later was ensconced in a bar in the East Village. Time for a few anaesthetising beers before bed. Hell, he was supposed to be on vacation. Well, strictly speaking he was supposed to be in London. It had been a stupidly long day.

Dear Sam
Re: Application for Position of Trusted Companion/Love Interest/Fun Guy to be With
Please accept the enclosed for review. While I understand that there may not be an immediate vacancy for this position, I would appreciate it if you could take a look and at least keep my details on file in the instance that one should one arise.
Should you require any further information, please be aware that I will be available in person at Coffee Shop, Union Square at 16th, on Thursday 10th May between noon and two p.m. (ECT) to answer any questions you may have.
In anticipation,
Ben Fisher
For references please apply to Mrs Alexandra Henderson or Mrs Susan Fisher.
Disclaimer:
Direct communication with either of these parties is likely to result in cross-examination on your knowledge of and intentions toward the applicant (at the very least) or a firm diary date for dinner (highly likely). The candidate cannot in any way take responsibility for either of these eventualities. He knows better.

It would appear Ben had a serious allergy to the postal service. The Atlantic clearly wasn't wide enough to deter a hand-delivery, and while it was the grandest of gestures, just turning up didn't come without a certain amount of pressure. Propped up by a mountain of pillows, Sam started reading the attached pages. At least with a duvet to hand she'd be able to cope with anything. Or at least she was hoping so. She really wasn't quite sure what to expect.

Name: *Benjamin (Ben) Henry Rudolph Fisher*

She smiled. Rudolph. Still, at least it was Rudy, not Randy.

Age: *31*
Birthday: *February 26th*

Sam grabbed *Elle* and flicked through in search of the horoscope page. Apparently that made him a Pisces. Which meant…? And were horoscopes even unisex? Sam peered at the alarm clock and counted forward in her head. Two a.m. in London. Maybe Gemma would be up watching a late-night film. And maybe she could just manage on her own—at least until the morning.

Dual Nationality: *Mother:American. Father: British. Sister: Bossy.*
Currently paying council tax to the London Borough of Hammersmith and Fulham. First eleven years of life spent in New York City.
Qualifications: *10 GCSEs, 3 A-levels. 1 at A Grade, 1 at B Grade, 1 at C Grade.*
Leeds University 2:1 International Broadcast Journalism—honestly not just watching television and listening to the radio in different countries.
Cycling Proficiency Badge
Grade 1 piano (it's a free country, they couldn't force me to practise)
Full UK driving licence.
PADI Diving certificate.

Sam settled back. All pretty straightforward so far.

Bad Habits Include (am sure there are more—referees should be able to help with these):
—Never unscrunching socks before washing them.
—In fact, pretty much wearing every sock I can find (at least once) before washing them.
—Buying expensive trainers.
—Never ironing bedlinen, or really ironing in general—philosophy is to own very little that would need ironing in the first place.
—Watching WWF.

Sam really didn't get that. But lots of ostensibly normal, intelligent people had a soft spot for it.

—Voting for participants in reality TV shows.
—Entering competitions.
—Rarely actually putting a fresh loo roll on the holder.

Whoever said people can't change didn't mean little things like that.

—Hoarding Sunday papers. Hoarding generally.
—Folding over the corners of pages in books instead of using a bookmark.
—Never finishing a cup of coffee.
—Two sugars in a cup of tea.

Desk drawer sugar sachet mystery solved.

—Talking about writing screenplay instead of actually doing it.

Screenplay? Interesting. And hopefully the action wasn't all set at the Playboy Mansion.

—Visiting tanning salons—not regularly, but with dark colouring look much better in winter with light tan. Helps to

avoids green/grey tinge that otherwise seems to develop in depths of British winter.

Hilarious.

—Clipping nails (into bin) while watching television.

The bin element had to be a good thing.

—Sulking when one of my teams loses a game (but only if they played well enough to win it).
—Cheating at Trivial Pursuit—well, if you don't cover the back of the card with your hand, I reckon it's just using your initiative.
—Collecting Christmas Number One singles. Have every one since 1985. I don't regard this as a negative, but past experience has revealed that plenty of people do.

Which meant he had one sleigh bell too many in his music collection.

Good Habits Include (am sure there are more):
—Cooking—house specials include Thai green curry and any sort of pasta with a sauce.

Suddenly Sam was hungrier. How long could it take to make a Club sandwich?

—Washing up (within twenty-four hours of cooking).

Twenty-four hours was far too long to allow bacteria to breed. The man needed a dishwasher.

—Responsible about bill-paying and all things financial. Even have ISA and house file.

There was no way it was going to be as comprehensive as hers.

—Setting the video for multiple recordings—even when on holiday.
—Labelling recorded videos.
—Remembering family birthdays and sending cards appropriately.
—Keeping CDs in alphabetical order by artist. (On reflection maybe this is a bad habit).
—Brushing and flossing teeth 2x day. One filling in thirty-one years can't be bad.

Excellent news. Sam had dismissed many potential suitors on the basis of bad oral hygiene.

—Returning calls when I say I will.
Relationship History:

Sam sat up and crossed her legs, which had already started going to sleep. She didn't have time to deal with cramp now.
Serious exes: Three.
Kirsty Flowers: met age 17. Dated for ten months (doesn't sound that long but it was the whole virginity thing—hers and mine). Now married with two children. No longer in touch, although we did exchange Christmas cards until a couple of years ago. Reason for relationship ending: we grew apart (and were far too young).
Lisa Denton—two years, two months. Met age 24 through friend of friend. Lived together briefly while I was between flats. She ended it (said she needed more space in our relationship. Later discovered that this space was required because she was sleeping with someone else). No longer in touch.
Julia Phillips—Eighteen months. Ended February this year. As previously discussed. We grew apart.
Pet hates in relationships:
—possessiveness.
—not listening.
—not letting me finish my sentence.
—listening to music really quietly.

—not listening to music at all.
—girls who don't eat.
—apathy.
—eyeliner and mascara on white towels.
—the answer 'I don't mind.' when asked about where they would like to eat/sit/go on holiday. It simply can't be true.
Miscellaneous:
—My legs and chest were waxed once as a dare on a stag night—never again—I can summon tears at mere thought.
General quickfire trivia:
Coca Cola or Pepsi? Coca Cola
Star Wars *or* Star Trek? Star Wars
Nike or Adidas? Nike
Crisps or chocolate? Chocolate
Tea or coffee? Coffee in the morning, tea in the afternoon.
Peanut butter or Marmite? Peanut butter. Don't get Marmite.
White wine or red wine? Red wine
Bitter or lager? Lager. Don't understand attraction of warm, flat brown beer.
Theatre or cinema? Cinema. Not a great fan of the subtitle.
Vodka or gin? Vodka
Tonic or soda? Soda
Cats or dogs? Cats in the city. Dogs in the countryside

Sam laughed. So far so good.

Also thought the attached might be of interest. Fair's fair.

New Year's Resolutions:
—Drink less. Or at least have two or three, or one or two, nights a week where drink nothing.
—Work out more, maybe on those nights?
—Be true to self.
—Save money for travel opportunities and plan one major trip every two years.
—Shoot hoops.

—Finish screenplay—if only for personal feeling of accomplishment.
—Never give up.

Monday March 5th

Work, pub, fell asleep watching DVD of The Matrix. *Must learn to not lie down on sofa if want to stay awake.*

Thursday March 8th

Work, thought about going to the gym. Home, thought about cooking, ordered takeaway, worked on screenplay. Really enjoy it when I give myself chance and stop pretending I am too busy/tired/untalented to try. Whole thing is confidence trick. Know tomorrow I will look at it and think it is positively mediocre. Need to move forward in plot rather than revise earlier parts. Can tidy whole thing once it has an end.

Wednesday March 14th

Spoke to Mum and Dad. Spoke to Ali. Booked flight for NY. Haven't been away, just the two of us, for a good ten years. Can't help feeling that might be for a reason. Anyway, she'll be working so should get some time just to hang out alone. Played catch-up at work all day. Met Ali and David in Notting Hill for dinner and then saw a movie at The Electric. This is the future of cinema. Leather armchair, footstool and wine cooler, and no more expensive than Leicester Square. Plus you can park on a yellow line on Portobello Road after six-thirty. I want a season ticket.

Sam smiled to herself and if she'd had a white flag, she'd have waved it. They had all been right. This stuff was mundanely addictive.

Saturday March 24th

Amazing to be in New York. Should come back more often. Strangely familiar and yet different. Ali being surprisingly laid back. Didn't even seem to mind I spent over an hour in Nike-Town. Mind you, she had just done marathon shop in Banana Republic. Diary is gripping. Know I shouldn't really be reading it. Ali freaked when she found out.

Sam knew she'd liked her straight away.

Have decided not to hand it in but to post it when back in London. At least that way, I know it's taken care of.

Wednesday March 28th

Back home. Have yet to post diary. Think will drop it round there tomorrow after work. Know this is probably crazy idea, but fascinated to see how real person lives up to my mental picture. Bound to end up posting it through letterbox, but at least I will have tried and at least it will be done. Over.

And Gemma could so easily have been out.

Tuesday May 8th
two a.m.

Can't sleep. Have been staring at ceiling, listening to the radio. Every song lyric seems to have a message tonight, whichever channel I tune in to. I guess I really thought this was it. A contradiction in her own terms but a perfect conundrum. Three dimensions of complexity, but I'd had privileged, if illegal access to the user guide. At first glance in the flesh she wasn't my type, or at least not a type I had sampled before. On a first meeting you might assume that she is only interested in herself. Probing deeper, there is so much more.

Maybe my mistake was thinking I stood a chance in the first place. But if I don't put myself on the line for her, how can I expect her to do the same for me? We could definitely learn from each other. Yet, conversely, I have never felt so defeated. It's apparently an impossible situation. I've apologised and yet we can't move forward. Or she can't. In my head it all seems so simple. To her it is so complex. Yet, if you peel away the layers, I believe our end goal is the same.

I know I should walk away. But it's not about winning or losing, or even the thrill of the chase. I think I fell in love right before she fell out with me. Now it looks like the most useful thing I can contribute is my absence. If she doesn't trust me, if she doesn't trust herself, I can't see a way out. I can do solid, trustworthy, dependable, and my intentions were good, if poorly executed. I didn't think all this through at the beginning and now I wish I had.

★ ★ ★

Sam checked the envelope thoroughly for more, before shakily liberating a vodka and tonic from the minibar. The see-saw of emotions was making her feel dizzy. A nervous pulse throbbed in her neck and yet there was a hint of a smile starting somewhere in her stomach and slowly making its way to the surface. Re-reading the contents, she started to understand better. And now, when she wanted him to be there, he wasn't. Unless…

The envelope was handwritten. So presumably he must have been in the hotel earlier. She picked up the phone and crossed her fingers.

'Front desk.'

'Good evening. Do you have a Mr Ben Fisher booked in to the hotel this evening?

'One moment, please.'

It was one of the longest moments Sam could remember.

'No one of that name has checked in, and there is no booking listed.'

'Thank you.' As Sam replaced the receiver a wave of disappointment threatened to engulf her room. And it served her right. Although there was nothing disappointing about his behaviour this week

Sam checked the covering letter again. Lunchtime. Same time as 'just call me Harvey'. Could she meet the fund for lunch at twelve and leave by one? Heart versus head. The showdown they'd all been waiting for.

A knock at the door.

Outplayed. He won.

Sam grinned as her heart skipped a beat and she opened the door with a hint of a flirt. 'Do you never, ever give up?'

'Room Service?'

Flushed with embarrassment, Sam waved the waiter in. She wished it was lunchtime.

Chapter Thirty-One

Ben attempted to watch the television suspended in the bar area. Determined to dissolve the tight knot of anticipation in his chest, he sipped at his beer. But after a few minutes of watching the clock in the bottom left-hand corner of the screen he refocused on his magazine. 12:46. He'd said he'd be there until two. But from twelve. And now it was nearly one. This could well end up being the most expensive drink he'd ever had.

'So, you're looking to stay in New York for a while?' Harvey leant back against the high wall of the booth as Sam relied on her legendary will power to prevent her from glancing at her watch. So far there hadn't been a moment to say anything. But they hadn't ordered yet. Just drinks. And the discussion seemed to be shaping up quite well.

'It was time for a change. London was feeling a bit claustrophobic, and as we've got an affiliate office out here it wasn't like I was taking a huge risk.'

'But you'll be doing more of the same?'

'I imagine so. I'll know more when I've met Charles and the

rest of the team tomorrow. I think it's likely to be more of an advisory role—unless, of course, they want to pay for me to do the State Bar. But I doubt they'll want to replicate what they already have.'

'And they'll still let you advise us, I hope?'

'If you request my services, I'll be only too happy to help. I feel like I know you all and your requirements pretty well now.'

Harvey smiled and nodded. 'We're quite keen on keeping you close to hand. The chairman trusts you.'

Sam blushed. 'Thanks. He runs a tight ship.'

'Hey, he takes his money very seriously…and his team.'

'And so he should.'

'And you've never thought about going in-house?'

'The right opportunity has yet to present itself.' Sam felt very cut-and-thrust.

'I think we should keep talking. But let's order.'

Sam picked up the menu, simultaneously glancing at her watch as subtly as she could. One fifteen. And eagle-eyed Harvey had noticed.

'Is there a problem?'

'Of course not.' A counterfeit smile.

'Are you sure…?'

'Of course.'

What did she think she was she playing at?

'Well, actually…' Sam addressed Harvey, not at all sure what she was going to say. This was a whole new experience for her.

13:20—Sam was immediately aware of the digital clock winking at her from the news-stand as she emerged onto the street, a wave of warm air unsettling her after the air-conditioned sanctuary of the restaurant. Yet, standing on the sidewalk, she was frozen in panic as a film of sweat crept up the nape of her neck and the heat haze from the traffic fumes threatened to wreck her perfectly straightened hair.

There was no shortage of cabs, but the traffic was gridlocked as far as the eye could see. The klaxons and sirens only added to her soaring stress levels. Union Square was too far away for a power-walk, not even taking her inappropriate footwear into consideration, and time was running out. She had to move fast. Or at least shrug off the paralysis that was threatening to steal the moment from her.

Grabbing the letter from her briefcase, Sam sprinted to the nearest payphone and prayed it was working. Having obtained the number, she found a quarter in her purse and dialled. 13:24.

'Cwarffee Sharp?'

'Hello?' Sam could barely hear a thing. She pressed a hand over her other ear to try and improve the situation, even though the noise was all at the other end. 'Hello…?' Dial tone. Sam crashed the receiver back to its base as, swearing, she searched for more change.

This time, closing her eyes to focus her hearing, she felt sure that the other pedestrians thought she was in some sort of prayer to a telecommunications guru.

'Cwarffee Sharp?'

'Hello? I need your help.' Sam was shouting. She didn't care. 'I'm looking for Ben Fisher. He should be there, waiting for me.'

'I don't know, ma'am. It's lunchtime, we're busy. Thanks for call—'

'Please, don't hang up.'

No dial tone. She must have sounded desperate enough. Sam continued tentatively.

'I've got a meeting with him. Or at least I'm late for our meeting. I need to get a message to him. It's urgent.'

'Well, I guess I can take a quick look. What's his name?'

Sam pictured him in her mind.

'Ma'am?'

'Ben Fisher. Dark hair. Greeny-blue eyes. He'll be sitting on his own. Take him a beer. And tell him he's got the job. That's really important.'

'Ben. Dark. Got the job.' She repeated it slowly.

'Yup. He's hired.'

'R-i-i-ight. So, Ben's hired.'

Sam couldn't help feeling that the waitress wasn't taking this very seriously.

'Tell him to wait. I'll be there as soon as I can.'

The line went dead. Sam had only the vaguest idea of where she was in relation to where she was going, or of who she was any more. Rummaging in her briefcase for her mini city guide, she squinted at the subway map and, already walking to save time, headed in what appeared to be a good direction. A few moments later she walked past the same spot facing the opposite way, her finger planted firmly on the map. She only hoped the New York Subway was more efficient that the London Underground.

The waitress looked round the busy joint. There was a cluster of men watching the television, plenty on their own, but peering into the table area and there was only one guy, and he was kind of cute-looking—if you liked that sort of thing.

'You Ben Fisher?'

Ben looked up at the accusation and nodded. His insides felt like pâté. This didn't sound like good news.

'Some Brit chick just called.'

He couldn't believe she wasn't even going to come in person. He concentrated on keeping all salt water away from his eye area. He was a guy. He could do that sort of thing.

'She sounded stressed-out, man. Anyway, she said she'd be with you as soon as she can.'

'She did?'

'Uh-huh.'

'Are you sure?'

'I guess. And she said to bring you this. I'll bring you the cheque.' The waitress made her way back to the bar area, shouting over her shoulder, 'Oh, and by the way, you're hired.'

If she hadn't left a fresh bottle of Budweiser on the table Ben would have struggled to believe that he hadn't hallucinated the entire exchange.

* * *

Sam surfaced from the Subway at Union Square, totally disoriented and breathless from taking the stairs two at a time. To her dismay, from this exit, even at ground level, she couldn't see this Coffee Shop place—or even a square, for that matter. A quick squint in each direction and she went with right. Good instinct. A few moments later she was at the south west corner. She needed to cross the road.

Don't Walk.

A sign? Yup, a road sign. And an alarm? Now she was hearing things. Unless…? Her phone. Sam grabbed it from her bag.

'Sam Washington?'

'Yay, we've got her!'

'Gemma?'

'It's all of us. A conference call.'

'What's going on?' Sam shook her head at her stupidity. She'd had a mobile in her bag the whole time she'd been in the call box.

'Nothing. This isn't me. You haven't heard from us. But how is everything?'

'Look, now is really not a good time. I've got, like, minus two minutes to hit a deadline. Can I call you all later?'

'Have you seen him yet?'

'What did you say, Soph?'

'Has Ben found you?' Not quite eighteen hours, but Gemma couldn't wait any longer.

'Well, right now I'm looking for *him*… But how do you…? Did you all know?'

'Gemma spoke to him last night. It's so exciting.'

'Look, I'm running really late. I was in this work meeting—I think I might have been offered another job already…'

'The fund boys?' EJ was as focused as ever.

'Yup.'

'I had a hunch they might. What are the terms like?'

'I'll call when I know more, EJ. I had to reschedule my lunch halfway through. And at this rate I'm going to miss Ben altogether. And, Gem, he's a Pisces—whatever that means…'

Sam thought she could hear Gemma whoop.

'Can't you just call his mobile?' Sophie. The voice of reason.

'His mobile…' Sam smacked her palm against her forehead. Her lateral thought must have become dislodged somewhere over the Atlantic. 'Jesus, I am such a muppet. Thanks, Soph. Look, so great to hear from you all, but I've really really got to go now. Lots of love.'

'Good luck.'

'Call us later.'

'Be nice.'

Sam smiled at Gemma's sign-off. If she ever got there she fully intended to do better than that.

The sign was still telling her to stand still, yet the traffic was barely moving due to roadworks she could see to her left. There was a truck revving menacingly right beside her, waiting for the merest opportunity to pull out, and beyond that she couldn't see. And this appeared to be the only crossing point for at least fifty metres. Sam stepped off the kerb just at the point when the wall of traffic accelerated towards her. Jumping back onto the pavement as fast as she could, she took a few deep breaths to try and calm herself down without choking, despite the fumes the traffic was belching at lung level.

Sam dared to look at her watch. 14:14. Stabbing at her phone keypad in search of Ben's number, she felt her pulse quicken as she waited for him to answer. Voicemail. That waitress had better have tried damn hard to find him or she might well have a homicidal lawyer on her hands.

He drained the beer bottle. There was no sign of the waitress. And no sign of Sam either. He didn't know why he was so surprised. Sam wasn't Gemma or Robert. Nor did he want her to be. But he couldn't sit there any longer. Leaving enough bills on the table, he headed for the bathroom.

Sam raced in as fast as her thighs could propel her, given the narrowness of her knee-length skirt. Clearly the legendary New York power-lunch had been replaced by spirituality and a sandwich. She'd just sprinted through a power Pilates class taking place in the square and now at a standstill, she was starting to sweat profusely. Furiously scanning the faces at the tables and the bar, it only took her a few moments to realise that he wasn't there. Stumbling back across the road blindly, she deposited herself on the first bench she came to and, kicking off her heels, brought her knees up to her chest and rested her chin on them, staring at the doorway she'd just exited as she waited for her breathing patterns to return to normal.

Ben reached the sidewalk. Left or right? It must have been her. No one else did a bar in fifteen seconds. The waitress hadn't even had a chance to offer her a table. His phone was out of juice and he hadn't packed a charger. He hadn't packed at all. He opted for left. And if he had no joy in the next few blocks he was going to sit it out at her hotel. Ben shook his head. He'd only been gone for a few minutes.

'Ben? Benjamin Henry Rudolph Fisher?'

He stopped and squinted. There was a woman standing on a bench waving her arms and a small crowd was gathering. Ben smiled. She definitely looked familiar.

'Hey.' Turning on his heel, he walked to the edge of the kerb.

'Hi.' Sam had been thinking about this moment for the last seventeen hours. She'd wanted to be there first and she'd wanted there to be a moment when their eyes locked. Now there was traffic, she was shouting, and her arms were apparently above her head, moving of their own volition.

'Hey, lady, are you waving at me?' Ben jaywalked towards her.

Sam nodded as she jumped down from the bench, forgetting she had taken her shoes off. But Ben finally made it across the road, and the plight of her feet failed to make an impact as an unexpected tidal wave of feelings surged to the fore.

'Hey, gorgeous. You look suitably ruffled.' He kissed her. 'And sweaty…'

The one time she wished she could have sustained the sophisticated approach.

'And I quite like it…'

Well, at least that was something.

'You don't even want to know what happened. You won't believe this, but I got totally lost on my way here—'

'Stop talking.' Taking her into his arms, Ben kissed her firmly as the cluster of onlookers applauded and whistled, much to Sam's embarrassment. She pulled back.

'I tried to squeeze in a work lunch, only I realised that was impossible, but then suddenly I was heading uptown instead of downtown, and...and I thought you'd have gone.' Tears pricked Sam's eyes as her emotions finally started to catch up with the rest of her.

'I *had* gone...to the bathroom. And it would appear Mademoiselle Impatient couldn't wait for one or two minutes.' A cheeky grin.

'I thought you'd given up. And I couldn't blame you. I mean, if I can't even make a two-hour deadline when you've come all the way from London...' Sam shook her head. 'I'm so sorry to have kept you waiting for so long, but somehow it was two-fourteen by the time I arrived. Pathetic.'

'But it's only two-eleven now.' A helpful, if pedantic, timekeeping citizen intervened.

'It is?'

Checking his own watch, Ben nodded as Sam shook her head. Fooled by her own over-organisation. From this minute forward, real time would suffice.

'Well, you certainly know how to keep a man guessing. So, you weren't just debating whether to come along or not?'

'Of course not.'

'And here I was, seriously beginning to wonder whether I'd lost you for good.'

Sam shook her head, her eyes meeting his. 'That was never going to happen.'

'Really?' Ben's expression was a serious one. Heartfelt and hopeful.

Sam nodded as his eyes searched hers and he pulled her in tightly for another kiss. More applause. This time it was Ben who pulled away. Sam was lost in the moment.

'Hey, guys, show's over.' The circle broke up as Ben returned his attention to Sam. He took her hand. 'Let's get out of here.'

Sam forced her feet back into her shoes and attempted to tease her hair into less of a clump. Rummaging for her sunglasses, she used them as an impromptu hairband.

Ben watched her attempt at a makeover with affection. 'You should have called. And, just for the record, I would have waited all afternoon.'

'It didn't even occur to me to try your mobile until Gemma suggested it a moment ago.'

'And she gave me her word that she wouldn't interfere for at least thirty-six hours.'

A flicker of disappointment in Ben's eyes. Sam couldn't bear it. 'She didn't. I promise I was already here.'

'Besides, my phone's out of power.'

'I know how it feels. So you didn't get my message at all?'

'Only something about being fired.'

Sam might have been shaking her head, but her eyes were smiling. 'Hired.'

Ben grinned as he led her towards a taxi. 'I was hoping that's what you'd say.'

Name & Address Withheld

Jane Sigaloff

Life couldn't be better for Lizzie Ford. Not only does she have a great job doling out advice on the radio, but now she has a new love interest *and* a new best friend. Unfortunately she's about to learn that they're husband and wife. Can this expert on social etiquette keep the man, her friend *and* her principles? Find out in *Name & Address Withheld,* a bittersweet comedy of morals and manners.